TANGLED ASHES

Michèle Phoenix

Tyndale House Publishers, Inc.
Carol Stream, Illinois

Visit Tyndale online at www.tyndale.com.

Visit Michèle Phoenix online at www.michelephoenix.com.

TYNDALE and Tyndale's quill logo are registered trademarks of Tyndale House Publishers, Inc.

Tangled Ashes

Copyright © 2012 by Michèle Phoenix. All rights reserved.

Previously published by Dog Ear Publishing, LLC, under ISBN 978-1608440917.

Tangled Ashes first published in 2012 by Tyndale House Publishers, Inc.

Cover photograph of flag copyright © Robert Wilson/iStockphoto. All rights reserved.

Cover photograph of letter copyright © Jill/Veer. All rights reserved.

Cover photograph of landscape copyright © javarman/Veer. All rights reserved.

Cover photograph of field copyright © CandyBoxImages/Veer. All rights reserved.

Cover photograph of woman copyright © Dornveek Markkstyrn/Getty Images. All rights reserved.

Author photograph copyright © 2011 by Michael Hudson. All rights reserved.

Designed by Beth Sparkman

Edited by Kathryn S. Olson

Published in association with the literary and marketing agency of C. Grant & Company, www.cgrantandcompany.com.

Tangled Ashes is a work of fiction. Where real people, events, establishments, organizations, or locales appear, they are used fictitiously. All other elements of the novel are drawn from the author's imagination.

Library of Congress Cataloging-in-Publication Data

Phoenix, Michèle.
  Tangled ashes / Michèle Phoenix.
    p. cm.
  ISBN 978-1-4143-6840-5 (sc)
  1. Castles—France—Fiction. 2. Family secrets—Fiction. 3. France—History—German occupation, 1940-1945—Fiction. I. Title.
  PS3616.H65T36 2012
  813'.6—dc23   2012011472

Printed in the United States of America

18   17   16   15   14   13   12
7   6   5   4   3   2   1

For David, who foretold, and Mari Ellen, who believed.

Heaven is richer for your music and laughter.

Acknowledgments

SPECIAL THANKS TO:

My parents, for allowing me to grow up in the magic of Lamorlaye.

Michelle, Renée, and Greg for enthusiastic first readings.

Ginger Johnson, for divine appointments.

Jan Stob, for this miracle.

Kathy Olson, for masterful understanding of story and mechanics.

Daryl Conklin, for expertise in the art of construction.

Dr. Kathleen Diehl, for surgeries that "de-cancered" me.

My Lord and Savior, for every day I live. May I make each breath count.

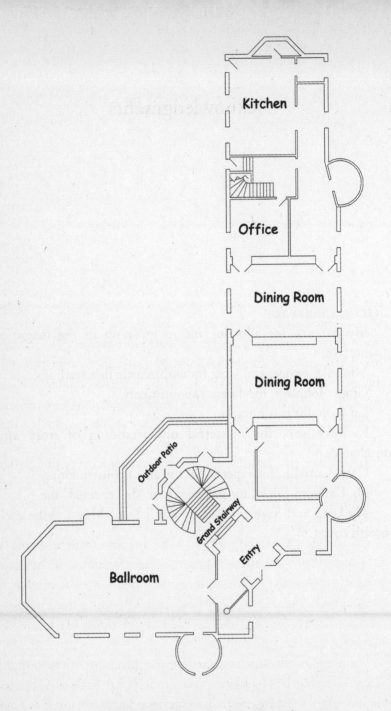

The Lamorlaye Castle

PROLOGUE

MARIE STOOD IN the shadow of the grand staircase and held her breath. The lights were out—they had been all evening—but the ochre glow from the flames on the patio illuminated the polished wood and chiseled stone that loomed around her with threatening austerity. Beyond the window, two columns of wide-spaced guards funneled a stream of nurses and maids from the castle's rear entrance to the fire that burned like a funeral pyre, exploding tiny, arcing embers into the warm night sky. Each woman carried a box of papers past guards who were alternately turned inward and outward. Those facing the coming and going kept their eyes on the documents the women dumped into the flames, sometimes ordering one of them to retrieve a sheaf that had fallen too far to burn. Those guards who faced outward kept their eyes on the woods at the outskirts of the castle grounds, their bodies rigid, as if the senses they trained on their surroundings were fueled by the tension in their muscles and nerves. They held their MP 40s in front of them, fingers near the triggers, and peered into the thick, black tree line with eyes and ears and minds.

A sound near the castle's front door snapped Marie's head around. She pressed harder against the cool stone at her back and scanned the entryway for movement. Two rats scurried across the floor and disappeared into the circular sitting room in the east tower, twittering like bickering lovers. Marie expelled her breath and turned to glance again at the procession outside the windows. The nurses' white wimples glowed orange in the night, lit by the flames that rose several feet into the sky. No one saw her. All eyes were on the urgent task before them and the unseen threat from the nearby woods.

When Marie stepped away from the wall, her shoe squeaked on the smooth granite floor. She reached down and removed the brown leather slip-ons she'd been given with her uniform eighteen months before. Glancing around the entry hall one more time, she moved out of the shadows, climbing the marble steps that led her to the landing from which the elegant stairway swooped around in two graceful arches that met again at the landing above. Across from the stairway was the castle's main entrance with its large double doors flanked by tall windows. The moon glanced off dozens of trucks and town cars parked outside, poised for the next day's evacuation.

In the stream just beyond the front doors, a duck rose from the water, clapping its wings and quacking loudly enough that the guards must have heard it. Marie froze. Though the ducks were a common element of the castle's soundscape, any noise on this night would be enough to arouse suspicion and reveal her presence. She stood conspicuously on the landing, visible from the front doors but still mostly hidden from the windows behind her and the glow of the fire. Blood pumped so loudly in her ears that she had to quell the impulse to cover them with her hands.

When a minute had passed, then another, Marie allowed herself to relax a little. She peered around the edge of the staircase's railing. The fire seemed to be smaller now; the procession of nurses was slowing too. She had to act quickly. Without another look out the window, she moved on stockinged feet toward the nursery. There was no time for fear. The brass knob on the nursery door was cold to her touch. When she entered, the large, ornate room was quiet but for the sound of small lungs breathing and infants' mouths suckling thumbs. This was a ballroom designed for luxurious events, not for eerily quiet children—Nazis in training. The silence in the nursery had always astounded Marie. Even in the daytime, in those hungry minutes before feedings, the babies had seldom cried. It was as if they knew their crying would serve no purpose in this place where their lives merely served to advance political agendas.

Marie moved swiftly past the night nurse's empty bed and the cribs of the children, each draped with a navy-blue blanket adorned with an eagle holding a wreath of oak leaves that framed a swastika. She knew the sleeping forms by name. Petra. Inge. Karl. Ulli. Marie longed to reach out and stroke each blond head and hold each slumbering child now that no nurses or officers were there to stop her. But she couldn't. Not with tomorrow dawning in just a handful of hours.

Squaring her shoulders, Marie quickly moved past the remaining cribs, each holding a child whose sleep was as deep as it was despondent. The small wooden beds were arranged in two neat rows with a wide aisle down the center that ended at a fireplace as tall as Marie. There were eight cribs in all, far fewer than at the height of the program's glory. These infants were the prized products of the castle. The perfect ones. The promise of the Aryan people.

A dog barked in the courtyard. Marie heard the Generalmajor's voice ordering two guards to investigate the ruckus. There was the sound of running feet, shouts directed into the woods, then the dog's whimper as a rifle's butt connected with its flank. The tenuous, tense calm that had held the castle in a vise since noon was broken by the disruption. The procession that had been conducted in silence until then ended in shouted orders and a flurry of movement around the remains of the fire. Generalmajor Müller's voice rang out again, ordering the women to their quarters and sending the soldiers to join the others who had been stationed around the perimeter of the castle for the better part of the afternoon and night.

Marie panicked. There was no time. Once the additional guards sealed the gaps in the ranks around the château, her escape route would be closed. She hurried to the last crib on the right and pulled back the fabric shielding the baby from view. The three-days-old infant lay utterly still, its tiny white fist curled next to its cheek, its rosy lips parted and slightly curved upward. A smile in this context was an astonishing sight.

Marie took the blue blanket from the crib and ran to lay it open on the night nurse's bed. Then she hurried back and lifted out the sleeping infant. It stirred and whimpered but didn't wake. Returning to the bed on unsteady legs, she placed the child in the blanket and swaddled it tightly, grateful that the dark fabric would further mask their escape. Then she stripped the sheet from the nurse's mattress and folded each corner over the baby.

With the château's front door patrolled by guards and the back door too visible, the only exit was through the window to the left of the fireplace. There was no need for silence anymore. The grounds were alive with the sounds of moving soldiers. Marie slipped her shoes back on, opened the window, and leaned out, looking left, then right. There was a six-foot drop to the path beneath. The fire was close by, barely hidden by the curving end of the building. Without taking the time to second-guess her plan, Marie sat on the edge of the window and swung her legs around. She reached back and gathered the four corners of the sheet, forming a sort of sling in which the baby lay. She lifted it out the window and held it down as far as she could, but it still didn't reach the ground.

Marie slowly lowered her body out the window, twisting as she did, so that she hung by the shoulder that straddled the windowsill. She knew she'd have to straighten her arm to lower the baby to the ground without jarring and waking it. Her muscles rebelled and shook as she grabbed the window ledge with her hand and gradually began to straighten her arm until it was fully extended. The fingers holding the ledge began to bleed as the rough wood cut into her skin. She gritted her teeth and strained farther, trying to lengthen her body without losing her grip. Her eyes stung with the pain and effort.

Just when she thought she'd have to drop the baby and deal with the consequences, Marie felt its weight lessen. The improvised sling had found the ground. Marie dropped the rest of the sheet, then let go of the windowsill, pushing herself off the wall as she fell, conscious that the baby lay beneath her. She crouched on the ground for a moment, catching her breath, blotting her bleeding palm and fingers with the sheet, and trying to calm her nerves.

When she opened the bundle and took the baby into her lap, open and alert eyes met hers.

"Shhh," she soothed softly, scanning her surroundings. She could see three soldiers heading away from her across the clearing on the other side of the river. Marie realized that they'd be looking for intruders coming *into* the property, not exiting. That would surely play in her favor. Just around the corner from where she stood, the officers stamping out the fire set off toward the woods to join their comrades in wait for the inevitable. Both clearings were too exposed. There was nowhere Marie could go but into the river at her feet. Though the locals called it a *rivière*, it was really more of a wide, slow-moving stream whose depth and width varied as it snaked through the property and around small islands.

Marie bundled up the white sheet and jammed it under a bush, then made her way down the river's steep bank, holding the baby close. She slid and had to catch the root of a willow tree with one hand to steady herself. The baby whimpered, frowning, its eyes mere slits. "Shhh," Marie soothed again, steadying her footing on the riverbank. "It's okay. I'm right here." The frown dissolved. The baby stared. Marie let go of the tree root and touched the infant's chin with her finger, bringing her face closer and lowering her voice to a calming pitch. "I'm going to get you out of here, okay? But you have to help me. You have to be quiet." The unblinking stare lengthened. Marie looked at the black water beneath her and shook her head at the folly of her plan. "I'm going to try really hard to keep you dry," she promised the child. Then she looked up at the stars and pleaded for help.

Her feet slipped on the mud as she descended the remainder of the slope, but she regained her footing and waded quietly into the water. The thick layer of silt on the bottom made Marie lose her balance and sucked the shoes off her feet before she'd taken three steps. She walked out until she was hip deep in the murky darkness, her bundle held tight and high above the river. She moved at a slow and deliberate pace, testing her next step before she trusted it, and progressed steadily out of the castle's night shadow and into the deeper woods. Every time the baby whimpered, she hushed it with a soothing sound and kept moving.

As Marie reached the outer perimeter of the property, she heard whispers in the darkness and paused to catch her breath under a wooden bridge. The voices came from both sides of the river, soldiers predicting what the new day would bring, their eyes trained on the walled boundary she had to reach. Marie knew they would see her if she emerged from her hiding place. The moon was too bright. The woods were too calm and motionless.

The baby gurgled again, and Marie clamped a hand over its mouth. "Shhh," she murmured as the baby started to protest. It tried to twist its head away from her hand and arched its back when it didn't succeed. "Please," she whispered, staring frantically into the baby's eyes. "Please." The baby twisted again, a strangled sound escaping from under Marie's hand. She pressed harder against its mouth. *"Please . . ."*

On the bridge above her, a branch snapped under a soldier's boot.

1

JANUARY 2001

MARSHALL BECKER PLANTED both palms on the impossibly shiny surface of his friend and business partner's cherrywood desk and leveled the kind of look at him that made foremen quake and contractors relent.

"Say what?" His voice was low, but it packed all the threat of his glare.

Gary pushed back from the desk, the wheels of his leather chair soundless on the Oriental rug that covered the office's Italian tile floors, and crossed his arms. He glanced out the window at the breathtaking sunset view of Boston's ice-covered Charles River and the waterfront homes that still sported their Christmas lights. Then he looked back at Becker, resolve in his eyes. "It's for your own good."

"You didn't just say that!" Becker snapped, smacking the desktop with his hand.

Gary sat forward in his chair, elbows on the desk. He met Beck's stare with practiced calm. "Will you let me explain?"

"You can explain all you want. The answer is still going to be a resounding no."

"Dude . . ."

"*Dude?* What are we—twelve?"

"It's a sound business decision. We need this contract."

"The Sag Harbor project is nearly finished. You can't pull me off that now."

"Kevin'll take over for the homestretch."

"And the deal on the Annapolis Inn . . ."

"We haven't signed off on it yet. Even if we do, you know there's months of preliminary work before we can start the remodel."

Beck stepped back from the desk and crossed his arms. He could feel a vein pulsing in his forehead and a telltale flush moving up his neck. "We're equal partners."

Gary raised an eyebrow. "Yes."

"We both make the big decisions. We *consult*."

"Yes."

"So . . . ?"

"So this is an obvious call, and if you were being logical, you'd agree."

Becker sighed. They both knew that neither logic nor rational choices had been a high priority for him in months. Maybe years. He was past caring. "We're pulling out," Beck said. He jutted his chin toward the phone. "Go ahead—pick it up. We're pulling out."

Gary looked him straight in the eye. "I've already signed the contract."

"What?" Beck stared at him in disbelief. "Let me get this straight—you get a call from some guy you met at a convention offering you a job in a country where neither of us has ever stepped foot, and you—without consulting with me—sign on the dotted line? Seriously?"

Gary nodded. "That's the gist of it."

Beck hissed out a lungful of frustration and dragged his fingers through his hair. His eyes settled on the wall to the right of Gary's desk. Stalking around the desk, he grabbed a plaque from the wall. "You see this?" He pointed at the names engraved in the polished copper, his finger spearing at the company logo. "T&B. Gary Tyler and Marshall Becker. Tyler and *Becker*!" He accentuated his own name. "I'm in this too, *dude*," he sneered, "and unless you plan on taking the *B* off this plaque, you don't make any decisions without consulting me. And certainly not if they involve *me* flying halfway around the globe to do the work!"

He hurled the plaque across the desk. It sailed off the edge, upsetting a pile of *Architectural Digest*s, and fell nearly soundlessly to the silk rug on the floor.

"Get ahold of yourself." Gary's voice was low, his eyes burdened.

Becker glared a moment longer, lips pursed, before moving to retrieve the plaque. He brushed it off and, with great precision, hung it back on the wall. Fingers unsteady, he spent an inordinate amount of time leveling it before stuffing his hands into his pockets and walking over to the panoramic window with its priceless view across the river, his body so rigid that he could feel his muscles spasming. He gazed out from the eighth floor of the Back Bay brownstone that had been the first and finest renovation of their twelve years of collaboration, his mind less on the view than on the dilemma at hand.

"What if I refuse?" he asked quietly. "What if I call your stuffed shirt myself and tell him T&B has changed its mind?"

Gary moved to the front of the desk and leaned back against it, facing his friend with a mixture of concern and determination on his face. "We risk losing his business."

Beck turned on his partner, eyebrows raised, ready to make that sacrifice, but Gary put up his hand in caution. "This is just *one* contract, Beck. But the guy owns half the historical properties in that part of the world. It might be hundreds of thousands—maybe millions—we're throwing away. Not to mention getting our foot in the door of a European market."

Beck leaned back against the window. "Why'd you do it?"

"Why did I commit?" Gary pursed his lips for a moment. "Because you need to get away from here. And because you're the right guy for the project. And it wasn't going to happen unless I—me, your business partner—took the initiative."

"It's a straightforward renovation gig. Any one of our guys could head it up."

"Number one, castle renovations are never straightforward, and number two, none of our guys have been project managers for jobs this size. None of them are the master craftsman you are, *and* none of them speak the language."

A long silence settled over the office. An antique grandfather clock ticked sullenly in the corner, a gift from one of their most prestigious clients.

Beck finally spoke, weariness in his voice. "So you think I need to get away from here."

"And the sooner the better." Gary pushed off the desk and moved to stand by his friend at the window, staring out as night fell over the stately homes of Arlington Street. "Seriously, Beck. You're the one who can pull this off. He doesn't want industrial efficiency. He wants traditional workmanship. You're the best guy for that."

"Not by myself—not this big of a job."

"He's got crews there who can do the bigger stuff. You'll oversee the project and personally take care of the more tricky renovations."

Beck nodded and pressed his lips into a hard line.

"It's what you do best," Gary repeated. "It's what your passion was at Dartmouth—before you became the tyrannical moron you are now."

The men stared at each other for long moments.

"I want lodging on-site."

"So you can avoid sleeping by working all night?"

Beck raised an eyebrow.

"Done," Gary conceded. "I'll talk to the owner myself."

"Meals provided."

"I'm sure that can be arranged."

"Transportation?"

Gary winced. "You can't drive here, so why should you drive there?"

"Because my DUI doesn't count over there?"

"They have taxis. Use them. We're not in any shape to deal with a lawsuit if you tangle with French policemen."

"Fine, but T&B foots the bills."

"Done."

The two men stared each other down, Gary's blue gaze holding Becker's amber glare without the slightest trace of capitulation.

"You're talking about a pretty big step here," Beck finally mumbled.

"It'll do you good."

"And you know that because . . . ?"

"Trish told me it will," Gary said. Trish was the sweetest woman Beck had ever met, and he wondered how she'd put up with Gary for nearly ten years.

"You bypassed me completely on this one."

"For your own good, Beck. Come on—give it a shot."

Beck shook his head and stared up at the ceiling.

"What do you have to lose?" his friend added.

That was just it. He had nothing to lose. Except frustrating jobs, tedious social engagements, and endless nights staring at his TV or computer screen. "What do *you* gain from this?" he finally asked.

Gary shrugged. "Not sure. But this is about you, man. And the welfare of the contractors you've been terrorizing." He shrugged when Beck cut him a disparaging look. "I can't afford to lose another one to emotional distress. Not good for business."

"You're full of it," Beck mumbled.

"Besides—Trish's been planning an intervention for months now. So that's your option. Either you go off to France like a good little boy and bring in some dough for our retirement funds, or you stay here and have a horde of do-gooders descend on you to commit you to a Doofus Anonymous center."

Beck rolled his eyes. "Nobody says *doofus*."

"I'm an innovator."

"You're full of it."

"So you've said."

Beck leveled a laser-sharp stare at his friend and held it for a moment. They squared off like wrestlers in a ring, both above six feet and built like quarterbacks. If things had ever come to blows, it was anybody's guess who would have come out on top. "Don't ever overstep me again," Beck said with unmistakable gravity. "Not for my own good. Not for T&B's good. We're equal partners. Just be happy I'm in the mood for a change of scenery this time."

"Agreed." Gary went around the desk and retrieved a manila folder from one of the drawers, then slid it across to Beck. "Here's what you need to know. Ticket's in there too. You leave February 2, two weeks from tomorrow."

"Are you kiddin' me?"

"First class. To *Paris*. Stop your whining."

Beck leafed through the documents in the file and took a closer look at several photos. "This is big," he said without looking up.

"But you love it, right? Do I know you or do I know you?"

Beck pointed at his friend with the folder. "If this thing goes bust, the blame's on you."

"Fair enough."

Beck moved toward the door, grabbing his jacket off a leather chair and casting a disparaging glance at Gary's shoes. "And buy some real shoes, will you?" he said. "Those shiny Italian things are for sissies."

"You know what, Beck? Go to—"

"France? Why, I believe I will." He gave his partner the you-owe-me-one look that had gotten them through the worst hurdles of their collaboration and opened the door.

The two weeks before Beck's departure passed in a frenzy of work-related pressures—tying up loose ends on nearly finished projects, handing others off to collaborators, and postponing those that didn't require immediate attention. Beck and Gary pored over what few blueprints they had of the castle in France, comparing visions and arriving at creative compromises that were both pragmatic and artistic. There was little they could truly predict from a continent away, but what *could* be anticipated was meticulously planned out. Turning a castle into a high-class hotel and restaurant, of course, was primarily a business proposition, but the hotel needed to be true to its origins if it was going to attract the clientele its owner hoped for.

Beck entered the Lucky Leprechaun two days before his departure and took a stool at the end of the bar.

"Hey there, Beck," Jimmy said from the other side of the counter. "The usual?"

"Yup."

"Knockin' off early?" Jimmy asked, cutting a glance at the Miller Lite clock on the wall above the door.

"Just pour the beer."

The bartender saluted. "Aye, aye, sir."

There was some pleasure in watching the foam pour over the

top of the tall glass and edge down its side, eventually soaking into the coaster's smiling leprechaun.

"Just past three and boozin' it up? What are we celebrating?" Leslie asked, sliding onto the stool next to his.

"My partner's insanity."

"Well, here's to the productively insane! If you two get any more successful, you're going to have to develop big-shot attitudes." Beck raised an eyebrow at her. "Never mind. That ship has sailed." She lifted a hand to get Jimmy's attention and pointed at Beck's beer. "One more."

Becker's eyes were on a recap of a Celtics game on the TV screen in the far corner of the room, but his mind was on the chore at hand. He hated this kind of thing. The artificial sincerity of cutting ties with the unimportant. He glanced at Leslie. Her eyes were on the game, her manicured fingers idly turning the glass of beer in front of her. Quarter turn, quarter turn, quarter turn. Her platinum hair was overteased and sprayed hard. Her makeup was garish—too bold and somehow geometric to actually flatter. Her business suit was expensive and sleek, cut to enhance her toned and trim physique. If he kept his eyes on that and away from her calculating gaze, he was okay. But if he met her dollar-sign stare for more than a few seconds at a time, the beer soured in his stomach.

"So talk fast—I'm between meetings. What's Gary's harebrained scheme this time?" she asked, swiveling toward him on her stool, legs crossed, the tip of her foot sliding around his calf. "Turning another dilapidated factory into a schooner museum?"

Beck turned to dislodge her foot. He dispensed with subtlety—wasn't in the mood for it anyway. "I'm heading to France. For a few months. Big project for one of Gary's contacts."

Leslie raised a perfectly arched eyebrow. "Nice. Can I come along?"

On the television screen, Paul Pierce took a shot from the top of the key and failed to make a basket. "I leave in two days. Thought you should know."

There was a pause while Leslie absorbed the information. Then she leaned in, her mouth close to his neck, and whispered, "Guess we'd better make the most of the time we have left, huh, slugger?"

The beer on her breath repulsed him. The way she touched his thigh did too. Then again, he'd never been more than mildly intrigued by her. Theirs was a cynical arrangement of convenience and distraction. He got the distraction and she got the . . . He wasn't sure what she got, actually. It wasn't predictability and it certainly wasn't entertainment. More often than not, they used more words ordering their drinks than they did having a conversation. That's where the convenience came into play. Hours of company and no need for small talk. Didn't get any better than that.

"Actually," he said, taking a long swallow from his glass, "I'm going to be swamped, so . . ."

"There are a lot of hours in a couple of days," she insisted, her voice dropping a notch or two as she traced the veins on the top of his hand with a fingertip. Whoever said a person couldn't live on hope alone had never met Leslie. She'd known him for several months and still lived with the delusion that she'd get him into bed. "What are you—a monk?" she'd asked one night, when he'd driven her home in the wee hours after a protracted cocktail party and dropped her at the curb. He'd driven off without answering, watching in his rearview mirror as she stomped her foot on the wet sidewalk. But she'd recovered fast enough and somehow made peace with the situation. As long as they played with fire on a regular basis, she seemed happy to be his drinking partner and social accessory. Suited him just fine.

Beck downed the last of his beer and dropped a twenty-dollar bill on the polished surface of the bar. He stood, grabbed his jacket off the stool next to him and moved toward the door.

"What—no 'See ya later'? No 'Nice knowin' you'?" Leslie swiveled on her stool, hands out in amazement, a flush of red high on her cheeks.

Beck gave her a long look, racking his mind for something meaningful to say. But he could no more validate their relationship with declarations than he could end it with regret. He shrugged, averted his eyes, and turned to go.

It hadn't taken long for Beck to say the rest of his good-byes. Most of them had required no more than a few words of instruction and a casual wave. Such was the nature of his friendships. They were about work or about distraction. Period. They didn't keep him warm at night, but they sure made transcontinental moves less complicated.

2

THÉRÈSE GALLET FUMBLED with the oversize key and carried on a flurry of conversation as she tried to unlock the castle's front door. Beck stood by with waning patience. He'd been through the same drill minutes before at the castle's main gate, and the routine was getting old. Jet lag was weighing him down, and Thérèse's inefficiency was stoking the kind of anger that made him miss his punching bag.

Thérèse spoke English with the crisp, staccato diction of a chirping bird. They had started out in French as they drove from the train station in Chantilly to Lamorlaye, but when fatigue had interfered with Beck's rusty linguistic skills, they had switched easily to the language he'd spoken since his parents had moved from Canada to Chicago when he was only ten.

"All the château's doors need to be replaced," Thérèse twittered, her fingers easing the key in and out of the lock, turning,

11

then turning again, hoping to catch the ancient mechanism hidden inside the antique white door. "It's really quite astounding that there hasn't been more vandalism in all these years," she said, her voice sharp and high-pitched, her eyes unfocused as she leaned into her task. She was a slight woman, probably pushing sixty, but she moved with a speed and an erect posture that belied her age.

Beck peered through the window while Thérèse fumbled with the lock. He tuned out her babbling and squinted into the shadows beyond the castle's door. He saw a sweep of stairs framed by an archway, stone floors, and little else. Thérèse had explained on the way to Lamorlaye that Gavin Fallon, a British expatriate and wealthy real estate tycoon, had purchased the dilapidated property several months before and had only recently decided to begin the renovation process.

"Eureka!" Thérèse cried when the key finally turned. She pushed down on the brass handle and motioned for Beck to precede her inside. "Here it is," she said with a more dramatic flourish than Beck thought necessary. "It's not much to look at right now, but it does have potential, wouldn't you say? Look at those carved banisters. And these *windows*! Here—let me switch on the light so you can have a better look." She hurried over to the wall next to the door and flipped a switch.

Beck had somehow expected more than a single bulb hanging from a wire to illuminate the space. But there it was—as out of place in this historical context as a corn dog at the Ritz. And sadly, all it did was further reveal the castle's disrepair.

"How old is this place?" Beck asked, interrupting Thérèse's chatter.

She took a notebook from her purse and flipped through a few pages. "I thought you might want some historical background," she said, smiling pertly. "I jotted down some notes that you might find interesting." She seemed proud of herself, a trait Becker found annoying. When she'd turned to the desired page, she said, "It's quite complicated, really. The foundations date back to . . . it looks like the twelfth century. It was a fortress, originally."

"The twelfth century?" Beck was stunned.

"Yes, but the current structure is much more recent. The fortress was mostly destroyed during the Hundred Years' War."

Beck shook his head, astounded.

"You've heard of that, I'm sure?"

Ignoring her question, he pursed his lips and stepped farther into the entryway, taking stock of the limestone walls and the detailing on the staircase. He'd pictured something old by American standards, but this felt more like archeology than architecture.

"The part we're standing in was rebuilt during the Renaissance," Thérèse continued, "and it looks like the final restoration . . ." She flipped some more, tucking back a strand of graying hair that had escaped from her rather austere chignon. "Yes, that's right. The final restoration came in 1872. It was really quite extensive, as you'll see. They added the entire north wing and modernized the overall look of the castle." She glanced up at Beck and frowned at the disbelief she saw on his face. "I'm sorry—were you not aware that the structure was . . . historical?"

"Oh no," Beck assured her, shaking his head and looking around at the centuries-old walls within which he stood. "I knew it was a historical monument. It's just . . . In the States, anything that predates McDonald's is considered ancient history."

Thérèse looked around too, but she appeared to be scanning for rodents more than admiring the decor. "Well, yes. Of course. It's quite old. And dusty. And damaged." She pointed at the graffiti-covered walls, the broken windowpanes, the yellowed marble floors, and the evidence of a fire on the grand staircase. "I'm not sure Monsieur Fallon understood the full scope of the challenge, taking on this renovation, but I presume it will keep us all busy for . . . a while."

Beck stopped listening. He was picturing the finished product in his mind and calculating what it would require to see the work to completion.

"Of course, how you're going to accomplish it all by April is a mystery to me," Thérèse said. "But I'm sure you know exactly what you're doing."

It took a moment for what she'd said to register, but when it did, Beck snapped his head around and squinted in the half-light. "Did you say April?"

"Well, yes, I . . ." Thérèse was flustered. She consulted her notebook again and nodded. "Yes. It says it right here. Monsieur Fallon wants it finished by the twenty-third of April, for his wife's fortieth birthday."

"You're a dead man, Gary," Becker muttered under his breath as he turned away from Thérèse, hands on hips, and contemplated the enormity of the task ahead of him.

"Pardon me?"

He raised his arms out to his sides and turned in a slow circle. "There is absolutely no way that I can get this place ready in three months. None!" He brushed disintegrated mortar from between the angle stones in the wall nearest him and watched it sift down to the floor. "Look at that!" He turned on Thérèse, his voice rising in frustration. "And that staircase?" he continued, striding over to the cherrywood structure and pointing at the large area of carved wood that had been destroyed by a fire. "This is hand-carved. We're talking dozens of man-hours just to fix that three-foot gap!"

Thérèse referred back to her notebook. "But Monsieur Fallon said . . ."

"*Monsieur* Fallon," Beck interrupted, "is not the guy who's supposed to pull off a miracle."

"Well, no, he isn't, but . . ."

He'd heard enough. "Is there a phone in this place? Seriously—is there a phone?"

Thérèse fingered the locket around her neck, her eyes wide and darting. "Yes—I'm sure there's one in the office upstairs . . ."

"Up here?" Beck asked, taking the steps two at a time. He stayed on the right side of the wide expanse, keeping his weight away from the fire damage, then followed the right arm of the structure around to the next floor.

"Monsieur Becker," Thérèse called from below. "The stairs are damaged. You shouldn't be . . ."

"Which door is the office?" Beck leaned over the railing at the top of the stairs and sent Thérèse the kind of glare that had made foremen break into a sweat.

"It's right there in front of you, but you'll need the keys . . ." Thérèse put a tentative foot on the first step as if she expected it to give way under her weight.

"Madame Gallet!" He tried to keep his tone friendly, but there was a growing hardness to it that he couldn't control. "The stairs held me, and I'm three times your weight. Just get yourself and the keys up here, will you?"

Thérèse stopped where she stood and propped a fist on her hip. "Monsieur Becker," she said in a clipped, offended tone, "it may be all right for you to speak to Americans in that manner, but you will not—"

"Okay, fine!" Beck threw his hands up. "Just—if you could get me into the office so I can use the phone, I'd be most grateful." The effort of putting a polite sentence together had cost him the few remaining shreds of his patience. "I stopped getting reception on my cell halfway here from the airport."

Thérèse harrumphed and lifted her chin a little higher. She moved up the steps at a cautious pace, muttering under her breath, until she reached the landing. When she finally stood beside Beck, she met his glare with a withering stare and somehow managed to look both angry and apologetic as she shrilled, "You will not treat me like your maid, Monsieur Becker. I am Monsieur Fallon's interior designer *and* your liaison with the outside world for the duration of this project. I am not, however, your slave."

She drew the last word out so long that it almost made Beck smile in spite of his mounting fury.

"Fine," he said, reining in the urge to bust through the office door without the benefit of a key, if only for the release of adrenaline it would ensure. "Now, will you please," he said, barely controlled, "show me to the office?"

Thérèse gave him a wide berth as she moved to the door right across from the landing. She fumbled with her keys, her fingers less than steady, and finally opened the door of the tiny room. There was nothing there but a phone on the floor, connected to a wall jack, and a window with a view of the broad marble stairs outside the castle and the small river beyond.

"I thought you said this was an office. . . ."

"Precisely. This *was* an office."

Beck was pretty sure he'd heard sarcasm in her response, but there was no smile to validate his suspicion.

"I'll wait outside," she said, leaving the room.

"Madame Gallet!"

She poked her head around the doorframe. "Yes?"

Asking for help had never been one of Beck's strong suits. Asking for help from someone like the high-strung interior designer was even more of a stretch. "What do I dial to get out?" he asked.

"Two zeros and a one. Then your area code. And it's Thérèse," she corrected him. "If we're going to be speaking to each other in English, we might as well be American about it, wouldn't you say?" Her mouth pinched into something that might have been an attempted smirk, though it never made it to her eyes. "I'll just be outside the door, then—Monsieur Becker."

If she'd been expecting Beck to reciprocate her first-name invitation, she was going to be disappointed. "No need for 'Monsieur,'" he said. "'Mr. Becker' is fine." He held her confused gaze for a moment, then waited silently until the door clicked shut.

Beck dropped to a sitting position on the floor under the window and took several deep breaths. Then he reached for the phone. The process of dialing a rotary phone had an exacerbating effect on Beck's already-strained nerves. By the time he'd entered the last digit and waited for the dial to turn, he was taking more deep breaths and practicing restraint.

"'Lo!"

"Eleven weeks?! Less than three months to get this place whipped into shape? Are you out of your mind?"

"I take it you've been introduced to the . . . Château de Lamorlaye!" Gary's attempt at an authentic French accent made Pepé Le Pew sound like a linguist.

"It's not the castle I'm worried about; it's the amount of work to be done by an impossible deadline."

"So you know about the wife's birthday bash."

"I do. But I didn't until a couple minutes ago, and I certainly didn't when you talked me into this!"

"Did Fallon explain it to you?"

"Haven't met him yet! I spent last night at a hotel near the airport and only got here this afternoon. This woman—Thérèse—picked me up at the train station. It can't be done, man. No way." The connection crackled and popped, but Gary's chuckle still made it across the ocean and into Beck's ear. He bristled. "If you're laughing over there, Gary, I swear I'll . . ."

"Listen to me," Gary interrupted. "When are you meeting Fallon?"

Beck covered the mouthpiece. "Thérèse, when am I meeting Fallon?"

"Monsieur Fallon will be by this evening," she replied, the wooden door somewhat muting the sharp edges of her voice.

"This evening," Beck repeated into the phone, doing a perfect imitation of Thérèse's snippy tone.

"He'll fill you in. Listen, you're not supposed to have the whole project finished by April. He's pretty adamant about having a reception for his wife on the ground floor and portraits taken on the staircase, but the rest of the work can take longer. And if you can't get it all done in the time you've got, you can pass it off to someone else when you leave."

"Portraits?"

"Yeah. You know—pictures."

"I'm going to work myself ragged to get a castle ready for a rich woman's portraits?"

"So the change of time zone hasn't improved your disposition."

"Gary." There was a warning in Beck's voice.

"He's turning the castle into an exclusive restaurant and hotel. The party and portraits are just an afterthought."

"This is a massive project, Gary. This place is older than America."

"And we've sent Rambo to beat it into shape."

"Not funny."

"Not in the least."

"I'm going to need some extra help on this one."

"Talk to Fallon. I'm just the architect on this project. If you want to redesign the floor plan, I can help you with that. Otherwise, this one's all yours."

Beck looked around the diminutive office and took stock of the high ceiling, the ornate molding, the ancient wallpaper, and the hardwood floor.

"Still there?" came Gary's voice.

"Yeah." He stood up, the phone in his hand, and turned to look out the window. In the small river below, a handful of ducks paddled lazily around a pint-size island. "What have you gotten me into, Gary?"

"Change. That's what. Change of scenery. Change of focus. And if we're lucky, change of attitude."

"You're a moron."

"And as an equal partner, I'm a moron with clout. So stop your whining and get to planning your project. Remember that the only alternative to France is Doofus Anonymous."

Beck sighed and raked his fingers through his hair. "I'll do what I can," he conceded.

"Attaboy."

After Becker retrieved his suitcases from Thérèse's car, she led him to his quarters.

"Monsieur Fallon will take you on a *tour du propriétaire* when he arrives," she said as she preceded him down the long hallway leading from the second-floor office through the north wing of the castle. On one side was a series of closed doors, and on the other was a long row of windows, paint peeling and putty crumbling. Some of the windowpanes had been broken and now sported roughly cut pieces of plastic to keep the elements out. Beyond the windows was a view of the castle's back acres, a large clearing that led into dense woods. Thérèse paused when she saw Beck stop to take in the sights.

"Not much to look at right now," she said, scanning the flat expanse that extended out of the V formed by the castle's two wings, "but back in the seventeenth century, there were eight elaborately designed flower beds back here. A sort of mini Versailles, if you wish."

"How do you know that?"

"Pictures in the *mairie*."

"Next thing I know, Fallon's going to be wanting me to restore the gardens, too."

Thérèse smiled a little wistfully, her eyes still on the darkening property. "Wouldn't that just be sublime?"

When they arrived at the end of the hallway, Thérèse led him down a narrow wooden staircase near the castle's north tower to a small apartment that extended out a half story lower. Someone had tried to clean up the space by scrubbing the floors and clearing the cobwebs, but it still looked like it had been uninhabited for decades. Thérèse opened the doors to each room as they passed. All three faced different directions, and none of them gave any particular clues as to their former use.

"We set up your bed in this one," Thérèse said, motioning into a bedroom that faced the stables and the large circular drive at the front of the castle. "There's a *salle de bain* right across the hall, so this seemed most convenient."

Becker stepped inside. He immediately recognized the smell of plaster and fresh paint. "Remodeled?" he asked.

"Monsieur Fallon paid a local company to come in and redo the walls for you. I promise you it's unrecognizable compared to what it looked like a week ago."

Becker took in the gouged hardwood floors, the seafoam-green walls, and the handful of frames that hung here and there. The art looked like something his mother might have bought for a quarter at a garage sale. "You do the decorating?"

Thérèse harrumphed again. "Mr. Becker, I assure you that my work is far superior to what you see here."

"Whatever. There's a bed and a chair. Good enough for me."

"I'm sure you'll be quite comfortable. If you'd like me to replace the . . . art . . ."

"Don't bother. I won't be spending much time in here anyway."

"As you wish."

"Was the bathroom redone too?" Beck asked, stepping back out into the hallway. He stopped short. "What's that smell?"

Thérèse reached for her necklace, toying with it. She seemed to be struggling for the right words to answer his question. "Well," she intoned, taking her time, "it seems that the hooligans who spray-painted the front entrance might have . . . stayed . . . here for a while."

Beck looked around. "Here? In this room?"

"Actually, it appears they might have spent less time in this room than in the one at the end of the hall. . . ." Her voice trailed off.

Beck moved quickly to the door at the end of the hallway and pushed it open. The stench there was far worse. The walls were covered—*covered*—in obscene graffiti, and the wood floor in one of the corners looked eaten by acid.

"Monsieur Fallon didn't think you'd want to live in this bedroom," Thérèse said, looking over his shoulder.

Beck pointed at the repulsive corner. "Didn't you say there's a bathroom right across the hall?"

"Well, yes," Thérèse said, still fidgeting with her necklace, "but it dates back to the beginning of the last century, so nothing actually worked until Monsieur Fallon had a repairman in last month. He also had all the wiring and plumbing redone in this part of the castle." She hesitated. "So you'd be more comfortable."

Beck raised an eyebrow. "Well, I appreciate the wiring and the plumbing, but there's no way I'm living with this stench."

"There are other rooms, I suppose . . . ," she began.

"Yeah, a few dozen from what I've seen so far."

"But this toilet is the only one that's functional right now. So if you need to . . . you know . . . in the middle of the night—"

Beck held up his hand. "All right—I get it."

"Maybe if you sealed the door with tape? Perhaps that would keep some of the smell from getting into the rest of the apartment."

"Or maybe if I got a room in town." He shrugged. Thérèse was silent for a suspiciously long moment, and Beck narrowed his eyes at her. "What?"

"Nothing," she said, turning away from the foul-smelling space and closing the door. "If you'll follow me, I'll show you to the kitchen. It's right beneath this apartment, just down another flight of stairs."

"Thérèse." The command in his voice made her stop in her tracks and turn to look at him. "What aren't you telling me?"

She pinched her lips together for a moment. "I wouldn't presume to tell you what to do, Mr. Becker. Monsieur Fallon said you wanted to be lodged on-site, and that's probably most practical. But . . . if it were me," she said, her eyes darting up and down the stairs, "I'd most certainly consider alternative lodging." She looked at him out of the corner of her eye. "There have been some . . . strange happenings in this castle of late." With that, she turned back to the stairs and descended them at an alarming pace, leaving a perplexed and disgruntled carpenter on the landing behind her.

Where the worn wooden stairs ended, a tiled floor began. Thérèse led him through two sets of doors and down several more steps before they entered the kitchen. Beck looked around in surprise. "This is pretty modern," he said.

Thérèse nodded. "It was remodeled—rebuilt, really—in the sixties, when some Swedish entrepreneur thought he could turn the château into a conference center, but he ran out of funds before he got much farther than the dining halls. That phase of the castle's history only lasted for about a year."

Beck scanned the modernized space. The appliances were dated but far from derelict. The walls were fairly clean. The tile floor just needed a good scrubbing. There was mold, of course, and oil stains above the stoves, but the space reassured Beck nonetheless. There was one room—one room—in the castle that wouldn't require as much work as all the others.

Fallon found them in the fruit cellar, a cave carved out of a raised mound just outside the kitchen's entrance. It smelled of earth and decay.

"Getting the grand tour, are you?" came a jovial, loud, regal-sounding voice from the top of the stairs leading to the cellar.

Thérèse threw her hands up in the air. "Monsieur Fallon!" she shrilled, as if the Messiah himself had appeared before her. She hurried up the stairs, exchanging a kiss on each cheek with the owner of the château. Beck followed and held out his hand. No kissing for him. He didn't care how customary it was in France. Fallon shook his hand with a firm and friendly grip. He was a tall, burly man, though his girth was somewhat mitigated by the well-cut suit he wore. He'd lost the majority of the once-red hair on his head, but his mustache showed no signs of imminent graying or thinning. It did handlebars proud.

"Mr. Becker, I presume?"

"Beck."

"Welcome to France, my lad."

Beck resisted the impulse to cringe at the loudness of the Brit's voice.

"Has Thérèse introduced you to the project of your lifetime?" There was a twinkle in his eye that Beck found disconcerting. "It's going to be smashing, isn't it? Just smashing."

Beck didn't want to dampen the man's enthusiasm, but he felt that honesty was the best approach. "Well, sir, it probably can be, eventually. But it's the time factor we might have trouble with."

"Come on inside," Fallon said, smacking Beck on the shoulder and motioning him back into the kitchen. "It sounds like we've got some negotiating to do!"

The three of them passed through the kitchen and returned to the bottom of the stairs, where a door led into what must have been a small drawing room at some time. It was on the same level as the château's entrance hall, though on the opposite end of the north wing, so the ceilings were tall and the windows elegant. This space too had been scrubbed down and emptied, except for a large desk, a couch, and two upholstered chairs.

"Welcome to your office," Fallon said, his voice just shy of a bellow.

Beck cut Thérèse a glance. "I thought the office upstairs was the only one in the castle," he said.

"It's the only one with a phone," Thérèse answered with more petulance than was entirely necessary.

"Nonsense," Fallon said, pointing to a small table next to the window, where a wireless phone sat in its cradle. "We're also trying to have high-speed Internet installed, but it appears that's a little more complicated than I thought. Small-town technology, you know? And installing a satellite dish on top of the town's most visible landmark is apparently a matter for much discussion! Sorry we couldn't have it up and running by the time you arrived. Still, if you'll be needing the Internet—" he paused, and Beck nodded— "you'll be able to connect using dial-up, at least until we get the other worked out."

Beck mumbled some threats aimed at Gary under his breath.

"Monsieur Fallon," Thérèse said, "if you'll excuse me, I'll leave you two gentlemen to your . . . negotiations."

"Thank you, Thérèse. Would you like me to see you out?"

She waved her hand in dismissal. "*Non, non!* No need for that. I'll see you tomorrow then, Mr. Becker." And with that, she turned crisply and left the office.

Beck waited for the sound of the back door closing before turning fully to face Fallon. "She's the interior designer on the project?"

"She is indeed. And she's also agreed to be something of a liaison."

"Between . . . ?"

"You and me, for one. I can't be on-site every day, and she has a fairly good idea of what I'm looking for. And between you and your contractors as well. She's fluent in both English and French and will be invaluable in ordering supplies and negotiating prices."

Beck had visions of suppliers canceling transactions just to get away from Thérèse. "I speak French too," he said.

"Yes, of course. Mr. Tyler mentioned that. But you'll have your hands more than full with the renovations, won't you?"

There was some logic to what the jovial Brit was saying, but Beck still disliked the idea. The couple of hours he'd just spent with Thérèse had left him craving a beer. Or something stronger.

"What do you say, lad? Should we talk business while we finish looking around?"

It took another couple of hours for Fallon and Becker to complete the tour of the castle. Beck was pleased to discover that not all the rooms required extensive work. The large adjoining dining rooms still bore the elegance of their glory years. The plaster of their ceilings was crumbling, and the floors and walls needed repair, but these were straightforward jobs that he could easily delegate to others.

He'd already seen most of the second floor, so they moved on to the third. It was a series of sixteen rooms, all with small dormer windows, alternately circular and rectangular. The ceilings in these rooms were low, making the spaces feel smaller than they actually were. It would take some artful remodeling to turn these into bedrooms for which patrons would willingly pay top dollar.

The last place they visited was the former stables. They were located in a long, two-story building just to the left of the château. The bottom floor boasted ceilings and doors tall enough to allow riders on horses to circulate without impediment, and the upper floor was another series of small, mostly dilapidated bedrooms. Fallon cautioned Becker to avoid walking near the orange plastic cone on the landing. "Watch your step there, lad. There's a rotten spot in the floor. It gets worse in the east end, I'm afraid. A former owner sealed off the communicating door in the hallway to spare visitors from injury. You can see it boarded up down the hall there."

Becker glanced down the dark hallway and saw the crisscrossing planks that had been nailed across the doorway leading to the far portion of the corridor. This was a dormitory space where jockeys had been stacked like lumber in poorly constructed cubbyholes. The garish wallpaper peeling from thin partitions further proved that little decorative effort had been invested in these rooms.

"This will be phase three of the project," Fallon said. "If we get that far," he quickly amended.

Beck looked around. "What do you see happening here?"

"I'm not quite sure," the Brit admitted. "Maybe some on-site lodging for the personnel on this level? A small spa and a museum in the stable space downstairs? You'll find that every shovelful of dirt you raise on the grounds will hold artifacts dating back a couple hundred years, so we could stock a few display cases fairly fast."

Beck nodded. He could see the potential for a striking museum in the elegant arches and molded ceilings of the bottom floor, with smaller, more intimate rooms at the opposite end, where guests would be pampered in a high-class spa. But there were more pressing matters on Beck's mind than massages and pedicures. "If this is phase three, what's phase one and two?" he asked.

Fallon led him back to the stairs, skirting the plastic cone. "Phase one is getting the ground floor ready for my wife's birthday, of course," he said, moving down the stairs. "We'll need the château's entryway, the large dining rooms, the ballroom, and the grand staircase to be finished by then. That's April 23, by the way."

"Not much time."

"Your partner seemed to think you could pull it off. What's your opinion?"

"My gut feeling? Doubtful."

"And how often is your gut right, lad?"

Becker considered the question for a moment. "These days, not very often," he said with utter honesty.

"All I ask is that you give it your best effort," Fallon assured him. "Your partner made it very clear that you wouldn't be staying longer than your contract demands. If you can finish phase one, I'll be satisfied. And if you can lay the foundation for phase two while you're at it—"

"Phase two?"

"Transforming the second and third floors into guest rooms and common areas. I presume you've seen your partner's blueprints?"

Beck nodded.

"His drawings completely alter the floor plan without losing any of the château's old-world charm. He's really quite a visionary, isn't he?"

"That's one word for him."

"Tearing down walls and replacing support beams are both major tasks, from what I've gathered. You're going to be a very busy man."

Beck shook his head. "You realize this is virtually impossible, right?"

"Preposterous. Exactly. But your partner, Mr. Tyler, struck me as a man who likes a challenge when I met him last year—a trait I quite fancy—and it seems to me, from our brief interaction, that it might be a trait you share with him."

"How many extra laborers are in the budget?" Beck asked.

"I've already got a crew working on the plumbing and electric,"

Fallon responded. "A couple others are ready to get to work on the rest of the project as soon as you're ready for them."

Beck nodded his approval as they stepped out of the stables and stood looking at the château. Night had descended, and the moon cast stark shadows on the limestone walls.

"Imagine it," Fallon said, pointing his chin toward the slumbering towers and windows. "A hotel. A spa. Tennis courts out back. Gourmet cuisine. Louis XIV furniture in all the suites. This can be a gem, my lad. And a lucrative one at that!"

They walked across the circle of grass in front of the castle and stopped when they stood dead center, facing the centuries-old building.

"There's only one problem," Beck said.

"What's that?"

"My apartment. It smells like a urinal."

Fallon let rip with a roaring laugh and smacked Beck on the back so hard that the younger man lost his balance. "Well, that can be remedied easily enough! We'll tackle it in the morning." He stood there chuckling, his hand patting Becker's shoulder, his eyes soft on the castle before him. "We're going to make this happen, lad. And it's going to be just grand."

3

THE MANOR STOOD on a hill high above Lamorlaye, its graceful lines and manicured lawns hidden in a thick forest of oak, beech, and chestnut trees. It had been built in 1912 by the Meunier family, but they'd had no choice but to surrender the property to Heinrich Himmler's Waffen-SS when the Nazis had invaded Lamorlaye in 1940. The SS had begun as a small paramilitary force devoted to Hitler but had grown into a formidable symbol of Nazi power that no one dared oppose. Kommandant Erhard Koch had quickly made the manor his headquarters, a guarded estate few were permitted to see and fewer still to enter. Even the Wehrmacht cavalrymen who had made their home in Lamorlaye's nearby castle and stables were unwelcome guests at the manor.

It wasn't really by choice that the girls had ended up working there. Like most of the villagers, they had seen the Germans arrive in town and had assumed they'd stay only a few weeks, maybe months. But more than two years after the Occupation had begun, they'd had to resign themselves to the fact that the Germans—the boches, as the French Resistance pejoratively called them—were there to stay.

It was during a Saturday-morning market that one of Koch's men had approached the stand Marie and her mother were tending. With the war, fruits and vegetables had become scarce—eggs and meat even more so—and the once-thriving market had been reduced to a handful of farm stands from which the rich and the occupiers bought rationed food at exorbitant prices. That morning, Koch's guard had informed the women that Kommandant Koch needed help at the manor and that he was willing to pay for the services of volunteers with food and modest salaries. Marie had signed up on the spot, and though her mother hadn't been enthusiastic about her choice, the handouts she'd brought home had quickly quelled any misgivings. Those were lean years in Lamorlaye, and every extra loaf of bread was a rare luxury.

Two weeks later, when Koch had commanded Marie to recruit additional help, she'd asked her friend Elise to join her at the manor. The two sixteen-year-olds had spent every day since then working together. They'd commiserated over the workload and made faces behind Koch's back on days when he'd stormed around the premises barking orders and thundering his displeasure. And they'd kept each other going on days when all they wanted to do was quit. Their hours were long and they were treated like slaves, but they knew their families counted on them to supplement the meager resources they had.

It was in early July that they sensed a change coming. It was nothing they could point to—they still spent each day cleaning, doing laundry, and meeting every need the Kommandant brought to their attention. But there was a feeling of anticipation in the manor, a lightness among the SS and their staff that was so uncharacteristic that it worried the girls. In their experience, anything that made the boches *happy was to be feared.*

The trucks arrived on a Friday, loaded down with furniture and boxes of strange-looking instruments. Elise and Marie watched soldiers unload them under Koch's watchful eye and carry their contents up the stairs to the second and third floors of the manor. No one mentioned the activity to them, and they knew better than to ask questions. A few days later, when they'd stayed late ironing SS uniforms for an event the next day, the girls had snuck up to the second floor and, hoping Koch and his acolytes had retired to their quarters for the night, had started opening doors.

"This is strange," Elise said, standing just inside the first room they'd explored. Marie had suspected that the SS were turning the manor into a hotel, but the large assortment of medical equipment in that room convinced her otherwise. The girls looked around, wide-eyed. The hospital-style bed, the examination table, the surgical lights, the instruments . . .

"You think we're going to become nurses next?" Elise asked, a nervous giggle in her words. "I mean, they've already made us into maids and cooks and seamstresses and gardeners. Why not nurses too, right?"

Marie stepped into the room and looked more closely at some of the instruments. "I don't get it," she said. "Why would they bring their wounded all the way here from the front? They'd die on the road."

Elise shook her head. "I don't like this. Whatever they're doing, it's going to mean more work for us."

The other rooms on the floor held none of the medical equipment. They'd been exquisitely furnished with comfortable beds and plush couches and chairs, their walls adorned with expensive artwork and their floors covered with imported rugs.

"Probably all requisitioned," Marie said, glancing around the fourth bedroom they'd entered and moving to sit in the chaise lounge by the window. "I bet there's a family somewhere in Chantilly wondering who stole their chair."

Elise giggled again. "So what do you think?" she asked, plopping down on the bed and testing its springs. "Are they turning the manor into a hospital?"

"I don't know."

A day later, a handful of German nurses moved into the servant quarters at the back of the manor. And two days after that, the "residents" started to arrive. As each Daimler-Benz limousine drove up to the front steps, Kommandant Koch rushed out to greet the new guest, escorting her personally to the room that would be hers for the duration of her stay. Though the first women who arrived spoke German, others seemed to struggle with the language, and Elise and Marie took great joy in watching Koch trying to communicate with them without losing his aplomb.

The girls tried to be inconspicuous as they observed the comings and goings, a task made more difficult by the presence of Frau Heinz, a solidly built, middle-aged German nurse with graying blonde hair who took control of the running of the manor on the day the first resident arrived. She was a commanding presence, her voice gruff and her orders succinct, and though she spoke in an almost friendly manner to the women who were guests of the manor, she addressed Marie and Elise with a sort of professional contempt.

"I liked it a lot better around here when Koch was the only barbarian," Elise said one morning as the friends were making up yet another bed in one of the upstairs rooms.

Marie wasn't as concerned about Frau Heinz as she was about the residents. "Did you see Frau Bouret arrive this morning?"

"The pregnant one?"

"Pregnant to her eyeballs."

Elise took special care folding the sheet around the corners of the *bed, lest Frau Heinz deem their efforts substandard and have them repeat the task, as she had on several previous occasions. "Koch was all over her the moment she arrived."*

"Maybe it's the blonde hair."

"She does look like an American movie star."

Marie had spent several days trying to make sense of the new activity in the mansion, and Frau Bouret's distended belly had provided her the puzzle piece she lacked. "Do you think the others are pregnant too?" Marie asked.

Elise stopped in the act of pulling a pillowcase over a down pillow. She looked at her friend. "What are you thinking?"

"I'm thinking that there's a room on this floor that looks an awful lot like a delivery room and that the only residents are women, one of whom is visibly pregnant."

"Frau Rieux might be too. Either that or she's built kind of strange." Elise paused, squinting her eyes with the effort of analyzing what she'd observed since the first resident's arrival. "Why would they be coming here to have their babies?" she asked. "Couldn't they just find a hospital nearer to where they live? I mean, Frau Janssen is Dutch—surely there are working hospitals left in Holland!"

Marie shrugged. "Maybe she needed to get away for some reason."

"I could ask Karl," Elise suggested.

"You're still seeing Karl?" Marie was appalled. Elise had met the young German soldier when she'd made a delivery to the castle several weeks before. The way she told it, there had been an instant attraction between them, Karl immediately approaching her to comment on the yellow dress that had caught his attention. But Marie distrusted the slight, tense Nazi whose Schütze rank was among the lowest in the Wehrmacht.

"We ran into each other at the market last week," Elise said breezily. Too breezily for Marie's liking.

"And you talked?"

"For a while," Elise giggled, blonde curls bouncing. She caught Marie's concerned glance and waved her suspicion away. "Oh, don't be a mother! I've got one of those already, and she's more than enough." She tossed a pillow at Marie, followed by a pillowcase. "Karl hasn't been anything but polite—you have nothing to worry about."

Marie took a long look at her friend, registering Elise's heightened color and dancing eyes, and wondered just how worried she really ought to be.

4

BECK'S FIRST NIGHT in the château was memorable. In the early-morning hours when sleep had eluded him, he'd had all the usual impulses—find an open bar, surf the Internet, order up some late-night takeout. And each one of his cravings had been foiled by his new location. There was probably no such thing as Chinese takeout in Lamorlaye. No more than there was high-speed Internet in the castle or a bar around the corner—though he planned on investigating that tomorrow.

Somewhere around 4 a.m., after he'd dragged his mattress away from the stench of his apartment and up to the second-floor hallway, sleep had finally claimed him. The combination of jet lag and nervous exhaustion rendered his slumber dreamless and deep, so deep that the sound of footsteps on the stairs the next morning didn't wake him until two pairs of sneakers—one white and one pink—stood in front of his face.

He focused on the shoes while fragments of reality swirled in his mind and finally fell into place. He was in a castle in France, lying on a mattress in a hallway and staring at what appeared to be two pairs of children's feet. As he had no particular fondness for children, the feet were not a welcome sight. His displeasure was only compounded by the lack of sleep he'd suffered during the night.

Feeling like his eyelids and brain were weighed down by cement blocks, he closed his eyes just long enough to gather courage, then opened them again resolutely. Grunting into a sitting position, he gave his scalp a vigorous scratch, ran a hand over the stubble on his cheeks and jaw, and stretched his stiff back, still avoiding looking directly at the children standing next to him.

"He's ignoring us," one of them said. It was more a statement of fact than a complaint.

"He might be deaf," said the other, just as matter-of-fact as the first. "Or blind."

Beck drew back his blankets and stood, a little unsteadily at first. He stretched his neck to one side and felt something pop. His morning disposition was seldom very people friendly, and waking up to pint-size strangers wasn't improving his mood. He raked his fingers through his hair and bent over to pick up his mattress, sheets and all. "Get out of my way," he said, cutting a look at the children.

The little girl, redheaded and freckled, stared at him with wide, surprised eyes. The little boy crossed his arms and jutted out his bottom lip, a study in childhood defiance. "That was mean," he said more forcefully and loudly than Beck thought was strictly necessary. "I'm going to tell Jade!"

Beck wasn't sure who Jade was, but he was convinced that a beer would make it matter less. Or a glass of red. Anything to dull the drumming in his skull and the ache in the small of his back. "Sure . . . whatever, kid," he said absently, moving with his mattress toward the narrow corkscrew staircase that led down to his apartment. He peered over his shoulder before taking the first step. The boy was still standing there, arms crossed, glaring at him, and the girl stood just behind him, peering around her brother at the scary stranger carrying his bed down the castle stairs.

He had just dropped his mattress back on the bedsprings and pulled off his T-shirt to head to the bathroom when light footsteps ran up the stairs and past the door to his apartment. "Philippe! Eva!" It was a soft voice, nearly a whisper, but it commanded attention. "What are you doing up here? I told you to wait in the kitchen!"

The children launched into simultaneous loud reports as Beck stepped onto the landing to hear what was going on.

"There was a man on the floor . . ." Beck was fairly sure that was the boy.

"With a mattress and a blanket . . ."

"And he was mean to me."

"Really, really mean."

"And then he got up and said, 'Get out of my way!'"

"Yeah, just like that!" the little girl chimed in.

"And then he carried his bed downstairs. He has a really lot of hair."

"And he's not happy."

The other small voice repeated with emphasis, "Not—happy!"

Beck tried to duck out of sight as the trio came into view, but the boy saw him before he could retreat. "That's him!" he yelled, pointing at the disheveled and now mildly uncomfortable Beck. "He's the one who was mean to me."

The woman descending the stairs with one child's hand in each of hers seemed as discomfited by the encounter as he was. She paused briefly and glanced in his direction. "I'm so sorry, Mr. . . . ?"

"Becker."

"Mr. Becker. I instructed them not to come up here and bother you, but . . ." Her dark ponytail bobbed with the sincerity of her apology. Her wide-set brown eyes and small, upturned nose accentuated her youthful look, and Beck found it hard to believe she'd be celebrating her fortieth birthday in just over two months.

Realizing he was standing there in his flannel pajama bottoms, bare chested and unshowered, Beck figured it might be best to postpone official introductions. "No problem, Mrs. Fallon," he said gruffly, gradually closing the door to his apartment as he spoke. "No harm done. . . ." She opened her mouth to speak, but he cut her off. "Just have to—" he motioned over his shoulder toward the bathroom—"take a shower."

He closed the door and leaned his forehead against the wood, the stench of the rear bedroom nearly distracting him from the awkwardness of his first encounter with his boss's wife. "Nice job, Becker. Brilliant." He bounced his forehead against the door a couple times, a sort of penance for his self-humiliation, then padded off to the bathroom on bare feet. His first day as an official castle renovator was starting off pretty inauspiciously.

It was a clean, shaved, and dressed Marshall Becker who strolled into the kitchen several minutes later, his mood only slightly improved by his shower in a space that was too confining for his large frame. He'd followed the smell of coffee to the kitchen, his need for caffeine overpowering his aversion to early-morning conversation.

"Beck, my boy!" Fallon exclaimed when he appeared. "Come," he said, patting a stool next to the stainless-steel table in the middle of the kitchen where he sat. "Pull up a stool. We've got some introducing to do!"

The two children sat across from Fallon, each dipping a buttered piece of French bread in a large bowl of what looked to be chocolate milk. There was a butter slick on top of the brown liquid, but that didn't seem to be bothering anyone. Fallon's wife sat next to the boy, instructing him to use his napkin on his chin. Only a small amount of the hot chocolate the bread was absorbing was actually making it into his mouth.

"You've met my children, I hear." Fallon beamed, his chest puffed out with pride.

"And your wife, yes," Beck said, taking a seat next to his employer, reaching for the pot of coffee in the middle of the table and hooking the empty mug next to it with his finger. "We ran into each other upstairs."

Fallon's wife ducked her head and blushed, shooting a look at the children, who were suddenly hiding giggles behind their hands. Fallon himself wasn't quite so subtle. He roared so loudly that it made Beck jump. And then he smacked him on the back with unbridled joviality, his guffaws subsiding into chuckles.

"Something I said?" Beck asked.

"Becker, my boy, I'd like you to meet Jade Loubry. My children's nanny and our family friend."

So this was the Jade the kids had mentioned earlier. Jade wiped some milk off the little girl's chin with a napkin and smiled up at Becker from under thick, straight bangs. Her voice had the melodious lilt of the French language, but her English was nearly flawless. "I would have explained earlier," she said quietly, still a little embarrassed, "but you seemed in a hurry to shut your door."

Becker dropped his chin and rolled his head back and forth. This day was starting off just swell. Not that the night had been anything to brag about. Its only saving grace had been the absence of dreams.

"Tell Mr. Becker your names, children."

Becker looked up and met two pairs of curious eyes.

"Philippe?" Fallon prodded.

Philippe looked at Jade, who nodded. "My name is Philippe," he said. Then he poked his sister with his elbow.

"Ow," she whined.

"Can you tell Mr. Becker your name?" Jade coaxed.

The pale, freckled redhead rubbed her arm where Philippe's elbow had connected with it and looked cautiously at the stranger across the table. "Eva," she said. Then, on a courageous streak, she added, "I'm six. Philippe too."

"So you're twins?" Beck asked, trying to appear friendly.

Eva looked up at Jade as if the question were too ridiculous for her to waste her time on. "Yes, they're twins," Jade said.

"But you'd never know it to look at them, would you," Fallon said. He was right, of course. Philippe's light-brown hair and blue eyes were a stark contrast to his sister's red hair and direct brown gaze. He was as stocky as she was delicate and, apparently, as little-boy as she was little-girl. Beck had the feeling that the average woman would have oohed and aahed all over herself at the sight of these two kids, but all they inspired in him was prudence. It wouldn't be a good thing to antagonize the boss's children.

"Come on, you two," Jade said, standing and motioning the children out of the kitchen. "Time to get some work done. We'll clean up later."

They grabbed their large bowls with both hands and downed the last of the buttery hot chocolate. Eva reached for her napkin to dry off her chin, while Philippe opted for the elbow of his long-sleeve T-shirt instead.

When they'd left, Fallon moved to the other side of the broad stainless-steel table and pushed a basket of bread toward Beck. "The children usually study at home in the mornings, then have the afternoon for other activities, but now that Sylvia is expecting our third, we've had to somewhat change the arrangement."

Beck felt surprise cross his face and quickly schooled it into something looking more like idle curiosity. "Your third, huh?"

Fallon leaned in conspiratorially. "It was my wife's idea at first, but I'm quite delighted about it now."

"Yeah? Congratulations." Beck focused his attention on buttering his bread and not imagining a forty-year-old pregnant woman posing on his grand staircase on her birthday.

"The timing is actually quite convenient," Fallon continued. "Sylvia is getting more and more tired as time passes and would prefer some peace and quiet around home, so it seemed like a perfect solution to have Jade and the kids spend their days here. The grounds are safe and secluded, and the castle is every child's dream playground."

Beck swallowed the chunk of buttered bread lodged in his throat. "They're going to be here?"

"Yes, of course. But they'll be doing lessons with Jade during the morning—probably right here, as it's out of the workmen's way. And in the afternoon, they'll play on the property."

"Every day?" Beck had never tried to complete a major renovation while a child-care facility operated on-site, and he wasn't too enthused about this first experiment of the sort.

"Most days. That won't be a problem, will it, lad?"

"I guess it's fine." His tone held little sincerity or confidence, despite his greatest efforts to sound accommodating.

"Right, then. And your reward for so much flexibility will be Jade's cooking. She needs to feed the children anyway, so I've suggested that she just make a little more to feed you, too."

At this, Beck raised an eyebrow and gave the arrangement a second chance. If Jade was any kind of cook, her meals would be a welcome change from the restaurant and takeout food on which he'd lived for the past ten years.

Beck and Fallon spent the rest of the morning discussing the finer details of the renovation as they pored over the drawings and blueprints Beck had brought with him from Boston. They wandered the castle, this time in daylight, comparing ideas and reaching compromises that both preserved the authenticity of the site and increased its profitability. The local company Fallon had hired to redo the wiring and plumbing had started two weeks before with Beck's apartment and were well into the mammoth operation. With Fallon's wealth and renown—not to mention the prospect of additional jobs in the future—companies seemed to be tripping over themselves for a part in the project, deploying large crews and doing the work in record time. That was just fine by Beck. The more of the grunt work they did, the freer he'd be to concentrate on the historical details of the daunting renovation. Once the new wiring was in place, Becker would be able to begin work in earnest. That left him with just a couple days to settle in, gather supplies, finish sketching his plans, and begin the process of turning a centuries-old château into a modern enterprise.

Thérèse arrived at noon, looking exactly as she had the day before. Her graying hair was in its tight, formal chignon, her clothes impeccable and her face set in a haughty and mildly condescending expression. None of the nervousness he'd witnessed when he'd arrived was evident. She seemed more subdued, though she still moved with the speed and energy of a woman half her age. In the States, someone her age would have been eyeing her 401(k) and planning a move to Florida. But Thérèse seemed to have no such plans.

Beck stood with Fallon and the interior designer in the entrance of the castle and read aloud the list of "assignments" for Thérèse that he'd jotted on a notepad. Beck was pleased to be able to pass a few of the responsibilities off to her. They included ordering materials, renting power tools, hiring labor for basic tasks around the castle—like painting, stripping wallpaper, and sanding floors—and getting the château connected to the Internet. He'd need it for research, communication, and *consultation* with Gary. One of them was big on that.

He ticked off each of Thérèse's assignments as he quickly and curtly explained them to her, lapsing into the construction/renovation jargon that was his bread and butter. He was nearing the bottom of the first page when Fallon cleared his throat in a very deliberate manner. Beck stopped midsentence and glanced up at his employer, a little put out by the interruption.

"Lad, I know you know what you're talking about," he said, one hand in the pocket of his cashmere pants and the other held up, urging caution, "but . . ." He looked pointedly at Thérèse, who stood wide-eyed next to Beck, still staring at the list of duties he held in front of him. "It might be helpful to slow down a little and allow for some questions," Fallon suggested in a mildly insistent tone.

Beck had been so intent on getting through his list and moving on to the next item on his own agenda that he hadn't been aware of the growing discomfiture of the woman standing next to him. Though her poise was unaffected, there was a small muscle twitching at the corner of her mouth, a subtle symptom of the nervousness he'd seen the evening before.

"Sorry, Thérèse," he said, feigning good nature. "Let me slow it down a little for you. I know it's early in the day and all."

It was far from early, and she was far from slow—and the statement had the desired effect. Her composure crumbled a little around the edges as she pulled herself up straighter, the muscle spasm more pronounced. Her face seemed to shrink into a pointed mask of pursed lips and narrowed eyes. "There's no need to slow it down, Mr. Becker," she said, darting a glance at Fallon. "All I require is more ample information. I am not the imbecile you suggest, but this is all rather . . . outside my realm of expertise."

Fallon stepped in before the situation could escalate, giving Becker's arm a warning squeeze. "Miss Gallet, would you mind making a couple calls to the Internet company and seeing what they've come up with? The phone number for my contact with Wanadoo is on the desk in the office. Henri, I believe, is his name."

She marched off in the direction of the office, her heels clicking primly on the castle's marble floor.

Beck dislodged Fallon's hand by reaching for an imaginary itch on the side of his neck.

"What was that?" Fallon asked, not so much angry as confused.

"We, uh, got off to a rough start yesterday," Beck said, scanning the notes he'd jotted down earlier.

"Well, do what you have to do to unroughen it, Mr. Becker. I leave for England in the morning and don't want to return to a war zone in five days."

Becker hung his head and bit back an unnecessary retort.

"Listen," Fallon said, lowering his voice. "Thérèse appeared on my doorstep a year ago and offered me her services based solely on hearing that I'd acquired the château. This is her dream project and she was a godsend—I wasn't even in the market for an interior designer at the time. Her résumé is impeccable and her expertise in the field is well established. I assure you that Miss Gallet's assistance and connections in the community are going to be important for your work."

Beck nodded. "I understand."

"Just . . . give yourself some time to get used to her, lad. And try not to hurt her feelings. I get the impression they're rather . . . fragile."

"Of course," Beck said with just enough conviction to assuage his employer. He turned his attention to the staircase that rose with sweeping grace from marble floors to molded ceilings.

Fallon took the hint. "One more thing before I leave you to

your craft," he said, motioning for Beck to move with him to the entryway doors. He pointed at the dilapidated gatehouse attached to the tall wrought-iron fence that guarded the entrance to the castle grounds.

"You want to remodel that too?" Beck asked, starting to wonder if his boss had delusions of grandeur.

"Oh, no! Heavens, no. You just need to know that Jojo lives there. A strange old fellow who sort of . . . came with the property."

Beck gave his boss a questioning look. "Jojo?"

"The old boy has lived in that poor excuse for a house since as long as anyone can remember around here, and no one seems inclined to evict him. I briefly raised the issue in one of our negotiations for the acquisition of the castle, but the reaction was so strong that I decided to let the poor soul stay put."

Beck squinted at the old building, noting the broken windows, the rotten thatched roof, and the overgrown path that led to its peeling door. "Well, as long as he stays out of my way . . ."

"That's why I'm telling you about him, actually. He tends to . . . wander. Usually at night, mind you. And he isn't much for talking either. The townsfolk seem to think he's either mute or a ghost."

Beck remembered Thérèse's remark about finding alternate lodging and wondered if this "ghost" was what she'd been referring to.

"Either way," Fallon continued, "he wouldn't hurt a fly, but he could scare the wits out of you if you didn't know to expect him!"

"Well, now I know."

"Just consider him another historical feature of the Château de Lamorlaye," Fallon said dramatically, tracing an invisible marquee in the air in front of him.

"Sure, I'll do that," Beck said. But he still planned on sleeping with a crowbar near his bed.

5

WITH THE TWINS out playing in the park, Jade had put some elbow grease into scrubbing the smell out of Becker's apartment. When he entered his quarters after a long shopping expedition with Thérèse in search of the perfect wood to repair the main staircase, he found Jade backing out of the room, spraying an air freshener as she went.

She heard him coming and turned, smoothing the fabric of her khaki skirt over her hips. "Mr. Becker—I'm just finishing up here. . . ."

Beck tossed his coat and wallet onto the chair just inside his bedroom door, then moved down the hall to where Jade stood.

"I scrubbed the room with vinegar and soap. Including the walls. And I used bleach in the corner with the . . . pee in it." She seemed embarrassed to have to use the word. "I read online that baking soda helps, so that's what you see on the floor over there. It's supposed to sit at least overnight. And you might want to leave the window open too. Just to air it out. I'll be back in the morning to mop up the soda."

She'd scarcely made eye contact with him while she spoke. She'd taken in his faded jeans and the white T-shirt he wore under an unbuttoned plaid shirt but had merely skimmed his face.

"I didn't expect you to—"

"It's nothing." She smiled a little and bent over to toss her supplies into the yellow bucket on the floor. "Mr. Fallon doesn't like his employees to complain that their rooms smell like urinals."

Beck wasn't sure what she wanted from him. An apology? A more heartfelt thank-you? Whatever it was, he wasn't inclined to play along.

After a moment of silence had passed, Jade pulled down on the hem of her pale-blue long-sleeved T-shirt and smiled tightly. "If you'll excuse me, I need to finish supper. It will be served at six, if you care to join us." She paused. "Or I can bring a tray up to your quarters for you if you'd rather eat alone."

She brushed past him on her way to the stairs, leaving a hint of lily of the valley in the castle's stale air. He watched her go, her ponytail swinging and her head held high.

He dropped a pair of pink rubber gloves on the sink when he entered the kitchen half an hour later.

"You left these upstairs," he said.

Jade gave him a look and tossed the gloves into a bucket beneath the sink. "Thank you, Mr. Becker."

The kitchen smelled of onions and basil. A thick stew bubbled on the stove, and lettuce floated in a sink full of water under a window with a view on the outside corridor that led to the fruit cellar.

"So what are you, exactly?" Beck asked, kicking himself moments later for his lack of tact. *Nice job, Becker.*

Jade turned to look at him, brow furrowed, and repeated, arms crossed, "What am I?"

Becker conceded the point. "Okay, that was poorly put," he said. "What I meant to ask is, what exactly do you do?"

"Aside from graciously scrubbing the pee off a perfect stranger's floor?" she asked sweetly.

Beck paused, trying to guess at the subtext of her statement, then giving up. "Yup, aside from that," he said.

Jade turned back to the sink and began to take lettuce leaves from the water, checking each one for dirt and bugs before tossing it in the basket of a spinner. "Well, Mr. Becker, since you ask so kindly, I'm a bit of a . . . what would you call it? A home assistant, perhaps."

"*Une femme à tout faire?*" Beck asked in perfect, albeit *québécois*, French.

Jade's head snapped around, then tilted to one side, eyes narrowed in suspicion. "That's a good French term, Mr. Becker. 'A woman who does everything.' Not the type of French an American student would normally learn in basic language studies."

Beck decided he liked the precise and delicate way she shaped her words. It made her English sound somehow daintier and lighter than the language Americans spoke. "I was raised in Québec," he finally said. "Just until the age of ten, but I thought you should know." Jade looked at him questioningly. "You know—in case you get tempted to talk about me behind my back or something."

"I'll try not to talk about you at all," she said with a sweet smile, turning back to the lettuce in the sink. "Yes, I am indeed a *femme à tout faire*, though the term is often used in a derogatory way."

Beck held up his hands. "Hey, no offense . . ."

Jade looked at him pointedly. "I love kids. I love teaching. I love cooking. I love cleaning. If I can make a decent living doing what I love, I'd prefer to call it a career rather than label it a social status."

Beck considered her statement for a moment, surprised again at the fluency of her English. He eyed the clock. Twenty minutes 'til six. He'd miscalculated this move. Twenty minutes of conversation seemed an overwhelming prospect.

"And you, Mr. Becker? Is your trade a calling or a status symbol for you?"

Beck opened his mouth for a sarcastic reply, but Philippe and Eva interrupted his retort with a flamboyant entrance into the kitchen. "Jade, Jade! We found a giant snail!" Philippe yelled as he ran up to the sink, the pride of the hunter on his face. "Look!" He held out his prize, a nondescript snail of fairly large size—but to his eyes, it seemed to be a fantastic dinosaur.

Jade took a step back. "That's—hmm—that's lovely, Philippe," she said, clearly not inclined to get a closer look at the snail.

"Can we cook him and eat him?" Eva chimed in, her British accent round and rich.

Jade put a hand to her chest in mock horror. "What?" she squealed. "You want to kill the biggest snail this castle has ever seen?" The children's eyes grew wider. "You want to eat the largest creature you've ever trapped during your fierce hunting expeditions in the woods?" She was making the statements so dramatic that even Beck found himself getting caught up. The children began to shake their heads, her words elevating their common snail to the rank of mythical beast. "You want to slaughter the king of this venerable castle for *meat*?!" she finished with great flair.

Eva and Philippe stared, wide-eyed, as her words settled over the kitchen. When they finally spoke, it was in a machine-gun fire of overlapping statements.

"We're not going to eat him!" Philippe declared.

"No, we're really, really not!"

"We're going to make him a crown . . ."

"And build him a little mini snail castle . . ."

"And dig a moat around it and put water in it . . ."

"And call him King Snail."

Philippe paused long enough to give his sister a disparaging look. "We can't call him King Snail."

"Why not?"

"Because it's too normal," he said, drawing out the last word. They both stared at the snail for a while, trying to derive inspiration from its dull brown shell. Jade looked on in amusement, and Becker tried hard not to find the scene endearing.

Eva's face was pinched in thought, her freckled nose wrinkled with concentration. "I know!" she finally squealed, clapping and skipping a little where she stood. "We can call him . . ." She paused for dramatic effect and lowered her voice to utter, "King Kong!"

"That's a monkey," Philippe said with obvious disdain.

"Yeah, but it's a really big monkey," Beck muttered, surprising himself and earning a surprised look from Jade.

"It's a good name," Eva persisted. "It's a really, really good name!"

But Philippe was still racking his mind for a better one. "King . . ." It looked like the perfect name was trapped inside his mind, and the mental constipation was turning his face red. "King . . . Rover!" He punched his fist into the air in victory and did his own little dance. Eva looked like she was about to disapprove of his choice, but she opted to join in the victory dance instead.

Jade placed a hand at the back of each of their necks and steered them toward the kitchen door. "Great. King Rover it is. Wonderful name, really. Now why don't you find just the perfect place to put him and call it his castle?"

The children looked at each other in anticipation of the task ahead. Apparently communicating without words, they both took off running at the same time, in the same direction, yelling, "To the castle!" at the top of their lungs.

"But come back quickly—dinner's almost ready!" Jade yelled

after them. When she heard no reply, she closed the door and turned slowly to face Beck. "I suppose I'm going to have to go out and fetch them in a few minutes, aren't I?"

Beck shrugged. "Probably." He'd been a kid before—eons ago. He remembered how it worked.

They stood in awkward silence for a while. "I guess I'll . . ." Jade pointed toward the salad still floating in the sink and got back to work. "Oh, to be a child again, right?" she asked when a few more seconds of silence had passed.

"Actually, it's been so long that . . ." He found himself tempted to pull up a stool and shoot the breeze—and the notion halted him midsentence. For a brief, uncomfortable instant, he realized that the thought of being alone in his apartment seemed less inviting than sitting in the garishly lit kitchen with a woman he barely knew. Jade looked over her shoulder at him with a puzzled expression. Beck allowed the usual mask to come down over his face.

"I'm going up to my room," he said, moving toward the door.

"Will you be coming back down for . . . ?"

"No." It came out more curtly than he'd intended.

Jade bobbed her head, slightly perplexed, and turned back to the sink. "I'll bring a tray up to you, then," she said.

Becker nodded and left the kitchen.

Beck didn't drag his bed up the stairs that night. Though the smell persisted, it was much more bearable thanks to Jade's intervention, and with his window open despite the February cold, he fell asleep fairly quickly.

And then the dreams came again. Beck's dreams had alternating plot lines. Some began in a college cafeteria. Others started in the restaurant atop the John Hancock Center. The worst began on a

Sunday morning in Maine. All of them ended with Beck jerking awake, drenched in acrid sweat, a horror so heavy in his stomach, so constricting in his chest, that he had to lie still for a while and fight nausea with deep breaths. It was in those wrenching moments, with the images and emotions of his dreams receding like pale ghosts into his subconscious, that Becker felt most agonizingly alive.

In the early-morning hours of his second night in the castle, Becker reached for the light by his bed, threw back his covers, and let his sweat-soaked body cool. The breeze from the window was wintery and chilled him until he shivered. He neither closed the window nor covered himself again. He preferred the body-numbing cold of reality to the fevered torment of his dreams. After several minutes of the self-inflicted torture, when he could trust his legs to support his weight again, Beck turned off the light and moved from the bed to the window. He draped a blanket over his shoulders and stood by the old-fashioned radiator, looking out.

A heavy fog covered the castle grounds. He could barely discern the circular patch of grass around which the driveway curved. The two guard towers, standing at attention on either side of the château's front gate, were eerie sentinels guarding the property with gun-slit eyes. The fence, a collection of wrought-iron spikes, ran along the road outside the castle grounds. It stood at least eight feet tall and was mounted on a low stone wall that curved in a perfect arch. If it meant to intimidate, it did a fine job.

It was only after his eyes had adjusted to the dark that Becker noticed a faint light coming from the gatehouse. It shone, wavering, out the side window. A candle, perhaps, or light from a fireplace. Beck thought he saw a figure crossing the lawn in the fog, heading toward the stables with purpose and stealth—no more than a moving shadow in the stillness of the night—but he couldn't be sure. The fog swirled on a soft, cold breeze, and the apparition vanished into the mobile gray.

Becker pushed the window nearly closed and returned to his bed. He held a hand up in front of his face. It shook visibly. He needed a drink—he needed it badly. But he'd been so busy during the day with planning and shopping for supplies that he'd forgotten how difficult his nights were without booze. He lay back, an arm bent behind his head, and tried to keep himself awake by planning for the work that would begin in just a few hours. As long as he didn't sleep, he wouldn't dream. And as long as he didn't dream, he'd be okay.

Morning came as a relief. So did the smell of coffee and eggs wafting up the stairs from the kitchen. Becker got up quickly after merely dozing for a good portion of the night and rejuvenated his spirits with a long, hot shower. His mother had always told him that a cold one would do even better to wash away the cobwebs in his mind, but he wasn't willing to test her theory quite yet.

He entered the kitchen with still-wet hair and the firm intention of being civil, which usually required limited contact with humans. His resolution teetered a little when he found Thérèse sitting at the table. Jade was slicing bread at the counter.

"Good morning," he said, stopping just inside the kitchen's archway, eyeing the pot of coffee still in the percolator and the pan of eggs on the stove. He glanced at Thérèse, who sat starchily across from the twins. She nodded her greeting. The twins watched him with a mixture of awe and caution. He looked at Eva. She immediately averted her gaze, dropping her chin and letting her eyes drift toward her brother. When Beck looked at Philippe, the six-year-old crossed his arms and stared right back. He was wearing the same outfit as his sister, though his sweatshirt was blue and hers was red. But the jeans and sneakers were pretty much the same.

"Shouldn't you be reading or writing or something?" Beck asked. He wasn't crazy about talking to kids, particularly not first thing in the morning.

Eva, whose hair was pulled back on the sides with barrettes that matched her sweatshirt, leaned across the table toward him and spoke in a secretive voice. "Jade said we don't have to start until eight thirty. That way she can make breakfast for everybody and get it cleaned up."

"Yeah?" Becker wasn't exactly pleased by the news. "Sounds like a good reason to eat somewhere else," he muttered. "That way you two can start your lessons earlier."

Eva's eyes widened. Eating in another room was apparently frowned on. But Jade turned from the counter with a basket of bread in her hands and deposited it on the table with a smile that held a bit of a challenge. "You, Mr. Becker," she said, "are a grown-up. You can eat wherever you like."

"Good," he said. "I'll take it in my office, then."

Jade's smile got deeper and, somehow, a little icier too. "I'll bring it right in," she said with utter courtesy.

Becker turned toward the door.

"In case you're wondering," came Thérèse's shrill voice, "I'm waiting on a crew from the satellite company in Chantilly. They're sending someone over to install the dish. Should be here any minute." Her voice trailed off as Becker slipped out of sight. He was fairly sure he heard her harrumph and the children giggle before he closed the door.

Jade entered his office a few minutes later, holding a tray loaded with breakfast. Beck was sitting at the desk, having moved it closer to the window for better light, and was finishing the sketch he'd started the day before of the elaborate woodwork of the staircase. He didn't look up when she asked, "Would you like it on the desk or on the coffee table?"

"Coffee table's fine."

She deposited the tray on the marble slab that sat on brass legs and turned to Beck, stuffing her hands in the pockets of her wraparound apron. She wore a plaid skirt in browns and beiges and a deep-green cardigan that made her already-dark eyes seem an even deeper shade of walnut brown. Her slender feet were clad in low-heeled pumps. The better to run after the twins, no doubt. "How's the smell in your apartment?" she asked, not in the least put out by the lack of eye contact and communication coming from the other side of the room.

"Better," Beck said, following the flowing curve of the banister with his charcoal pencil. He looked up. "I'll actually be tearing most of the floorboards out of that corner this afternoon. Get rid of it for good." It was a decision he'd reached around dawn.

"Tearing up the floorboards?"

"Uh-huh."

"Just . . . tearing them out?"

He looked up. "Is there a problem?"

"You can't tear up those floorboards. They've been there for centuries!" There was genuine distress in her voice.

Becker put down his pencil. "It's going to happen eventually anyway. It's no use trying to restore boards that are that damaged."

She eyed him with suspicion. "I certainly hope you know what you're doing," she said. Something sparked in her eyes. "This castle is like a living organism, and I'd hate to see you amputate something that can't be replaced."

Beck smiled a little at the intensity of her expression and tried to mirror it with his own. "I'll do my very best not to amputate any major organs," he said with exaggerated seriousness, like a television doctor in a tacky reenactment. "You have my word, *ma'am*."

Jade gave him a sidelong glance and undid the strings of her apron. She pulled it over her head as she moved to the tall door of the office. "I'm off to teach the children," she said, adding "sir" in a pointed way. "The satellite people arrived, by the way. I'm sure Thérèse will be in to inform you of their progress. Just leave the tray by the door when you're finished, and I'll take care of it later."

As she was pulling the heavy door closed behind her, Becker called her back. "Jade." He hadn't said her name before. It sounded foreign and somehow intimate on his lips. He didn't like the feeling. "It's a standard renovation process," he explained as she stood in the doorway with a hand on her hip. "By the time I'm finished with that floor, you won't be able to tell where the original wood is missing."

She wrinkled her nose at him. "We'll see."

6

IT WAS KARL who finally shed some light on the goings-on that Kommandant Koch and Nurse Heinz so meticulously oversaw. Elise had run into him during one of her shopping trips to town, and he'd offered to help carry the meager groceries she'd bought to the Horch staff car in which a German driver waited to take her back to the manor.

As they walked, Elise asked Karl what he knew about what was happening at the manor.

"They're SS," he said, his heavily accented French the product of four years of study in the German school system. "We Wehrmacht don't know what happens at the manor."

"But . . . aren't you all part of the same army?"

He smiled tightly. "We fight in the same war, yes, but I don't think your manor's Kommandant Koch and our castle's Generalmajor

Müller want any more contact than that. The SS consider themselves—how do you say it? Superior." It was a difficult word for the young officer to pronounce, and Elise had him repeat it twice before she was satisfied with his accent.

"There are new residents at the manor," Elise said as they approached the car that would drive her back up the hill and into the dense woods. "All women—all having babies," she added, remembering the tall blonde who was due any moment.

"German?" Karl slowed his pace to stretch the remaining time they had to speak.

Elise shook her head. "Mostly French. But some from Belgium and other places too."

"And what happens to the babies after they're born?"

"None of them have been born yet," Elise explained. "Why do you ask?"

Karl stopped walking and faced Elise, the basket of groceries in his hand somehow mitigating the austerity of his uniform. "There's a program," he said. "I've only heard of it, but . . ." He lowered his voice. "It's an SS program they call Lebensborn."

"Lebensborn?"

"'Fount of Life' in German. I don't know much, but your manor—they must be trying to start a Lebensborn in France."

"What are the Lebensborns for?" Elise asked.

Karl shot her a warning glance, then darted his eyes toward the car. He lowered his voice. "Their purpose is to expand the master race," he said. "Women go there to . . ." He searched for the right word. "They go there to deliver Aryan babies and give them over to the Reich—to be raised as Hitler would want them to be."

Elise wasn't sure she was understanding correctly. Part of her hoped she wasn't. "You mean—they're having these babies to help with the war?"

"It's an act of loyalty. Himmler has encouraged SS officers to father children with Aryan women in order to—how do you say it? In order to expand the race."

"Wait . . ." Elise shook her head, unable to grasp the significance of what she was hearing. "These women are coming to the manor to give birth to Aryan children?"

"Yes."

"And they're going to leave here without them?"

"It's a most noble gesture. Their children will be adopted by worthy German families who will raise them in comfort, with Nazi ideals."

There was a trace of pride in Karl's voice that startled Elise. "But why can't they raise the kids themselves?" She was appalled. "The husbands come to visit all the time—can't they take the babies home with them after they're born?"

Karl resumed walking. The driver from the manor saw them coming and got out of the car to open the back door for Elise. "They probably aren't the women's husbands," Karl said, his voice low. "Himmler made it clear that marriage was not to get in the way of the expansion of the Reich. The instructions are to procreate as much as they can, with as many devoted women as are willing to conceive."

Elise stopped abruptly. "Are you telling me that . . . ?" There were so many questions in her mind that she couldn't narrow them down, and the driver was waiting rather impatiently for her to climb into the car. "So what you're saying is that the manor is a—a baby factory?" she asked, her voice hushed with incomprehension.

Karl shrugged, his voice almost inaudible as she brushed by him to bend into the back seat. "It's a place where SS officers and the women they love can prove their allegiance to the Reich." Elise looked up and caught the glint of approval in his eyes. "There is no limit to what a true soldier will do for his Führer."

Elise tracked Marie down immediately upon her return to

the manor, filling her in on the sordid details she'd learned from Karl, but neither of them fully believed his story until the first of the mothers gave birth a week later. They could hear her moaning and screaming upstairs for hours, the nurses running in and out of the delivery room for most of the afternoon. Just before suppertime, Marie heard the sound of a crying newborn and shushed Elise, who had been engrossed in the telling of one of her lengthy stories. They both tiptoed out to the foot of the stairs and listened to the infant sounds reaching them from above.

The baby was immediately committed to the nurses' care, and though the mother stayed on at the manor for a few days following the delivery, neither Elise nor Marie ever saw her with the baby. It was the nurses who fed, bathed, and swaddled him, and once the mother was well enough to leave, she was escorted to the limousine by an ever-attentive Kommandant Koch. Her baby, a boy, was given the first crib in a nursery that held ten. Within a month, three more cribs would be filled.

Birgitt, one of the friendlier nurses at the manor, was the first to invite the girls into the nursery. Though she made it look like it was merely a friendly gesture, it quickly became clear that her ulterior motive was to garner some free help. After their third or fourth visit, she began asking them to perform minor tasks like emptying trash cans and changing diapers. As the baby population of the manor increased, so did the frequency of their visits to the nursery. But they had strict instructions not to play with the babies and to limit their attention to necessary contact.

The two girls were standing in the kitchen sterilizing bottles one morning when Koch came storming in, going straight to Marie and grabbing her by the hair. "You've been in the nursery?" he hissed.

"I—yes, Kommandant, I . . . ," Marie stuttered. "I've been helping with the babies. . . ."

"On whose authority?" he demanded, his fist tightening in her hair.

Elise stood across the kitchen from Marie, her eyes wide and the color draining from her face. "We were just doing what they asked," she said, barely above a whisper.

"Who?" he snapped, turning on Elise so quickly that Marie lost her footing as he yanked her hair. "Who asked you to help?"

The two girls stared at each other. "Birgitt," Marie finally said. "Birgitt asked us to help. But we don't mind," she quickly added. "We don't mind at all."

Kommandant Koch released her hair so suddenly that she stumbled and caught herself on the edge of the sink. He swiveled and marched out of the room, his boots thudding as he took the stairs two at a time.

It was Frau Heinz who convinced the Kommandant to let Birgitt remain at the castle, lauding her initiative in recruiting help for the nursery and assuring him that she was a valuable asset in the Lebensborn. She also persuaded him to let Marie and Elise continue helping with the babies, as the workload was increasing exponentially with each woman who gave birth. After some further discussion, Kommandant Koch agreed, but when he found Marie coming out of the nursery on her first day of official duty, he stepped in her way as she walked toward the stairs.

"If you breathe a word of what you see here to anyone—anyone—you and your family will suffer the consequences," he said, his breath foul against her face. "Is that understood?" There was an unmistakable threat in his eyes, and Marie and Elise pledged that day that the manor's secrets would be safe with them.

As time went by, the number of mothers at the Lebensborn increased, sometimes reaching fifteen at once. They spent their days strolling in the Japanese garden, reading in the library, or knitting in the conservatory. The SS fathers of the babies came only occasionally, usually bearing flowers and always looking a little tense. Their visits seldom lasted longer than an hour, and Marie and Elise wondered if their trips to the manor were motivated by desire or by duty. They had no such questions about the couples who came to claim the children they'd been given to raise. They arrived with hesitant smiles and left exuding pride, holding a weeks- or months-old baby in their arms.

"You think Lisbeth's going to be happy with her new parents?" Elise asked, blinking back tears as an older, regal couple bundled the baby into their waiting car.

"I don't know," Marie murmured. "And I don't think anyone really cares."

7

THE CASTLE NOW sported a satellite dish. It looked as out of place on the historic structure as a Santa costume in an Easter egg hunt, but it was the best and fastest way of connecting the château to the Internet. Two men had spent the better part of the morning finding their way onto the roof and installing the dish, then had to borrow a ladder from the fire department to run a cable along a drainpipe down the outer wall. It seemed they weren't accustomed to working on such imposing structures. They had finally drilled a small hole through the window frame of Beck's improvised office and attached the cable to a receiver and a wireless router.

Thérèse had supervised the installation with all the aplomb of a cawing magpie seeing its nest being defaced. It would have been humorous had it not been so distracting. She stood outside Beck's window and yammered, yelped, and shrilled until his pencil stood still, poised above the page, incapable of drawing. It was when he heard the sound of falling stone and went to the window to see part of the cornice lying in pieces on the ground that the tenuous hold he had on his patience snapped. "Thérèse!" he yelled, flinging the window open and pointing angrily at the vestiges of the cornice. "Tell your men to prop their ladder on something other than the cornice! Look at that!" He pointed again at the fragments of hand-carved limestone on the grass. "That's carved stone, Thérèse. It can't be replaced!"

Thérèse gave him an apologetic look and pointed up the ladder. "I'm afraid it's finished now," she said. "The workmen are just coming down. I'm so sorry, Mr. Becker. I've been trying to tell them . . ."

If he had been in Gary's office, he would have found something heavy to throw, but there was nothing here but antique furniture. With growing frustration, Beck stormed out of the office and into the kitchen. He had one very precise and very pressing goal in mind, one that had been nagging at his subconscious since his arrival at the château. "Where's the nearest bar?" he barked.

Jade looked up from the flash cards she was using to teach the twins the alphabet and raised an eyebrow. "At eleven in the morning?"

"Thérèse has been supervising the satellite installation. . . ." He let his voice trail off, figuring that information would be enough.

"Right. So it's an emergency."

"Correct." He tried to control his voice, but his request still came out sounding like an order. "Where's the nearest bar?" he repeated, his voice gruff and demanding.

"Mr. Becker," Jade said, placing her flash cards carefully on the table. He could tell she was trying to stay civil. "Do you think it's entirely appropriate for a man to speak of medicating his stress with alcohol—in front of young children—at . . ." She looked at the clock. "At eleven twenty-two in the morning?"

Beck felt familiar fury rising. "Miss . . ." He'd forgotten her last name, which slightly took the wind out of his sails. "Jade," he amended, cocking his head to glare at her, "do you think it's entirely appropriate for a woman to be lecturing a grown man about his choices in front of young children at a time in his life when he doesn't give a flying leap about her opinion?" He realized as he finished that his voice had gotten louder as he'd spit out his diatribe. Too loud. Eva had grabbed Philippe's arm and sunk down next to him. Philippe's eyes were glued to Jade, true fear in their depths.

Jade rose from the table and stepped forward until she stood so close to Beck that he could feel the reproach in her gaze. "Don't ever raise your voice in front of the children again," she said with deadly calm, her voice a little rough from restraint. "Not for alcohol, not to vent your frustration, and certainly not to insult me." She moved back to the table and placed her hand on Philippe's shoulder. He looked like he wanted to launch himself into her arms. "Find your own booze, Mr. Becker," she said. And with those words, she took the children by their hands and led them outside, pausing by the door to take their jackets from metal hooks on the wall.

Becker was still standing in the kitchen minutes later. He'd heard Jade murmuring to the children just outside, had then seen them running into the park, probably on a quest for another giant snail. He'd heard the satellite van start up in the parking lot beside the kitchen and drive off. He'd stood there oblivious to everything but the burn of humiliation. He wouldn't call it shame. Shame reeked of conviction. But humiliation—that was accurate.

The stupor finally seeped out of his mind, and he turned with purpose to exit the kitchen. Far from dulling his ache for alcohol, his embarrassment had fueled the fire. He took the stairs two at a time on the way to his apartment, grabbed his jacket off the bed, and left the castle in search of release. If it came in the form of a deep-amber liquid, all the better.

Lamorlaye was a small town. Its nine thousand inhabitants lived in close-set neighborhoods of old middle-class charm. Its main street was lined with small shops and restaurants, benches, artsy streetlights, and cobblestone sidewalks. Some people greeted him as he walked, and others didn't seem to notice him at all. Fine by him.

He chased down a deliveryman who was about to get into his truck. "Hey! Hey—is there a bar anywhere around here?" The question sounded desperate even to his own ears. He wanted to take it back. He wanted to take the past fifteen minutes back. But if there was anything he'd learned in two years of relentless nightmares, it was that there was no rewinding allowed, no undoing possible.

The man shrugged. "If you're not too picky, there's always Marcel's." He pointed with his chin toward a Heineken sign on the corner. "He's open all day."

He drove off leaving Beck still standing there. Still craving. Beck knew there was only one cure—for the craving *and* the regret. He crossed the street with heavy strides and, shaking his head, entered Marcel's.

Men were hard at work on every floor of the château. The plumbing had nearly all been repaired, which had involved removing much of the cast-iron piping that hadn't already been replaced in the 1960s renovation. After a hundred years, the cast iron had virtually crystallized, and the oakum and lead used to seal the joints had deteriorated too badly to repair. It seemed almost obscene to install PVC pipes in their place, but the budget would be better spent on more visible expenses.

On the top floor, a crew of carpenters was hard at work taking down flimsy walls and replacing them with solid ones, often combining spaces into larger living areas. In as few cases as possible, supporting walls were replaced with new beams that required more modern foundations. It was hard work, particularly in those cramped, low-ceilinged quarters.

The electrical work was progressing rapidly. Beck was still waiting for it to be finished before he could begin the artistic part of the renovation. The old setup had been less than sightly—wires tucked into corners and strung along ceilings, stapled to window frames and pushed through gaping holes in walls. Most of them needed to be replaced or concealed. The process was painstaking, but the results would be worth the wait.

With the clock ticking and several artisans ready to jump in at a moment's notice, Beck rode the electricians hard, often just standing by while they worked, exerting pressure with his presence. Thérèse kept them supplied with whatever they needed during her hours at the castle. As she was splitting her time there with a handful of other projects, she was an unpredictable collaborator. But as frustrating as she could be, Beck was quickly realizing how valuable her connections were. Whatever was needed, she knew someone who could provide it. There were no yellow pages as thorough as Thérèse's mind.

Meanwhile, Beck continued to fine-tune his drawings, making his choices according to the supplies he could find and the budget he'd been given. Fallon was due back from England at the end of the week, and Beck wanted to have a comprehensive plan in place by then.

Jade still brought the children to the château every morning. She brought breakfast to his office at 7:30 sharp and had his lunch waiting there whenever his midday break came. He wasn't sure how she knew exactly when to bring it, but regardless of his schedule, it was always there—hot and fresh. Now that the office was equipped with Internet, he was spending more time there than in his bedroom.

The evening meals had become simpler after the first few days. They were often just bread, cold cuts, and a salad. Jade left those in the kitchen for him and took the children home around four each afternoon. He filled the quiet time by playing music on his laptop and made believe that he was perfectly content. He was good at that. He'd been at it for a while.

Marcel's was his refuge of choice in the after hours, when he needed to step away from work. Although he'd promised Gary and Trish that he'd use this trip to lay off the alcohol, there were times when it was simply his only link to sanity. He hadn't gotten drunk—though he'd gotten close a couple times. That much of his promise to Gary he'd been able to keep. And he'd cut down a little. A lot. He wasn't sure. Once he started drinking, he stopped counting glasses.

Because Marcel's was a bit of a dive, there were fewer women there than in the sports bars he'd frequented in Boston, which suited him just fine. Those who did show up found his *québécois* accent too cute for his own good. He tried to counteract it by speaking less or not at all. Worked for him. If one of the women got too cozy, he paid for his bottle and took it back to the castle. He didn't really like company anyway. Or so he told himself. But on those days when he could hear the laughing and talking in the kitchen from his office, a small, intimate part of him longed for the courage to be there too.

He was sure he heard it that time. Beck turned off the desk lamp in the office and moved to the window, hugging the wall. There was no motion in the expansive clearing behind the castle. Not even the rabbits and foxes he'd grown accustomed to seeing in the middle of the night were out. On a hunch, he went through the door into the first dining hall and moved to the windows facing the front of the property. A dim light shone in the gatehouse, its flicker barely perceptible from this distance.

The sound came again. Like a chisel on stone. A few sharp strikes, then a pause. But it didn't come from the front of the castle. Beck moved through the second dining room on his way to the entryway. He slid behind the stairs, where a bay of French doors held a view of the small patio and the park beyond. The sound. Closer this time. There was no mistaking it for animal noises, and the wind wasn't strong enough on that night to blame it, either. Beck opened one of the windowed doors as quietly as possible. Warped by time and exposure, it groaned faintly as it swung inward. Beck strained his eyes and ears as he waited for an indication of the origin of the noise. Nothing.

He took a few steps out to the patio in his stocking feet. An owl hooted somewhere in the woods, and another answered from a different direction. Aside from that, the night was perfectly silent. Moving out to the edge of the small patio, Beck descended the four steps that led to the lawn. He thought he heard a rustle, but it was so muted that his ears didn't register location. He stood there for a moment longer, the cold of the starless winter night seeping through his clothing, then, hearing nothing more, went back inside.

He closed the door only partway, just far enough for it to catch again, then waited—wondering if whatever was out there would come out of hiding, thinking he had gone. But long seconds ticked by without any movement or sound. "You're losin' it, Becker," he finally mumbled to himself, pulling the door all the way and latching it shut. He walked back to the office, stretching his arms above his head and yawning so loudly that he startled himself.

Beck was scoring the wood on the staircase the next morning, still planning for its elaborate restoration, when a tall, elegant woman walked in. He looked up from his work, expecting a laborer. But she was most certainly not blue-collar. She walked with practiced grace on stylish heels—the type of shoes Gary might have appreciated—and though her clothes were cut with extra fabric to accommodate her swelling belly, they were nonetheless chic and sophisticated. Becker put down his tools and descended the stairs. He wiped his hands on the rag he took from his back pocket and stepped forward to shake her hand. This was the boss's wife, after all, and he was all about keeping his employers happy.

"Sylvia Fallon," she said in a perfectly modulated voice.

"Marshall Becker." Her hand was soft and firm in his, her gaze direct.

"So," she said, turning her attention to the staircase, "what are we doing here?"

"I'm just scoring the wood," he said, a little nervously. It wasn't a feeling he enjoyed, but he'd been taken slightly off guard by the unexpected guest. He stepped back and pointed to the marks he'd made. "We'll be taking out this entire section, from here to here," he explained, outlining the five-foot portion that had been so severely damaged by flames that there were empty gaps in the elaborate design, "and we'll replace it with wood that's been cut and carved to match the pattern of the rest."

"You're cutting out part of the staircase?" she asked, some concern in her voice. "Aren't these stairs at least two hundred years old?"

Beck braced himself. What was it with women and their desire to preserve old lumber? "Actually," he explained, "it's the only way to repair the damage and not lose any of the original look."

"Explain," she said, her forehead furrowed in thought. From anyone else, the one-word statement would have sounded like an order, but she had managed to make it sound calm and inviting.

"All right," Becker said, putting his immediate plans on hold for this impromptu carpentry lesson. "You can see where the worst of the damage happened." He used his pencil to point at various segments of the staircase. "The railing's burned away here, but even where there's still some left, most of the roundness of its original shape is gone. You can't just bulk up something that's been mostly destroyed by fire." Sylvia nodded, paying close attention. "And then there's all the decorative carving underneath." He pointed at the beautifully executed woodwork that extended from the railing to the base of the stairs. "It's been reduced to ashes for at least three feet, and what's left in the remaining foot on either side is too damaged to save."

"So you cut all that out . . . ," Sylvia mused.

"We cut out as little as possible, but the cuts have to be made in healthy wood."

She nodded. "And then . . . where do you find wood that perfectly matches this? And someone to carve those swirly bits?"

"Actually," Beck said, "I've already found some lumber that will be suitable once it's stained and treated to match the older portions. It's nearly impossible to get a perfect match out of woods that have a several-hundred-year age gap, but this will probably come close. As for the swirly bits," he quoted, smiling at the decidedly untechnical term, "that's my job."

Sylvia leaned in for a closer look at the design of curved lines and graceful forms. "How will you reproduce this? It's much too delicate for jigsaws and such, isn't it?"

Beck nodded. "Where I can use a router, I will, but it looks like I'm going to have to do the bulk of it by hand."

Sylvia stepped back, appraising him. "So you're a sculptor, too, are you?"

Beck was about to explain his expertise when Fallon came gusting through the front doors, dressed impeccably in a cashmere coat and a plaid scarf. With his brown tasseled loafers, expensive leather gloves, and felt fedora, he looked the epitome of the rich British gentleman. On anyone else, the attire might have appeared pompous, but on Fallon, it was merely part of the persona.

"Beck, my lad," he bellowed, stopping only briefly to shut the front door before he hurried over to Beck and shook his hand as if they were fast friends. "Tell me about our progress!" He looked around the entryway at the still-graffitied walls, still-dull floors, and still-burned staircase, and added, "Doesn't look like much of anything has gone on during my absence!"

"Well, you know what they say about when the cat's away."

"This particular cat has a million quid invested in this property, and he'd like to assume that the mice are aware of that!" He guffawed and smacked Beck on the back. He seemed to suddenly become aware of Sylvia's presence at his side. "By the way," he quickly said, lowering his voice a notch, "this is my lovely bride, Sylvia." His eyes danced as he added conspiratorially, "And that extra little bulge you're trying so hard not to look at is a Fallon-to-be."

Beck wasn't sure what to say. The only human beings who made him more uncomfortable than children were not-yet-born children.

"You'll understand, Mr. Becker," Sylvia said, looping an arm through her husband's, "that my husband's greatest pride is his progeny. And I—lucky me—get to be the human incubator of his children. It's a job I enjoyed a little more six years ago, when my body was younger, but it's a small price to pay for living in the lap of luxury!"

Again, her words, spoken by anyone else, would have sounded self-important and cynical, but she had uttered them with so much good humor and self-deprecation that Beck couldn't help but smirk. He was beginning to understand why Fallon was willing to move heaven and earth to see that his wife's birthday wishes would come true.

The three of them spent the better part of the next hour walking through the castle. Beck explained in detail what work had been done during the past week and answered each of Sylvia's questions as simply and thoroughly as he could. Fallon seemed pleased with the progress upstairs, particularly when Beck explained that the electrical work was actually a day ahead of schedule. He greeted the workers with typical joviality and asked questions of them to which Beck suspected he already knew the answers. If likability were an Olympic sport, Fallon would be working on a gold medal. Having walked through all three floors of the castle, they climbed down the small staircase at the far end of the north wing and finished the tour in the kitchen. When the kids saw their mother appear, they jumped up from the table, leaving half-finished tongue-depressor houses behind, and ran to wrap their arms around her waist.

"Three hours apart and you'd think she'd been gone for a week," Fallon said as he and Beck watched the happy reunion. "Do you have any children, lad?" he asked. He cocked his head to the side. "It strikes me that I really know very little of you at all."

Beck shook his head and cast a glance at Jade. She sat at the table with a nearly finished tongue-depressor house in front of her, but her eyes were on Sylvia and the children, something melancholy in her gaze. "Nope. No children," Beck said. Jade lowered her eyes back to her task.

With the whole family there, it was impossible for Beck to excuse himself to eat lunch in his office. They sat around the large table with room to spare, and though Beck and Jade said little, the conversation never waned. The children were animated and loud, and their parents reveled in the precocious entertainers' antics. While the Fallon family enjoyed a rare lunch together, Beck focused on the roast chicken and potatoes on his plate, and Jade kept herself busy by keeping everyone else supplied with food and drinks.

"Oh, go outside and run around for a while," Sylvia finally exclaimed. The twins had been bombarding her with an unending list of toys they wanted for their birthday, and their pitch had grown so shrill that Beck wanted to clap his hands over his ears—or their mouths.

"Yay!" the kids shrieked together, dashing for the door.

"Put on your coats!" Jade called after them, snatching their coats off the hooks and following them out. By the sound of the complaining, she must have caught them right outside the door.

Sylvia rose and began clearing the table. Her ease in performing so domestic a task surprised Beck. He had somehow expected her to leave such a menial duty to Jade. He rose to take his own plate to the sink.

"And how are your accommodations?" Fallon asked, gathering the children's plates and cutlery and stacking them in front of him. "Jade mentioned that you resolved the urine issue with a handsaw."

At the sink, where she was rinsing dishes, Sylvia said, "Gavin . . ." and wrinkled her nose.

"You know, when that partner of yours mentioned that you wanted to live on-site," Fallon said, "I put up a fairly decent fight. There are some very nice, very convenient hotels in town that wouldn't have had the bonus smells you've had to contend with, but he seemed adamant. He said you functioned best if you were near your work site."

"I do," Beck said, adding, "I don't sleep very much anyway, and once I get into carving and designing, my best hours are after midnight."

"But when do you sleep, Mr. Becker?" Sylvia asked from the sink, drying her hands on a towel. "If you supervise the project all day and carve all night . . ."

Beck shrugged, leaning back against the counter. "I sleep enough."

She leaned in, conspiratorial. "You need a mother." She winked and got back to rinsing dishes.

"Oh, I've got a mother," Beck said, shaking his head. "She's a cross between a mama bear and a pit bull, and I assure you we've had the sleep conversation a few times!"

"Clearly to no avail," Fallon said, depositing a stack of dishes on the drainboard of the sink.

"She learned long ago that I'm not easily persuaded." Beck smiled. On a whim, he asked the question that had been trotting around in his head since he'd heard the late-night noises around the patio: "Just out of curiosity, have you ever gotten reports about prowlers on the castle grounds?"

The Fallons looked at each other and shook their heads. "Just Jojo, on occasion. There were the vandals several years ago, of course," Sylvia said. "The ones who did so much spray-paint damage in the entryway. But I don't think there have been any problems since then."

"Why do you ask, lad?" Fallon moved to the counter where Beck stood, reaching for the carafe of coffee Jade had prepared during the meal.

"It's probably nothing," Beck said, sorry he'd broached the subject. "I've just . . . heard and seen a couple things since I've been here that had me wondering."

"Sylvia, my dear," Fallon said dramatically, "we might have ourselves a mystery." He lowered his voice and leaned toward Becker. "Tell me, lad, what have you seen?"

Feeling more than a little foolish, Becker waved it away and filled a cup with coffee. "Nothing. I'm sure I'm just imagining things."

8

As soon as the Fallons left, Becker wandered out the back door and strolled over to the small patio where he had heard the noises the night before. He looked around for anything that seemed out of place but saw nothing. All the windows were closed, the shutters fastened securely. He took a couple paces back to get a broader look at the area and noticed, just off to the right of the steps, a small opening that led under the patio. At some point it had been sealed with red brick and cement, but there was a hole in the makeshift wall and bits of broken brick lying near it on the grass.

Getting down on his hands and knees, he peered inside, but he couldn't see a thing. In a matter of minutes, he'd gone around the château to the front entrance, retrieved a flashlight, a crowbar, and a hammer from his toolbox, and returned to the opening. It was fairly small—maybe two feet by three feet. Beck made quick work of the remainder of the bricks, using his hands to pull them out after he'd loosened the cement that held them. When he was finished, he dropped to his knees again and shone the flashlight around the dank, dark space that ran the entire length of the patio. There were some old pipes, a discarded tire, and, in the far corner, something well hidden that sounded an awful lot like a family of rats. Beck was about to switch off his flashlight and get back to work when the beam glanced across something smooth and rounded.

He hesitated. The animal sounds coming from the rear corner nearly deterred Beck's sleuthing ambitions, but, if he was seeing right, his find would be worth the close proximity to rodents. "Come on, Beck," he urged himself on. "Just a few little critters. You stay out of their space, they'll stay out of yours. . . ." He got down on his stomach and crawled into the dark and musty shadows. The space became a little taller once he got through the arched opening. He only had to go a few feet on hands and knees before he reached the object of interest. He prodded it with his flashlight and rolled it over on its side.

Beck's eyes widened. It had deteriorated substantially in the time it had spent under the patio. Most of the leather elements were gone and all that was left was the metallic shell, its paint flaked off in many places, but the faded decal on its side was unmistakable. Two lightning bolts in a white shield. He was staring at a World War II helmet, one that had belonged to a Nazi soldier.

Beck backed out of the space with the helmet, feet first, and emerged to find two bemused children and a slightly annoyed adult staring down at him.

"Do you know how often I've had to order the twins *not* to venture into places like that?" Jade asked.

Becker squinted up at her. "A lot?"

She shook her head and looked skyward, a small smile tugging at the corners of her mouth. When she looked back down at Becker, it was with a little less annoyance. "What on earth were you look-ing for?"

"Did you find a giant snail?" Philippe demanded, eyeing the treasure Beck held.

"No, but I think I found a family of rats."

Eva squealed and hid behind Jade's legs, and Philippe's eyes got so big that Beck feared for their safety. Jade smirked.

"That's one hole you'll never have to tell them to stay out of again," he said, standing and trying to brush some of the stains from his knees and elbows. "Ever found anything like this on the grounds before?" he asked, holding out the helmet.

"Probably World War II," Jade said. "May I?"

Beck handed her the helmet, and she took it carefully, turning it to observe it from all angles. "This castle was a Kommandantur—a Nazi headquarters—during the war, you know. I'm sure this belonged to one of Hitler's prized Wehrmacht warriors." There was disdain in her voice as she handed the metallic shell back to him.

"Wehrmacht?"

"The Nazi military. This area is the horse capital of France, so they made Lamorlaye and Chantilly their cavalry's home base."

Beck shook his head, bemused and amazed. "I crawled into a hole and found a Nazi helmet." Something stirred in him that reminded him of childhood treasure hunts. He held the helmet up and turned it, taking in the decal, the chipped paint, and the rem-nant of a leather strap still attached to a rivet inside the shell. He tried not to sound too eager when he said, "You think I can keep it?"

Jade smiled sweetly and, he suspected, condescendingly, clearly lacking the enthusiasm the helmet had elicited in him. "I'm sure you can keep it, Mr. Becker," she said. The twinkle in her eye some-what softened the sarcasm in her voice. "But helmets like these, in this part of the world? They're really not that rare. Now—" Jade glanced down at his soiled clothing—"you'll need those washed," she said, turning her mind back to business. "There's a machine in the laundry room at the back of the kitchen. Anytime you need anything done, just leave it on the washer and I'll take care of it."

"I can do my own laundry," Beck said, oddly disgruntled by her offer. He rotated the helmet in his hands again.

"Suit yourself, Mr. Becker." She turned toward the kitchen. "Come on, kids. I promised you a video after lunch, and the DVD player is set up in the office."

"My office?"

"It has a couch in it. Do you mind?"

How could he say no when his was the only space in the château that held any comfortable furniture? As they were traipsing away, Philippe twisting in Jade's grasp to look over his shoulder at the strange grown-up who had crawled into a rat's dark hole, Beck shouted, "You can call me Beck, you know! Or Becker!"

Jade stopped and turned, smiling a little more kindly than she had of late. "Becker it is, then," she said. "Why don't you come inside and have another cup of coffee, Becker? You must have gotten chilled crawling around under the castle on your treasure hunt."

"So . . . you have lunch with your employers," Jade said a few minutes later, her lilting voice enigmatic, "and then, rather than, say, repair a dilapidated château, you decide to crawl under its patio. Is that about the gist of things?"

Beck poured himself a mug of coffee and reached for the cream. "I'm going back to work right now," he said. "No need to tattle on me to the boss." The excitement of his find had begun to wear off, and embarrassment at his temporary lapse had set in. He opened three drawers before he found the spoons.

"Why exactly did you do it?"

"Do what?"

"Why did you go spelunking?"

"I needed a change of scenery."

Beck hadn't been prepared for her laugh. Her frustration? Yes. Her dismissal? Absolutely. But her laugh? It froze him midbreath. It also made him want to say something else—and fast—to prevent her from laughing again. There was a strange kind of power in that sound. It made him feel less bulletproof. He didn't like it.

"I thought I heard . . . something . . . last night," he explained, focusing on answering her question. "It came from that part of the castle, so . . ."

"Something?"

He shook his head. "It was probably nothing. My imagination." He remembered the figure he'd seen moving through the fog nights before and wondered if he'd conjured that, too.

"Well, I know that Jojo sometimes wanders around at night, but I'm not sure he'd be noisy about it."

She had his attention. "You know Jojo?"

Jade shrugged out of the jacket she'd been wearing outside and went to hang it by the door. "Mostly I know *of* him. The people in town talk about him, you know, and if you live around here long enough, you hear all the stories."

"What kind?"

She paused, looking at him as if she were gauging his sincerity. "He's old," she said, coming back to sit at the table. "Nobody knows how old, of course. He's a bit of a mythical creature in these parts. The story goes that he turned up in the gatehouse decades ago. All of a sudden, he was just living there one day, as if he'd always been there. The castle was abandoned at the time, so no one really cared."

"Does anyone ever see him?"

"He isn't Boo Radley, Mr. Becker." She smiled, then caught herself. "Becker. Just Becker."

Beck took a slug of his coffee, a little embarrassed by his fascination for the urban legend that was Jojo. "So . . . you've seen him?"

"Quite regularly. There's a gap in the wall out there," she said, pointing to the carport outside the kitchen. "Monsieur Legentil owns the stables on the other side of the wall, and Jojo helps out with caring for the horses. You'll see him going through the gap a couple times a day. Nights, too—especially when there's a sick horse that needs tending."

"So he's a stable hand?"

"Not officially. I think he just likes horses."

Beck mulled over the information. It really raised more questions than it answered.

"Has he ever hurt anyone? Scared anyone?"

"Mr. Becker . . ." Jade caught herself again. "Becker. He's barely had the courage to speak to anyone since I've known of him, so scaring them or hurting them would be a little out of character, don't you think?"

"I just think it's strange," Becker said, heading toward the archway with his coffee cup. "A guy who appears out of nowhere and installs himself on private property—pretty much mute, from what you've said. No friends, no job, up at all hours of the night . . ."

"How do you know that?"

Becker turned. "I've seen the light on at his place—a candle, I think."

She smiled innocently. "So you were up too."

"Yes, but I don't prowl."

"You only crawl."

Becker heard himself chuckle as he was making his exit. The sound perplexed him. He was on his way to the entrance hall when he stopped. If Jade was surprised to see him back in the kitchen moments later, she didn't mention it.

"About the drinking thing . . ."

She didn't speak but merely waited for him to continue.

"I won't mention it in front of the kids again."

"Thank you," she said.

Becker stood there for a while longer, his cooling coffee in his hand.

"Is there anything else?" Jade asked after a long moment of silence had passed.

He remembered the anger in her eyes, the revulsion on her face, the threat in her voice. He wanted—somehow—to address those, too. But he didn't have the words. So he turned instead and walked away, leaving Jade sitting at the table, shaking her head.

It was the music that first alerted Beck that this was another dream. He was sitting in a circle of men. There were at least six of them. Maybe seven. He kept squinting, trying to make out their faces, but he couldn't seem to drag his gaze up past their chests. There was murmuring—something that bordered on chanting. In the background, he could hear the strains of a Barry Manilow hit being sung by a child. *"I can't live without you, can't smile without you. . . ."* He'd always hated the song. But she'd loved it. On this occasion, however, there was something desperately wrong with the recording. The infant voice warbled as it reached his ears. It was as if the song were being played too slowly and from a warped LP. *"I can't laugh and I can't sing. . . ."*

The man on Beck's right was wearing a blue suit. That much he could tell. He was speaking loudly into Beck's ear, trying to outdo the music, but all Beck could hear were fractions of sentences. "No point being a hero. . . . Take one for the Gipper. . . . The view from the bottom ain't bad. . . ."

The scene reeled and roiled, came in and out of focus. The next thing Beck knew, the man was holding him in a bear hug, pressing

Beck's face into his sweaty, foul-smelling chest, and repeating over and over, "There you go . . . there you go . . . there you go," as if he were comforting a baby.

The Barry Manilow song was louder now. It throbbed in Beck's head. He wanted to cover his ears, to blot out the noise of the music and the murmurs and the man in the suit's voice, but he was anchored to him and couldn't escape the stench or the chaos.

The world started to swirl. He saw the room pitch and turn, the vague, blurred faces of strangers staring. He couldn't catch his breath. He started to scream. He thrashed about, tried to stand and use his legs to pull away, but they wouldn't support his weight. He just kept getting drawn deeper into the suffocating mass that kept saying, "There you go . . . there you go . . . there you go . . ." while the child's voice rose to a fever pitch.

At first, Beck thought the faint keening sound was a remnant of his dream. He sat bolt upright, taking in the unfinished woodwork on the desk in front of him, his T-shirt clinging to his sweaty skin, his breathing fast and labored. He felt sick. Filthy. Frightened. He got up from the desk, cursing himself for having fallen asleep, and steadied himself while his back spasmed from several hours spent sleeping in an awkward position. His legs were wobbly. His head spun. He opened the window and took in a deep lungful of cold air, holding it for a moment, then expelling it forcefully as he bent his body forward over the windowsill. And he heard the keening again. It seemed to come from the area of the patio, near the crawl space he'd explored. Shaking off the vestiges of his dream, he stepped barefoot into his work boots and threw a coat on over his T-shirt. Whatever the expedition revealed, it would distract him from his subconscious, and he was eager for the relief.

Beck grabbed a heavy-duty flashlight from the windowsill and took the stairs to the back door of the castle. He opened it as quietly as he could and stepped out into the night air. The covered passageway outside the kitchen shielded him from view. He looked around the edge of the wall in the direction of the patio and saw nothing but the willow tree that bent over the river, its bare branches swaying lazily in the night breeze. The moon was out, so bright that it cast a stark outline of the château's chimneys and roofline on the lawn.

Beck moved out of the shadows, listening for the sound, but it was gone. A little spooked, he had to force himself to travel the short distance to the patio. The soggy earth was soft beneath his boots, its moisture gurgling with each step he took. He didn't turn on the flashlight. He could see better without its beam interfering with his night vision.

Beck was halfway to the willow tree when he took stock for the first time of what he was doing. He'd woken mere minutes before from a terrorizing dream, had thought he heard an unusual sound, and had exited the castle in his pajamas so fast that he wasn't sure what he hoped to accomplish once he got to the spot from which he *assumed* the keening had come. He was alone in the dark with nothing but a flashlight as a weapon, following something that might be much more real than mere vestiges of a nightmare. Every iota of logic he still possessed dictated that he should turn around and head back to the warmth and safety of the castle. But Beck was a stubborn man, and once he set out on a decided course, there was little that could deter him from seeing it through.

As he approached the hole under the patio, he turned on the flashlight, sweeping it quickly in an arc along the castle's outer wall, then over the creek and into the brush beyond. He followed the stream with the powerful beam. Nothing there but stagnant water and the reflected eyes of some small animal. There wasn't anything amiss—no intruder, no ghost, no danger at all.

Berating himself for his overactive imagination, Becker strode to the small opening next to the patio stairs and crouched down. It was time to prove to himself that his fears were unfounded. He turned on the flashlight again and shone the beam around the dank space. What he saw froze him to the spot. The rubble under the patio was still there, but nothing was as he'd left it on his last expedition. The tire had been flipped. The segments of pipe were several feet from where they'd lain before. Even the mounds of unrecognizable refuse seemed different. It looked as if someone had dug through the trash and the top layer of decaying soil in search of . . . something.

Without thinking twice, Beck crawled under the patio, shining his light ahead of him. Someone had been thorough. There wasn't a square foot of the space that looked untouched. He crawled deeper into the cavity, exploring the objects the intruder's search had exposed. There was nothing of value there. As he approached the far corner, his flashlight bounced off three small, pink forms lying on the dark earth. The rat's nest he had heard earlier hadn't survived the exploration that had turned the dark, musty space upside down. The three pups in his flashlight's glare were dead, probably from exposure to the cold. Their mother was nowhere in sight.

It was that thought that prompted Beck's hasty withdrawal from the crawl space under the patio. Ghosts and marauders were one thing. Angry rats were quite another. He sat on the edge of the patio for a moment, considering what he'd found. When the cold started to seep through his pajamas and jacket, he shone his flashlight in one last arc around the perimeter, then headed inside. He left his filthy pajama bottoms on the washing machine as he passed through the kitchen.

9

DECEMBER 1943

MARIE WAS GETTING used to the horrendous sounds that came from the room upstairs. At first, she'd been terrified by them, tried to stay as far away as possible from the screaming and moaning that bled through the walls and seemed to coat everything they touched. Marie and Elise had developed a sort of sixth sense for when the babies would be born. The swollen faces and increased discomfort of the residents played into their predictions, but there was something more—something intangible—that they recognized as impending birth. Most of the mothers seemed to settle somehow, to become more focused and brave, as if nature itself were preparing them for the ordeal ahead.

"I'll bet you my dessert that it's a boy," Elise said one day as they sat in the kitchen, polishing silver. The guttural sounds from upstairs were faint but unmistakable. Elise had her own theories about birth.

She thought she could tell the gender of the coming child by the pitch of its mother's screaming, and this mother's voice was low and hoarse.

Marie didn't particularly like dessert, even though it was a rare commodity in these days. "Fine," she said, extending her hand to shake on it. "Keep your dessert, though. You can give it to Karl if he comes by this afternoon."

Elise smiled and feigned confusion about the guard from the château who had become something of a fixture at the manor in recent weeks. "Why, what on earth might you be referring to?" The question aimed for innocence but fell far short.

Marie put down the silver platter and dipped her rag into the dish of strong-smelling blue liquid. "I'm not an idiot," she said, rubbing a particularly stubborn patch of oxidation. "I'm starting to suspect that he's bribing all the other soldiers at the castle to let him run their errands for them—especially when those errands bring him here!"

"He's sweet."

"He's infatuated."

"He's handsome."

Marie pursed her lips. "If you like Nazis, I guess."

"Marie!"

"What? You know he is!"

Elise's eyes lit up. "But he's not like the others! He's kind—and generous!" She put the silver dish down on the table and took a small vial of perfume from her pocket, pulling out the cork that kept it sealed. "Smell this," she said, lowering her voice nearly to a whisper and sliding the bottle across the table to Marie. "He brought it to me this morning, when he delivered a document to Koch's office. Just dropped it in my pocket as he walked by!"

The perfume smelled like lavender and lemon. "He's a guard—he can't afford perfume," Marie said.

Elise frowned. "Maybe they requisitioned the perfume factory in town," she mused, her expression serious—but not for long. Elise lived in the moment, seldom letting her spirits be bogged down by practical matters or excessive doses of reality. "Doesn't it smell divine?" she asked, taking the fluted vial back from her friend.

"It smells like my mother's underwear drawer and furniture polish," Marie said, earning a flick of Elise's rag.

They worked in silence for a while, the screaming and moaning upstairs having subsided to the occasional raised voice. When Marie spoke again, it was in the hushed tone the girls reserved for speaking of the Nazis while working in their manor. "Elise," she began, searching for the right words, "are you—are you serious about Karl?"

Elise smiled. "Perhaps," she said.

"You are," Marie said, dread settling in her stomach.

"Maybe."

"Be careful, all right?"

Elise shrugged.

"Elise, promise me you'll keep it quiet," Marie urged. "If your neighbors and friends find out that . . ."

"And what if they do find out?" Elise asked, dismissing Marie's concern. "I haven't broken any laws. Besides—" she rolled her eyes— "we're being discreet."

"You don't know how to be discreet, Elise. Anyone who sees you will know something . . . happy . . . is going on!"

Elise put on a sour expression. "Is this better?"

"Elise . . ."

"Oh, hush, Marie. Karl and I are being careful. The only time I've seen him outside of work was at the parade last week, and even then, we only had a couple of minutes together before he had to ride back to the castle. No one will know."

Marie was at a loss. Her friend was speaking of the soldier as if he were a harmless boy next door, not a footman in Hitler's army. "He's a Nazi, Elise," she said again, glancing at the doorway to make sure no one had overheard.

"So? You work for Nazis, and I don't see you considering quitting."

"There's a difference between working for them and falling for them," Marie said, hearing the futility of the argument as it left her lips.

"I don't love him," Elise replied, rolling her eyes again. "Don't be so dramatic."

"And yet—look at what you're risking for him."

Elise leaned across the table and grabbed her friend's hand, excitement dancing in her limpid gaze. "He's taking me to the ball!"

"The army ball?"

She nodded vigorously. "In the castle, with an orchestra and . . ."

"Elise." There was genuine worry in Marie's voice.

"Karl told me to wear my prettiest dress. Can you believe it? I'm going to a ball. . . ."

"Elise, are you sure?"

"Oh, Marie, stop being a nag!" Her frustration was growing.

"This is a big event. I know it's happening at the castle, but who do you think will be serving? There are going to be townspeople everywhere, and you want to attend it with your German boyfriend? Do you know what people will think?"

"Let them think what they want!" Elise said, her petulance loud and brittle in the quiet kitchen. "I haven't danced in forever, and I can't wait for the first valse musette!"

"Your friends will hate you. . . . Elise, surely you realize that."

"But you won't, will you?" The worry in her gaze wasn't feigned.

"No, of course not. Not me, but . . ."

Elise's face split into a wide, exuberant smile. "Then it's going to be wonderful," she said.

10

BECKER BREATHED A sigh of relief. The massive work that had prepared the skeletal structure of the castle for the renovations was
finished, and the army of carpenters and other artisans Thérèse had
so carefully selected for the next stage of the project were all on-site.
The real restoration could now begin.

The crews gathered in the ballroom in the west wing of the
castle, a vast, high-ceilinged space with creaky hardwood floors,
tall windows, and an imposing fireplace. The bare-bulb lighting
contrasted ridiculously with the carved ornamental molding that
framed the ceiling and the tall, elegant windows through which the
early-morning sunlight streamed. Beck was grateful for the change
in weather. He'd seen little other than rain and grayness since his
arrival in Lamorlaye.

When all the craftsmen had gathered, some of them new to the
work site, he gave them a brief overview of the weeks ahead. There

was a timeline on the whiteboard he'd brought in for the meeting, and he walked each group of workers through the tasks that would be theirs. It was important that they all understand the full scope and sequence of the project if they were to work together to meet their deadlines. Beck had laid out a series of drawings and plans on several tables at the front of the room and extended an invitation for the men to peruse them at their leisure. He introduced Thérèse as the person to go to with any purchasing needs or general concerns and warned them that because time was short, he would personally be keeping a close eye on the superhuman effort completion would require.

If the tradesmen were in any way put out by having an Américain giving them orders, none of them showed it. This was a big job that would result in big paychecks, and it was obvious that they were motivated to begin.

Once the meeting was over and the men had dispersed to tend to their responsibilities, Beck moved with two carpenters to the grand staircase. He briefly explained the cuts that needed to be made, and after they'd asked for clarifications and stopped just short of questioning his methods, they went out to their van to get the necessary tools.

Thérèse stood by, biting her lip and looking up at the graceful expanse of wood. She cleared her throat twice before actually speaking. "So . . . you're really going to cut that segment of the staircase out?"

Beck turned toward her, both hands on his hips. "Would you like to voice an objection? Every other female in the castle has, so you might as well chime in too."

Thérèse swallowed convulsively, clearly torn between insult and concern. "It's just that . . ."

"I know," Beck said, holding up his hand to halt her. "It's beautiful." She nodded. "It's old." Another nod. "And you'd hate to see it damaged."

"Yes. Precisely."

"Take a good look, Thérèse," he said, motioning toward the charred remains of railings and steps. "This staircase isn't exactly in prime condition anymore!"

Thérèse dropped her head. "I understand."

Her change of attitude did more to disarm Beck than her badgering usually did. He climbed up several stairs, making sure to stay away from the most damaged segments, and pointed to the sections to be removed. "We're just taking this out," he said, trying to sound conciliatory. "This part of the railing, these decorative pieces, and those eight steps."

Thérèse moved forward, paying close attention to what he was saying. "And the . . . underbelly?" She was referring to the masking wood on the underside of the staircase that followed the structure's curve and hid the steps from view. It was one of the design details that made the staircase seem so grand, as it provided a smooth expanse that curved around toward the landing above.

"We're not touching that," Beck said. "Just the steps."

"All right," she said, patting the hair around her tight bun. "I was just . . . wondering." And with that she turned and walked toward the dining rooms, her high heels clicking pertly on the marble floor.

Castle life began to fall into a routine after that. There were, of course, occasional delays and miscommunications that required immediate action, but the craftsmen Thérèse had hired were generally good workers who seemed to love their trade. Thérèse came and went several times a day, alternating being a nuisance at the château with harassing other workers on other sites, and, truth be told, providing more help than hindrance. Her background wasn't in construction, but it did give her a finer appreciation of the work being done, and she was an efficient and competent—albeit annoying—asset to the project.

Becker had started his own renovation routine in earnest. His office had taken on the look of a workshop. When he wasn't supervising the progress in the rest of the site and making adjustments where necessary, he was bent over the pieces of cherrywood he had bought to repair the staircase, meticulously carving out the shapes that would match them to the centuries-old woodwork in the entrance. It was laborious and finicky, the work so minute that he sometimes had to take a break just to release the tension he felt in his arms and head and stomach. Still, it was good work—satisfying work—and he found less need for distraction when he was engrossed in re-creating art. But the flip side of drinking less was that his hands were shaking more. He'd resigned himself to keeping a stash of bottles in his bedroom and retreating for a quick drink when the shaking started to interfere with his carving.

Jade continued to bring his meals to the office, and the clothes he regularly left on the washing machine turned up neatly folded on his bed several times a week. The stench in his quarters was nearly gone, though he still slept with the window open, and he was feeling less and less like running when the children were around. They still weren't the best of buddies, of course, but he was okay with that, too.

It was on another rare sunny day that the sound of voices in the kitchen finally forced Becker out of his comfort zone. He'd spent part of the night researching the mortar that had been used to cement the massive stones that formed the walls of the castle, trying to determine what would be the best way to clean the stones and reinforce the mortar without causing further damage. As he had suspected, the solution would have to be a compromise between primitive and progressive. He had Thérèse out gathering information from experts on historical reconstruction and hoped they'd have a solid plan in place by evening.

There was enough to do that his mind should not have been wandering, yet he caught himself staring at the same carving he'd already been staring at for well over twenty hours, incapable of focusing. He finally turned off the light above his workbench, pushed back the large suspended magnifying glass he used for the smallest details of his craft, and headed to the kitchen. He told himself that it was nearly lunchtime anyway and that this would save Jade a trip to his office.

When he entered the kitchen, he found Eva sitting on one of the long countertops, licking a wooden spoon with gusto. Philippe stood on a plastic footstool by the counter, a giant rolling pin in his hands, trying to flatten a big chunk of stiff cookie dough. Jade stood beside him, giving him instructions and laughing in a motherly way at his failed efforts.

"It's too hard," Philippe said, a little out of breath from the exertion.

"But it's good." This from Eva, the human powder puff. She was covered from head to toe in flour and seemed not in the least concerned about it. "It's really, really good. Can I have some more?"

"You," Jade said, poking at the little girl's stomach with a spatula, "can have one of the cookies when they're done, but no more dough for you!"

Eva giggled and scooted away from the spatula, her eyes darting toward the arch where Becker stood. She waved happily. "Hi, Mr. Helmet Man!" Her voice was as bright as the sunshine streaking through the window and casting dancing patterns on the kitchen floor.

Philippe didn't turn from his labor, but he chimed in too. "Hi, Mr. Crawls-under-the-Patio Man!" He blew his bangs up and kept trying to roll out the dough.

"Mr. Eats-in-His-Office Man," Eva said, the sugar she had just eaten fueling her boldness.

"Mr. Needs-to-Get-to-a-Bar Man."

Jade put a restraining hand on top of Philippe's head, but Eva wasn't finished. "Mr. Poopy-Head Man!" she said triumphantly, clearly the victor of her own one-upmanship.

"All right, kids, enough," Jade instructed, but the firmness in her voice was contradicted by her laughter. She glanced at Becker, still laughing. "I promise I didn't put them up to that!"

Beck leaned against the archway and cocked his head as he contemplated Eva's final moniker. "Mr. Poopy-Head Man?" he asked.

Eva ducked her chin and looked sideways at her nanny, a mischievous smile on her lips and in her eyes.

"Say you're sorry to Mr. Becker, Eva. It's not nice to call people poopy-heads." She looked at him with an *even if they've earned it* addendum to her statement.

Eva said a very halfhearted "Sorry."

Philippe was having a terrible time with his job. He'd finally had enough and shoved the rolling pin away, sending it careening across the counter and into the wall behind it.

"Philippe," Jade said, voice raised. "There's no need for that."

"It's stupid. It won't roll!"

"And what exactly does taking it out on the rolling pin accomplish?"

Philippe stood at the counter, his arms crossed tightly across his chest, his shoulders hunched, his eyebrows drawn downward in a fierce frown.

"Go sit in the time-out chair," Jade instructed softly. "I'll let you know when you can come back."

Philippe stalked over to a chair just outside the pantry door, and Eva looked at Becker, her eyes wide. The time-out chair was apparently a big deal in the Fallon household. Jade took over where Philippe had left off, rolling the dough into a circular shape with ease. She looked over her shoulder at Beck. "Anything you need, Mr. Becker, or is this just a social call?"

Beck had a sudden urge to return to his office. Or to the entryway. Or anywhere other than the kitchen, really, as this seemed to be a place of awkward silences and time-out chairs. "I was just wondering what time lunch would be today," he said, grasping at straws.

Jade propped a floury hand on her hip. "The same time it is every day," she said pointedly, glancing at the clock above the archway. "But the lasagna might be ready now. If you'll just give me a minute to cut the bread and get some coffee made, I'll bring it right in." She grabbed a hot pad and opened the oven.

Beck was discovering, as he had on some previous occasions, that the downside of being an intentional recluse was trying to become less of a recluse. It appeared to be one of those character traits so closely associated with a person that, unless there was consistent evidence to the contrary, it became indelible. The thought that he might be there for company had clearly not crossed Jade's mind, and short of saying, "Actually, I'd like to talk," he couldn't think of any expedient way of altering her expectations.

"Actually, I'd like to eat here with you today," he heard himself say. Shock froze him. Some small part of him must have known that he was going to say it, and that part had been sadly devoid of the kind of internal filters he liked to think he possessed. Three pairs of eyes—one at the oven, one on the counter, and one in the time-out chair—converged on him. "If—that's okay," he added.

Philippe was released from the time-out chair just in time for lunch. Jade had asked Eva to help "Mr. Becker" set the table, and the little girl had shown great patience in instructing him on the location of plates and cutlery. He was pretty sure she'd set the knife on the wrong side of the plate, but, given his inefficacy so far, he wasn't going to risk pointing it out. As Jade brought the pan of steaming lasagna to the table, Becker once again questioned the impulse that had landed him here. He sat across the table from not one, but two children, and he was about to spend lunch with them and their nanny. A businesswoman? A debutante? A calculating witch? Any of those wouldn't have shaken his confidence. But two children and a kind woman? He was out of his league and suddenly feeling much less hungry.

"I've been meaning to ask you how your spelunking expeditions have gone," Jade said as she was serving up the pasta.

Beck got suspicious. "Why do you ask?"

"Use your fork this time, Philippe," she said as she served. "And please blow on the food so you don't burn your mouth again."

Philippe nodded and used the edge of his fork to annihilate the previously perfect square of lasagna in front of him. He probably figured that kind of ventilation would cool it off all the faster.

Jade served herself last and sat at the end of the table, next to Beck. "I just ask because I wasn't aware that spelunking in pajamas was a recognized sport." She held up her hand. "At least, not in France. But is it very widespread in America?" She smiled sweetly and took a bite of food.

Beck pursed his lips to squelch his smile and nodded at the sarcasm. She'd obviously been a little surprised to find his muddy pajamas in the laundry, and he didn't blame her. "It's a growing trend," he answered her question. "Mostly just reserved for the incredibly wealthy, but they've allowed common folk like me to join their secret society." He took a bite and waved his fork, adding, around the hot food in his mouth, "As long as I go along with the human sacrifices and drinking of animal blood." He swallowed. "Wanna join?"

While Jade tried really hard not to laugh, Philippe and Eva let loose with a simultaneous "Eeeewwww!" and made gross-me-out faces at each other.

Jade put a hand on Philippe's arm to stem any further dramatics and turned on Becker, attempting—and failing—to be stern. "Mr. Becker," she said, "in the future, when you're trying to pull some adult legs, it might serve you well to remember that there are also children's legs in the room!" She turned her eyes on the twins. "Mr. Becker was joking when he talked about drinking blood and making human sacrifices. Weren't you, Mr. Becker?" She raised an eyebrow at him.

"I was," he conceded, shoveling another large forkful of pasta into his mouth.

"So, Mr. Becker—Becker," she said after they'd eaten in good-natured silence for a while, "to what do we owe this . . . pleasure?" She smiled again, that quizzical smile that seemed to indicate she was having some fun at his expense.

"Uh . . ." Becker wasn't sure how to respond. Getting into the kitchen and inviting himself to lunch had been a big-enough hurdle, and he hadn't contemplated the conversation that would have to happen next. It had been so long—so long—since he'd engaged in any form of casual small talk that he wasn't sure how to be natural. More important, he was suddenly unsure of the consequences that conversation might have or of the promises it might convey. He didn't need the expectation of a repeat performance, and he didn't want a new friend.

"Is there room for one more?" Thérèse entered the kitchen in a cloud of expensive perfume, her burnt-orange cashmere poncho somewhat louder than her voice. The twins gave each other a meaningful look while Jade smiled and motioned to the empty stool next to Beck.

"There's always room for one more," Jade said, smiling at Thérèse, then swinging her eyes to Becker, a message in their depths. "Isn't there, Mr. Becker?"

"Beck," he grumbled.

"I'm sorry. Beck," she corrected herself. "I don't know why I have such a hard time calling him by his first name," she said to Thérèse.

"Maybe because his first name is really his family name—or a chopped-off version of it," Thérèse said, a certain amount of disapproval mixed with her enjoyment at berating him. "Can you imagine calling me Gallet? Or just Ga?" She tsked and took the plate Jade handed her, then sat on the stool. "This looks wonderful. Thank you." She glanced over at the two children, both of whom were eyeing the cat-shaped brooch on her shawl. "And what have you two been up to this morning?"

"We made cookies," Eva said, then, without pausing, added, "Can I have your cat?"

Thérèse touched her brooch and looked toward Jade, who laughed. "Your brooch is safe, Madame Gallet. Eva—we've talked about this, right? You can't have things that don't belong to you unless they're given to you."

Philippe jumped in without hesitation. "Miss Thérèse, can you give Eva your brooch?"

Thérèse covered her mouth to stifle a disapproving gasp, and Jade jumped into the conversational void with a sharp "Philippe!" before launching into a lecture on the finer points of generosity and greed. Becker found himself dwelling a little too long on the light in her eyes, the dimple betraying a smile she tried to dissimulate with sternness, and the genuine kindness in her voice.

With Thérèse's appearance, the pressure for Becker to participate in the lunchtime discussion had lessened. He was happy to concentrate on his meal and listen to the banter of the children and the two women, answering when directly addressed but otherwise sticking to the outskirts of the conversation. When the children spoke with Jade, it was with a kind of reverence that took him aback. He'd seen her discipline them and teach them, and he knew she was firm when she needed to be, yet there was something simple and trusting about their communication. He wondered why her mothering gifts were being spent on the children of others while she invested her time in this less-than-profitable career.

Thérèse, on the other hand, pursued the children like there would be prize money for gaining their affection, and though the twins played along, it was fairly obvious that theirs was not a mutually enjoyable relationship. Becker wondered if it might make working with Thérèse easier if he were to revert to a more childish version of himself. Based on some of what she'd seen from him so far, of course, Thérèse might suspect that he'd already done so.

Jade caught him looking at her and smiled, offering him another piece of lasagna, but he declined. "I'll leave the leftovers in the small fridge—just in case you get a craving later," she said, motioning to the smallest of the three fridges that lined the wall by the door.

"Uh . . . sure. Whatever."

She sighed and rolled her eyes. "There's no obligation to eat it," she said. "I just don't want you starving to death up in your little apartment."

"I get plenty to eat."

"You're welcome," she said curtly, covering the leftovers with tinfoil. "Sometimes I wonder if I shouldn't just bring what we don't eat to the gatehouse. I'm sure Jojo would be more than happy to accept the kindness." She put extra emphasis on the word *kindness*, and Beck knew that was for him.

"Jojo?" Thérèse asked.

"The man in the gatehouse," Eva answered. She and Philippe were standing on stools by the sink just outside the archway, rinsing their hands with enough water to end the drought in Africa. The sink had a view of the front half of the castle property, and on previous occasions, while they scrubbed dirt from their hands, Beck had heard the kids planning the elaborate stories they would reenact in the guard towers and around the stables.

"Yes, of course," Thérèse said. "I knew there was someone who lived out there, but I had no idea he had a name."

"That's what the ladies at the butcher shop call him," Jade said, heading back to the table from the fridge. "It might just be made up, but it seems to suit him."

There was a flurry of activity over by the sink.

"There he is, there he is, there he is!" the twins whispered frantically, gesticulating with such force that they nearly fell off their footstools.

The adults in the room tried to maintain a certain amount of dignity as they rushed to the window, but each one of them failed miserably. Thérèse let out a high-pitched peep and covered her mouth, trotting over to join the children, and Jade grabbed Beck's arm with a hushed "Come on!" and moved in a mockery of stealth to the window. Much as he wanted to catch a glimpse of the château's resident stalker, Jade's hand on his arm took precedence in Beck's mind. It hadn't been that long since he'd felt a woman's touch, so it wasn't the contact that registered so fiercely. It was the person whose hand grasped his elbow who made the difference. The women he'd spent time with before arriving in France would have made of that touch something demanding and sordid, but with Jade it was as simple as it was unmeasured. He would have been more comfortable with the former.

Beck heard Thérèse take in a shocked breath and turned his attention to the window. Jade had to let go of his arm to lean forward, but not for long. All five of them leaned back when Jojo passed in front of them—just a few feet away. He was small, probably no more than five foot four, though he was so stooped that he might have once stood taller. He wore a moth-eaten, dark-gray coat whose hem had apparently fallen out quite a while ago. The dark-blue sweatpants underneath were stained with mud and touched the ground, the elastic at the ankles long gone. But it was his face that made Beck catch his breath. From the silence around the sink, he knew the others were affected as well.

Jojo's face was so deeply lined that dirt had lodged in the crevices, making it look like he'd painted the wrinkles into his skin. His eyes were sunken, as were his cheeks, and his mouth was a hard, thin line surrounded by coarse bristles. His hair was long, pulled back with a shoelace, and nearly perfectly white—it might have been, except for the dirt. But the steel-gray eyes that peered out of that face, heavy-lidded and sunken, were sharp and piercing, fully alert yet somehow turned inward. This was a man whose life only prolonged his suffering and who suffered with utter, complete awareness.

The five of them stood at the window long after Jojo had passed out of sight. Philippe and Eva had actually climbed into the low flat-bottomed sink and pressed their heads against the windowpane to follow his progress as far as they could. Thérèse fingered the pendant at her neck as if it were a rosary, looking spooked, and Jade's eyes had a soft, sad look about them. She ran a hand over Eva's hair before coaxing her down from the sink, then helped Philippe to jump out.

As for Becker, he stood slightly back from the others. There was a tightness in his chest and a heaviness in his mind that begged for release. He reached out to get Jade's attention, then withdrew his hand. His voice was gravelly when he said, almost too quietly to be heard, "You should bring him some food."

As he climbed the steps to his apartment, he could hear Thérèse cackling about how unsafe it would be to go near "that man's" house and how setting a precedent could have disastrous repercussions. Jade's calm voice followed. "We just saw him heading for the neighbor's stables," she said. "We'll leave a plate on his doorstep while he's gone. It will all be perfectly safe."

Beck closed his door and reached for the bottle in his closet.

11

THIS TIME, he could see people. They stood against a charred wooden wall from which small flames still ribboned upward, and they stared at him through the eyeholes of black ski masks. He couldn't see their faces, but their eyes . . . Their eyes were searingly familiar. He recognized the green of his mother's gaze. The gray of his father's. The blue of Gary's. Eva's deep brown. Jojo's frozen gray.

"Say something," he said.

They stared, immobile, expressionless, callous.

"Mom?" He pleaded with the blue-green eyes. "Come on, Mom, speak to me!"

She stared ahead without flinching.

"Pops. You recognize me, right? Pops?" He tried to step closer to the masked figures, but there was an invisible barrier shielding him from them. He touched it, and a shock of electricity burned through his body. He cried out and fell back against a toppled tree trunk, his heart pounding from the shock. He looked into each pair of eyes again, a frantic pulse beating in his ears, searching for any form of recognition, but he saw none. Even Eva's normally lively eyes were dim with dispassion and oblivious to his pleas.

As he paced in front of them, begging for connection, a door opened in a large tree next to him, its elevator chime dissonant in the walled forest in which he stood. Philippe stepped out. Then Jade. They looked him in the eye and knew him. These two, he could connect with. These two, he could embrace. But as he opened his arms to draw Philippe to him, he found that they weren't his to control. It was as a spectator that he watched himself taking a black ski mask from his pocket and slipping it over Philippe's head.

"No!" he screamed, ashamed and appalled. "No! Stop! *Stop!*"

But he couldn't stop his own body from performing the obscene task. He tried to warn Jade to escape. "Run!" he yelled at her. "Jade, get out of here! Run!" But even as his mouth said the words, his hands pulled a mask over her face. Over her dark hair, over her walnut eyes.

"No!" he screamed, the tortured sound of anguish pouring from his throat like blood. "No," he cried again, as Jade and Philippe were sucked into the row that lined the burning wall. "No . . ." It was a sob. A plea.

The flames grew brighter—bigger. They licked at the clothing of the masked lineup, burning their bodies until they turned a gruesome, charred black, then sifted to the ground, reduced to ashes. Beck sank to his knees, unable to breathe. Unable to breathe. Unable to breathe.

Becker woke with the feeling that his lungs were exploding. He rose onto an elbow and gulped in a deep breath. It rasped past his constricted throat, making him cough so hard that he could taste the bile in his mouth. He rolled out of bed and tried to make it to the door, but his legs buckled beneath him. It took several more breaths on his hands and knees before he was able to muster the strength to make it to the bathroom. He retched into the commode, then sat back against the wall, depleted.

An hour later, lamplight shone out the window of his office and cast a rectangle of light on the grass outside. Beck held a long, curved piece of wood in his hand, its shape becoming the swirl of the staircase's design. The hand that held the wood was fairly steady, but the one that held the razor-sharp lathe was not. Beck pressed his lips together and willed his fingers to obey his mind's commands. He shaved off one fine layer of wood after the other, a little less shaky when he exerted pressure, and slowly saw a form emerge.

The element of the staircase wasn't finished yet when the castle awoke in the morning, and, truth be told, it had taken him much too long to make the small amount of progress he had. But he'd made it through the night without a drink, scared dry by the dream that had shaken his equilibrium. Those few hours of sobriety were a significant accomplishment.

There was a light tap on his door. "Come in," he called out, his rough voice betraying his sleepless night.

Jade poked her head around the door. "Thought you might want to know that the plate I dropped off at Jojo's yesterday was waiting for me at the kitchen door when we got here."

It took a moment for Beck's mind to catch on. When he finally remembered yesterday's meal, he asked, "Was the lasagna still on it?"

Jade smiled. "It was all gone." She frowned at him. "And no, I don't think the neighborhood cats ate it!"

"Well done," he mumbled, getting back to work. "You've saved a perpetual trespasser from starvation."

Jade cocked her head and stepped all the way into the office. Beck glanced up, irritated by her lingering presence. She was wearing her hair down more these days, and its slick lines accentuated her features. Her eyes seemed wider set and her jaw sharper. Her skin, he noticed, looked paler. But that might merely be the dreary winter months taking their toll. "Been burning the midnight oil?" she asked.

He grunted his response and reached for a rag to dust off the fruit of his labor.

Jade stepped closer to his workbench and inspected the graceful arches and curves of his handiwork. "Becker, that's exquisite," she said, sounding surprised that a man like Beck could produce something so fine and artistic. "I had no idea I was feeding *Rodin!*"

Another grunt.

"Speaking of waiting on you, I was just coming by to let you know that we're having an English breakfast this morning. I'll still make coffee for you, of course, instead of tea," she added hastily, "but there will also be fried eggs and bacon and sausage and potatoes."

It all sounded good to Beck. "And you felt the need to warn me because . . . ?"

"Because I saw your light on when I arrived and I figured you'd been working most of the night. I thought you might enjoy having something to look forward to."

"Huh."

"Well, good. I'm glad we shared this moment," she said, exiting the office.

Becker smiled as he brushed wood shavings onto the floor.

He waited for nearly an hour for Jade to return bearing his tray. He fiddled on the Internet, sending Gary an update on the progress so far, entering new figures into his budgeting spreadsheet, and jotting down items he'd have to discuss with Fallon when he dropped by later in the day. He'd made it through the night without a drink, shielded from his cravings, in part, by his focus on his woodwork, but with the brutal light of day, his throbbing head and upset stomach were doing their best to foil his midnight resolutions. He felt weighed down and sluggish.

Jade's soft knock came as a relief. "Yes!" he shouted, probably more loudly than necessary.

She opened the door and gave him a questioning look. "Are you coming to breakfast? It's been ready for going on twenty minutes, and I'm afraid it'll be ruined if you don't come quickly. . . ."

"I thought you were bringing it to the office," Beck answered, a little put out by the assumption that he'd eat his breakfast in the kitchen.

"I . . ." Jade raised her shoulders in an apologetic gesture. "I'm so sorry. I just assumed . . . after yesterday . . ."

"Just because I eat one meal in the kitchen doesn't mean I'm changing my habits," he said, eyes narrowed.

Jade moved into the room and propped a hip against the backrest of the couch, crossing her arms and eyeing Beck as if she were assessing one of Thérèse's antiques. "You know, Beck," she said, for once leaving the *Mr.* off his name, "some people actually find it enjoyable to spend time with others."

He raised an eyebrow.

"I think you're the only person I've ever met who equates sociability with some sort of Chinese water torture." She smiled, her expression less pleasant than self-congratulatory, and Beck wondered how long she'd been practicing that line.

"Are you finished?"

She looked at the ceiling as if evaluating the necessity for further statements. "Yes," she finally said. "I'm finished."

"Best news I've gotten all morning."

"So are you eating in the kitchen—where the coffeepot is, by the way—or am I bringing you your breakfast on a tray?"

He would not be swayed. He leaned forward at his desk, eyebrows raised in something he hoped resembled disdain, and answered, "I'll eat it here."

Jade's eyes narrowed and she pursed her lips, looking as if she wanted to retort but was restraining herself out of deference for his position on the renovation team. "Fine. I'll be back in a minute," she said, her smile more forced this time. "Over easy all right?"

"Over easy's fine." His eyes were on his computer screen.

He heard the door click softly as Jade left.

Half an hour later, he was still sitting at his desk, staring out the window as he finished a sausage link and wondering what the payoff of his stubbornness had been. He'd spent the better part of the past two years being mostly alone and enjoying the benefits of his choices, but there was something about the banter reaching him from the kitchen that made him wonder if his self-imposed reclusion was entirely a good thing. He shook his head and dismissed the thought. No, this was what he wanted. Total independence. No one to tell him what to do or how to do it. This was the life he'd crafted for himself, and he was satisfied with it. It was simple. Straightforward. No excess baggage required.

The throbbing in his head and the shake in his fork betrayed his convictions. He took another slug of coffee and hoped it would still his nerves. Some heavy-duty labor might too. He'd join the carpentry team in the dining rooms this morning and exorcise his demons with some physical exertion.

Beck was just getting back to his breakfast when the door to his office burst open and Thérèse stormed in.

"Someone has destroyed the well!" she shrilled, pointing back in the direction from which she'd come.

Beck raised an eyebrow. "And that's my problem because . . . ?"

She squinted. "I understand that the cosmetics of this renovation are mostly my purview, Mr. Becker, but if you'll follow me,

I think you'll see that there is little I can do alone to resolve this matter!" Her voice rose to new heights on the last word.

Beck knew that no amount of sarcasm or soothing would talk Thérèse down, so he heaved a deep sigh and levered himself to a standing position. "Show me," he said, his voice that of a lamb being led to slaughter.

Thérèse preceded him briskly out the door at the bottom of the stairs, under the overpass outside the kitchen and into the parking area flanked by the carport and the old carriage courtyard. The children, who had been finishing up their breakfast in the kitchen, came running out to see what all the fuss was about, followed by Jade, who had been washing dishes and still sported pink rubber gloves.

Just outside the kitchen wall was a waist-high stone well, its wrought-iron tripod uprooted from the stone to which it had been anchored. Beck had passed by the well before, but had never paid close attention to it. This morning, however, he knew at first glance that the damage had been intentional and had probably required some effort. The heavy cement-and-stone slab that had covered the well's opening had been painstakingly pushed to the side, using something like a crowbar to displace it one inch at a time. There were sharp indentations where a hard object had scored the stone. The slab had been displaced so far across the well that, Beck suspected, it had teetered over the edge, dislodging one foot of the tripod in its fall. It had landed on the stone apron around the bottom of the well and shattered into several pieces.

Beck tested the solidity of the wrought-iron elements that rose like a teepee above the well, supporting in their center a pulley from which a bucket had once hung.

"Philippe," he said to the boy, whose eyes were wide and excited. "Run to my office and get the flashlight off my desk, will you?"

Philippe's little chest swelled with pride at his mission, and he took off running in the direction of the back door.

The wrought-iron tripod hadn't bent permanently when the cover plate had dislodged it from the stone. Beck quickly pulled the leg back to the hole from which it had been torn and dropped it into place.

"There," he said, casting Thérèse a "what's the big deal?" look. "Tragedy averted. Any other cataclysmic destruction I need to know about?"

Thérèse pointed at the well with both hands. "But don't you find it odd that—"

"Yes."

"And don't you wonder who would possibly—"

"Yes."

Thérèse's shoulders slumped, as if Becker had disappointed her dramatic expectations. In a much calmer voice, she said, "Well, I guess there wasn't any lasting damage done. Except to the cover plate."

Philippe came running back with a large black flashlight he held by its yellow string. "Here it is," he said breathlessly, holding the flashlight out to Beck. "Are you going to go down the well?"

From the look on his face, Beck could tell that the boy really considered Beck rappelling down the narrow well to be a possibility. "Not if I can help it," he said, shining the powerful beam down the three-foot opening. The shaft of the well was only about twelve feet deep, and there appeared to be a collection of debris sitting in a shallow puddle at the bottom. What caught Beck's eye was not the rotting wood and rusting bits of metal. It was the bright-blue nylon rope coiled on the mound of refuse.

He looked at Thérèse and Jade. "You sure this well was completely covered until this morning?"

"Yes, of course," Jade said, leaning over the edge and following the beam of Beck's flashlight to the blue rope at the bottom. "That rope looks new."

"Well, new or not, it's not part of the original design."

Jade peered more closely into the well. "Why would anyone want to go exploring in an old, dried-up well?"

"Jojo," Thérèse declared. "He'd do something like this."

Jade ignored her, taking the flashlight from Beck's hand and aiming it more specifically at a portion of the well floor. "Do you see that?" she asked.

Beck leaned in closer, a little uncomfortable at the proximity, but his curiosity was aroused by the surprise in her voice.

"What am I looking for?" he asked.

"That," Jade answered, circling an object on the well floor with the beam from the flashlight.

Eva, who had shuffled over to Jade, pulled on her arm and asked, nearly in a whisper, "Is it Jojo?"

The question made Becker smirk and Jade momentarily straighten to lay a hand on the six-year-old's head. "No, Eva, it's not Jojo." Eva seemed immensely relieved. "What I think it is, however," she said, leaning in again to get a closer look, "is a flashlight. And the flashlight appears to be tied to the end of the rope."

"Well, that's just preposterous," Thérèse clucked. "Who would lower a flashlight down a well and leave it there?"

"Jojo?" Philippe asked. The kids were clearly intent on making the mysterious old man the protagonist of this story.

"Whoever did it," Beck said, putting special emphasis on *whoever*, "probably didn't intend to leave the rope and flashlight down there." He glanced at the shattered cement slab lying at the foot of the well. "They might have been startled when the cover fell off and shattered. . . ."

"And they just let go of the rope?"

"It's a possibility."

"Interesting theory, Sherlock," Jade said. "Do you think we should dust for fingerprints or something?"

Beck turned on her, taking the flashlight from her hand. "You're mocking me."

She smiled. "I am indeed."

"Well, whatever the explanation is," Thérèse said, "I'm just glad the structure wasn't damaged. It might not look like much now, but with the right kind of landscaping around it and some creativity, it could make a stunning water feature."

Beck raised an eyebrow. "A well as a water feature? How original."

Eva hadn't finished working herself into a terror. "I think Jojo did it," she whispered loudly enough for all of them to hear.

Philippe nodded with the vigor of conviction. "He was looking for a treasure, but he didn't find it 'cause he dropped the flashlight."

"And now the treasure is stuck at the bottom of the well and nobody can get to it," Eva finished with the kind of dramatic flair that might have earned her a role on Broadway.

"Why does it have to be Jojo?" Beck asked them, hands on hips.

Twin sets of shoulders hunched up in an "I don't know" gesture that made Jade laugh. "All right, you two. Let's leave Mr. Becker to find the culprit and get back to our books."

"But . . ."

"I promise you he'll let us know just as soon as he traps the bad guy, Philippe," Jade added, lowering her voice to a dramatic purr on "bad guy." The boy seemed satisfied with the promise.

"You tell us, okay?" Eva's soft voice held fascination and command.

Beck snapped a salute as the trio walked away. "You'll be the first to know." As an afterthought, he added, "But don't go accusing Jojo of anything! There's no reason to think he did this!"

At least, that was what Becker chose to believe. There were so many tugs-of-war being waged in his head that he didn't need to add another to the mix. Whoever had done this must have had a good reason. Beck wondered as he walked away if it was the same reason that had prompted the late-night excavating under the patio.

12

MARIE WAS in the laundry room, scrubbing stubborn bloodstains out of cotton sheets, when Elise found her. She leaned back against the doorjamb, sighing dramatically, clearly waiting for Marie to ask her about the ball.

Marie wasn't in the mood for listening to her friend wax romantic about the Nazi of her dreams and was tempted to let the silence stretch until Elise got bored and went away, but it was not to be.

"Ask me about the ball!" Elise chimed when Marie failed to broach the topic. She had the look of a cat after a five-course canary meal.

Marie scrubbed a little harder, taking some of her worry for Elise out on the soiled linen. "Tell me about the ball," she mumbled.

"It was . . . grand," Elise gushed, her eyes on the ceiling, as if a reenactment of the event were being projected on its white surface.

"The castle was . . ." Her excitement got the best of her, and she ran behind her friend, wrapping her arms around Marie's waist as she continued to stare off at the scene she was reliving. "It was magical, Marie. There were lanterns all the way around the lawn out front. Flowers everywhere, even in the bathroom! And waiters and a chamber orchestra in the ballroom. And the canapés—Marie, you should have seen the canapés! They were tiny little edible works of art."

Marie pried the arms from around her waist and turned to face her friend, leaning back against the washboard. "I'm glad you had fun, Elise."

Elise studied her face for a moment. "No, you're not. You're not happy at all!"

"Elise."

"But if you had been there . . ." She twirled gracefully as if she were in her partner's arms on the ballroom's polished floor. "The ladies all wore dresses of the most exquisite fabrics. Silks and taffetas and Chantilly lace. And their hair. Oh, Marie, you should have seen their hair. It was all so . . . so elegant!"

Marie couldn't help but smile, albeit sadly. Her friend was entertaining on the most common of days, and this post-Cinderella's-ball version of Elise was as endearing as it was disquieting. "Did Karl treat you right?" she asked.

Elise paused in her exuberance and met Marie's straightforward gaze. "He treated me like I was made of china. Marie, he treated me like I was made of gold . . ."

Their gazes held for a moment longer before Marie turned back to her scrubbing, alternating salt and vinegar on the stubborn stains. "And is he a good dancer?" she asked. "Or do you have bruised feet to show for your adventure?"

"He dances like a Greek god," Elise breathed.

This made Marie pause again, hand on hip. "Elise, what on earth do you know about Greek gods?"

Elise giggled. "I know they dance like Karl," she offered. She took the sheet Marie had been working on to the tub on the tall counter by the window and immersed it in bleachy water while Marie riffled through a laundry basket for her next cleaning project.

"Were there any townspeople there?"

Elise was silent for a moment before answering, in a much more serious voice, "A few of them. The caterers who provided the wine and hors d'oeuvres . . . and a couple others."

"And they recognized you?"

"They spoke to me in French, so . . . yes, I guess they did." A sad edge had crept into her voice. It seemed her magical night had not been all magic after all.

Marie wiped her hands on her apron and moved to the window where Elise, arms folded over her stomach, stared out at the woods just outside the manor's gates. "What did they say to you when they spoke to you in French?" she asked.

Elise bit her lip. "They called me a traitor. . . ." She averted her gaze, but not before Marie had seen the tears gathering there.

"Elise," she said, her hand on her friend's back.

"It's not fair!" Elise protested. "I'm no less French than they are."

"But . . ." Marie didn't know how to make her see the villagers' point of view. "But they saw you dance with a Nazi," she finally explained, trying to sound sensitive, but intent on getting her point across. "They saw you talking with him and laughing with him. They saw you eating the food and drinking the champagne they had served the Nazis. They know you're French, but, Elise, if you work for the boches *and have a relationship with a* boche *and dance with him at a ball hosted by the* boches *for the* boches *. . . what do you expect their conclusion to be?"*

A tear rolled down Elise's cheek. "Maurice spit at me," she said, taking in a hiccupping breath.

"He did?"

She nodded. "He walked right up to me as I was waiting for Karl to come back with our drinks and he spit at me." She turned watery eyes on her friend. "And then he just—walked away."

Marie's hand traced slow circles on Elise's back. "Are you sure it's worth it?" she asked. Then, as Elise looked at her quizzically, she added, "Are you sure you love Karl enough to go through this—to risk what you're risking?"

Elise nodded, her blonde curls bobbing and her eyes determined. "He said he wants to marry me."

Marie felt her lungs constrict. "He wants to—?"

"Not right now," Elise added, some excitement coming back into her gaze. "But soon. When the war is over."

"Elise . . ."

"He said his family owns a lot of land near Heidelberg where we can build a home and breed horses." Cheeks flushed with excitement, she took her friend's hand and squeezed it. "And you can come and visit us. You can live with us if you want!"

"Wait! How can you be sure this is what you want? Why raise horses in Germany when your home is right here—in Lamorlaye—and your family—"

"Stop trying to be my conscience, Marie," Elise interrupted, her face and voice suddenly hardening. "You don't know what it is to love someone and to want to spend the rest of your life with him."

"You're right, but . . . Elise, he's a boche*!"*

Elise's face lit up with the kind of pride that made Marie's skin crawl. "He wants me to serve the Führer with him, to obey Himmler's order to bear children who will restore the Aryan race."

"Elise . . ."

She turned on Marie with a hysterical sort of intent on her face. "Don't try to talk me out of it!" she nearly yelled. "Just—don't! Karl says it's our duty to repopulate the Reich. Just like all the women in the manor are doing! You see how they're treated," she continued, her voice now nearly pleading. "They're special, Marie. They're doing something that has . . ." She searched for the right word. "Something that has a higher purpose. If I can bear a baby for the Führer . . ."

"Elise, stop it!" Marie grabbed her friend's arms and shook her, trying to jar the enraptured expression from her face. "You're talking nonsense. You're not old enough to have children. And the war isn't over. The Nazis might not win, you know. And then what? What do you do then with your bastard baby?"

The slap resounded in the room like the crack of a whip. Marie covered her cheek with a hand that shook from shock and horror. Elise raised her chin and gave Marie a look so cold that it sent a shiver down her spine. "Don't ever speak of my baby that way again," she said, her voice low and threatening. "Nor of the man I love, nor of the Führer."

"Elise . . ." Marie was at a loss for words. She knew her friend loved Karl but had never suspected that the love would lead to treason. "Just wait. Okay? Before you . . . do anything about having a baby. Give it a little more time."

Elise moved toward the door, stopping to turn to Marie before she exited. There was a dreamy smile on her face when she said, "It might already be too late for that."

13

THE PROGRESS BEING MADE in the castle was astonishing. On a rainy Friday morning, Fallon, Thérèse, and Becker toured the site, consulting with the artisans and master craftsmen they encountered and marveling both at the extent and beauty of the work already accomplished. In the two adjoining dining halls, the crown molding and wainscoting had been painstakingly removed and restored, several layers of paint steamed and scraped off each piece to return the artistic accents to their rich wood finish. Several layers of old wallpaper had also been stripped and the plaster beneath them prepared for the wall treatments Thérèse had ordered. They would be covered with two different historically accurate patterns printed on modern wallpaper and the artistic use of molding designs.

The passageway between the dining rooms and the kitchen had been used as a food preparation site in decades gone by. Originally, floor-to-ceiling built-in cupboards had lined one wall, and a giant cutting board across the room sported a sort of guillotine intended to make quick work of slicing French baguettes. The floor in this area had previously been covered in old, cracked tiles now replaced with small, unglazed marble tiles in shades of gray and brown. The cupboards had been ripped out, and Thérèse had ordered some new organizational features for the space. She liked to call the style she'd selected for this area and the kitchen *"nouveau vieux,"* which, translated, meant "new old." The men had to agree, almost reluctantly, that her choice was in keeping with the colors and lines of the dining halls, while modern and spacious enough to add practicality and efficiency to the room. Thérèse tried to hide her pleasure at their praise and failed miserably. She glowed with satisfaction and expressed her pride with a nonstop flurry of words that threatened to sap Becker of whatever sanity he still possessed.

Becker led the trio into his office to show Fallon the progress he was making on the staircase features. Fallon looked around, taking in the workbench crowded under the window, the thick layer of wood chips on the floor, and the draped sheets protecting the furniture in the sitting area.

"Made yourself at home, did you?" he asked, smiling.

Becker realized that he hadn't consulted with his boss before making the office his carpentry studio. "I just thought it would be more practical . . ."

Fallon interrupted his explanation with a hearty thump on the back. "No need to explain yourself, my lad. I can see this office is serving you well, and that's exactly what it was intended for."

They'd spent a few more minutes discussing the progress of the project when there was a quick knock on the door. Sylvia poked her head into the room. "I thought I heard my husband's voice," she said, smiling at him as she entered. "Mr. Becker," she said, "I hope you'll forgive me, but we have a doctor's appointment—" she glanced at her watch—"a half an hour ago, so I'm going to have to forcibly remove your boss from the premises!" She linked an arm through her husband's as she spoke and gently propelled him toward the door. "Nice to see you, Thérèse! That shade of red looks just beautiful on you." She was at the door now, pushing Fallon out. "I'm sure he was very pleased with your progress, Mr. Becker," she said, turning to smile at him, then calling out the door, "Weren't you, love?"

"I was indeed," came Fallon's jovial reply from the landing outside the office.

Sylvia was just about to pull the door closed when Thérèse took a few furtive steps forward and interrupted her. "Madame Fallon!"

Sylvia stepped back into the room, clearly preoccupied by the passing time. "Please. Call me Sylvia."

"Sylvia, then. I'm just wondering how you're feeling," she said.

Becker frowned and took a closer look at the high-strung woman whose eagerness to ask about her employer's wife's health seemed just a little excessive. She seemed to be torn between staring with odd intensity at Sylvia's swollen belly and averting her eyes from the sight.

"With the baby, I mean," Thérèse answered. "Is everything all right?"

Sylvia too seemed a bit nonplussed by Thérèse's concern. "I'm doing fine, Thérèse. I'm . . ." A thought struck her. "Oh—you're referring to the doctor's appointment!"

"Yes, of course. You mentioned that you were seeing him this morning, and . . ."

"Her. We're seeing her. And it's just a routine checkup. Nothing to worry yourself about."

"Oh, good." Thérèse sounded genuinely, deeply relieved. She fingered her pendant, a flush on her neck and cheeks, her eyes earnest. "One just doesn't know. Pregnancies can be so . . . unpredictable, sometimes. And even with modern medicine . . ."

Sylvia smiled and said, "I'm sure everything is just fine, Thérèse." She nodded at Beck. "It's been a pleasure seeing you both."

When the door closed behind her, Thérèse's tension collapsed in a visible way. She let out a shaky breath and grabbed the backrest of the couch with an unsteady hand.

"Thérèse," Beck said, a little embarrassed by the woman's behavior, "she's the pregnant one, you know. There's no need to work yourself up about someone else's baby."

"No—of course not," Thérèse conceded. "It's just that—you know—" She seemed to be racking her mind for a plausible explanation. "I've come to care about the Fallons, and I guess I get a little overprotective of those I feel close to."

"Yeah, well—your overprotective is someone else's over-the-cuckoo's-nest, so you might want to put a lid on the hysterics." He realized too late that his words had been unnecessarily harsh. He opened his mouth to apologize, but Thérèse cut in before he could say anything.

"If you'll excuse me," she said, her back once again ramrod straight, "I've got some wallpapering to attend to." And she marched out of the office.

Sundays were the only day of the week when his meal routine was altered. The kids were home with their parents on that day, and Jade spent only enough time at the castle to bring Beck croissants for breakfast and fix him lunch. They had agreed that he'd snack on leftovers for dinner and allow Jade to spend some time at home.

It was nearly one when he realized there had been no sign of life from the kitchen, and he went out to investigate. Jade's purse hung on the hook next to the back door and there were some groceries on the counter, but the kitchen was otherwise empty. Beck went to the sink to start some coffee percolating and looked through the bags of groceries. There was broccoli, potatoes, cheese, and a pot of cream. Anyone else might have known how to turn those ingredients into a meal, but Beck's culinary specialties were Kraft mac and cheese, microwave popcorn, and Thai takeout. Anything beyond that was Greek to him.

He had his head in the fridge and was scrounging for leftovers when he heard the door open. Jade smiled when she saw him and immediately raised a hand in apology. "I'm so sorry it's so late . . . ," she began.

"Well, it's about time you showed up. Look at me. One more minute without food and the UN would be sending in a humanitarian convoy."

Jade sent him a small smile and hung her coat on the usual hook, grabbing an apron and moving slowly toward the bagged groceries on the counter. "I'll have it on the table in fifteen minutes."

There was something in her demeanor that caught his attention. Maybe it was the slight shuffle of her feet or the look of forced concentration on her face. Or maybe it had more to do with the fact that she hadn't made eye contact with him since she'd arrived.

"Um . . ." He was slightly out of his league here. Sensitivity had never been a strong suit. "Are you sure you're up to cooking? I mean . . . there are leftovers in the—"

"I'm fine," she interrupted, her voice a little raspy.

"But if you're not feeling well . . ."

"I'm *fine*," she repeated.

He held up his hands in surrender. "All right. I'm sorry."

She sighed and turned away from the sink where she was washing the broccoli just long enough to cast him a weary smile. "I'm just a little tired. And church went late, so . . ."

He thought he saw something more than fatigue in the dullness of her eyes and smile. From the moment he'd entered the castle and mistaken her for Fallon's wife, she'd had a sparkle in her eye—something infinitely alive and aware. He hadn't seen that just then. He'd seen something dim and forced. It had the dual effect of making him want to pry *and* flee. And since he was neither good at asking personal questions nor at beating hasty retreats, he was left anchored to the spot, at a loss.

At the sink, Jade filled a pot with water and seemed to strain as she carried it to the stove to light a flame beneath it. She took a cast-iron pan from the shelf beside the stove and poured a dribble of olive oil into it, placing it too on a flame. Beck watched her tear open the package of meat she'd taken from the fridge—it looked like steak—and sprinkle it with an assortment of spices. She seemed as unaware of him as he was aware of her, which left the onus of any conversation on Beck. Under other circumstances, he might have left her to prepare the dinner in silence, but there was a frailty about her that he hadn't seen before, and it made him feel . . . concerned. Granted, concern was a bit of a new emotion for him. At least, of late. And the coward in him would have preferred to ignore it. But as much as he had fought it, there was something about Jade that had gone beyond intriguing him. It had engaged him. And that small spark of new life in the high-strung void of his existence was reason enough to push past his reservations.

He walked over to the stove before he lost his resolve and leaned on the counter next to it, crossing his ankles in an attempt at nonchalance. From that distance he could see more clearly the pallor of her skin and the determination in her eyes. She was fighting some sort of battle, and he was watching from the sidelines. He grasped at conversational straws and finally settled on "So you go to church?"

She paused in the act of dropping diced onions into the frying pan and gave him a look. "You're making conversation?"

He had to admit that, given the tenor of previous interactions, she had a right to raise the issue. "I am," he said. "And I'm not sure why, except that you look like you've been broadsided by something really large and really heavy, and I figure if you won't tell me what it is, at least talking might get your mind off it. . . ." He let the sentence trail off, hoping for an "Okay, let's talk" or a "What, are you kidding me?" that would give him a clearer picture of what he was up against.

Instead, she said, "Yes, I go to church," and left it at that.

As far as conversations went, this one was shaping up to be painful. "Here in Lamorlaye?"

She gave him another look. Given the fact that she owned no car, the likelihood of going somewhere distant for church was slim. "Can you cut me a little slack here? I'm just trying to . . ." *Trying to what?* "I used to go to church," he finally said. The moment the words were out, he wondered where they'd come from. His churchgoing days were a farce to him. And certainly not worth discussing.

Unfortunately, Jade seemed to have a different opinion of the topic, and though she didn't regain any color and her eyes didn't recover their spark, there was a fresh focus on her face when she said, "Tell me about that."

Beck held up his hand. "Wait a minute—you can't turn the tables on me like that."

Jade smiled. "It's called conversation," she said, using a fork to transfer steak into the frying pan where the onions sizzled in the oil.

Beck was starting to regret the concern that had prompted his foray into verbal territory. "Actually, since I asked you first . . ."

Jade rolled her eyes, then put a hand on the counter, as if the eye motion had set her off balance. "Okay," she said, a sheen of perspiration breaking out on her upper lip, "what do you want to know?"

Becker shrugged and contemplated possible scenarios that would put an end to this conversation. Before he'd opted for any of them, Jade went on.

"I've attended church since I was . . . I can't remember, actually.

Since I was a child." She looked at him and smiled, a vestige of her usual feistiness in her gaze. "Why did I go to church, you ask? Because my parents dragged me there, kicking and screaming, every Sunday. Why was I kicking and screaming, you ask?" She smiled again, enjoying the conversation "they" were having without any need for Beck's participation in it. "Because I thought church was this austere place where people went when they didn't have anything better to do, or—worse yet—when they were so lonely that the only company they could find was the priest who sat in the confessional." She let a moment or two pass while she flipped the steak and seasoned the other side, then washed a potato and placed it in the microwave. She glanced at him and said, "It's your turn to ask a question." She dropped several broccoli florets into the pot of simmering water.

Beck, who had been considering his own definition of church, shifted against the counter and said, "So . . . you're Catholic?"

"Good question, Mr. Becker."

"Beck."

"Beck. I was Catholic. Then I was agnostic. Then I went through a bit of an atheistic phase—my mother died and I had to hate somebody, right? And it was easiest to hate God because he doesn't fight back. And then I found . . . something else. Not so much a religion as a place where life is valued and hope is pursued and . . . and there's peace. I'm a big fan of peace," she concluded.

Beck found himself envying the simplicity of her statement. He couldn't help saying, "So now you're Buddhist."

At this, Jade laughed. She laughed and again caught the edge of the counter. This time, Beck could see what little color was left draining from her face. He moved quickly, catching her arm as she swayed and hooking a stool from the table with his foot. "Here. Sit," he said, hoping the roughness he heard in his own voice didn't sound like anger to her.

Jade sat and leaned forward, her hand on the table's edge, as if she might fall from the stool. Beck opened two cupboards before he found the glasses. He filled one with water and brought it to the woman who sat bent over, taking deep breaths. He knelt down in front of her to push the hair back from her face and assess the situation, but she immediately pushed his hand away.

"I'm just . . . ," he began.

"I'm okay," she said.

Beck handed her the glass and she took it gingerly, her eyes unfocused, her breathing deliberately slow and deep. After a few more moments, she took a sip and closed her eyes as she swallowed. She let go of the table to blot at the patches of sweat on her face with her fingers. "That's attractive, isn't it?" she said with a weary smile.

"Jade . . ." He didn't know what to do or how to ask whatever questions needed to be asked in a situation like this.

"See what happens when you get smart-alecky in conversations? Somebody always gets hurt."

He didn't know where she was finding the strength to poke fun at the situation. She looked—depleted. Worn out. Another wave seemed to hit her and she bent over again, her hand clutching the edge of the table for support.

"Do you need me to help you to the bathroom?" Beck asked, becoming truly concerned as the episode wore on. He reached for her elbow and started to help her up. "Here, let me . . ."

She motioned with her hand for him to stop. He stood beside her as she took several more deep breaths, then straightened.

"I'm calling the Fallons," Becker said when she seemed to have regained her balance. "They've got to know a doctor you could see on a Sunday."

"Don't." Her voice was firm, her eyes trained on a fixed point in front of her, as if trying to keep the world from spinning. She didn't move her eyes when she motioned toward the stove with her hand, fingers flapping. "The steak!" she said.

Beck quickly removed the pan from the fire, the very-well-done steak a little seared around the edges. "You're sitting here about to pass out and you're worried about the steak?"

"I'm a cook. It's what we do."

Beck thought he saw a trace of color returning to her cheeks. "Have more water," he instructed.

She drank a little. "I think it's passing," she said, tentatively moving her eyes away from the fixed point at which she'd been staring.

"What's passing? What was that?" Now that she was starting to look better, Beck wanted some answers. He went to the counter and tore off a paper towel, handing it to her to blot her face. "Does this happen often? 'Cause really, you need to warn me next time." He attempted a lighthearted chuckle, but it got caught somewhere between his mind and his throat. His legs were shaky and his heart was racing. He'd wanted to—help, somehow. To comfort her or warm her or touch her. But he hadn't been able to do anything but stand by and watch her suffer. He tried to counteract the powerlessness with purpose. "Okay," he said, "how 'bout we try to make it to the office. You can lie on the couch in there for a while and see if this really passes."

"I'll be fine. . . ."

"You're going to the office. Now."

He was relieved to see that Jade knew an order when she heard one. When he placed a hand under her elbow and helped her stand, she didn't resist. They made it to the office, where Beck pulled the protective sheet off the couch, moving around it with her and helping her sit. "Still okay?" he asked. She nodded. Beck handed her the glass he had carried with them from the kitchen and offered to get her a blanket.

"No, I'm fine," she answered. "It's almost passed now."

"At the risk of repeating myself . . . *what's* almost passed?"

She looked at him with the enigmatic expression that was so

typical of her and smiled a little weakly. "It's nothing to worry about. I promise you."

Beck pulled the sheet off one of the armchairs and sat across from the woman whose face had, moments before, been frighteningly white. Though some color had returned to her cheekbones and the tip of her nose, she still looked far from healthy. "So I'm not calling the Fallons?"

She shook her head. "It's nothing to panic over, I assure you."

He attempted some levity, if only for his own good. "Maybe somebody spiked the holy water at church."

She gave him a look that warned him not to joke about her religion. "For your information," she said, her voice gaining back some of its strength, "we don't have holy water at my church."

He was curious. "A confessional?"

"No."

"A priest?"

"No."

"How 'bout those incense things. You got some of those? Or a crucifix?"

Another smile, this one nearly amused. "No and no."

He smiled back. "So what's left?"

Jade took another deep breath and shifted, sipping from the glass of water, her eyes evaluating him. "I'm not sure what you really want me to say, Beck. I mean, I can give you a fairly thorough overview of what I believe and how it is lived out in my church and beyond, but . . ." She hesitated, sipping again. "Something tells me that you're just looking for one more topic to turn into a joke."

Beck considered this for a moment, admitting to himself that probably would have been the direction the conversation took. He realized there were few topics of any substance that he could approach without ridiculing them.

"Am I right?" Jade asked.

It was Beck's turn to take a deep breath. He saw the sincerity on Jade's face and gave himself the challenge of hearing her out without turning her words into weapons. "Fine," he said. "I promise to be good." He thought of his own checkered past where church and religion were concerned and added, "I'd actually be very interested in your point of view."

Jade put her glass down on the coffee table and rubbed both hands over her face. "Here's what I know," she said, leaning her head back against the couch. "My parents used to read me Jesus stories when I was little. Then I went to Sunday school and heard more Jesus stories. And when my mom died when I was fifteen, I heard more Jesus stories about how she was with him and he was comforting me and . . . and then I decided I didn't want to hear any Jesus stories anymore. Ever." Another deep breath. Another sip of water. "So I went a few years being angry at God—literally cursing him and accusing him of all the horrors in the world— and all that time . . . all I wanted, all I craved, was for someone to tell me another Jesus story." The eyes that had been so dull until moments before now filled with tears and certainty. "They aren't just stories, Beck. I know that now. They're promises. And without those promises and the God who made them . . ." She shook her head.

Beck swallowed hard. There were no jokes needing to be stifled. Only a yawning void at his core. He nodded, incapable of doing much more.

"And at your church?" Jade said, pulling her legs up onto the couch next to her. "Were there priests and incense balls and crucifixes?"

"The ugliest crucifix you've ever laid eyes on!" He managed a chuckle.

"I loved the Catholic church," Jade said. "Still love a lot of aspects of it—the reverence, the mysticism. . . . But those Jesus stories told me that he's right here, as real to me as you are. And I didn't want a secondhand connection to him."

Beck had a few questions he wanted to ask, but he didn't voice them. He had avoided this topic for two years now—when he hadn't been using it to vent his frustration on the pious and self-righteous. He'd allowed Jade to speak for reasons he couldn't understand, but it wouldn't go any further. The God thing was dead to him. Life made more sense that way.

Jade gingerly sat forward on the couch. "I think I'm okay," she said, moving to stand up.

Beck was on his feet in an instant, reaching for her arm. They stood there together while Jade seemed to gauge her stability. "I'm fine," she finally said, this time with more conviction.

Beck stopped fighting his frustration. "Okay, so now that it's behind us, will you tell me what that was?"

Jade walked toward the door, Beck close on her heels. "First, I'm going to walk you through the rest of the meal preparation. It's almost finished anyway, and you might as well learn a few tricks while I sit on a stool and bark orders at you. The broccoli's going to be overcooked, by the way. Second, you're going to take a plateful of food over to Jojo's and leave it by his door."

"Wait, I'm not—"

"Oh, hush. I've been taking food over every day since that lasagna and I'm still here to tell the tale. And third, I'm going to go home, put my feet up, and not move again until tomorrow morning."

"Sounds like a plan," Beck said. "But it doesn't answer my question."

Jade sighed loudly, turning exasperated and revived eyes on Becker. "Will you shut up about it if I tell you it's female problems?"

He wasn't convinced—but by that point, he'd used up all the courage required for follow-up questions.

It was the children's screams that alerted Becker that something was not right. He was up on a ladder helping install the renovated molding in one of the dining rooms when Eva and Philippe's frantic voices reached him. They were calling Jade with such urgency that he jumped off the ladder and rushed to the French doors that led from the dining room to the front of the castle. The first thing his eyes registered was Eva holding on to two bars of the closed gates, her face pressed into the space between them, immobile. Philippe stood a little closer to the castle, his attention torn between the frantic pleas for help he was yelling toward the château and the tense scene beyond the castle gates.

A terrified stallion stood in the center of the large four-lane boulevard just beyond the castle, probably escaped from the racetrack on the other side. He had a racing saddle still strapped to his back, but his jockey was on foot nearby, flanked by other men, arms outstretched, who were trying to corral him away from the traffic. Amazingly, though many of the cars had pulled off to the side, others still sped past the hysterical animal, too eager to get where they were going to wait until the drama was resolved. As the men stepped closer, nearly encircling the black, wild-eyed stallion, he bucked and whinnied and burst through their ranks, narrowly avoiding a collision with an oncoming car and coming to a stop in the middle of the short, broad passage that led from the castle's front gates to the boulevard beyond. His flanks quivered with panic and his nostrils flared.

The men who had been trying to surround him were so busy shouting strategies at each other that they didn't initially notice the hunched form that emerged from the gatehouse and moved toward the horse. The children, who had been pressing their faces between the bars, didn't see him either until he had grasped one side of the ten-foot gate and pulled it open. They fell back a few steps and stared, gape-mouthed, at the apparition.

By this point, Beck had run across the circular lawn and, with a "Stay here!" barked at the children, was about to follow Jojo into the street. The older man's eyes were focused on the horse with an intensity that made the jockey and men stop their bickering and watch. Beck was just passing through the gates when Jojo, without a backward glance, held out his hand in an unmistakable order for the younger man to stay where he was.

The horse, the kind of spirited thoroughbred that Lamorlaye and neighboring Chantilly were famous for, made a couple lurching bounds away from Jojo as he approached. Jojo stopped, his lips forming inaudible sounds, his hand outstretched, palm down, toward the fierce animal whose coat shone with sweat. When the horse snorted and stamped a hind leg, Jojo moved forward again, one soft step at a time, his gaze so powerful that Beck wondered if its trajectory could be seen if he concentrated hard enough.

In the boulevard, cars had resumed their noisy travels, oblivious to the drama being played out just feet away. The men who had previously failed to contain the thoroughbred now stood several paces behind Jojo, some of them eager to step forward again but a couple of the others ordering them to stay put. The old man in his worn wool coat was now just four or five feet away from the racehorse. He stopped again, lowering his hand this time, his lips still moving, his eyes still connected as if by a tangible thread to the horse's gaze.

At the castle gates, Beck stood with a twin on either side of him. Eva had pressed up against his leg and grabbed one of his hands, but he'd been so focused on the rescue taking place and Jojo's nearly hypnotic powers that he'd done little more than acknowledge her hand with a slight squeeze of his own. On his other side, Philippe had climbed onto the lowest crossbar of the gate, his face still pressed between two wrought-iron bars, his eyes wide and fearful. He looked over at Beck every so often, as if he needed to remind himself that there was a strong man nearby, then swiveled his head again to watch the unfolding drama.

Jade hurried out of the castle and ran to the gate. Like Beck and the children, her attention was quickly riveted on Jojo.

"Is Jojo going to save the horse?" Eva asked, awestruck, at Beck's side.

Jade smoothed a hand over her hair. "I don't know, Eva. But I think he's going to try." Beck felt her small hand clutch his more tightly, and something softened in his chest.

Immobile but for the motion of his lips, both hands hanging loosely at his sides, Jojo stood four feet from the still-quivering horse. The stallion's nostrils flared again and he looked about to take another startled leap away, but something stilled the impulse.

After what seemed interminable moments and without any visible impetus from Jojo, the stallion shook his mane and seemed to stand down. He took a couple of tentative steps toward Jojo, his gaze as unwavering as the old man's, then closed the distance and nuzzled the recluse's chest with his nose. Jojo lifted a hand to rub the stallion's neck and reached for his bridle with the other. He turned to the jockey and his companions and walked the now-docile racehorse across the space that separated them, handing the reins over to the stunned professionals. Then he turned on his heels and headed back toward the gatehouse, passing through the castle's gates with a wink aimed at Eva and Philippe and a nod toward Beck. He cast a sideways glance at Jade and nearly smiled. Then he was gone, hunched over and worn, his shuffling steps inaudible on the lawn's thick grass.

14

THE RACEHORSE INCIDENT had elevated Jojo to the rank of demigod in the children's eyes. They now spent much of their outside time in the front of the castle rather than in the park at the back, whiling away the hours climbing trees and going on treasure hunts, always with an eye trained on the gatehouse in case Jojo might make another miraculous rescue.

After lunch every day, Philippe and Eva walked with Jade to Jojo's dilapidated home, eyeing its broken glass, sagging shutters, and rotting wooden door with a sort of rapt repulsion. The path leading to the door was overgrown with young oak shoots, brambles, and weeds. Smoke occasionally drifted up from the chimney that seemed to teeter precariously on the decomposing roof lacking many of its shingles. A little unnerved by the structure and the mythical creature inside, the children usually stood back a few paces while Jade left a plate of food on the stoop, then spent the return trip to the kitchen looking over their shoulders just in case Jojo might be following them home.

A day without a Jojo sighting was a wasted day to the twins, yet as much as they anticipated his next appearance, it came only occasionally. The sole advantage of their obsession was that it kept them from hanging around the work site as they'd been tempted to do before, which left Becker to focus uninterrupted on his work.

With the carved elements of the staircase nearly finished and only the railing and assembly still pending, Beck was able to spend more time lending a hand with the rest of the work going on in the castle and making sure each aspect of the renovation was as meticulously executed as if he were doing it himself. He had started to eat his lunch in the kitchen occasionally, mostly on the days when his repeated attempts at weaning himself from the bottle played havoc with his mind and made concentration impossible. His longest dry spell to date had been three days—three full days of more or less visible tremors, raging headaches, and frustrated, sleepless nights. Those nights were the driving motivation behind his experiments in sobriety. If he wasn't sleeping, he wasn't dreaming, and a night without dreams was a rare and welcome luxury. The discomfort was a small price to pay.

On those nights when his body was so strung out that being still became a physical ache, he spent the hours carving in his office or running sprints in the long hallway upstairs. Morning always came with glaring clarity, the victories of the night tempered by fatigue that made insurmountable obstacles of minor setbacks.

It was on one of those days that Philippe came bursting into his office, emboldened by excitement over his latest discovery. "I found a saber," he yelled, rushing to Beck. "I found it in the guard tower!"

Eva came in close on her brother's heels, obviously trying to match his enthusiasm over his find. "It's really, really old!" she exclaimed.

Beck, who had been using a router to carve an artistic flourish into a fragile piece of cherrywood, was so taken aback by their entrance that he jumped at the saw, causing the cut to go off course. He felt anger rising in him like bile and fought it down. This was about his nerves and cravings, not about Philippe's intrusion, and he knew it—still, the gash in the cherrywood was an unforgiving flaw.

"Philippe," he said, trying to maintain a friendly tone with the beaming boy who held his treasure out on the palms of both hands, "I'm busy right now." He hoped the statement would indicate to the boy that his timing was bad and send him running to Jade for the praise he obviously wanted.

"But look—I found a saber!" Philippe repeated, stepping close enough to Beck that he could hold the rusted object up to his face.

Eva stepped forward too. "Philippe said you could tell us if it was a treasure." She was so enraptured with their discovery that she fairly shrieked the words.

Beck could tell at first glance that this was not a historical artifact. It looked like an old farmer's knife, its wooden handle mostly rotted away and the blade rough with corrosion.

"Do you think it goes with the helmet?" Philippe asked.

"It's just a normal knife," Beck said, eager to get the consultation over with and evaluate how much damage had been done by the slip of the saw.

"But it's old, right?" This from Eva, the light beginning to dim in her eyes.

"Sure, it's old. Look at it—it's been in the ground for a while. But it's just a knife."

"It's a saber," Philippe said, his jaw beginning to jut out in defiance.

"Philippe . . ." Becker didn't have the time for the boy's stubbornness.

"It's a saber." Eva parroted her brother, crossing her arms and daring Beck to contradict her.

Philippe wasn't finished yet. "You don't know what you're talking about! It's a saber! It's a saber!" He leaned in, looking straight up at Beck, the rusted knife clenched in his hands.

"Yeah!" Eva seconded, in frail support of her brother's belligerence.

Becker's thin control over his temper snapped. "Out!" he said in a clipped, no-nonsense voice, pointing at the door. "Both of you—out. Now!"

Philippe was so angry that it took him a couple seconds to draw in a breath and find something strong enough to blurt at the man who had so heartlessly dismissed his discovery. "You're . . ." He sputtered. "You're *mean*!" he said with all the sincerity of a hurt six-year-old.

Eva, still not to be undone, yelled, "Yeah!" but there was a quiver to her chin that made Beck wonder if he'd been too blunt.

He took a calming breath. "Look," he said, trying for a kinder voice and holding his hands up in apology. "I'm sorry that your knife isn't a saber, but . . ."

The damage had been done. To the children's minds, a grown-up had insulted and hurt them. "I think you're stupid," Philippe said, squinting with rage, "and I'm never going to talk to you ever again!" With that, he spun around and sprinted out of the office, leaving Eva standing there fighting tears and unsure what to do.

Beck sat down and let out an exasperated breath. He'd been called a lot of insulting things before, but none had pierced his armor like that well-aimed *stupid* from a six-year-old. He contemplated the fight for composure being waged on Eva's face and wondered what a normal person would do. Go to her? Probably. Hug her? Maybe. Somehow find a way to comfort her? Absolutely. The best he could muster at that moment was a gentle dismissal. "It's okay, Eva," he said. "You can go find your brother."

And with a bit of a hiccup, she did just that.

Becker was calculating the amount of damage done to the carving when Jade pushed the door open with more force than she'd used before and came to stand a couple of feet away from him, arms crossed and eyes ablaze. Beck was again taken aback by the pallor of her skin and the circles under her eyes, but repeated inquiries had yielded only instructions to mind his own business. On this particular day, he had a feeling Jade was about to mind it for him.

"You feel better now?" she asked.

"Not particularly, no."

"Well, good, 'cause I've got two kids in the kitchen that I've just sent to the time-out chair, but I'm thinking I've punished the wrong culprit!" She was as angry as he'd ever seen her.

"Why did you send them to the . . . ?"

"Because they disobeyed me," Jade exclaimed, throwing her hands up. "They know not to disturb you in your office, and they did disturb you in your office, so now they're sitting in the kitchen wondering why *you* were the mean guy and *they* got the punishment. You explain that to me, Mr. Becker!"

"Are you finished?" he asked, an eyebrow arched as anger once again mounted inside him. "'Cause I'm not one of your kids, Jade, and I'm not sure I enjoy being chastised by their nanny."

"They found a saber," she exclaimed, as if the statement held all the explanation he needed.

Beck snorted. "They found a knife," he said under his breath.

"Whatever!" Jade wasn't in the mood for his sarcasm. "To them, it was a saber, and they brought it to *you* because they think you're pretty cool. 'Beck's so great.' 'Beck's our friend.' 'Beck's funny.' 'Beck's brave,'" she mimicked, a bit of a sneer on her face. "And when they come to you to show you their big discovery, you tell them to get out? Well done there, Mr. Becker. Very impressive. I'm sure your precious work hours aren't going to be disturbed again."

She turned to storm out of the office but stumbled a little, catching herself on the back of the couch. Beck was off his chair and by her side in an instant. "You okay?"

She shook off the hand on her arm and leaned on the back of the couch for a few moments, taking slow breaths. "I'm fine," she said, her voice hoarse. After a few more breaths, she turned to look into Beck's face, one hand still on the couch, and asked, "Why do you do it?"

"Why do I . . . ?"

"Why do you limit every single one of your responses to cynicism and anger?" She took another deep breath while she waited for him to answer. "I'll tell you why," she said when he turned slightly away, staring at the floor. "It's the same reason you're chained to your bottles—and don't go thinking I haven't seen them when I've taken your laundry to your room—because you're scared." She walked to the door, still a little unsteady. "Well, let me introduce you to a world bound by fear, Beck," she said, turning. "It's a very lonely place." And she closed the door with a decisive click, leaving Beck standing in an empty room, utterly alone.

He needed to get away. That was the bottom line. He needed to catch a cab to the train station, take the RER into Paris, and let his mind focus on something other than the job and Jade's warning. Things were moving along smoothly enough with the renovation that a day in the city wouldn't even be noticed.

He called a cab before Jade and the kids arrived the next day and was on his way to Paris by seven. The RER car was loaded with passengers on their way to work, either holding copies of *Le Monde* like shields in front of their faces or staring at the tiny screens of their PDAs. By the time the train arrived at the Gare du Nord, a tentative sun cast vague shadows on the bustling streets of the city where car horns and yelled threats seemed to be acceptable forms of navigation.

Beck had no plans for his day. His RER ticket gave him full use of the Métro, but he opted to wander on foot for a while rather than ride the subway, absorbing the energy and culture of the City of Lights. He had a rough idea of where the Latin Quarter was and set off in that direction, making sure his wallet was out of reach of the pickpockets who swarmed the streets, particularly in the city's most touristy places. It didn't take long for Beck to realize that his best friends on that day would be the sidewalk salesmen, all immigrants from Africa, who started lowering their prices before he even began to bargain with them. They seemed to possess the inimitable talent of being able to close up shop and blend into the crowd at the first sight of police, even if they were in the middle of a transaction at the time. Beck merely ignored them as they spoke to him, somehow guessing that he was American and lapsing into a truly comical version of the language. "Yoo want Aifool Tawah? I geev yoo Aifool Tawah! Twantee ooros. Feefteen? Feefteen ooros."

As he walked, Beck passed bar after bar, loud music and heavy smoke billowing out the doors as patrons entered and exited. There were sports bars and racing bars and Irish pubs and gay bars and dating bars. He'd never seen such a plethora of drinking establishments in the States, all crammed tightly into expensive pieces of real estate. It was easy for him to pass the first one without stopping. Jade's comment about being chained to the bottle had cut a little too deep, particularly as it had come on his third day of abstention. Much as he wanted to prove to himself that he was not as chained as Jade had suggested, he knew that third day always came, and with it the inevitable capitulation to the comforts of the buzz. He hated to admit it, but the best part about sobriety was the moment he decided to break it.

Beck wandered through the Latin Quarter with its assortment of small boutiques and exorbitant prices. He stopped at a café for the strongest espresso he'd ever tasted and bought a croissant from an expensive *boulangerie*. *"When in Paris,"* right? And then he turned a corner onto the rue de l'Esplanade and stopped dead in his tracks, staring awestruck at a rear view of Notre Dame Cathedral. It would have been impossible for a man in his line of work to remain unmoved by the fragile balance of power and grace in the cathedral's flying buttresses and spires. It was, in real life, much grander than the pictures and documentaries he'd seen could have conveyed. The sheer magnitude of its presence on the edge of the Seine took his breath away. The stained-glass windows glinted in the pale noonday sun as the bells incredibly high up in its towers rang the hour. For a brief moment, nothing else mattered but the vision of architectural splendor before him. He shook his head in awe and crossed the street.

He walked by a row of small booths as he made his way to the front of the church, each one of them displaying a random assortment of books, antique postcards, porcelain figurines, and works of art. Much as he wanted to stop and browse, the cathedral drew him on toward its gargoyle-shielded entrance and the vast beauty inside. Beck entered, glancing at the signs that forbade photography and eating on the premises, and moved to the back of the neatly aligned chairs and benches that covered much of the cathedral's floor. There was little light in Notre Dame other than the glow of candles and the sun's weak rays slanting through the stained-glass windows that flanked both sides of the space. There was a reverent stillness—as if the tourists who milled in its aisles had been stunned into silence.

Beck followed the perimeter of the church, past crypts and monuments to the dead, under inestimable statues, and around limestone columns. He stopped occasionally merely to absorb the atmosphere of serenity and security, emotions that were so unfamiliar to him that they made him mildly uncomfortable. He passed an empty confessional and tried to resist the ridiculous urge to step inside for a few moments, just to sit and still his mind. It was with a self-deprecating sigh that he finally gave in and pushed the privacy curtain aside. A nun hurried up to him. *"Non, non, non, monsieur,"* she whispered. "No priest, no priest." Becker nodded and waited for her to walk away before taking a seat in the confessional and pulling the curtain closed. He leaned his head back against the carved wooden wall and closed his eyes, the exhaustion of the past few weeks catching up with him. The small space smelled of wood polish, and the curtain muted what few sounds reached him from the cathedral floor.

He sat there for long minutes, his mind drifting in and out of a deep rest, his spirit somehow soothed by the darkness and the intimate aura of grace that permeated the church. He thought briefly of addressing the God who was rumored to like that kind of thing, but it had been so long since his last prayer, so brutally long, that he knew it would border on blasphemy. If he didn't have the words to address children like Philippe and Eva, how was he supposed to find his way around talking to the Big Guy?

Beck heard someone enter the other side of the confessional and pull open the partition. He could see only a vague shadow beyond the screen. The presence on the other side waited for Beck to speak, while all that flashed through his mind was the pressure to say something. He knew the words. "Forgive me, Father, for I have sinned." Weak words. Pathetic words. Rebellion descended on him with anger. Who was this priest? What good could *he* do for the demons that plagued Becker?

"How can I help you, my son?" came a soft voice from beyond the dividing screen.

The serenity that had blanketed Beck moments before erupted into full-blown rage. Not trusting himself to speak, he tore through the curtain and stalked out of Notre Dame on stiff, wooden legs, ashamed at the peace he'd allowed to soften him.

Becker must have veered off the beaten track as he made his way back to the Gare du Nord that evening, several beers warm in his gut and his mind filled with the architectural wonders of the ancient city. It was nearly 11 p.m. when he found himself staring at a long cobblestone street lined on both sides with Paris's women of the night, hookers who stood in doorways wearing little more than fishnet stockings and shreds of cloth as the night's temperatures descended toward freezing. The prostitutes called him and pouted at him and posed for him as he walked by. He saw a couple johns, both of them engaged in bargaining for the favors they desired, their language faintly slurred, their stance a little less than steady. Beck took a better look at the second john as he passed him. He seemed to be about forty. His cologne smelled expensive. He was clean-shaven and dressed for a respectable job. The man glanced at Beck and shouted, "What're you lookin' at?" Beck changed sidewalks and walked more briskly, eager to reach the streetlamp at the end of the block. A hooker called out to him, offered him a discount, told him she liked his shoes. By the time he reached the brighter light of the intersection, he felt dirty, guilty by association, and scared out of his mind.

Beck spent the next three days in frenzied labor. He stopped only for a few hours of exhausted sleep in the middle of the night, then got up again and resumed his work. The banister, carvings, and steps were nearly finished. He'd checked and triple-checked them against the remaining elements of the original staircase and was fairly sure they would fit seamlessly. All that remained to be done was the staining and polishing that would give the new segments the same antique look as the rest of the woodwork. When he wasn't in his office, Beck was lending a hand in every aspect of the labor being done around the château, climbing scaffolding, sanding floors, mixing wallpaper paste . . . whatever would keep him busy. And still the battle in his mind raged on.

The dining rooms were nearly finished too, with two and a half weeks to spare before Sylvia's big party. The next item of business was to sand down the herringbone parquet and treat it again. The purpose here wasn't to restore the wood to looking like new—Thérèse had decided that leaving it with some small signs of age and wear would only increase its visual appeal—but the new boards they had installed to replace the damaged ones needed to be blended in with the original wood, and the larger stains, some of them centuries old, needed to be sanded out.

Thérèse wasn't in much better shape than Beck, though he couldn't understand what had her so sullen. This should have been her favorite part of the project, the part when the heavy construction and renovation were finished and the interior decoration could begin in earnest, but she stalked around the castle giving one-word answers, shrilling orders, and making her displeasure known when things didn't look the way she wanted them to.

There had been little communication between Beck and Jade since the saber incident. She had dutifully provided meals for him and been polite as she'd delivered them, but there hadn't been any banter lately, no attempts to destabilize him by calling his bluffs as she had so many times before. She'd gotten another haircut—Beck had noticed that much—a short bob that framed her face. He suspected she'd had it dyed too—not that it was any of his business. It was just that with so little talking going on, all he had to occupy himself was observation.

The children, too, had been less than cordial, but he figured they weren't much different than a beaten dog steering clear of people with sticks. They'd been hurt once by the big man they considered a hero, and they wouldn't soon put themselves in a position for it to happen again. Beck realized the burned bridges that surrounded him—every single one of them—had been damaged by his own actions.

There was something else that had been plaguing him since his day in Paris. Something dark and sordid that had shaken his already-fragile equilibrium. He kept picturing the john bargaining with the prostitute on that ill-lit street in the city. The designer clothes. The appearance of confidence and charm. He'd seen a man who probably had all the earmarks of success yet had been reduced to paying hookers for company. The thought repulsed him, but no more than the easy parallel he could draw between that man and himself. The bottle was his gratuitous release, and he knew that when it failed to distract him and warm him, the Internet would become his fallback plan. Oh, he'd never spent hours on adult sites as some of his coworkers had, nor engaged in the salacious business of online depravity, but he'd taken a few glimpses of the alternate universe that provided escape for other wounded souls. Those brief brushes had left him feeling defiled. And yet—he knew it wouldn't take much for him to join the ranks of those whose lives were captive to the perversion of their imaginations. One major failure. One jarring disappointment. One more crisis that couldn't be medicated with overtime and rigid expectations. One day too many spent in self-imposed isolation.

Becker didn't realize how deep-seated his fear was until he saw Jade alone in the kitchen one evening and submitted to the need to connect with her. He opened the door gingerly and gave her an "is it safe?" look. She turned from the grocery bags she was unpacking just long enough to acknowledge his presence, then got back to work. Becker stepped into the kitchen and closed the door behind him, determined to bridge the chasm that had caused their silence.

"What can I do to make things right with the kids?" he asked.

Jade's hand stilled, then resumed its activity. "Why do you ask?"

"Because I know I . . ." He searched for the words. They weren't a natural part of his vocabulary. "Because I think I hurt them."

Jade turned and raised an eyebrow at him. "One small step for man . . . ," she quoted.

"Is there—" A sudden thought halted his question. He glanced at the clock above the door. "Wait, what are you doing here? It's after your normal hours, isn't it?"

Jade carried a bag of lettuce and a wedge of Brie to the refrigerator, showing traces of the tiredness he'd come to recognize. "I won't be here until late tomorrow morning. I have an appointment and Mrs. Fallon is keeping the kids. I figured I should do the grocery shopping tonight." She turned around with a saucy look on her face. "Is that a problem?"

Beck smirked in spite of himself. Jade was of that rare breed of people who somehow managed to be endearing even on their ornery days. He raised his hands in surrender. "Hey, no problem at all. You haven't missed a day since I've been here, so . . ." He ran out of things to say. And yet there was still so much that remained unspoken and urgent in his mind.

"You could begin by apologizing to them," Jade said. "That goes a long way with kids."

"Okay."

"And none of that condescending 'Hey, sorry, kid,' approach either. They know when they're being manipulated."

Beck gave it some thought and concluded that she was probably right. Still—a heartfelt apology? To a six-year-old? This might take some scripting. He drew himself up short at that thought. Who needed a script to acknowledge a failure?

"And the work is progressing well?" Jade asked, trying to make a smooth transition away from more delicate matters and somehow managing to make it feel awkward instead.

"It's . . ." Becker didn't have the courage to attempt trivial conversation. There was too much else that needed words put to it to waste them on status updates and the weather.

"I want you to know that I get it," he said, using up a good portion of whatever courage he still possessed. He leaned back against the fridge. "I get the alone thing."

Jade moved to the table and sat on one of the stools, head propped on fists, listening with the kind of sincere concentration that made him feel . . . heard.

"And you're right," he continued. "Do you know how much I hate saying that?" He smirked. "You're right. I've got two moods: cynical and angry."

Jade finally smiled. "And don't forget stupid. Philippe would vote for stupid."

"And stupid."

Jade turned her palms toward the ceiling and shook her head in confusion. "Why? How did you end up with only those two?"

"I don't know." From the way Jade looked at him, he could tell she knew he was lying. "But the payoff. The payoff isn't exactly what I hoped it would be."

"You thought this would be beneficial in some way?" Jade asked, amazed.

Beck pressed his lips together. "I saw a guy in Paris the other day."

"I presume you saw more than one."

He held up a hand. "Will you let me? Please."

Jade wiped a film of perspiration from her upper lip and motioned for him to continue.

"This guy was . . . hiring a prostitute." He saw Jade raise an eyebrow, but there was no judgment in her gaze. "And it occurred to me . . ." This was the type of conversation he'd seldom had before, and he couldn't seem to find the right words or to phrase things that made sense.

"You're doing fine," Jade said, a small smile playing around her lips.

"And it occurred to me," Beck said again, "that if I don't do something drastic, I'm going to become him. I mean—not that I'd go out and hire a prostitute," he quickly amended, "but . . . I could become the guy who's so desperate for friendship that he has to buy it." He paused. "I don't know how to say this except that—I know I need to have . . . people. In my life."

Jade stood and took a few steps toward him, stopping just in front of where he leaned against the fridge. "I think you're right," she said. Her eyes softened as she added, "And I think it's good that you've gotten to this point—to the point of seeing your need." Beck was about to respond, but she held up her hand to halt him. "But I'm not going to be your new best friend, Becker."

He was stunned. And suddenly defensive. "That's not what I was—"

"No, but I'm guessing it might have been your next conclusion. I know you're lonely and I know you're trying, but . . ."

"What?" Beck asked, frustration tightening his voice.

"I'm tired. And you . . ." She looked him straight in the eye, defying him to contradict her. "You are a drunk. A functional drunk, but a drunk. And you're a coward who hides behind his anger to skim the surface of real life in the real world." He opened his mouth to protest, but she shook her head and laid a gentle hand on his arm. "You want to hang out in the kitchen and shoot the breeze? I'm your girl. But I've got enough problems right now, and I can't shoulder yours too. I can't step into your stuff and help you carry it. Figure it out, Becker," she said, using his name in a way that made his lungs constrict. "Do what you need to do to gain a foothold, and then do something about whatever it is that killed your spirit and left your body alive. And when you've figured it out—" she squeezed his forearm to make sure he knew she meant it—"I want to be your friend. But I'm not going to be your counselor, I'm not going to be your scapegoat, and I'm not going to be your priest." She saw the anger hardening Becker's gaze and said, "What? What are you angry about?"

Beck tried to control his voice, but the effort made it shake. "I come in here holding out an olive branch, and you tell me to get lost?" His breathing was faster with the effort of maintaining his cool. "You—"

The word he used seemed to hit Jade like a physical blow. She pulled back from him, immobile for a while, then went to the counter, stowing the grocery bags in their proper place and reaching for the light switch. "If I became your best friend right now— your Band-Aid—I'd only be taking the place of your bottle. And, Becker," she added, expelling a sad breath, "I have more important things to do with my time."

She flipped the switch.

15

MARIE AND ELISE sat in the paneled library on a June afternoon. They had been sitting in silence for a while, Marie lost in the pages of a Victor Hugo novel and Elise fiercely focused on the knitting stitches some of the other women had taught her. Once she perfected them, she'd begin on a pair of booties, using the green yarn that had just been delivered that week.

The two girls had finally become accustomed to their afternoon sessions in the library. When Elise had been admitted to the manor as a resident, the sudden switch of roles had thrown them both for a loop. Marie had remained an employee, while Elise had suddenly found her rank elevated from maid to loyalist. The baby that rounded her belly was a child of the Führer, and it had been her ticket into the opulent and leisurely lifestyle of the Lebensborn's elite. After a couple weeks of utter boredom, Elise had finally requested *that Marie be relieved of some of her duties in order to spend time with her. Koch had refused at first, but when Elise's loneliness and the hormones coursing through her body had combined into several difficult emotional outbursts, he had relented. It was better to have a part-time domestic and a content expectant mother than to put up with the kind of drama that had disrupted the manor's serenity on those occasions.*

Elise glowed with pride and the faint flush of motherhood. The first time Marie had seen it, she'd correctly guessed that her friend had acted on her intentions, choosing to bear a Nazi child for the recognition and honor the Reich had promised. But while most of the unwed mothers who came to the manor to give birth had conceived their child with members of the SS, as per Himmler's orders, the child Elise carried had been conceived with a German soldier of inferior rank. Because of this, there had initially been a bit of a scuffle about her admission to the program. The Lamorlaye Lebensborn preferred to limit its activities to the children of high-ranking officers. Mere soldiers in the Wehrmacht's cavalry were only tolerated on-site if they were running brief errands, then swiftly departing, so hosting one of their mistresses posed a dilemma, particularly when the soldier in question submitted an official request to be allowed to spend extended time with Elise as her pregnancy progressed. A compromise had eventually been reached—Elise and her unborn child would become pampered residents of the manor, but her boyfriend, the soldier, would have to limit his presence to one short visit per week.

Of course, the process of being admitted to the Lebensborn hadn't been an easy one. Frau Heinz first had to ensure Elise's worthiness. She measured her face, eyes, and nose to make sure the young mother met Aryan standards. She compared strands of her blonde hair to charts that displayed acceptable shades. She also put the girl through a battery of tests to determine whether she would be able to carry the baby to term, since her youth increased the risks of her pregnancy.

The worst of the vetting process had been the requirement that she provide proof that there was no Jewish ancestry on either side of her family for three generations back. It was that stipulation that had orphaned Elise in the eyes of her family. In a single conversation, she'd had to inform her parents of her clandestine relationship with one of the Führer's men, divulge her pregnancy, and request that they produce paperwork that would prove her flawless lineage. When she told Marie about it the next day, it was with copious tears.

"What did you expect?" Marie asked, patting her friend's hand but shaking her head in disbelief.

"I don't know!" Elise wailed, her emotions so far out of control that she hadn't been able to reel them in for the better part of the past hour. "I guess I—" She hiccupped. "I hoped they would be happy. This is their grandchild!"

"Elise . . ."

"Don't say it! I don't want to hear it! This baby isn't just a boche's child—he's my child too. With the man I love."

"To whom you're not even engaged . . ."

"That doesn't matter! We love each other. And Himmler said that as long as we produce heirs to the Aryan race, there's no such thing as moral or immoral. It's a noble cause, Marie. It's my duty as a . . ."

Marie frowned and pulled back a little to take a better look at her friend's face. "As a what, Elise?"

"As a daughter of the Reich," she said quietly.

Marie stood and took a couple steps back from her friend. Elise looked up and attempted a tremulous smile. Marie didn't answer it. "Elise Dupuis, you are not a Nazi. You are not one of them!" Shock made her voice tremble. "You're just as French as I am! We were born in the same hospital in Chantilly, we went to the same kindergarten and primary school, we had crushes on the same boys, and we both got jobs here when the Germans invaded Lamorlaye because it was the only way to provide for our families, but we're not Nazis!"

"Speak for yourself," Elise said, her face wet with tears but defiance tilting her chin a little higher.

Marie moved back to her friend's side, desperate to say something that might change her thinking. She knelt in front of her chair and grasped Elise's hands in her own. "Elise . . . they might give us extra rations and treat us kindly when we're here, but they're—they're assassins. You've heard the rumors about Poland and Germany—the BBC says they're all true! The massive arrests, the work camps, the public shamings . . . You must have heard the reports!"

"It's all for the cause," Elise said, her eyes sparking. "It's all so the world can be rid of the vermin and restored to what it should have been!"

"You don't mean that." Marie sat back and stared into her friend's face, looking for the smallest vestige of the girl she used to know. It was there—hidden under layers of a resolution born of necessity and fear.

"I do."

"Why don't you take some time to think? Call in sick and go back to your parents' house for a while. They'll help you to see . . ."

Elise stood so quickly that she toppled her chair. "They don't want me back!" she yelled at her friend, her face contorted with grief, fresh tears on her cheeks. "They called me a prostitute and told me never to show my face again. Never!"

Marie was speechless. The Dupuis family had always been loving, welded together by adversity. She couldn't imagine the power of emotion it must have required for them to disown their daughter. "Oh, Elise," Marie said, going to her friend and embracing her. "Maybe they'll come around. Maybe—if you just give them time . . ."

Elise shook her head. "I had to sleep at my aunt's last night. They *sent all my stuff over to her house." She took a tremulous breath. "And now she wants me to move out too." More tears streaked down her cheeks. "And I can't even move in here because I don't have the papers they want."*

"We'll figure it out, Elise," Marie said, holding her friend closer. "We'll find a solution."

As it turned out, it was Marie who had been able to convince her friend's parents to provide the manor with proof of their daughter's heritage. They had answered the door with suspicion on their faces, and Monsieur Dupuis had tried to shut it before Marie was inside when she'd told them the reason for her visit. It was Madame Dupuis's hand on her husband's arm that had prevented it. "Let her speak," she'd said, deadness in her voice.

Marie had spent just a few minutes in their home. She'd listened to the mother's anguish and been stunned by the father's anger. But when she'd asked for the paperwork Elise needed to be admitted to the manor, they'd relented. Their daughter was a traitor and an unwed mother, but she was still their child.

So in a matter of hours, Elise had gone from maid to resident, and she now lived as one of the Führer's prized daughters in this place of birth, this "Fount of Life" operated by the army of death. Though Marie had initially balked at the idea of being Elise's companion for fear of being associated with the rest of the manor's occupants, her friendship had dictated the risk. She still saw Elise's parents on occasion—they crossed paths in the street or saw each other during Mass on Sunday mornings—and sometimes, Madame Dupuis whispered an inquiry about her daughter. But aside from that, the family ties were severed. The longer the chasm existed, the easier it was for Elise to accept. She was steeped in a place where the higher goals of the Führer trumped familial loyalty, and Marie could see her friend's zeal increasing with every day that brought her closer to giving birth.

16

It was the moment of truth. The new steps were installed, and with the help of two carpenters, Beck was assembling the staircase, simultaneously aligning each of the interlocking parts and fitting them into place with the portion of banister he had finished just days before. He'd been meticulous in the staining and polishing that had followed completion and had sanded down a section of the existing staircase on either side of the gap, applying that same stain and finish to it. The slightly distressed, deep-colored new cherry-wood was a near-perfect match to the rest of the antique structure.

As if they'd sensed the importance of the moment, both Fallon and Thérèse had materialized to watch the installation. They stood on the marble steps leading up to the staircase, pleasure on their faces. A little farther back stood the children and Jade. There had been a slight thaw in Beck's relationship with the kids since he had appeared in the kitchen on the morning after his confrontation with

Jade and, as best he could, blurted out an apology. He'd sat down at the table opposite both kids and tried not to register the chocolate milk dripping off their chins. He'd folded his hands in front of him and let a few moments pass while he'd selected the words he would use for the first apology he'd made in recent memory.

"I was wrong to yell at you," he said, looking sincerely into the widening eyes across the table from him. "I was wrong to yell, and I was wrong to tell you to get out of my office. And I should have taken a closer look at your knife—" Somewhere behind him, Jade cleared her throat. "At your *saber*," he amended, "because you'd gone to the trouble of bringing it to me. You probably wanted me to be excited for you. Which I should have been. But I wasn't. And I'm sorry."

Though Eva blinked, there was little more coming from the twins to prove they were alive and had been listening. He turned to Jade and asked, "Did I say too much? Not enough?"

She pointed with her chin toward Eva. The little girl had gotten off her stool and walked around the table to Beck's side. Then she'd taken Beck's hand, saying as maturely as a six-year-old could, "We'll forgive you once you've spent an hour in the time-out chair." And with that, she'd pulled him to his feet, marched him to the chair that stood by the pantry, and instructed him to sit and not talk until he was released.

At the sink, Jade had watched the exchange with a combination of horror and delight. When Becker had looked to her for rescue, she'd merely thrown up her hands, shaken her head, and let Eva exact the punishment she felt the infraction had warranted. But after Beck had sat on the small chair for a few moments, she had finally suggested to the twins that they reward his "great apology" with a little lenience.

Philippe had come marching up to the chair and said, "You can get out of time-out if you say my saber was a saber!" And then he'd crossed his arms again, a position Beck had come to recognize as his "don't mess with me" stance.

Looking the little boy straight in the eyes, Beck had said, "To you, it's a saber. And that's all that really matters."

With that admission, Philippe had run to the window ledge where the "saber" now rested and climbed on a footstool to reach it.

"Careful," Jade had mumbled under her breath.

Back in front of Beck, Philippe had laid his rusted knife on the sitting man's shoulder and declared, somber and serious, "I dub you ready to get out of the time-out chair."

So as the kids stood by on the day Beck reassembled the stairs, the caution between them had vastly decreased. His interactions with Jade had gotten a little easier too, though they'd never referred to their brutal conversation again. He'd tried to mitigate the harshness of his words with deliberately cordial exchanges in the ensuing days, and Jade had responded in kind. He was still processing her comments—though not out of choice. He wanted to forget what she'd said and go on with his life, but the moment his mind was unoccupied, her words came back to haunt it. Between that and his cycle of drinking and desperately trying to quit, his head was not a pleasant place to live. He'd finally assuaged some of the chaos with a couple swallows of whiskey that morning. A little bit couldn't hurt.

While two of his men held the ornamental pieces in place, Beck and another carpenter slowly lowered the banister section into the gap. Several holes had been routed into the underside of the carved wood. The tips of the sculpted accents would fit into the holes, locking the elements into place like a giant jigsaw puzzle. It was the kind of work that required complete coordination and the smallest of adjustments. In other words, it was the worst possible task for large men who lacked experience. The presence of the usual group of onlookers, gathered to watch the pivotal moment, only exacerbated the tension. Beck ignored the audience as best he could and snapped instructions at his helpers as if he were the skipper in a boat race. "Lower. To the right. Hold it still. No—go back." It was essential that each piece be exactly aligned and vertical before the railing could be put in place.

When one of the workers lost his focus, an expletive erupted from Beck like a gunshot. "Come on, man, hold it still! Every time we get within a millimeter of getting it right—" He halted, becoming aware of the group around him. The twins stared at each other wide-eyed and Fallon's smile showed signs of strain. Thérèse looked anywhere but at Beck.

Tempering his impatience, Beck growled, "Let's try it one more time," and he removed the banister to start over again.

Jade, apparently deciding the children's vocabulary didn't need any more expansion, propelled them toward the château's doors. Just as they were about to exit, one of the craftsmen who were sanding the floors in the ballroom came hurrying out. "We have a problem," he said without preamble. "The plaster at the floor line in the ballroom is bad. It's frittering away every time we come near it with the sander. You know what that could mean. . . ."

Beck paused, still bent over his work. "How bad is it?"

"We won't know until we tear up the floorboards, but the deterioration runs the length of the room. No visible dry rot in the boards that I can see, but if the plaster's going, you know there's something major happening down there."

Beck knew the news wasn't good. He also knew it should have been discovered weeks before. "Didn't they just redo all the wainscoting in the ballroom? Tear it off the walls and restore it?"

"Sure—and it's going back up when we finish the floors. Don't know how the guys didn't catch it."

Beck managed to maintain his composure, but there was a rigidity developing in his shoulders and neck that belied his calm tone. "Who was the project leader in that room?"

"Christophe."

"The same guy who assured me last week that he'd inspected the work himself and it was all in order?"

"Same guy."

"And where is he now?"

Jacques looked unsure. He glanced at Fallon.

"Jacques!" Beck snapped.

"He's on a coffee break."

Beck, still holding the portion of the banister in place, looked over his shoulder at the craftsman. "He's taking a coffee break?" he asked, incredulous. "You're telling me that we might have to tear up parts of the floor to find God knows what under them, and while you're telling me this, Christophe is out in the truck having a coffee break?" The menace in his voice was unmistakable.

"Actually," Jacques said, "I think he might have gone home for something. . . ."

Beck tried to stem the outburst he knew was coming. He felt the fury rising but was powerless to contain it. Throwing the banister to the floor, he turned on Jacques and let loose with a dressing-down worthy of any sailor.

The craftsman was taken aback by the outburst. "Hey, man, don't shoot the messenger."

"Get on the phone!" Becker bellowed, veins beginning to stand out in his neck and forehead.

Jacques squared his shoulders and pulled himself up taller. He took a step closer, pointing at himself and yelling a defiant "Don't talk to me like I'm your lackey!"

"Excuse me?" Beck was incredulous.

"And you know what? You can call him yourself!"

Fallon stepped in. "Lads—"

Becker pointed a finger at Jacques. "Listen, man! As long as

I'm the project manager on this gig, you do what I say! Get on the phone! Now!"

The craftsman stood in defiance for just a moment longer, then stormed past Jade and the kids on his way out of the castle, slamming the door with so much force that Beck was surprised the glass didn't break. Jade laid a hand on each of the children's heads and, with a quietly spoken "Let's go through the dining room," led them away from the entrance hall.

Fallon was as serious as Becker had ever seen him. "Give us a moment, gentlemen?" he said to the workers who still stood by, halfheartedly holding the elements of the staircase. They were only too eager to go. That left Becker and Fallon facing off on the marble steps with Thérèse fidgeting nearby.

"I'll just . . . go make some calls." As no one was paying any attention to her, she meekly turned and left.

"Not exactly the most inspirational performance I've ever witnessed," Fallon said.

Beck turned on him. "Not exactly the most qualified workers I've ever dealt with either!"

"I suggest you get yourself in hand before you say anything else." The suggestion was spoken softly enough, but it held the kind of authority Fallon had seldom demonstrated before. "Now, I've been in the business longer than you have, lad, and I know there are some things we can't anticipate. It's how you deal with those—and with your men—that truly tests your mettle."

Becker looked skyward and let out a frustrated sigh, a vein still pulsing at his temple. "Yeah, sorry about that." It was a mechanical response devoid of any trace of remorse.

Fallon wasn't so easily pacified. "'Sorry about that'?" he inquired, his voice sharp with an edge Becker hadn't heard before. He pointed at the section of railing lying on the stairs. "You have a temper tantrum that might have damaged the pieces you've been slaving over for weeks, antagonizing craftsmen we still need on this job and possibly further slowing a project whose deadline is fast approaching, and your response is 'Sorry about that'?"

Becker held up a hand. "I shouldn't have lost it. . . ."

"Well, what you call 'losing it,'" Fallon said softly, "could also be construed as harassment, and that kind of thing doesn't belong in this line of work."

"Christophe should have caught the problem when he was renovating the wainscoting!"

"Jacques isn't Christophe!" Fallon said, his voice rising in frustration. "I might understand better if your anger had been directed at the person who rightfully deserves it, but you yelled at the wrong man! And," Fallon added, his impatience showing in the intensity of his expression, "you blew up in front of my children! Whatever that was, lad, you've got to get it under control!"

Coming from anyone else, the order might have been easy to dismiss, but Fallon had been nothing but good to Becker since his arrival in Lamorlaye, and the least he owed him was honesty. Becker rubbed his hands over his face and hung his head. "You're right," he said. "I know you're right."

"I think you also know that I'm not the type of chap who likes to prance around giving orders, but I'm going to break with that tradition just this once."

Beck met his gaze, trusting the man enough that he was ready to follow his orders. "Okay," he said.

"I'm not one for ultimatums, but for the sake of this project and your welfare—not to mention the children who witness your childishness—here's my final order. You treat people with respect. You check your anger at the door—run it off, sleep it off, will it off—whatever it takes. I don't want to see it or hear of it again." He paused, staring Becker in the eye, then took a step closer. "And your breath stinks of whiskey, lad," he said, equal measures of disgust and compassion in his voice. "If I smell that again, you'll be out on your ear." Fallon looked as if the diatribe had cost him dearly. He added, "You're a brilliant artisan. You're also a man approaching forty with nothing to show for your life but expertise in your field. Given the sums I'm paying you, I appreciate that trait, but what's keeping you safe isn't keeping you warm. And until you get to the root of that, you'll have nothing of value to offer anyone."

With those words, he slapped Becker's shoulder, his hand lingering a moment longer in a show of support, and then he was gone.

There had been no drinking for Beck that night. So what if he wasn't the clinical drunk who couldn't go an hour without alcohol. Big deal. Whether it was a day or a week, if it eventually sucked him back in, there was a problem. And he didn't want that problem to be his anymore. After the public humiliation of the afternoon, with Fallon's words still fresh in his mind, he'd been spurred on to give it one more shot. As fragile as he was, his desire to buck the demon off his back felt strong enough to warrant one more attempt. One last-ditch effort to become human again. He'd done it before. He'd gone four days—five—without a drink, but much as he'd tried to convince himself that those days proved he wasn't an addict, he knew that each relapse was evidence that he was. He wasn't sure if his resolve was strong enough this time to resist the lure of the bottles in his closet, but he had no other alternative than to give it another try.

Becker didn't empty his bottles down the drain. He didn't remove them from his apartment either. That would have felt too much like capitulation. How would resisting something that wasn't there prove any degree of sobriety? No, he wanted to do this the hard way. So he moved the bottles to the unused bedroom next door and shut the door on them—just to muffle their voices. And then he went up to the second-floor hallway and began running sprints, as he had on so many occasions before.

When Beck returned to his bedroom, thinking he was winded enough to sleep, he found that his mind was alert and taunting. He tried to ignore it. Then he tried to discredit it. Then he got up again, threw on some sweats, and headed outside. There was a circular path that led through the woods behind the castle. It started at the kitchen door and, after a large loop, ended at the castle's main entrance. Beck took it slowly the first time, but by his third lap, he'd reached full speed. His lungs rebelled, his head throbbed as his feet pounded the dirt path and his arms pumped furiously. He stopped counting after the eighth lap, when the exertion that had temporarily rid his mind of its ghosts sent it instead into overdrive.

As his steps thumped dully on the packed earth, images began to run like a slideshow in his mind. He saw Northwestern's football field, the flash of pom-poms, heard the boom of the game announcer's voice over the loudspeakers. He saw the segment of bleachers where Amanda always sat, blonde hair impeccably coiffed and makeup perfectly applied. He saw the smile she returned every time he looked in her direction, the knowing wink, the vicarious pride.

The slide show fast-forwarded to a frigid December night atop the John Hancock Center. There was lobster and fine wine and crème brûlée. There was the outline of platinum and diamonds in the bottom of a glass, distorted by the champagne bubbles that danced around it. There were kisses and promises and dreams.

And then, as Beck rounded the castle one more time, his muscles cramping and his vision blurred with sweat, there was a summer day in Maine. The conference center. The flowers in his hand. The fifty to the cleaning lady to have Amanda's door unlocked.

He'd walked into the room, his smile anticipating the surprise he'd planned for weeks. But it was a disheveled and somewhat-pale Amanda he'd found in the hotel bed, CNN on the TV and a bottle of Aleve on her nightstand.

"Amanda—?"

At the sound of his voice, her head snapped toward the doorway where he stood. The room was curtained, the fan on high. "Beck, I . . . Beck! What are you doing here?"

He held up the bouquet in an attempt at getting his imagined scenario back on track. "Surprise?" What had been intended as a "mission accomplished" statement came out as a question.

"I—" Amanda straightened against the pillows and reached for the remote, muting Al Gore mid–stump speech. "What are you *doing* here?" she asked again, her expression showing none of the excitement he'd expected. In its place was something that looked a lot like uneasiness.

"I got a few days off to spend with my wife," he said, attempting another smile. "Figured we could grab some time between your meetings. Maybe drive up the coast . . ." Beck glanced at the pill bottle on her nightstand again and stepped forward. "Are you sick?"

"I . . . Yes." Her eyes darted to the door behind him.

Beck half turned, but there was no one there. "Have you seen a doctor?"

"Beck." There was an edge of desperation in her voice. "You've got to go."

"What?"

"You can't be here, Beck." She looked around the room. "This is—"

"Listen," he said calmly, "we can stay put until you feel better. I've got three days."

"Beck . . ."

The door opened so fast behind him that it knocked him off balance. He put out a hand to steady himself against the closet door.

"Got your prescription, but the cashier was—" The lanky man drew up short. He looked at Beck, then at Amanda. "Who's this guy?"

Amanda's head fell back. She closed her eyes and pressed her lips into a thin line.

Getting no response from her, the man in cargo shorts and a T-shirt turned on Beck. "You got a name?"

Beck's thoughts ricocheted against his emotions. He saw the challenge in the man's eyes and the drugstore bag hanging from his hand. "I'm the husband," he said. "The better question is, who are *you*?"

He snatched the bag and held it up to the bathroom light. "Doxycycline?" His razor gaze went from the tall stranger to Amanda. "Convince me this guy is just a deliveryman from the pharmacy."

Something cold came down over her face. She raised her chin and looked him straight in the eyes. "I think it's time for you to leave, Beck."

With a cocky swagger, the stranger stepped to the door and depressed the handle. "Here," he said, "Let me get the door for you."

Beck slammed him back into the door with both fists on the man's chest and held him there for a moment, eye to eye.

"Let him go, Beck." Amanda sat up and raised her voice. "Beck! Let him go."

Beck did just that, turning and marching over to stand by the bed, sickness in his gut. "Wanna explain this?"

"He's . . ." Amanda frowned and seemed to be searching for an answer. "He's here to help me. I asked him to come."

"Help you with what?"

"Becker . . ."

"*Who—is—he?*" Beck's jaw was clenched, his nerves raw.

"I'm the guy who was here for your *wife* when you were too busy to be," came a sarcastic voice from behind him.

Beck swiveled and planted a hard finger in the middle of the man's sternum. "You. Shut it," he growled. Then he turned back on Amanda, his voice low and forbidding. "One more time. Who is he?"

"He's Jeff. He's . . . a friend."

Beck wanted to hurl the lamp across the room, but he restrained himself. "Define *friend*."

She didn't look away. She met his gaze and shrugged a shoulder in a mockery of apology.

Becker dropped his head and expelled a loud breath. His voice was gravelly when he asked, "How long?"

Amanda didn't answer.

"Those business trips," he said, conscious of the man standing just a few feet away with a smirk on his face. "Like this weekend. You were . . . ?" He looked at Amanda as a muscle twitched in his jaw.

"Becker."

"You were with him?" he asked, trying to make some sense of the scene.

"Why wouldn't she be?" This from Jeff, still standing by the door.

Becker stared at his wife. She stared right back, unflinching. It was he who looked away first, his eyes glancing off the drugstore bag he'd dropped next to the bouquet on the floor.

"You should go," Amanda said.

Jeff took a step forward. "Why don't you pick up your flowers and get out of here," he said. "A woman needs a real man around when she's taking care of business."

Beck's jaw clenched. "Business?"

Amanda sighed, but there was more exasperation than contrition in the sound. "You don't want to do this, Beck. Just go home."

"What kind of business is he talking about?" Beck could feel his incredulity giving way to a burning rage.

"Hey, the lady said go home."

"Amanda." There was a command in Beck's softly spoken word. Jeff cleared his throat. "Listen—"

Beck swiveled on him. "If you say one more word—"

"I was having an abortion, Becker." Amanda's voice was steel edged. "Jeff was here to help me get an abortion."

The words shattered what was left of Beck's composure. He hadn't ever been much for having kids, but to hear that she'd gone off and gotten pregnant with . . . He felt his stomach churn and his muscles go slack.

Jeff shrugged and smiled, something resembling self-satisfaction on his face.

Bile rose in Becker's throat. He swallowed it down and stared at Amanda's blanket-covered stomach. "You're—" He shook his head. "You were—"

The stranger leaned against the hotel room door. "Preggers, knocked up, in a family way . . ."

"You," Beck rasped, a long, drawn-out sound. "You son of a—" He surged across the space between them, slammed the other man into the door, and crashed a fist into his face, images of Jeff and his wife together incinerating his restraint.

"Becker!" he heard Amanda yell.

He brought his fist down again, then again, as Jeff raised his hands in a futile attempt at self-defense and slid down the door. Beck saw blood and felt cartilage break. It didn't matter. He kept slamming his fury into Jeff's cowardice, for the future he'd annihilated and for the baby he'd conceived with Beck's wife and then killed.

"Becker, stop! *Stop!*"

Beck looked over his shoulder at Amanda, halted by the vehemence in her voice.

Amanda held two fistfuls of blanket in a white-knuckled grip.

"It wasn't his, Becker!" she yelled, anger and disgust dueling on her face. "The baby was yours!"

Beck increased his pace again. He pushed his strength to its limit and his muscles to their breaking point. He ran as if his strides were hammer blows that shattered each of the images in his head. He ran until his labored lungs constricted one last time in a guttural, primal cry that tore from every loss and shrieked from every wound and howled from every life he had assaulted with his pain. And on his knees on the dark forest floor, he capitulated, body and mind, and let the merciful night invade his soul. His last conscious words, hurled at the sky in a maelstrom of aggression and contempt, were saturated with despair. "I—hate—you!"

In the torpor of his mind, there was a commotion at the track. Jockeys and stable hands and trainers had gathered around again, all intent on stilling the escaped steed. As Beck tried to see more clearly, their faces kept morphing into people he recognized—the prostitutes from Paris, Gary, Fallon, Trish, Philippe, Amanda, and Sylvia. They waved their arms and yelled instructions and barked orders and all began to converge on the trapped animal. In a flash of full vision, Beck realized the animal was he. He was the frantic, frenzied, and trapped one. The more the approaching friends and strangers tried to soothe him, the more he quivered and jolted with fear, until, backed into a corner between a tall hedge and the highway, he knew he might trample them all in his desperation to rush through their closing ranks.

There was only one onlooker who neither gesticulated nor

screamed. She stood by the castle gates, arms at her sides, eyes focused on him, lips moving. He couldn't hear her over the noise the others were making, and he strained to see the words forming on her mouth, but he couldn't read them from such a distance.

He tried to say, "Come closer! I can't hear you!" but his lungs couldn't hold enough breath to form sounds. He tried to send her signals with his mind—"Come closer! Please!"—but realized his thrashing might not let her near. She finally moved. Imperceptibly at first, as if she glided just off the ground. Then she hovered in his direction, mercifully blocking the others from view. She didn't smile. Her eyes were tired. Her hair seemed matted and dull. She glanced over her shoulder at the assembled jockeys and trainers clamoring to help him. Then she looked back at him with so much pity that he felt an aching void open up in his chest. She began to glide away.

"No!" he cried. "Come back!" But she was at the castle gates again, back inside the property. Out of touch. His bucking and howling increased until those who had been trying to calm him stepped back too.

Sunday peered over the horizon with timid rays that shone faintly through the fine mist over the racetrack. It was the cold that finally drew Beck out of his inertia. He looked up from the forest floor on which he lay, his body chilled and sore, and stared at the patches of brightening sky he could see through the branches. He wasn't sure how long he'd been there. He wasn't sure of what had caused his blackout. He wasn't sure of anything, really. It was that thought that gave him pause and filled his mind with dread. If he were to do this thing—if he were to battle his need for the relief of alcohol—he'd have nothing left. No certainties. No escape plans. Nothing.

Beck was shivering when he finally turned over and pushed onto his hands and knees, the muscles in his calves and thighs protesting. There was a branch in his hand—he must have grasped it while he was out. He cast it aside and saw it reflect the faint light of the morning sun. This was no ordinary branch. It appeared smooth and pale, incongruous in the dark and sullen woods. Beck stumbled to his feet and approached the discarded object, his breath catching in his throat. He lifted it into a pale ray of sunlight piercing through the trees above him, stunned by what he saw. It was small and delicate and perfectly formed. A figurine of a rearing horse, intricately hand-carved out of cherrywood, exquisite. The mane flowed gracefully out behind its head. Its nostrils flared as its hind legs braced a nearly tangible weight. Its back arched, angry and unyielding. Beck knew enough about sculpture to recognize a work of art. This one had inexplicably been placed in his hand while he was blacked out, and the fascination it caused followed him into the next day.

There were no croissants waiting for him in the kitchen when he came down after a long, warm shower and a couple hours of sleep. A little surprised, he rummaged through the fridge and found enough to eat. He was in the entry hall, sanding the seam between the old and the new railing, when Fallon came bursting through the doors with the twins hot on his heels.

"Come on, lad. Put down that sandpaper!" he bellowed in his good-natured way. "It's Sunday and we're going on a picnic!"

Beck could tell that the kids were as excited about the picnic as they were uncertain about him. Their faces were all smiles, but their eyes were guarded.

"Come again?" Beck said.

"Jade's taking a bit of a break, so your options are us—" he motioned to the twins—"or starvation." Beck eyed the threesome with suspicion. "Listen, Becker," Fallon said, taking a step closer. "It's a beautiful day. The birds are chirping. The flowers are blooming—or they will be any week now—and it would be a great injustice to leave you holed up in here working when the rest of us are out enjoying the first days of spring." He raised an eyebrow, clearly expecting Beck to drop everything and go.

Beck stared at his employer long enough to ascertain that this wasn't a joke. Then he glanced down at the children. They stood a pace behind their father, eyes on him. "A picnic?" Beck asked.

Eva had finally had enough of her standoffish routine and burst out with "We're going to the Château de la Reine Blanche!"

The White Queen's Castle, whatever it was, was clearly one of her favorite places. Beck hedged. "I have an awful lot of work to do before the deliveries tomorrow, and . . ."

"Put it down," Fallon commanded, pointing at the sandpaper still in Beck's hand. "This is an order, lad, and I'd hate to have to fire you for picnic insubordination."

Becker couldn't help but smile at that. "I'd sue you for everything you've got," he threatened, winking at the kids.

"Splendid! You can start just as soon as we get back. Now come on, lad! Hop hop! Sylvia's in the car, pregnant to the gills, and we've got to get this picnic in before she bursts."

17

Though Becker had generally had amiable relationships with his employers, he'd never been invited on a picnic by any of them. So it was with a bit of discomfort that he got into the backseat with the two children, who were still keeping a safe distance, and buckled himself into Fallon's Mercedes for the short drive to the White Queen's Castle.

Sylvia turned cumbersomely in the front seat, just far enough to smile her greeting. "It's about time we tore you away from that castle, Mr. Becker. Don't you think?"

"Don't ask him that," Fallon warned. "The boy has been tethered to that staircase for so long that I'm sure he feels incomplete without it! Consider this an intervention, Becker, my friend. We're about to prove to you that there's a whole world outside of banisters and parquet flooring!"

They arrived just a few minutes later and the children scampered out, yelling, "There it is! There it is!"

Beck got out of the car and prepared himself for his first glimpse of what he presumed would be a Versailles-esque vision of historical architecture, then stopped short. This was by far the smallest castle he'd ever seen, no larger than a middle-class house, though its four towers and sky-reaching lines were graceful and elegant.

Beck turned to his boss. "Was the White Queen poor or something?"

Fallon, who was helping his wife out of the front seat, chuckled. "Not big enough for your American tastes, is it?"

"What can I say? We like our cars long, our music loud, and our castles . . . Well, if we had any, we'd want them to be a little more castle-ish than this!"

"Actually, it was built to be a hunting lodge and the architect clearly got carried away," Fallon said, joining Becker where he stood, "but I think it's stunning—something straight out of a fairy tale—and neither Eva nor Philippe would contradict me on that."

The children had run up the stairs to the front door of the castle and were trying the handle.

Mrs. Fallon smiled up at Becker. "Next thing you know, they'll actually get in and we'll all be arrested for trespassing!" She walked off toward the twins, a little more teetery than she'd been a week before. "Philippe! Eva! Get away from the door! I'm sure there's a very good reason why they keep it locked!"

The castle's prime feature was its location. It stood at the head of four picturesque man-made reflecting ponds, each rectangle nestled in the dense forest that flanked it on two sides. On that sunny Sunday, fishermen cast their lines into the dark water, their brightly colored lawn chairs out of place in the lush natural environment.

The children ran on ahead as the Fallons and Beck made their way down the path along the side of the ponds, Fallon carrying the large basket they'd brought along and Becker the blanket and chairs. They found a spot under a lime-blossom tree and set up their camp while the kids raced each other around the nearest pond.

The conversation was a bit awkward at first, as Beck and the Fallons had never interacted outside of the other castle's confines and the topics of their conversations had until then been about work. But as the children returned to eat and they all indulged in the sandwiches and salads Sylvia had prepared, things got decidedly lighter.

It was after lunch, when Fallon and the twins were off chatting with a fisherman, that Sylvia said, "So, Mr. Becker, why is it that you're so uncomfortable around children?"

As discussion starters went, it was a bullet between the eyes. Becker choked a little on the mineral water he was drinking and contemplated her question. When he took too long to answer, she continued. "Not that it's any of my business, of course, but it's been my experience in life that a man who doesn't like children is not to be trusted. And I want to trust you, Mr. Becker. It's just that the children have been coming home with some tall tales about you that have aroused my curiosity." She waved at Eva, and the little girl returned the gesture with all the excitement a six-year-old could muster. "Would you mind if I taught you something about children?" she asked.

Becker swallowed. "I'd actually be thrilled if you did most of the talking on this topic," he answered with a kind of desperate sincerity.

"First, tell me this," she said. "Why are you so . . . standoffish with them?"

Still at a loss for words and fighting the urge to get defensive or rude—the most expedient way out of uncomfortable conversations—Becker shook his head and raised his hands. "I just don't have it in me," he said.

Sylvia laughed. "I assure you it's not a matter of having it or not.

Children are not much different from horses, you know. If they smell fear, they balk."

Beck jumped to his own rescue. "I wouldn't say I fear them," he interjected.

"So what is it? You dislike them?"

"Not . . . entirely."

"You distrust them."

"Probably part of it. One minute they're sky-high, and the next they're pouting in the time-out chair."

"So you see yourself in them. Is that what you're saying?"

Beck hung his head and managed a half smile. "They don't like me much."

"Oh, being liked is the easy part. Pay attention to what they're saying. Get down on their level and ask them questions. Get a little silly when you can, and establish firm boundaries. I'm sure you've noted that though they hate the time-out chair, they're really quite fond of the woman who puts them in it most often! The two are not exclusive."

Becker considered her words and nodded, lips pursed. "And if I do that, children will suddenly love me?"

"Maybe not. But they won't be as hesitant to come near you. Predictability also goes a long way with the twins—and with adults, too, if truth be told. Once you master that and actually communicate with them, you might find that your distrust turns to a sort of . . . reluctant fondness."

"Reluctant fondness."

"With room for improvement. But that's already a big step up from mutual suspicion!"

Sylvia leaned her head back in her chair and observed her husband and children as they watched three swans floating on the placid surface of the nearest reflecting pond. "They're really not very complicated creatures," she said. "They need to feel known, they need to feel loved, and they need to feel safe. Look at Philippe out there. He's the toughest little boy I've ever known—and I used to teach kindergarten, so I've met a few! He acts like there's no fortress he wouldn't be ready to storm and like there's nothing anybody can say that could possibly pierce his invisible armor." She looked at Beck. "Right?"

He hadn't actually spent much time analyzing the boy, nor had he been tempted to, but he figured a mother is always right when it comes to her children. "Sure," he said.

If Sylvia noticed the evasiveness of his answer, she didn't mention it. "Well, for all his bravado, that child is as fragile as his sister. Probably more so because he fears it so much. You see, Mr. Becker, when he feels backed into a corner or unsafe, he does what all men tend to do."

Beck didn't like where this was going, but he knew a shift in topics was not in the stars for him. "Okay."

"He fakes it. He puffs out his little chest and waves about with his little arms and raises his little voice and makes believe he's so tough." She smiled a little sheepishly and took a bite of Brie.

"Talking about me again?" Beck said, his eyes narrowed with suspicion, but strangely unthreatened by the obvious parallel she was drawing.

"You? No, I assure you I'm speaking of Philippe." She glanced over at her son. His father had just lifted him to hang from a tree branch, and he was dangling there doing his best to mimic Tarzan's cry. He came across sounding like a pubescent hyena instead. "I'm concerned about what he said to you—that day in your office when he brought you the knife."

"The saber," Beck corrected.

"The saber. Indeed." She leaned sideways in her chair, a move that visibly cost her much effort. "Eva told me what he said to you, Mr. Becker. And I want you to know that it was fear that made him lash out. Not genuine dislike." A lengthy silence settled between them. They kept their eyes on the twins' escapades and let it stretch. When Fallon finally herded the children back toward their picnic spot, Sylvia said, "I guess that was my attempt at apologizing for my son's behavior. And begging your indulgence—as yours sometimes isn't much better." She cocked an eyebrow. "Right?"

Beck hung his head a little. "You could probably say that. Actually, Jade would certainly say that."

"Which brings me to the second reason I brought up this topic."

Becker threw up his hands. "Great! Kick me while I'm down!"

"Jade." Sylvia said the name with so much affection that it gave him pause.

"What about her?"

"She's going to be . . . taking a couple of days off. Probably Monday and Tuesday. We'll make sure your meals are provided, of course, but . . ."

"This is about meals?"

"No, Mr. Becker," she said, her gaze soft and compassionate. "She's a dear girl. A much-loved extension of our family, really. And . . . well . . . I don't know what your thoughts are about her, but I beg you, Mr. Becker, to keep that blasted temper in check when you're with her."

Though he felt his privacy was being invaded, there was something about Sylvia that made it impossible for him to resent her. "I know I've hurt her," he said, surprising himself again with the genuineness of his answer. "And I know I need to be—kinder," he added.

"That would be a lovely start," Sylvia said. "And one more thing," she added, as the children rounded the last corner of the pond and made their way back to their mother. "We never, at any age, outgrow the rules that apply to children. We need to feel known, we need to feel loved, and we need to feel safe. That's true for Philippe. It's true for Jade. And, Mr. Becker, like it or not, it's true for you."

In retrospect, the picnic had been the lull before the storm. With daylight on Monday morning came several items of bad news. The first came from Thérèse. She'd arrived early that day with photos of the antiques she'd purchased to furnish the castle. With the deadline becoming a greater concern, she needed to have the interior decorating planned and ready to go the moment the rooms became available. She found Beck working on the grand staircase.

"I'm afraid I have some news," she began, looking like she was braced to sprint away if Becker unleashed anything unpleasant on her.

Beck looked up, eyebrow raised. "Well? Spit it out."

"I received a phone call from Christophe last night. It appears . . ." She took a breath and blurted, "He and his men have decided not to work here anymore."

This got Beck's attention. "Come again?"

"After the—how shall I put this—after the unpleasantness the other day, I think he opted to focus his energies on some other projects in the area."

Propping his fists on his hips, Beck gave Thérèse an evaluating stare. "You mean he walked off the job."

Much as she clearly wanted to deny the statement, it was obvious that there was no way around it. "Yes," Thérèse said, her pointed chin bobbing up and down. "It's really quite unfortunate."

"Unfortunate?" Beck heard the volume of his voice rising and reeled himself back in. "This means that Jacques and his crew of incompetents are going to have to fix Christophe's mess!"

"I realize that."

Beck rubbed his scalp and gave the situation some consideration. With the dwindling time remaining, there was no way they could find another crew. He looked at Thérèse. "Anything else?"

"Just—one more small item."

"What is it?"

"It's Jade, Mr. Becker. Monsieur Fallon wanted me to remind you that she won't be coming into work today but that Madame Fallon will be dropping off your meals."

Beck was about to thank Thérèse for the information and let her go when he realized that she might be the informant he was hoping for. "Thérèse," he said, coming down a few steps to the entryway where she stood, "do you have any idea what's wrong with Jade?"

She looked flustered. "No, of course not. I'm sure it's a private matter, and I wouldn't want to pry."

"But you've noticed it, right? How pale she is? How she seems tired? And her eyes—they're . . ."

He was halted in his questioning by Thérèse's surprised expression.

"Something I said?" he asked.

"Not at all. I'm just wondering how many men would notice such subtle changes as coloring and . . . eyes." There was little of her usual high-strung energy in the comment, as if Beck's question had lulled her into a more human countenance.

"I was just wondering," Beck said, hoping the birdlike woman wouldn't read too much into his questions. "But since you don't know any more than I do," he said, "I'll just get back to work."

18

THE MOOD IN the manor was somber. While the nurses and aides tried to keep the expectant mothers comfortable and calm, there were meetings in the offices upstairs that lasted for hours. Though the SS tried to spare the residents from the drama in the news, Marie made it a point to keep her friend abreast of the biggest developments. They'd take long walks in the Japanese garden, their conversations muted by the waterfalls and foliage.

"Didier's uncle is in the Resistance," Marie said one July morning. "He says the Allies have landed in Normandy. Thousands and thousands of them."

Elise, with just over two months to go before her due date, held her friend's arm as they walked slowly down the shaded paths. "Are they coming this way?"

"They only landed a couple weeks ago, but . . . yes. Yes, I think

they are!" She couldn't contain her excitement, though she knew the news would not be entirely welcome to her friend. "Elise, they're fighting the Germans, liberating towns as they go, and they're rolling toward Paris. Do you know what that means?"

Elise stopped and pressed a hand into her back. "All I care about right now is popping out this baby. . . ."

"Elise!"

"What?"

"Would you just—I don't know—think beyond your baby for a minute?"

"And think about what?"

"Your country!"

Elise smiled. "I don't want to think about my country," she said. "Or about the Allies or Normandy or anything! I've got this child to bring into the world."

"And then? Elise, this baby is only going to be yours for four or five days after you give birth. After that, it's the Führer's and you're out of the manor. And then what?"

Elise never responded well when Marie tried to talk about life after the baby. Marie wondered whether she was having second thoughts about giving it up for adoption, now that she had spent the past months feeling it move inside her.

"I'm not talking about this," Elise said. "Not today."

The two girls strolled in silence for a few moments, each lost in thoughts of a future they couldn't fathom. It was Marie who finally spoke.

"Elise . . ." She hesitated. In the months she'd spent keeping her friend company, she had tried to avoid reporting anything to her that might trouble her. She'd learned that lesson the hard way when she'd told Elise that her parents had moved to Brest to live with her grandparents, fearful that the situation in Lamorlaye would deteriorate if

a liberation movement were ever under way. It had taken days for Elise to get over the shock of the news, and when she'd finally come out of her depression, she'd been more militant than ever, vowing that her parents were dead to her anyway and that the only family she needed was Karl and his beloved Reich.

Marie had been selective ever since then in reporting the stories she heard in whispered conversations behind closed doors, afraid of sending her friend into another tailspin. But as news of an Allied invasion had started to spread over the radios and in the broad communication network of the Resistance, she'd wondered if her sensitivity had been misguided. Elise needed to know. If Paris was liberated, if the boches *were sent running, what would become of her friend and the baby she carried?*

"Elise," Marie said again, with more conviction this time, "there are some things you need to understand—before you have the baby. Before the Allies get here. Before you and Karl make any more plans together. While you've been in the manor, the world has been falling apart. Because of your Hitler. And not just in Paris."

"The Führer is fighting for us, Marie. For all of us."

"But at what cost?"

"'Strength lies not in defense, but in attack,'" she said with near reverence, her words a verbatim quote from the man whose folly had caused so much destruction.

Marie's blood ran cold. "You don't know what you're talking about, Elise."

"I do," Elise protested, her tone lighthearted and bright. "You're forgetting that I spend much of the day reading."

"But what you read isn't the truth. It's the boches' *sugarcoated version of their crimes! It's lies, Elise. Surely you realize that!"*

"Oh, Marie. Always so dramatic."

"Dramatic? Telling you that 'bad things' are happening is not

dramatic. But if I were to tell you the truth, if I were to tell you that thousands of people have been ripped away from their homes and sent to work camps in overloaded trains, never to be heard of again—that would be dramatic! Telling you that people right here in Lamorlaye, some of the families we've known forever, have been kicked out of their homes and forced to live on the streets because everyone is too scared to take them in? Telling you that there are torture chambers in Paris where members of the Resistance are put through hell just for the fun of it and long after they've confessed all they know? Or telling you that your precious Führer has said it's okay to rape women and get them pregnant and keep them prisoner in places not much different from this one as long as it expands his Aryan race? That, Elise," Marie concluded, breathless, *"would be dramatic."*

Elise had stopped walking and was staring at her friend with mounting horror. *"You're lying,"* she said.

"Elise, there are trains full of French men and women being sent to work camps, and no one knows where they really are. Francis's father was taken just last week, and he's not the first and surely won't be the last. They don't ask any questions—the men and women and children just get rounded up and carted off without any explanations."

"Francis's father?"

Marie nodded, letting the truth sink in. *"Those stories you read aren't true. Hitler isn't making this world a better place. He isn't building the foundation for better lives for all of us. People are starving right here in Lamorlaye. And they're terrified. I can't tell you how many of our friends huddle in the dark around their radios late at night listening to the BBC and praying—praying—that the Allies will get here soon. I'm sorry to tell you this, Elise, but the Führer who plans on stealing your baby has already stolen thousands of lives, and those weren't given up voluntarily."*

"Why are you telling me this?" Elise asked, torn between denial

and horror, her voice a whisper. She placed a hand on her stomach in the protective gesture of a loving mother. "Why are you telling me this?" Her voice rose and broke. Tears flooded her eyes.

"I wasn't going to," Marie admitted, taking her friend's hand and pressing it firmly. "I didn't think the Nazis would ever leave, and I figured you'd find it easier to live with them if you didn't know all they were doing. But now—now that the Allies have breached the beaches of Normandy and are dead set on making it to Paris? Elise, when the Germans are run out of town, you'll need to know—you'll need to understand that . . ." Her voice trailed off.

"That I'll be considered one of them," Elise said with monotone sadness.

"You might be," Marie corrected, trying to remain positive for her friend's sake, but fearing much worse.

Elise's eyes widened, and she grasped Marie's hand more tightly. "Marie!" she said, horror in her voice.

"Is it the baby?" Marie asked, glancing down to see if her friend's water had broken.

"No—I mean, yes. I mean—" The tears that had been gathering in her eyes dropped onto her cheeks. It was in a nearly inaudible voice that she whispered, "My baby will be one of them too."

They stared at each other for a long moment, each trying to conjure a solution, before hugging in a frightened, desperate way. Marie was the first to offer hope. "We'll figure something out," she said, her gaze determined. "If it comes to that—if the Allies get here and chase out the boches—we'll figure it out."

Elise nodded, her eyes still glazed with fear. "We'll figure it out," she parroted, dipping her fingers in one of the Japanese fountains and soothing her face with the cool water.

The girls walked back to the manor, hand in hand.

19

BECK STOOD NEXT TO the gaping hole in the ballroom floor with dread in his gut. That which he had most feared had, as the saying went, come to pass. Jacques and his crew had torn up some of the floorboards in the far corner of the room, and what they'd found had thrown a wrench in any expectation Beck had had that the project would finish on time. Though the boards themselves were in fairly good shape, the plaster where the walls met the flooring had offered a subtle, nearly missed clue that all was not well underneath. In the space where the floorboards had once lain, Becker saw what he presumed to be a widespread condition. Some of the joists that sat on heavy beams were still in decent shape, but a majority of them were so eaten away with dry rot that they wouldn't have lasted much longer.

"Can we save any of them?" Thérèse asked.

Beck shook his head, his lips pressed tight in frustration. "If one's infected, they all are. And that's not counting the beams and the columns they rest on. We'll have to check those, too. Worst-case scenario?" he said, rocking his head side to side and feeling something pop. "We get down there and find out the foundations are compromised. If there's sitting water in the basement, we're in big trouble."

Fallon nodded. "So, lad. What do we do?"

Beck raised his shoulders in a gesture of defeat. "We probably reschedule your wife's party," he said. "Or at least move the venue to the dining rooms. I mean, we'll get down there and figure out exactly where the problem lies, but . . . I don't know. It doesn't look good."

The three of them stood there for a moment, each lost in thought. Beck subconsciously registered the intricate woodwork that bound the joists to each other with nothing more than wedges, pins, and dowels, each one perfectly cut to fit the giant puzzle hidden under the hardwood floors. The design mastery that had gone into it had been foiled by a microscopic organism that had slowly eaten the substance out of the wood and, most probably, started up the walls as well.

"What's the next step?" Fallon asked.

"We get Jacques and his seven dwarfs into the cellars and figure out where the problem is. I thought we'd given them a good once-over before we started, but—" he looked out the window to situate the ballroom in reference to the rest of the structure—"I don't think the cellars we explored extend this far. There might be a separate entrance somewhere, or a blocked one. Once we know what state the support columns are in, we'll also know if we need to start from the foundation up. If we're lucky, we'll just have to rip out all the joists and flooring, plus a good portion of the floor-level plaster, and start from there."

Thérèse was already moving toward the door. "I'll get Jacques."

The problem with nights at the castle was that they were completely still. In the two days of Jade's absence, Beck had eaten all his meals alone, without the usual short exchanges with Jade that had until then accompanied their delivery. Sylvia and the children had come by every day, but Beck had found himself missing Jade's presence in a nearly visceral way. And then, when the workers and Thérèse had gone home every evening, he'd found himself alone within the constantly creaking and settling halls of the castle. Those were the hardest hours. He'd known they would be and had braced himself for the inevitability of the cravings that would leave him holding his head and pounding walls with his fist, but even with full knowledge that the weaning would be torture, he'd been surprised.

On the first two nights, he'd taken to the woods again, his pounding feet imprinting the path with the ferocity of his determination. On the third night, his body too exhausted by resistance to run again, he tried to dull the ache with Internet searches that only served to accentuate the permeating sense of aloneness that made of his battle a very private hell. Every hour that passed was a new record, and every day without an outburst was his prize.

Beck was quickly finding out that raging headaches could be crippling. He medicated them with caffeine and the aspirin Thérèse had donated from her purse. He'd also learned that tremors couldn't be suspended, not even if an urgent task required stable force. He'd hidden the affliction behind a semblance of teamwork and encouraged others to do the jobs he would normally have done himself.

He'd been practicing new skills on an oblivious Thérèse, sometimes stunning her into silence with questions about her work, her home, and her family. She'd been particularly taken aback when he'd said, "So, tell me about your parents," during a grueling conversation in which she'd assaulted him with so many details about the kitchen's new appliances that he'd wanted to strangle her with his bare hands. After the question, though, she'd fallen silent—and Beck had thanked his lucky stars for Sylvia's instructions to "get down on their level and ask them questions."

He and Jacques had spent most of Monday afternoon exploring the musty space again, entering each of the small, arch-ceilinged cellars and looking for any passageways into the area beneath the ballroom. One cellar led into another, debris hampering their progress until they got to the southernmost room. There, Beck tried to gauge their position under the castle. He looked up. "You think that's the ballroom above us?"

Jacques hadn't answered. His eyes were on a pile of old bookshelves stacked against the far wall. "Help me move those," he said.

Becker found it refreshing to have someone else giving orders for a change and moved quickly toward the other end of the room. They dispensed with the wood in record time and stood staring at the brick wall that spanned a rounded opening.

"My guess is that the ballroom is through there," Jacques said, a pleased glint in his eye. "You want to get some hammers?"

They worked off some of their frustration tearing through the wall, and when the final fragments of red brick had been broken off, made their triumphant entrance into the cellar beneath the rotten joists. Beck was relieved to find that the floor was dry and the columns seemed solid enough to support the floor for at least another century or so. But there were watermarks on the rough walls that proved the space had not always been dry. "Any history of floods in this area? Does the river ever jump its banks?"

Jacques shrugged. "Not in my memory. But the castle's been around for a couple hundred years and I haven't."

Beck shone his flashlight in a slow circle around the foundations. "Looks like it was about a foot deep at some point," he said, following the light beam. "There's a good chance they built that brick wall to prevent any more flooding from reaching the rest of the basement."

"Meanwhile, the damage was already done in here. You leave a foot of water sitting for however long it took for it to go down, and it's prime conditions for dry rot."

Though the discovery hadn't solved the problem, it had at least relieved Beck's mind. With the plaster-covered stone columns still in good shape, "all" that would have to be replaced were the supporting beams, the joists, the floorboards, and portions of the plaster on the walls. The work would have to cover the entire ballroom, and Becker was glad to hand the bulk of that job off to Jacques and his men with strict instructions to work as quickly as they could.

Now, as Beck sat at his computer distracting his mind with online research, he heard something in the basement that made his ears perk up. It wasn't unusual for small noises to rise up through the floors, but they usually sounded like scurrying rodents or shifting floorboards. On this night, however, the sound was loud enough that it startled Beck and sent him to the basement for the second time that week.

He entered through the door just around the corner and down a couple steps from his office. As the basement wasn't wired for lights, he carried in his hand his trusty flashlight, sweeping the floor with its beam as he went. The first room held nothing suspicious. Just the usual debris that had accumulated over years of use as a repository for unwanted items—wooden planks, broken flowerpots, an old length of rope. The next two rooms seemed equally undisturbed. Beck shone the flashlight into the corners of each room, and though a rat or two scurried through holes in the walls, there was nothing else moving there.

As Beck got to the final cellar that led to the space under the ballroom, he noticed that the stack of old bookshelves he and Jacques had displaced Monday afternoon had fallen. They'd been propped up against the wall when the two men had left, but now they were scattered on the floor. He stepped into the dark and musty room ahead with a little less confidence in his gait, grabbing a two-by-four from the pile near the destroyed wall. There was nothing in the farthest cellar that hadn't been there earlier. Beck stood in the doorway and shone the flashlight around, letting the beam alight on the rocks and pieces of timber that lay here and there on the floor, vestiges of the construction that had taken place so long ago. Nothing amiss. Nothing remotely interesting either. A little embarrassed by his eagerness to pursue ghosts through the château's dungeons, he turned and retraced his steps, wondering if his newfound sobriety might be causing more hallucinations than the drinking had.

When Jade arrived at the castle the next day, Beck was in the kitchen. He'd made the coffee and generally cleaned up the mess he'd left there in the three days of her absence. The night before had been another rough one, starting with the basement expedition.

Beck wiped bread crumbs off the kitchen counter and tried not to let his nervousness disarm his most honorable intentions. He remembered what Jade had said during their heart-to-heart and wasn't about to go against her wishes by dragging her into his battle for wholeness, but he also remembered what Sylvia had said. Her words had anchored themselves in his mind during those sleepless hours when he'd had to weigh oblivion against returning to the ranks of the living, and they had swayed him toward the courage the harder path required. *We need to feel known, we need to feel loved, and we need to feel safe.* He hadn't felt any of those things in recent memory, and he wasn't sure if they were in the stars for him, but the look on Jade's face when he'd so ruthlessly disparaged her had left him yearning to offer at least some of those things to her. The list of Becker's altruistic élans in recent years was short indeed, but he didn't question the impulse.

Jade arrived shortly before nine. She carried in her arms three full plastic bags from which baguettes, leeks, and rhubarb extended. If she was surprised to see Beck standing by the sink, she didn't show it. "Sorry I'm a little late. I needed to wait for the stores to open. Are you hungry?"

"Just . . . cleaning up a little before you got here." He cursed the nervousness that nearly made him stumble.

"No need to clean up on my account," Jade said, emptying the bags and stowing the groceries. "It's what I'm paid for, you know."

"Are you feeling better?" The moment the words left his mouth, Beck wondered what had prompted him to say them. He'd wanted to shoot the breeze for a while and make a smooth segue into asking her about herself, but that plan had been shot to smithereens by his agitated state of mind. He knew the challenge he'd put before himself was not solely to blame for the jitters that had his brain working overtime. He knew that because the craving for a strong drink was increasing with every moment that passed.

Jade turned from her groceries long enough to give him an inquiring look. "Yes, I am." She searched his face. "Thank you for asking."

The subtle approach wasn't working. Beck didn't want to muck around with pleasantries and talk slow circles around the real reason for his presence in the kitchen. Taking a resolute breath, he marched over to the counter, then balked, his courage dimming with the proximity to Jade. But the stubborn streak that had mostly harmed him came to his rescue this time. He wanted to reach out and turn her toward him but ended up touching her arm rather gingerly and asking, "Can I say something?"

Jade looked up, startled. "You can say anything you like, Mr. Becker. France, like the United States, is a free country, after all."

"Jade," he began, feeling his determination ebb as she raised an expectant eyebrow and leaned a hip against the counter, arms and ankles crossed. Beck closed his eyes and reminded himself again of the rationale that had led him to this critical point in his life. What he did right now—this moment—would be the hopeful precedent on which future courage would be based. And if he failed, if he cowered and hid behind his usual scare tactics, he'd never know if he possessed the strength true vulnerability required. "I need to tell you something," he said when the dueling voices in his head had called a truce.

"So you've said."

He held up a hand in warning. "I know we don't know each other very well, but it doesn't take a genius to figure out that talking is not my forte, so if you'll keep your witty little quips to yourself for just a minute . . ." He looked at her expectantly.

Intrigued, Jade nodded her consent and made a zipping motion across her lips. "Please," she said, clearly perplexed. "Be my guest."

Becker took a moment to observe the woman who stood before him. Her color seemed a bit improved since the last time he'd seen her, but her face was still gaunt. Her eyes had a spark in them despite the dark circles and dullness that hadn't entirely disappeared. She wasn't the fresh-faced, energetic sparring partner she'd been when he'd first arrived, but this woman casting him an inquisitive smile was still the incentive he needed to be bold.

"Okay," he said, then let out a breath. "I'll try to make this really quick because I know you have work to do and I have work to do and . . ." He stopped himself. "Actually," he admitted, "that's not true at all. I'm trying to make this quick because I am so far out of my element right now that the faster I get this over with, the faster I'll be able to make a beeline out of this kitchen and hide in my office for the rest of the day." He offered a tentative smile and was pleased when she returned it, though her answering smirk held a little more good-natured mockery than he liked.

"Mr. Becker, if you're going to ask me to marry you, the least you can do is get down on one knee," Jade said with such a deadpan expression that Beck nearly started to protest.

It was the mischief in her gaze that finally eased Beck's mind. A little chagrined to have been duped so easily, he blamed his naïveté on the strain of the moment and forged ahead. "Nice. Go ahead and kick me while I'm down."

"Sorry," Jade quipped, duly repentant. "Please, Mr. Becker, do go on."

"I know you don't want to be my best friend," he said, quoting her.

She shook her head and reached out to stop him. "Mr. Becker, about that. I didn't mean to be rude, and I realize that—"

"No, you were right. If you became the person who somehow made the rest of my life bearable, you really would be just a substitute bottle."

"But I shouldn't have said it so—"

"Could you just be quiet until I'm finished talking? Please?"

Jade ducked her head. "Yes. Of course."

"I've . . ." He hesitated. "I've been doing a fair amount of soul-searching in the past couple of days, and . . ." He took a deep breath. "And I want you to know that I know how rude I've been to you. How cold and unpleasant. And I've taken frustrations out on you and the kids that you had nothing to do with. And that's . . . uncool." He saw her smile a little at his word choice but didn't let it deter him. "There's been stuff in my life that I haven't been proud of. In fact," he added as an afterthought, "most of the past two years are a complete wash. But there's something . . . something—I don't know—*happening* that I don't quite understand."

"Something happening?" Jade was confused, and he didn't blame her.

"Something good. Like I'm . . . wanting to be alive again—or something. I'm not very good with words." He finished on a frustrated sigh.

"I think you're doing just fine."

"I want to be able to . . . communicate again. And not just with sarcasm and barked orders. And I was wondering . . ." This was where his vulnerability would either take a beating or be validated, so he paused, contemplating the precipice at the edge of which he stood. "I was wondering if I could start on that with you."

There was a long silence—longer still in Becker's mind—while Jade appeared to rummage through the plethora of words he'd just blurted to get to the crux of his point. "You want to communicate with me?" she finally asked, looking at him a little askance.

He threw back his head and expelled a loud breath. "Maybe this was a mistake," he said, staring at the ceiling. He looked back down at Jade and tried again. "I want to be able to talk—just . . . talk—with you. And not just for the practice, though God knows I need that, but because . . . because . . . because I want to talk with you!"

"And you need my permission to speak?"

Beck turned briskly to the table, pulled out two stools, and motioned Jade to take one of them. "Sit!" he ordered.

"Care to rephrase that?" she asked, one eyebrow raised.

Beck held up his hands. "I'm sorry! Getting a little carried away." He tried again. "Would you mind sitting here? Just for a minute."

Jade moved to the stool and sat down. It dawned on Becker that she was still wearing her jacket.

"Do you want to take off your coat or . . . something?"

"I'm quite comfortable with it on, thank you."

Becker sat heavily on the other stool and leaned forward. "How are you?" he asked.

Jade's giggle brightened her eyes and brought color to her cheeks. "I'm quite well. And you?"

Beck raised both hands, palms upward, in a give-me-a-break gesture that made Jade giggle again. "Come on . . . I'm not just being polite. I really want to know."

Jade squinted into his face to gauge his sincerity. "I'm really fine," she said after a moment. "I wasn't great last week, as I'm sure you noticed, but . . . I'm feeling better today."

There was a pause while Beck took stock of the alterations he'd seen in her since he'd first met her. "Can you tell me what's wrong?" he finally asked. "I mean—I don't want to be insensitive, but . . . I've noticed that you seem . . . less well than you did a few weeks ago."

"I look sick," Jade said, her tone pleasant. "That's what you mean to say, right?"

"No, I—" Becker started to protest, then stopped himself.

"It's no secret. I know I do."

"Is it . . . something serious?" Beck asked, genuine concern sharpening his focus.

Jade bit her lip. "I'm sorry, Mr. Becker. I'm not quite sure I can tell you about that yet." She reached out to lay a hand on his arm. "I'm not telling you to get lost," she added hastily. "I'm just saying that . . . I'm not quite to the point where I can discuss it yet."

Beck nodded. "Okay. But if you need anything—anything at all . . ."

"I'll be sure to tell you."

Beck suddenly remembered that the children hadn't arrived with her. "Are the twins not coming today?"

Jade rose and went back to the task of putting away the groceries she'd brought with her. "The children went to a doctor's appointment with the Fallons. They'll get to see an ultrasound of their new brother or sister—which should have them hanging from the rafters when they return." She shuddered.

"You're good with them," Beck said, still sitting at the table. "Mrs. Fallon tried to give me pointers on how to be more comfortable around kids, but . . . we'll see."

Jade suddenly paused in her work and leaned back against the tall counter, her face a shade paler.

Beck started to rise from his stool, but she motioned him back down. "No need to trouble yourself. It'll pass," she said, taking a flyer from one of her bags and fanning herself with it, eyes closed.

"Jade . . . ," Becker began, the act of pronouncing her name again doing strange things to his stomach.

"I'll be fine," she said, letting out a long breath and pushing away from the counter.

"You sure you shouldn't sit down?"

Jade ignored the question and finished emptying the last bag, then retrieved a carton of eggs from the fridge. "Scrambled eggs and bacon okay for you this morning?"

"I had some leftovers before you got here. I'll be fine until lunch."

"Oh—all right then," Jade said, returning the eggs to the fridge.

Beck smiled and picked up his coffee cup. The conversation hadn't lasted long, but all things considered, it had gone fairly well. He realized, as he placed the cup in the microwave and waited for it to heat, that he'd been so distracted by the conversation he'd been having with Jade that he'd almost forgotten the booming in his head—and had completely forgotten his schedule for the day. He picked up his reheated coffee and told Jade he'd be ready for lunch around twelve thirty. "If that's okay with you," he added as an afterthought.

Jade smiled. "That's just fine," she said.

Beck left the kitchen and headed for his office. When he got to the door, he paused, considering the one act of courage he'd been too hesitant to perform. With determination in his stride, he returned to the kitchen, marched up to the woman who stood drying dishes at the sink, and without preamble said, "I haven't had a drink since Saturday. My head feels like someone's using it as a soccer ball, and I might throw one of Jacques's guys through a window at some point this morning, but I haven't had a drink. Just wanted you to know. It's not a best friend thing or a counselor thing. It's just a fact." He looked upward as if he were checking his mind for anything else that remained to be said. Finding nothing, he turned and walked out of the kitchen as quickly as he'd entered, leaving Jade grinning by the sink.

The demolition in the ballroom was well under way when Becker joined Jacques and his men. They'd ripped up most of the flooring, starting at the fireplace and moving back toward the doors, and were plotting the best way to get rid of the rotten joists and support beams. With most of the rest of the room already finished, it was all the more important to reconstruct the floors with minimal damage to the walls, windows, and fireplace. These were not by any means ideal circumstances.

With the ease of a carpenter, Beck walked on the bare four-inch-wide joists toward the front of the room, where Jacques and one of his men were planning the heavy-duty sawing that would remove the large timbers one piece at a time. He noticed a frayed rope hanging over one of the joists. "What's the point of the rope?"

Jacques shrugged and pointed at him. "We thought you left it there."

Becker was stumped. What was a clearly ancient piece of rope doing draped over the woodwork that supported the ballroom floor? He reached for the rope and pulled it up, coiling it. He was about to dismiss the whole thing as an unimportant detail when he remembered his midnight exploration of the basement the night before and the old rope he'd seen in the first room of the maze of cellars.

"What?" Jacques asked, seeing the look of concentration on his boss's face.

"It was hanging there when you got in this morning?"

"Sure. Just where you found it."

"And it wasn't there when you left last night."

"Nope. You got a theory?"

Becker did, but he didn't know if he should believe it or not. He hadn't seen anyone loitering in the series of small cellars when he'd given them a cursory once-over. But what if someone had been down there? Maybe hiding behind a pile of old wood . . . or behind the support columns in the space beneath the ballroom. Beck had locked the basement door on his way out, having found it unlocked on his way down. And if someone had truly been hiding in the dank shadows, they would have had no means of escape but through the torn-up ballroom floor.

Becker looked down into the darkness beneath the joists. It was at least seven feet from the support beams to the floor. Whoever had used the rope to make an escape—*if* anyone had used the rope, he corrected himself—had been mighty determined.

20

Buoyed by the morning's conversation, Becker decided to eat lunch with Jade and the twins. All in all, it was a fairly drama-free meal, and though time-outs were threatened—for the kids, not him—they didn't actually occur. Eva spent the bulk of the time retelling the visit to the doctor's office, then launching into an endless list of possible baby names for the little boy she'd seen on the TV screen. It was Philippe's order to "shut up" that had brought the time-out chair into the discussion, but a hasty retraction had deferred the punishment for the time being. Becker's stomach still churned with the restless need for alcoholic relief, and he found the condition both remedied and exacerbated by protracted time with the kids. They were in turn entertaining and annoying. Their entertaining phases were a welcome distraction from the turmoil inside, but the annoying episodes made it hard for him to maintain his tenuous grip on his temper. He decided halfway through the meal that an after-lunch run through the woods would probably be a good idea.

He was getting ready to go up to his apartment and change when he noticed the plate Jade was preparing.

"For Jojo?"

She nodded.

"You know, he seemed to be pretty well-fed before you came along." As soon as the words were out, he regretted them. His intention had been to relieve her of the obligation to feed the old man who lived in the gatehouse, but he deduced from the look she gave him that he'd somehow fallen short.

He quickly raised a hand in self-defense. "I didn't mean—"

She interrupted him with a well-aimed "Have you taken a good look at him lately?" She raised her eyebrows and gave him a moment to consider the question, much as she did when she was reprimanding Philippe. "He may have found ways to feed himself before I 'came along,' as you put it, but something tells me he could use the act of kindness."

"I was just trying to say that if it's too much for you . . ."

"It's not," Jade said, pulling plastic wrap out of a drawer. "The walk will do me good." She covered the still-warm food on the plate and looked up at him with challenge in her eyes. "Anything else you'd like to confront me about? Giving to charities? Paying my taxes?"

Though the words sought to be humorous, there was an edge to her tone that made Beck want to get hostile. Given his precarious disposition, he knew that any retort would probably be overkill and stifled the impulse to defend his motivations. Retreat, he figured, was probably the best option. "I'm going for a run," he said by way of parting words.

On his first pass in front of the castle, just when he was starting to feel the burn in his legs, he saw Jade heading across the lawn with the plate for Jojo in her hands. The children were playing something that looked like cowboys and Indians on the large island in the river, and Jade yelled at them that they had ten minutes before they had to come inside.

On his second pass in front of the castle, the children had crossed the small stone bridge that led from the big island to the tiny one that stood at the widest part of the creek, not far from the gatehouse. It was really a rocky protrusion off the river floor, maybe six feet across, and it had long been a refuge for the château's ducks and ducklings. The bridge that led to it looked to be centuries old and was nothing more than a large, long rock spanning the gap, moss-covered and age-worn.

Beck was finishing his third lap when he heard Eva scream. He'd been within earshot of the children playing often enough to recognize that this wasn't the usual juvenile drama. There was something in her voice that chilled Becker's blood and sent him racing toward the last place he'd seen the twins. He rounded the castle and saw Eva squatting on the stone bridge, her face frozen in horror, screaming, "Philippe! Philippe!" as she stared into the water beneath her.

Beck didn't take the time to scan the water for the boy. He ran so fast that he stumbled, his legs unable to match the commands coming from his brain. When he got to the river's edge, he didn't stop, splashing into the murky water with powerful strides as his eyes skimmed the space under the small stone bridge for any signs of the six-year-old. What he saw, through his panic-sharpened vision, was Jojo, fully dressed and chest-high in the river, his hands gripping the back of Philippe's blue jacket as the boy lay facedown in the water.

"Let him go!" Becker cried, his voice hoarse from exertion and fear. "Get your hands off him!"

He covered the last few yards in a surge of water, arms and legs pumping against the river's restraint, feet straining to break loose of the heavy silt that pulled them downward. Jojo lifted Philippe from the water and was turning him over when Beck's fist connected with his jaw and sent him reeling backward into the muddy, opaque river. On the bridge, Eva screamed again, more loudly this time, then clapped a hand over her mouth, her eyes impossibly wide as she watched Becker carry her brother to the river's edge. She crossed the tiny island until she stood as close to her brother as she could, the river still separating her from him.

Beck deposited Philippe on the grassy riverbank as soon as he was out of the water and knelt down, his ear to the boy's chest, trying to perceive movement or a sound that would attest to the boy's breathing.

"Ow . . ."

Beck snapped his head up and looked into Philippe's face. The boy's eyes were open and squinting, his face contorted in pain.

"Philippe?" Beck said, still breathless from his run and the fear that was cramping his legs. "Philippe, can you hear me?" He grasped the boy's chin and moved so he could look into his eyes. "Are you okay? Where do you hurt?"

Philippe raised a wet hand to his forehead and touched the growing purplish knot just below his hairline. The gesture broke through his semiconscious haze. "Ow . . ." This time, it was a wail that grew into sobs. He looked up at Becker with so much pained surprise in his tear-filling eyes, begging with his gaze for some sort of comfort, that Becker froze. As the boy's sobs grew louder, Eva, still on the small island, joined in, her crying pitched higher but just as gut-wrenching as her brother's.

As Becker sat next to the sobbing boy, a hand on the drenched arm of his jacket, he found himself paralyzed, incapable of thought or motion. In his peripheral vision, he saw Jojo, who had been standing waist-deep in the water just beyond the island, wading toward the spot where Eva knelt, hand outstretched, wracked with terrified sobs. She didn't see the man approach her and hardly reacted when he lifted her off the rocky edge of the island and carried her across the expanse of stream to the shore where her brother lay. Becker watched him, saw the gentleness in the man's touch and the compassion in his eyes as he carried the child across the water. Their eyes met.

"You weren't harming him," Beck said, dismayed, his voice barely above a hoarse whisper. "I shouldn't have . . . I assumed . . ."

Jojo lowered Eva onto the riverbank with so much tenderness that she looked up into his craggy face with surprise, her weeping suspended by his kindness. At his nod, she turned and ran to her brother's side, taking his hand in hers and joining her tears to his. Beck met the old man's gaze and saw nothing but kindness there despite the red imprint of his fist on the stubbled jaw—no reproach, no defensiveness. He knew there were words he needed to say. Words of apology. Words of explanation. Self-deprecating words about snap judgments and fear. But there was a child lying in the grass in front of him, paralyzing him with his need, and Becker's mind could formulate little more than panic. With a nearly imperceptible smile and a last glance at the children, Jojo walked away toward the gatehouse, his clothes dripping.

Philippe's sobs had become less frantic once his sister reached him. His tears still flowed and his chest still heaved, but he seemed somehow soothed by her presence. Beck checked the boy's scalp for any other bumps and found none, but the one on his forehead was growing. He needed to get some ice on it. Fast. Beck gingerly snaked one arm under Philippe's shoulders and the other under his legs to lift him and carry him back to the castle, but as soon as the boy felt Beck's arms holding him, he turned and burrowed into his chest, his hands clutching the front of Beck's sweatshirt and his legs curling up until he half sat, half lay against Becker's body. It was such an unexpected act that Beck's instincts took over. Rather than standing with the boy in his arms, he merely held him more tightly, dropped his chin onto the boy's wet hair, and stayed seated with the shaking form in his arms. The fragility and need of the weeping boy broke adrenaline's grip on his emotions, and he found his own body shaking in time with the child's.

Beck sat for a moment longer, cradling the frightened boy. Eva had scooted over on the grass and leaned against him, her small, white hand patting her brother's shoulder, her sobs now mellowed to occasional hiccups. Beck tried to meet her wide-eyed gaze with soothing confidence and wasn't sure if he succeeded. There was little peace in his mind and even less in his water-chilled, shocked muscles.

The cold eventually brought the world back into focus. It seeped through his wet clothing, relentless. They all needed to get inside, and quickly, before the air temperature did more damage than the water already had. Beck was about to stand, holding Philippe, when he sensed movement and looked around to see Jade standing just a few feet away, her face pale, her arms wrapped around her middle, her eyes intense. He wasn't sure how long she'd been standing there, but the tug-of-war between fear and surprise in her eyes indicated that it had been a while.

She hurried forward when he stood, still holding Philippe, and bent down to scoop Eva into a tight hug. The little girl clung to her. "What happened, Eva? Eva—look at me."

The child, whose head had been pressed into her nanny's neck, pulled back, a hiccup convulsing her little body. "We were on the bridge," she said, fresh tears welling in her eyes, "and then he slipped on the moss."

Jade saw a chill quake through Beck and said, "Come on. Let's go inside and get everybody warm, okay?"

Beck walked briskly toward the château's front entrance, opening the door with his elbow, then hurrying through both dining rooms with the boy in his arms. Eva didn't stop talking as she and

Jade followed, but little of what she said registered in Becker's mind. There was something about a space landing and having to walk on a bridge from the spacecraft to the surface of Mars. Then something about Philippe slipping off the bridge and hitting his head on the stone as he fell into the water below. Jojo and "Mr. Becker" were the heroes in the rescue, but he didn't care about that, either. All he wanted was to get the boy into the warmth of his office and still the shaking he could feel through their drenched layers of clothing.

He kicked the office door open when he got there and put the boy down on the couch.

"Take his clothes off while I get a blanket," he instructed Jade, his throat still constricted by the emotions of the past few minutes. Jade was installing Eva in an armchair when he left the office. By the time he came back down, Philippe had been stripped out of his cold, wet clothes, and Jade was holding him close to her, rubbing his back and arms vigorously. She took the blanket from Beck and asked him to sit on the other side of Philippe while she wrapped it around the shaking boy.

"Now rub his back and arms while I call the Fallons, will you? We need to warm him up." She went to the desk and picked up the phone. Eva slid off the chair and went to press against her.

The task of warming Philippe's shocked body lay far outside Beck's comfort zone, but the welfare of the now-silent boy super-seded his druthers. He rubbed his bony back with restraint, afraid to rub too vigorously, but as his palm circled, he felt some of the tension seeping out of the boy's waterlogged body. Philippe scooted a little closer, then closer yet, then so close that Beck couldn't reach his back anymore. There was nothing left to do but hold the boy against his side while Jade finished explaining what had happened to Mrs. Fallon and asked her to bring dry clothes.

The flurry of activity that followed was a welcome respite from the slow-motion aftermath of Philippe's adventure. The Fallons arrived in a whirlwind of concern. Eva promptly burst into tears when she saw them, and it was all Fallon could do to calm his daughter. He finally gained moderate success by promising her a pizza for dinner. Even Philippe perked up at that news. After gathering what information Jade had about the accident and placing a call to the doctor, informing his receptionist of their imminent arrival, the Fallons loaded Philippe into their car, still wrapped in the blanket, and drove off, leaving Beck standing in front of the château with Jade, utterly spent.

Beck went up to his apartment to shower and change, telling Jade he'd be right back for the coffee she'd promised. Over half an hour later, he heard her footsteps on the stairs. She went to his bedroom first and knocked lightly on the door, calling his name when there was no answer. He heard her move to the bathroom next. The door was open, and he wasn't there either. Her footsteps moved back toward the stairs, then paused. He heard them come back in the direction of the extra bedroom where he stood, motionless.

Jade reached the doorway and stopped. "Becker?"

He didn't move. His wet clothes clung to him, a cold straitjacket that mimicked the vise grip of shock that had seized his mind shortly after he'd reached his apartment. He'd stood in his bedroom for a while, his thinking blanked by the assault Philippe's accident had waged on all his senses. He'd told himself to move—to go to the closet and take out dry clothes, to head to the bathroom for a long, restorative shower. . . . But the shrieking static in his mind had propelled him instead to the bedroom where five bottles stood lined up on the windowsill. He felt as if his eyes bulged and his skin throbbed from the intensity of need.

"Becker," Jade said again, stepping into the room.

A constricted breath quaked into his lungs, then hissed out again. His eyes were riveted on the lineup of bottles as if by a powerful magnetic force. He couldn't shift his gaze away from the source of guilt and solace that waited, dull amber and diluted gold, for his capitulation. He felt Jade move out of sight for a moment. Then she reentered the room and draped a blanket over his shoulders. "Becker," she said, her voice firmer, more demanding this time. "Look at me." She tugged at his arm. "Look at me," she repeated. He looked down at her small hand where it gripped his arm, and something in that connection weakened the power of the static over his mind just a fraction. When she tugged again, he swayed, stumbling a little as he lost his balance, his gaze skipping from her hand to her face. Her eyes were steady and her expression unyieldingly soft. "You don't want to do this," she said.

"Yes, I do." His voice sounded frayed.

There was an undertone of worry in her voice when Jade coaxed, "Come on, Becker. Just take a shower. Get warmed up. I have hot coffee for you downstairs. We can talk about this. . . ."

At that, his mouth twisted into a rictus that might have been a smile under different circumstances. "We can't talk about this," he said. "We're not that kind of friends."

He heard her sharp intake of breath and was somehow pleased to have hit home. After a moment of silence, Jade said, "Right now—this moment—we can be that kind of friends. I'm not leaving you here to mess up your life."

His eyes darted back to the bottles on the windowsill, the static growing in his mind again, swelling behind his eyes. He saw a flash of Philippe floating facedown in the river, then another of the boy's lifeless body as it might have looked had Beck gotten there just a few seconds later—blue lips and open, empty eyes. "Just go away," he said to Jade, the static rising to new pitches.

"Philippe is going to be fine. Mrs. Fallon just called, and aside from that bump on his head—"

"Get out."

"Becker."

He felt the relief of rage building inside him and didn't begin to resist it. "Get out of here!" He spat the words in Jade's direction as he stalked to the window and grabbed a bottle of whiskey, pulling out its cork. He pointed at Jade with the hand that held the liquor and growled, "Don't give me that look. Just . . . don't!" Then he raised the bottle to his lips and took a deep, burning swallow of the amber liquid.

The look on Jade's face when he glanced at her again made him pause in the act of raising the bottle for another swig. The pallor of her skin accentuated the depth of sorrow in her eyes. She watched him as if he were a jumper leaping to his death from the railing of a bridge. Horror and grief dueled in her gaze, but Becker saw nothing comforting in the concern they expressed. He kept his eyes defiantly on hers as he tipped the bottle and took another swallow of tranquilizing shame.

Jade took a step toward him, so much compassion on her face that he held her off with a pointed finger. "Don't!" he barked.

"But, Becker—"

"I don't want to hear it!"

"But it's been days. You've managed to go without for days, and you're going to give it all up for this?"

"Were you there?" he asked, his voice edged with acid. "Did you see what happened—what nearly happened in the river this afternoon?"

"I did," she said softly, tears choking the words. "But he wasn't seriously hurt. He's probably home with his parents by now, demanding to have ice cream with his dinner to reward him for his bravery." She was at his side, covering the hand that held the bottle with her own. "I know it rattled you," she said, "but . . . Becker . . . you don't have to do this."

Her hand on his was torture. Her voice, her eyes, her nearness were too. "Get your hand off me," he said through clenched teeth. "You're neither my best friend nor my counselor, remember?" he grated, sending her a look so filled with venom that she released her hold and took a step back.

"I . . ." She looked as if his words had physically struck her. Her shoulders seemed to slump and her focus to turn inward. There was something so broken about her that Becker nearly retracted his words—nearly begged her to forget them. But the familiar balm of fury prevented him from surrender.

"What do you want from me?" he sneered, tension mounting. "What is it you're so convinced I can do?"

She swallowed. "I just want you to . . ." She reached out a hand and steadied herself on the wall. "I want you to know that you can cope without . . ." She pointed her chin at the bottle in his hand. "Without hiding away inside that."

"This is coping!" he bellowed, the alcohol beginning to loosen his clenched muscles and shocked nerves. "This is being able to deal with life when kids like Philippe come this close—" he held up his thumb and finger, a fraction of an inch apart—"this close to drowning in a muddy river. This is being able to forget that I punched an old guy who was trying to save the kid because I'm too much of an idiot to—" He didn't finish. The memories were causing the static to start up again. He moved to the window and looked out over the castle grounds. "This is the only way I can do it," he said after a moment, his breathing ragged and shallow. "It's the only way I know."

"Then it's all you'll ever have."

It wasn't so much the words that made Becker turn toward Jade as the tone in which she'd said them. The compassion and concern he'd seen on her face before were gone. There was a hard tilt to her chin that reflected the glint in her eyes, and though tears hung on her lower eyelids and threatened to drop onto her sallow cheeks, the set of her jaw belied no weakness. She took three steps that ended just a few inches from where Becker stood, prying his fingers from around the bottle with more strength than he'd suspected she possessed and slamming it down next to the others on the windowsill.

When she spoke again, her voice was higher and harder, her words deliberately chosen for maximum impact. She pointed at the alcoholic lineup and sneered. "Take a good look, Becker," she commanded. "Those bottles? They're all you're going to have left when this is all over. They're going to be the only friends you ever have— the only family—the only children—the only woman. You want to dive into their oblivion because life is too hard?" she demanded, sneering the last two words as if they were the excuse of an idiot. "Well, dive away, Mr. Becker. Go ahead and lose yourself again. Give in to whatever demons made you into a drunk. You're a fool. A first-class coward who's going to die completely alone because you're too weak to get a grip!"

Becker held a finger an inch from her face. "You don't know anything about my life! You know nothing about me!"

She swatted his hand away with enough vigor to startle him. "Oh, shut up!" she spat. "Stop your whining! You want your life to turn around? Start living it—not avoiding it! There is nothing this life can throw at you that gives you the right to waste whatever years you have left on booze!"

"What do you know about that? What do you know about pain and suffering? You're a nanny, Jade," he said, hands on hips, his voice derisive. "You're a perfectly capable woman who chooses to spend her life wiping kids' noses and cooking for guys like me when you could probably do anything you set your mind to. So don't lecture me about retreating to a bottle when you spend every day of your life hiding away in a kitchen!"

"Shut up!" she yelled at him, tears overflowing her eyes and coursing down her cheeks. "Just . . . shut up!"

"Why? Why should I shut up when you've spent the better part of my time in the château lecturing me about my character flaws? Why should I shut up when all you've done is yap about how I need to change and become a better person and conform to whatever standard it is you have for the perfect strangers who cross your path? You're a fraud, Jade! You know nothing of what surviving in this world really demands! So don't tell me to shut up, and stop preaching at me about being a coward!"

He was so engrossed in his verbal lashing that he didn't see her vacillate until she'd nearly reached the ground. His arms shot out to help her the moment he realized her knees had buckled and her face had gone ashen, but she was a deadweight. All he succeeded in doing was going down with her and breaking her fall. She never fully lost consciousness, but her eyes were blank and her body listless as she leaned, half-sitting, in the corner formed by the bed and the wall.

"Jade," Becker cried, searching her face for signs of returning awareness. "Jade!"

Becker was trying to decide whether he should leave her alone long enough to go downstairs and call an ambulance when she took a shuddering breath and focused her eyes on his face. "Jade?" She seemed to be fully aware again, her eyes darting around the room.

"Did I . . . ?" she asked, her impossibly pale lips stiff as she tried to form the words.

"You passed out . . . I think. Sort of." The blood was pounding in Becker's ears. His hands shook as he helped Jade straighten into a sitting position against the wall. "What do you need? What can I . . . ?" He eyed the bottles on the windowsill and cringed. "Would a sip of something strong—?"

"No!" She held up her hand as she leaned her head back against the wall. "It'll pass," she said. "Just give me a minute."

"I'm calling an ambulance," he said, rising to a standing position.

"No, you're not." Her tone was unyielding.

"Jade, you just—"

"Had an episode." She inhaled a deep breath and let it out slowly.

"You virtually passed out!"

"Yes—but not for any reason an ambulance could cure."

"You need to see a doctor."

"No," she said, pulling herself up a little straighter and expelling another deep breath. "What I need is to get enough strength back to yell at you."

Becker took a closer look at the pale and shaken woman on the floor. "I'm pretty sure there are some more pressing things you could be doing with your time."

"You're a moron, Mr. Becker," she said.

He was tempted to agree. "Can we shelve the rest of our argument until you're well enough to put up a decent fight?" he asked.

"No," she said, her gaze serious. "I'm not much for shelving anything these days."

"I've noticed."

"But if you take another sip from any one of those bottles before I'm finished saying what I have to say, I promise you that you will never have to put up with my 'preaching' again."

Becker looked away and mumbled, "I hoped you were already unconscious when I got to that part."

"Oh, I heard every word you said." She took another breath and patted the floor next to her. "Have a seat, Mr. Becker."

He couldn't very well refuse a woman who had passed out moments before, but it was with a certain amount of trepidation that he lowered himself to the floor next to Jade and leaned back against the wall. "You're sure you don't want to wait until . . . ?"

The eyes she turned on him held the kind of clarity and certainty that made his question moot. "I heard every word," she said again. "And I particularly enjoyed the bits about hiding away in my kitchen and wasting my life caring for children."

"Jade, I—"

"Did you miss the part where I told you to shut up?"

Whatever traces of weakness had been there moments before had vanished. Becker clamped his lips shut.

"You might think caring for children is a dead-end career for dunces, and you might think taking a job that keeps me chained to the castle's stove is one step up from slave labor, but I assure you that both of those choices were made not out of fear but out of purpose." She turned her head against the wall so she could lock eyes with his. "I have a degree from the Sorbonne in international relations and was, until six months ago, working on a doctorate in business management from Oxford. So yes, you were right when you suggested that I could probably do anything I set my mind to." She paused while Becker absorbed the information, his mind reeling. "But when you said that I had no idea about the tough stuff this life has to offer, Mr. Becker, you were way off base."

She bent her legs and used the bed next to her to pull herself up to a standing position. Becker quickly got to his feet and assisted her effort, though she shook his hand off her elbow as soon as she was upright. "I don't know what your demons are," she said, looking so directly at him that he had to quell the impulse to glance away. "And I suspect that you don't easily express that kind of thing to anyone, let alone a kitchen-chained nanny," she added, a derisive smile tugging at her lips. "But I'd hate to see you storming around here feeling like you're the only person who's ever gotten a taste of the worst life has to offer."

"Jade, I didn't mean to insult you by . . ."

She held up her hand to silence him, the softness and compassion back in her gaze. "Life isn't fair. Life hurts. Life tears us up, sometimes. We all have our crosses to bear, Mr. Becker." She caught herself. "Becker. Some of us respond with anger and addictions." She could see that Becker wanted to protest, but he held his tongue in check. "And some of us respond by choosing to spend our lives with people we love, in places we love, for however long life lasts." She walked toward the door, her steps slow and determined, and turned back with her hand on the doorknob. "It might look like cowardice to you, but I assure you it feels like living to me. Really living. Living with purpose. It's messy and it doesn't pay as well as some of my other ambitions might have, but it makes my days count." She reached up toward her head, hesitating as she cast him a glance that was, once again, filled with tears. Then she took hold of her hair with shaking fingers and slowly removed it from her head.

Beck felt his stomach clench and his breath freeze as Jade pulled off her wig, a combination of shame and defiance on her face. She looked him straight in the eye, tears on her cheeks, and attempted a shaky smile. "I was diagnosed six months ago," she said, "and it didn't take me long to figure out that I wanted to spend however many months or years I have left investing in something I love that truly makes a difference. Dying rich and alone . . ." She swallowed hard and shook her head. "Not much of a priority anymore."

Becker stood there staring at her, his mind a reeling kaleidoscope of questions and emotions.

"My doctors are still trying to adjust the medication so my chemo doesn't take so much out of me, but sometimes . . ." Jade pointed to the spot where she'd fallen in a near faint. "I've been doing as well as I can."

Becker was too stunned to utter more than "You have cancer?" The huskiness of pain in his own voice startled him.

Jade nodded and looked down, idly turning her wig in her hands. "Breast," she said. "And I'm going to be fine—I think," she added, looking back up at him. "But . . . maybe now you'll understand a little better why I can't stomach seeing someone—anyone—throw their life away. And why I've been . . . why I've been selective in . . . well, in just about everything, really."

Becker was dumbfounded. There was an acid taste in his mouth, a weakness in his legs, and a numbness in his mind that robbed him of the ability to say something—anything—that might express all he wanted to convey. "Jade, I . . ." Nothing more would come out. He was utterly, painfully empty.

Jade cast him a weary smile and said, "I should probably be heading home. There are leftovers in the fridge, if you don't mind eating those tonight."

"That's fine," Becker said, the intensity of his emotions audible in the words. He softened his tone and said again, "It's fine, Jade. Really." Again, he tried to formulate words that would express the maelstrom in his mind, but he simply couldn't.

In the doorway, Jade nodded her bare head, her eyes enormous, and for the first time, Becker noticed that her eyebrows were mostly gone. How many signs had he missed? How could he not have known? "I'll see you in the morning," Jade said softly. "You really should take a hot shower." She cut her eyes toward the bottles on the sill. "If I can do this, so can you," she whispered. Then she was gone.

21

THERE WAS SOMETHING stirring in Lamorlaye that felt a lot like hope. The small town's inhabitants had until then responded to the German occupation with reluctant, imposed submission. But since news of the Normandy landings had reached them, their attitude toward the unwelcome presence of the Wehrmacht had begun to change. It was visible in the glances shopkeepers shot at their German customers and in the whispered conversations that happened behind shielding hands as officers and soldiers walked Lamorlaye's streets. The tolerance of the French for their invaders had reached its end.

At sundown, neighbors crowded into the homes of those who owned radios and listened for the latest news of the liberation that seemed to be happening on multiple fronts. The Canadians were moving into Alsace. In southern France, combined forces from the United States, Spain, and Poland pushed through the impressive

German resistance in the Pyrenees and began herding the Nazis eastward. The French Resistance grew so quickly and so enthusiastically in those weeks that even a small town like Lamorlaye saw dozens of its young men and women join the cause. There was a brightening in the spirits of the inhabitants that was evident in brisker steps and friendlier greetings. The end, it seemed, was imminent, and though no one could predict what the après-guerre might bring, they were eager to discover it.

At the manor, there was none of the levity Marie had witnessed in the streets. With the relentless approach of the American, British, and Canadian forces, the mood was heavy with a mixture of dread and determination. The Kommandant had so far issued no orders to dismantle the Lebensborn, but several of the new mothers had been sent home sooner than usual, leaving their babies in the nursery. No new residents were being accepted. There was a bravado-fueled wait-and-see attitude that only imminent danger would disarm. The latest news placed the liberating armies still 150 kilometers away, so Koch's determination to stay put was holding.

With just four expectant mothers remaining, one of them Elise, the manor was not the bustling place it had been weeks before. A handful of the nurses and maids had been released with the decreased workload, and Marie had been given even greater leeway to spend time with Elise. There was no real generosity in the allowance. As the seventeen-year-old's due date approached, she was finding it more and more difficult to control emotional outbursts born of frayed nerves and maternal indecision. Although it might have been easier for Koch to send her home to her estranged parents, the child she carried was an Aryan, and with the viability of Hitler's dreams for a world-dominating master race now widely questioned, every child needed to be counted.

The girls were strolling just outside the manor's front doors on a sunny morning in August when a military jeep carrying Kommandant Koch careened into the yard and came to an abrupt halt outside the manor. The vehicle had barely stopped moving before Koch catapulted out of his seat and took the steps to the front door three at a time. No sooner inside, he started bellowing orders for the staff to be summoned immediately to his office.

Marie and Elise exchanged worried glances and made their way back over the manicured lawn and graveled driveway to the manor's doors. Climbing stairs had become a bit of a challenge for Elise. With the baby's birth just five weeks away, she suffered from swollen limbs and imbalance. Her face and neck were rounder than ever, and her gait was sometimes so comical that Marie had to exert tremendous self-control to refrain from laughing at her whalish friend. When they'd finally made it up the front steps and into the manor, they took a seat on one of the Louis XIV divans in the entryway while Elise caught her breath, and waited.

It wasn't long before Kommandant Koch's office disgorged its assortment of nurses and officers. They came bustling out with focused expressions and hurried steps. Frau Heinz saw Marie sitting in the entryway.

"Marie! Get upstairs right now and help pack up the—"

"But she's supposed to be—" Elise wasn't pleased to have her friend sent off on an errand during their allotted time together.

"Elise," Frau Heinz snapped, turning on the frowning girl with a pointed finger and raised eyebrows, "we don't have time for any of your complaining today!"

"But Kommandant Koch said Marie could . . ."

"Elise! Be—quiet!"

The young woman's eyes opened wide. She looked from Frau Heinz to Marie, then back again.

"Go up to Frau Carpentier's room and start packing her things, then do the same for Frau Lejeune," Frau Heinz instructed Marie. "Their suitcases are in the attic."

"Are they leaving?" Marie asked, suspecting much more was going on than the mothers' departure, but afraid to overstep her bounds.

"We're all leaving," Frau Heinz replied, her jaw set.

"What?" Elise pulled herself off the divan, grunting with the effort.

"Everyone?" Marie asked.

Frau Heinz didn't seem inclined to explain more fully. "We're closing down the manor," she said. "The Americans are moving in this direction and could be here in as little as two days." She hurried toward the stairs.

"Wait! Where are we going?" Elise called after her.

Frau Heinz turned at the stairs. "The château," she said. "We'll be safer there until Kommandant Koch decides what to do next."

"But . . ." Elise's eyes were wide and terrified.

"Should I pack Elise's suitcases too?" Marie asked, hoping it would calm her friend's mounting panic.

Frau Heinz didn't turn from her ascent of the stairs as she answered, "Not yet. First, the other mothers and the contents of Kommandant Koch's offices. Elise will go after that."

"Wait," Elise protested again, "why not me? Why can't I go with the other mothers?" Her voice was teary and sharp, but Frau Heinz disappeared up the stairs without a backward glance.

Marie hurried to her friend's side. "Don't worry about it, Elise. You'll go right after the rest of the mothers. There's still time—the Americans might be here in two days, but it could take longer, too."

"But why aren't they sending me with the others?" she asked again, lips trembling. "Why do I have to wait?"

Marie helped her friend sit on the divan again and took a seat next to her. "Elise, listen to me. I don't know why they're doing it this way, and it doesn't really matter. You're going to get out just as soon as they've cleared the offices and sent the other mothers to the castle. There's plenty of time." She tried to smile reassuringly as she patted her friend's shoulder.

"It's because I'm not one of them," Elise said, her chin quivering and tears forming in her eyes.

"Elise . . ."

But the emotions that had plagued the young mother for months could not be contained. "I'm not one of them," she said again, her voice approaching a wail. "Their babies' fathers are SS, and mine is just . . . Karl." She started to cry in earnest.

"Elise . . ."

"You know it's true!" she wailed.

Marie grabbed her friend by the arms and shook her hard. "Listen to me, Elise!"

Elise gulped and stared, wide-eyed.

"It doesn't matter! Okay? It doesn't matter. Whether you go first or second or last—Frau Heinz said you'll be moving to the château too, so don't worry about it!"

"But—"

"I've got to help Frau Carpentier pack. Why don't you go to your room and start on your own things? Elise?" Elise was staring into space, a blank look on her face. "Elise!" Marie shook her friend again. "Come on—I'll help you up the stairs so you can start packing. Okay?"

"What's going to happen when the Americans get here?" Elise asked, genuine concern in her voice.

Marie didn't know, but she suspected the next few days wouldn't be easy. Elise was, after all, a Nazi sympathizer whose baby had been conceived out of wedlock with one of Generalmajor Müller's men. Whatever good Lamorlaye's liberation would bring, there would be *little mercy shown to young ladies like Elise. Even Marie might be less than welcome among her countrymen.*

"I'm not sure," Marie said, trying to sound reassuring. "But the best thing you can do now is get moved to the château. It's safer, and you'll be surrounded by the Wehrmacht's best soldiers." She coaxed Elise toward the stairs that led to her bedroom.

"I'm scared," Elise said, grabbing her friend's hand and pressing it hard.

"I know, but being scared isn't going to help anything. Come on—let's get your baby to the castle, and then we'll figure out what to do next."

Elise leaned on her friend as they made their way up to the second floor.

22

FROM THE SOUND of Philippe's voice, the boy hadn't suffered any permanent damage in his aquatic escapades. Beck could hear him yelling at Eva from the bottom of the stairs.

"Come on, you baby! See if you can beat me to the attic!"

"No!" Eva was clearly not in the mood for a race.

"I'll give you a head start. You can start five steps up."

"Ten!" Eva countered.

"Fine. But I get to say go!"

"Why do you always get to—?"

"Go!" Philippe bellowed before Eva had the chance to finish her complaint.

Twin pairs of feet pounded up the tightly wound staircase, past the door to Becker's apartment and upward toward the top floor and its attic. He suspected that their loud presence in the castle that morning had everything to do with yesterday's adventures and that the two troublemakers wouldn't soon be allowed to play outside unsupervised again.

The night had been . . . grim. After Jade's departure, Beck had nursed his bruised ego and shocked mind with the kind of self-loathing that had left him numb. To have once again fallen off the wagon was humiliating enough. But to have taken out his frustration on a woman whose ill health he should have been able to see—and not just yesterday, but since his arrival in Lamorlaye—that was unpardonable. He was a jerk of colossal proportions. Worse, he was a drunken jerk. The label afflicted him.

He'd spent the night's hours doing research into breast cancer and had come away with more questions than answers. In its most vicious form, it was a fatal condition that could kill in weeks if discovered too late. But there were lesser forms that seemed more treatable—more merciful. Much as he wanted to know everything about Jade's condition—and quickly—he knew those questions might be better answered secondhand.

He hadn't mentioned the previous day's exchange when Jade brought his breakfast to the office, somehow guessing that he'd want to take it there that morning. They'd been cordial and stiff, skirting true contact by limiting their interaction to hellos and thank yous. Beck had tried to surreptitiously take stock of the changes in Jade's appearance since he'd arrived, and now that he knew what to look for, the evidence was flagrant from the vantage point of hindsight. Her new hairstyle, the thinned eyebrows, the loss of weight, the sweating, the fatigue, the dizziness. They all pointed to what he now knew to be true. How could he have been so self-absorbed that he had missed the significance of such blatant signs?

The sound of Jacques's men hard at work forced Beck out of his self-accusation. There was just over a week remaining before Sylvia's birthday, and though the mountain of work still to be done seemed an insurmountable obstacle, he hadn't given up yet. He was on the way out of his office to the ballroom when the phone on his desk rang.

"*Allô,*" he said, strapping on his tool belt in anticipation of the work waiting for him in the ballroom.

"You still alive over there?"

Beck smirked and leaned a hip against the desk. "Back at ya."

"Oh, so we're going to blame me for the radio silence, are we?"

"You're the guy with the cell phone," Beck answered. He heard his friend laugh on the other end of the line and was somewhat comforted by the familiar sound. "What's up, Gary?"

"That's my question. What's going on over there? Just got off the phone with Fallon, and he seems to be wondering if this thing's going to get off the ground."

Becker felt a pang of anger. "What—did he call you to tattle on me?"

"No, I called him to ask him some billing questions. He was pretty upbeat, considering he's not sure if it'll get finished on time."

"You'd probably be wondering the same thing if you were here."

"Um . . . not music to my ears, my friend."

"We had a setback with the flooring in the ballroom. The guys missed dry rot the first time around, and we've had to tear it out and start over."

"All of it?"

"Yup."

"So . . ." Gary let a leading silence lengthen.

"So we've got a challenge on our hands," Becker finally said.

"A 'we can do this' kind of challenge or a 'we're in trouble' kind of challenge?"

"Call me back in a week and I'll let you know."

"Again—not music to my ears."

"Listen," Beck said, trying to sound reassuring, "we're as close to on schedule as we could hope for, given the setback. If the floor hadn't had to be redone, we'd be right on target."

"What's left other than that?"

"Putting the wainscoting back up once the floor is done. We're cleaning and restoring the walls and marble floors in the entryway now."

"Has the interior designer started moving furniture in yet?"

"Starts tomorrow. Right now, we're still installing light fixtures and window dressings, but I think she has a truck coming in the morning with a couple full loads." Becker considered the woman's recent propensity for chatter and added, "That should keep her out of my way for a while."

Gary laughed. "Not your type?"

Becker paused. "Remember that guy senior year who fired potato cannons at campus security and couldn't figure out why he got in trouble?"

"Billy Bloom?"

"I think Thérèse would be his type. Anyone more cerebral than Billy might have trouble falling for her."

"Wow. . . ."

Neither man said anything for a moment. "You still there?" Becker finally asked.

An ocean away, Gary sighed. "All right, this is your partner signing off and your friend signing in. Anything else I should know about?"

Becker smirked. "Subtle there, buddy."

"Just lookin' out for you."

"Nothing else you should know about."

"Really?"

"Just ask your question already," Becker finally ordered, knowing full well that his friend's curiosity was more pointed than general. "What do you want to know?"

"Drink much?"

There was a pause while Becker squelched the impulse to blurt an obscenity and hang up the phone.

"Beck?"

"I'm here."

"Hey, I wouldn't have asked, but Trish made me swear I would, so . . ."

"Is Trish there now?"

"Technically yes, but it's just past 2 a.m. here, so I don't think you'd want me to put her on the phone. She loses most of her social graces when I wake her up in the middle of the night."

"What are you doing still up?"

"Finishing the blueprints for our Nantucket renovation."

"Looking good?"

"What kind of a question is that?"

"Right. I'm sure they look great."

"So, about that other question."

"I'm working on it," Beck said.

"As in you've quit, or . . . ?"

"As in I'm working on it." Beck's hackles were rising. "You ever see me butting into your business?"

"You don't have to—that's why I married Trish." There was a long silence while each of the men considered his own life. "We're just worried about you. That's all."

"Hey, have you two ever known anyone who had breast cancer?"

"Come again?"

"Breast cancer."

"Yeah, I got that part, but . . . Why do you ask?"

"Would you just answer the question?" Becker snapped.

"Hey—chill."

Beck dropped his head and took a breath. "Never mind."

"No, not 'never mind.' What's going on?"

"Nothing you can do anything about." Beck glanced at his watch. "Listen, I've got to get to work. We're not going to make that deadline if I spend all morning on the phone."

"We've been talking five minutes!"

"And every one of them counts."

Gary laughed, and Becker could imagine him throwing his hands up in surrender as he had so many times before. "Always a pleasure talking with you, dude. Let's not do this too often, okay?"

"Sounds like a plan," Becker answered, a reluctant smile in his voice. "I'm on top of things," he assured his partner, "and I'll let you know if for some reason we're not going to make it on time."

"Sounds good."

"Okay—I'm outta here."

"Call if you need anything—oh, and since I've seen you up against hard deadlines before, try not to bite anyone's head off, okay? Especially Thérèse. She might be Billy Bloom's long-lost bride, but you still need her."

Sylvia Fallon appeared the next day with a plate of pastries in a fancy bakery box. She waddled quite happily into the castle's foyer, where four men on scaffolding were busy washing down the limestone walls with a muriatic acid solution. The stones they'd already treated were several shades lighter than those remaining to be cleaned, and the effect brightened the tall, austere space considerably. She intercepted Beck as he was leaving the ballroom.

"Mr. Becker!" she called to him, approaching lumberingly and handing over her plateful of treats. "I told my husband that we should buy you a Porsche or a villa in Tuscany for saving our Philippe, but he suggested pastries instead," she said with a broad smile.

Beck was embarrassed. "You didn't have to . . .".

"Well, neither did you, but you jumped in anyway." She patted his arm. "This is a very small expression of my undying gratitude, Mr. Becker. Were it not for you . . ." Her smile slipped a little.

"You should give these to Jojo," Beck said quietly. "He got there before I did."

"That's what Eva said," Sylvia acknowledged. "That man does seem to appear at the most opportune moments!" She winked at Becker. "And sometimes gets punched in the face for his efforts, from what I've heard."

Beck hung his head. "It was a reflex."

"And one born of concern for my boy, I presume, so I appreciate it." When Beck shook his head and averted his eyes, she said, "Walk me to my car?"

He pointed over his shoulder. "I've got to make sure the guys are—"

Sylvia raised a perfectly sculpted eyebrow. "Just two minutes."

Beck hesitated only briefly before reaching around Sylvia to open the door. She walked out of the castle and down the marble steps with surprising ease, considering her condition, and headed toward her small silver Mercedes. "I had a long chat with Jade last night," she said when they'd reached the car. "She told me about your conversation."

Beck felt a humiliated heat in his chest and averted his eyes. "I . . ." He hesitated. When had his demons become a matter of general knowledge? "I haven't been drunk on the job," he finally said, his voice tight and his jaw clenched. "I'm trying to quit." When he glanced at his employer's wife, he was surprised to see a look of surprised confusion on her face. "What?" he asked.

Sylvia shook her head and hunched her shoulders. "Actually, Mr. Becker," she said, a sad kindness in her gaze, "Jade didn't mention anything about drinking."

Beck raked his fingers over his scalp and stared at the ground. "I thought you meant . . ."

"No need to explain yourself, Mr. Becker. If you tell me it's under control, who am I to judge?"

"It's . . . I'm working on it," Beck said, unwilling to lie to pacify his employer.

"Well, that's a good start, isn't it," Sylvia said, her eyes a little more intense than usual, as if she were trying to gauge the severity of his addiction from his expression. When a few seconds had passed, she nodded, then said, "What Jade and I talked about was her illness."

She had Beck's undivided attention, the discomfort of their previous conversation paling in comparison to the urgency of this topic. "She told me she had cancer. Last night."

Sylvia turned to lean against her low-riding car. "The way she remembers it, you were fairly stunned."

At that, Beck let out a chuckle that was self-deprecating and devoid of humor. "Yeah, you could say that."

"I know it might be a difficult subject for you to talk about with her. It's in the breast, after all, and you Americans seem particularly awkward when discussing some parts of the human anatomy. So . . ." She paused long enough to dig her fingers into the back of her waist. "Sorry," she said. "Muscle spasm." A few moments later, when it appeared to have passed, she continued. "There are a couple things I want to share with you. That way you'll know the basics and won't have to bother Jade for the information."

"Okay." Beck wasn't sure where she was going with this, but he was grateful for any information she might share.

"We've known Jade for several years," Sylvia said. "We've attended the same church since we moved here, and when she was earning her master's degree at the Sorbonne, she did an independent study on the differences between the English and the French approaches to business. My Gavin was one of her main resources, and the interviews she did with him led very naturally into a wonderful friendship for all of us. She was so enamored with the twins when they were born that she volunteered to watch them for us whenever we needed help. So when we started to travel with the children, it seemed only logical to ask her to come along with us and help care for them—if her studies allowed."

Sylvia paused while a delivery truck from a local lighting store passed through the château's gates and made its way around the circular drive to the front door. Thérèse came rushing out in a flurry of waving arms and enthusiasm, shrilling instructions at the deliverymen before they'd even exited the truck.

"She's a character, isn't she?" Sylvia asked.

Beck nodded.

"And the best at what she does," she added.

"About Jade . . ."

"Yes—where was I?" Sylvia ran her palm over her belly in a circular motion. "This little one is eager to get out!" she said with a bright smile. "Either that or he's working on his air guitar in there!" She saw Beck's serious expression and got back to the topic at hand. "Up until six months ago, Jade was headed straight for a stellar career. Her doctorate was right on track. Prospective employers were lining up to hire her the moment she became available . . . and then she found a small lump in her breast. She was brave enough to see a doctor immediately, and the rest . . . Well, you know the rest."

"Is it bad?" Becker asked.

"It's not as bad as it might have been had she waited longer to seek medical help. But it's cancer. Cancer is never good—and it's always frightening. Because her mother died of breast cancer, Jade opted for a double mastectomy—about three months before you arrived here—followed by chemotherapy. They hope those measures will spare her from any recurrences, but . . . one never knows with these things. It sure is taking a toll on her."

"Then why is she still working?" Becker asked, finally voicing the question that had plagued him since the night he'd found out about her cancer.

"That's probably a question best answered by Jade. Do you mind if we walk a little?" she asked, applying pressure to her back again. "It seems to be better for me than standing still."

"Sure."

Sylvia led off toward the clearing on the far side of the stream. "When she asked to see us a couple weeks after her diagnosis, we figured it was to tell us that she wouldn't be able to travel with us for the foreseeable future. Imagine our surprise when she informed us instead that she wanted a full-time job taking care of the twins. We'd just announced that I was expecting number three, although it was fairly obvious by then."

"And you just said, 'Sure, you can work for us while you go through chemo'?"

Sylvia paused and looked at him with long-suffering kindness. "We're not tyrants, Mr. Becker." As she resumed walking, she added, "It took us a long time—and many conversations with Jade—before we offered her the position she now holds. And it came with some pretty strict rules. She was to quit the moment it became too much . . . but you saw what happened the last time she got really bad. She took a couple days off, then was back on duty as soon as she could stand up straight again."

"Why?" Beck asked. "Why does she want to be working when she should be home resting?"

Sylvia considered his question for a moment. "That's probably another one of those questions you should ask her," she said. "But from what she's explained to me, it comes from the new set of priorities her cancer inspired. I think that, when she came face-to-face with her mortality, she tried to figure out how she wanted to spend the remainder of her days—particularly if they were limited. And that led her where she is now—working with children she adores in a setting she's loved since she was a child."

"She needs to take a break," Becker said, his voice firm. "She practically passed out the other day, and I don't think—"

"It's her decision to make," Sylvia interrupted.

Becker didn't like the disclaimer. "What—so you're going to stand by and not step in while she wears herself out? How can you do that?"

"Sometimes helping others isn't controlling them, Becker. Sometimes it's supporting them until they can reach their own conclusions, in their own time." She stopped and faced him, eyebrows drawn together in sincerity. "I won't let Jade harm herself for the sake of my children. Neither will Gavin. But we're both committed to letting her make her own decisions as she battles this deadly disease. It's the least we can do for someone we love." She gave him a pointed look. "Isn't it?"

This again, Becker thought as he stretched out his hamstrings in the dim glow of a full moon. The Internet had exhausted its distractions hours ago and so had the accounting ledgers he'd pored over while the sun had set. That had left him with nothing but the castle's noises to occupy his mind, and it had drifted toward the usual quagmires. On the one hand was the lure of alcohol's anesthetic. He was back to fighting it, having so blissfully indulged in it the night after Philippe had fallen into the river. And on the other hand was his preoccupation with Jade. *Preoccupation* probably wasn't the right word, but it was a safe word. Safer, anyway, than the alternatives.

As Becker set off at a slow trot around the now-familiar circuit through the woods, he tried very hard to focus on the efforts of his legs and lungs, on the sounds of night owls and the shadows the moon cast as it pierced, smokelike, through the branches above him. There was no evading the nagging in his mind, the wordless onslaught of question after question that rang like a metronome in his thoughts.

He'd been drawn to Jade since the first day he'd met her. That much he knew. But the attraction had shifted somewhere along the way, from curiosity to a deeper desire to shield and protect. These were frightening emotions to Beck, both because of what they said about him and what they said about Jade. What they said about him was that his defenses had weakened at some point during his time in Lamorlaye, leaving him exposed in a way he had avoided at all costs for the past couple of years. What they said about her was that she was dangerous to him. Both conclusions left him with only one option that would satisfy his need for independence and invulnerability: flight. And with that word came the craving for escape he'd been battling again in recent hours, the need for a drink that would allow him to be absent without leaving the château.

Beck picked up his pace and focused harder. He needed to man up. Get back into the swing of hard labor and keep his eye on the end goal. He'd been weakened by the luxury of thought and the softness of sympathy. He'd been . . .

The pep talk was pointless. As he raced through the woods on straining legs, the image in his mind wasn't of the château's renovation or the prospect of insanely busy days ahead. It was of Jade—soft eyes and enigmatic smile. He could tell himself all he wanted that his feelings for her had everything to do with the boredom of being alone, but he knew better. He'd been captivated from day one, and her recent revelation had only served to deepen his desire for a deeper, fuller connection. She was stubborn and contentious and often holier-than-thou, but there was something about her—something in the words she spoke and the way she looked at him—that moved him. He didn't like it and he certainly didn't want it, but the attraction was undeniable. So, flight? It was an urgent instinct to which only part of him wanted to yield. The rest of him, the part he couldn't control, was frighteningly content to dabble in the dangerous.

As Becker rounded the front of the castle, he saw a vague shadow crossing the lawn in the direction of the gatehouse. On a whim, he veered off course and headed toward the stooped figure in the ratty gray coat. The older man paused when he saw the change of course, and Becker couldn't blame him for stepping back cautiously as he drew near. He stopped a few feet from the man whose steely eyes, shaded by thick eyebrows, watched him with disturbing intensity.

Out of breath from the run, Becker greeted him, speaking in French. "I never saw you after . . . I should have . . ." He took a deep breath and held out a hand, causing the older man to step back again. "No, I don't mean any harm," Beck hastily explained, retracting his hand for fear of further spooking Jojo. "It's just . . . I shouldn't have hit you. It was completely a reflex. I saw you holding Philippe and . . . I didn't think."

Jojo nodded, but otherwise he stood stock-still.

"I'm trying to apologize here," Becker said after the silence had stretched into uncomfortable territory. "I hope I didn't hit you too hard. Like I said, it was—you know—involuntary."

Jojo nodded again and set off toward his house.

"So . . . no harm done?" Beck called after him.

The figure disappearing into the midnight mist merely held up a hand in acknowledgment. Becker figured that was as much communication as he could expect from the old man and turned to head back to the castle.

23

THE KIDS WERE off at a doctor's appointment with their parents again. Jacques's men were on their lunch break, and the crew cleaning the limestone walls in the entryway had finished with that task and moved on to the marble floors. Thérèse had decided that the chandelier above the grand staircase needed replacing after all—it was an argument she'd been having with herself since Beck's arrival—and had gone off to an antiques warehouse in Chantilly, where she'd eyed something suitable to grace the newly restored centerpiece of the castle's foyer.

Beck entered the kitchen so briskly and with such determination that Jade paused in the act of peeling potatoes, one eyebrow raised in question. Beck marched over to the sink and, with a look of ferocious concentration, proceeded to empty each of the five bottles he carried down the drain. He then placed them in the glass-recycle bin under the sink and turned to Jade, hands on hips, something resembling victorious frustration drawing his eyebrows together.

"It's too hard," he said.

Jade put down the half-peeled potato she was holding and wiped her hands on her apron before crossing her arms. "And yet you did it. Well done, Becker."

"Not that," Beck scoffed, motioning at the drain down which his collection of booze had disappeared. "You."

"Me?"

"I can't do this 'barely friends' thing. It's a ridiculous notion, and I think you know that."

Jade's chin rose a little higher. "And yet it's the choice I've made, so you really have no option but to—"

"What? Obey?" Becker asked.

"No, that sounds superior. *Concede* might be a better word."

"Let me make this very clear," Becker said, ignoring her. "Part of me doesn't want to be your friend. It doesn't want to worry about you, and it doesn't want to wonder what I could possibly do to make life easier on you."

"That's flattering."

"And I've got to tell you that I'd much rather storm around the castle half-sloshed with an assortment of reasons to mouth off at workers than be concerned about you, but you won't let me!"

"Excuse me?" Frustration and astonishment dueled in her gaze.

"You won't let me! You're all about laying off the booze and checking my temper at the door, which leaves me . . ." He paused, desperately searching for the right word and raising a finger in victory when he found it. "Which leaves me *raw*."

"Are you sure you haven't been drinking?"

"It's like every nerve ending and every synapse is alive, which means I can't turn my brain off, which means I can't just ignore that I want to . . . to . . . to help you somehow. If you hadn't spent all this time talking me out of drinking, I wouldn't be so incredibly aware every single minute of the day that you've got . . ." He stumbled on the word. "Cancer. You've got cancer."

"Yes, Becker, I know."

"So you're just going to have to come to grips with the notion that I want to . . . to . . ."

Jade raised an eyebrow, a smile playing around her lips. "Under any other circumstances, I'd suggest a word or two that might fit in that sentence, but this monologue has been so perplexing that I'm fresh out of ideas."

"Are you finished?"

Jade merely smiled.

Beck took a deep breath and continued. "You're going to have to deal with the notion," he began again, "that I want to—I don't know—help you. And maybe know you more. You tell me that's crossing some kind of point-of-no-return line, but it's a line I only want to cross when I'm sober, so really, you have no one to blame but yourself."

"What are you trying to say, exactly?"

"How many more months of chemo do you have?" he asked, surprising her.

"You want to know about my treatment?"

"I want to know about you. How many months?"

"Six more rounds." She seemed too taken aback by his direct question to evade it.

"And a round is a month?"

"Two weeks."

"How are you feeling?"

"Today, or . . . ?"

"Now. Right now. How are you feeling?"

The smile on Jade's face spread wider. "I'm fine, thank you very much."

"Can I do anything for you? You need to sit down for a minute or anything?"

"You could begin by letting me get back to my peeling. That's what I need from you, Mr. Becker. Nothing more." She reached for the peeler she'd set on the sink, dismissing him.

Something in Beck wanted to launch into a full-blown rant. Visions of tossing the potatoes across the floor surged through him, the anticipation of such behavior alone a welcome adrenaline rush. But he quelled the impulse with the kind of effort that left him feeling weak and took a moment to calm his nerves.

When Jade looked back at Beck it was with firm resolve in her eyes. "I think I can make the battle in your mind a little easier to manage," she said softly. "Becker . . . I've said it before. I know you think you want to know me better, but I assure you that I have no time for that right now. My life is fighting off cancer and caring for the twins. Anything more . . . complicated than that would be too much."

"Then why have you ridden me so hard about the drinking?"

"For the children."

Becker raked his fingers through his hair. "And in the spare bedroom the other night—with the bottles—before you passed out. That was just . . . for the children?"

"It was . . . a lapse. I shouldn't have gone up after you."

Becker took a few steps away from the sink, hands stuffed in his pockets, head shaking. "Who takes care of you when you're not here taking care of the kids?" he finally asked.

"The Fallons make sure I'm all right."

"Who else?"

"That's about it. My father lives in Normandy."

"And you're okay with that?"

"I am. Life isn't about being loved—it's about loving others."

Becker's eyebrows lifted suspiciously. "What do you mean?"

"I mean that being loved isn't a priority. It's a perk. Loving others? That's a responsibility I take very seriously."

"You know what one of the main perks of being sober is?" Beck asked, an angry undertone in his voice.

"I'm sure you're about to tell me."

"It's being able to tell when your pithy little statements are full of it."

She paused for a moment, then resumed her peeling.

"You know that being loved is more than a perk! If you've dedicated this part of your life to loving those kids, it's because you know it's good for them." He braced himself for the statement he had to make but dreaded voicing. "We . . ." Courage failed him for just a moment, but when Jade looked up at him with a challenging glare, he found the bravura to say it. "We all need to be loved. It's what feeds us."

Jade paused again in her peeling and murmured, "How ironic to hear those words coming from you."

Becker sighed. "I think your self-sacrifice is an admirable thing, particularly under these circumstances, and I realize it takes up a lot of your time. But I also think there has to be some other reason you beat me off with a stick every time I come near you. I don't know what it is—but I'm pretty sure it has nothing to do with your highfalutin altruism."

Jade dropped her peeler and turned to face him, her jaw set. "Dinner will be served in an hour," she said.

"Fine—I'll be in the foyer helping with the stone restoration. Might take my mind off the shakes and cold sweats. Thanks a lot for this sobriety thing."

This time, Beck called the police. The previous nocturnal visits had caused no damage to the castle and had done more to entertain his imagination than to harm the building. But when Beck rose at the crack of dawn the day before the Fallons' party and toured the castle looking for anything he might have overlooked in the last-minute rush to meet the deadline, he found a surprise waiting for him in the entryway that made calling law enforcement a no-brainer.

With Thérèse fully invested in a decorative frenzy, Fallon had taken it on himself to have all the doors of the castle replaced by new ones a local artisan had designed in conjunction with a security specialist. The doors matched the old ones nearly perfectly, but they also vastly improved the insulation and safety of the castle's entrances. Even the half-dozen French doors that led from the château's interior to the patios had been upgraded to modern, antique-looking replacements. The result, they all agreed, was stellar. Even more satisfying to Fallon than the antique appearance of the structures was the series of rods hidden inside each door that extended into the stone beneath and above it when the elaborate lock was turned.

The air grew cooler as Becker approached the foyer. He felt the hair on the back of his neck rising. He'd locked the doors himself the night before, and it was still too early for anyone else to have opened them. The first thing he registered as he reached the entryway was the glass lying on the floor just inside the front door. At some point during the night, someone had broken two vertical rows of the door's windows and apparently tried to hacksaw through the wood that separated them, finding only too late that the veneer concealed a metal core. Whoever had attempted to forge a wide passageway through the front door and into the castle had found their efforts thwarted by Fallon's fortified investment.

Beck turned to retrace his steps to the office and call his employer with the news, but he stumbled as he glanced into the sitting room Thérèse had installed in the circular space of the southeast tower. He'd been so focused on the front doors as he'd passed the room earlier that he hadn't noticed the displaced furniture and severely damaged wall. The Louis XIV divans and chairs had been pushed away from the limestone, and an entire section of carved stone had been pried out of the wall. The blocks now lay on the newly renovated marble floor, most of them chipped and broken from the fall.

Beck shook his head, incomprehension a bullhorn in his mind. The uniqueness of the wall had been pointed out to him the week before by Jacques's men. They'd discovered a section of smaller blocks that appeared to be chiseled sandstone. The contrast in size and color hadn't been very obvious until the walls had been cleaned, the limestone of the rest of the entryway turning a much lighter shade than the sandstone. The anomaly was about six feet in height and three feet wide, projecting up from the floor in the shape of a doorway. And though there was no expedient way of proving if it was in fact a walled-off door and if it led anywhere, the general consensus had been to break through it and see what treasures lay beyond. It had taken all of Beck's persuasive powers and the imminence of the looming deadline to talk the workers down.

Beck took a closer look at the damage. Most of the sandstone was still in place, but a chest-level section had been pried out, a couple feet wide and at least a foot deep. Though no larger than bags of sugar, the blocks of stone that now lay in a layer of their own dust on the castle floor must not have been easy to dislodge. Beck peered into the gap where they'd once been and saw nothing out of the ordinary. Just the marks left by whatever metallic tool had been used to pry them loose. Beck had a flashback to the well's cover and wondered if the castle's nighttime intruder had a thing for crowbars.

Fallon arrived within five minutes of Beck's call, entering the castle through the French doors in the dining room. The two men moved to the still-locked front doors and contemplated the damage.

"Well, they looked splendid for the few days we had them," Fallon said, his humor somewhat forced in light of the setback. He leaned in to peer more closely at what remained of the windows.

"Looks like our ghost tried to saw through the wood and widen the gap."

"That's what I figured," Beck said. "And I'm pretty sure he wasn't too happy when he found the security bar inside."

Fallon stepped back. "How wide do you think that gap is?"

Becker pursed his lips. "Ten inches?"

Fallon nodded and cocked his head to the side. After a moment, he said, "Given the damage to the wall, we know that whoever did this actually made it into the castle." He stepped forward and compared his paunch to the width of the opening in the door. "We can fairly safely assume that I'm not the one who squeezed through here," he said with a chuckle. "And I suspect Sylvia's out of contention too!"

"We need to call the police."

Fallon nodded, taking a cell phone from his pocket. He got through to the operator at the police station and explained the situation in British-accented French. "Jojo? No, I don't think it would have been him," he said after a brief silence. "The old chap's harmless." He paused, listening. "We'll be here," he concluded, ending the call. "They're on their way," he said to Beck.

While they waited, the two men examined the gouged-out hole in the wall.

Becker shook his head. "This doesn't look like something Jojo would do." He was surprised at the defensiveness he felt for the old man. "I know he's an odd character and all, but . . ."

"He's not a criminal," Fallon agreed.

"That why you haven't kicked him off the grounds?"

"He's part of the château's lore, really. And the French have strict squatter's rights that would make it illegal to evict him. As it is, I'm not sure he'd have anywhere else to go if I did force him to leave."

"And he'd have to get used to life without Jade's cooking."

Fallon smiled. "She's a bit of a saint, isn't she?"

The men turned and exited through the dining room doors as they heard a car coming to a halt outside the castle. They joined the two gendarmes on the front steps and answered their questions as best they could. Becker had trouble taking the men seriously. They were dressed all in blue—navy-blue pants and a pale-blue button-down shirt under a navy vest—and wore on their heads the kind of hat Becker had thought only existed in old movies. Their képis were ridiculous pillbox hats with gold trim and a small, hard bill. It was all Becker could do not to stare.

Fallon introduced them to Becker as Officers Vivier and Maréchal, then informed the gendarmes that there had been a few other minor nighttime incidents in recent weeks. He was soundly reprimanded for not reporting them. After taking pictures of the damage and discussing possible motives, the only conclusion all four men could reach was that a better security system would need to be installed, including surveillance cameras, particularly as Thérèse's antique furniture and decorative accents could potentially create more incentive for break-ins.

"We need to ask Jojo a few questions," the older of the two gendarmes, Vivier, said after they'd covered all the bases.

"There's no need for that," Fallon told the man. "He's never done any harm around here, and I doubt he'd be involved in this."

Maréchal looked at Fallon in surprise. "You seem fairly sure of him."

"I hardly know the old chap," Fallon said. "But he's lived here since Shakespeare was a child, so I can't imagine that he'd choose last night to begin wreaking havoc in the castle."

The gendarmes headed out of the castle and stowed their camera in the ridiculously common Renault they drove. Becker was certain he'd be able to outrun them on a moped. "We'll just drop by and ask him a couple questions," Vivier said. "See if he heard anything last night."

Becker had had enough. "He doesn't talk," he said, hoping the information would disarm the policemen's plans.

Vivier smiled a little too confidently. "We'll see," he said.

Fallon and Becker watched them walk the short distance to the gatehouse.

"Barney Fife has nothing on them," Beck said to Fallon, anger searing the edges of his consciousness.

"Barney Fife?"

"Never mind. American reference. But those guys are not the ones I'd call if I was in trouble."

Vivier walked up to the front of Jojo's gatehouse and pounded on the door. It took a second knock before it was opened. From where Becker and Fallon stood outside the castle, they couldn't hear what was being said. Jojo stood on the threshold, disheveled and squinting, shaking his head occasionally. Beck couldn't be sure, but he thought he saw Jojo's lips moving a couple times. He couldn't imagine what the old man's voice might sound like and had to resist the urge to stroll over to the gatehouse for a closer listen.

The younger policeman, Maréchal, finally closed his notebook, and, after a few more words, the two gendarmes walked back to the castle.

"Says he was in the barn across the way tending to a sick horse all night," Vivier said. "Didn't hear a thing."

Fallon nodded. "Probably true. He spends quite a bit of time over there, from what I've gathered. I can check with the owner if you'd like."

"No need for that. We'll swing by on our way back to the gendarmerie."

"Did you actually get him to talk?" Becker asked.

The gendarme shrugged. "Some. It got easier when I started asking only questions that required one-word answers. He's not much of a conversationalist, is he?" He crossed his arms and divided his attention between Becker and Fallon as he continued. "From what we've seen here, there's very little we can do. We'll keep our eyes open and make sure we send a car by at night. Are those gates always closed?" He pointed to the large wrought-iron gates that led into the castle grounds.

"I lock them every night after the workmen have gone and open them again in the morning before they arrive," Becker said. "Unless Thérèse or Mr. Fallon gets here first."

"And has it ever looked like someone had tampered with the lock?" Maréchal asked.

"Not that I remember. It's just a padlock."

"I'll look into having a better lock installed, gentlemen," Fallon offered. "And if you hear anything at all that might explain this break-in, do let me know. It's the oddest thing, really—going to all that trouble to destroy a section of wall . . . and just a day before the opening festivities. The timing couldn't be worse."

"You call us if you see anything suspicious—anything at all," Maréchal said, shaking Fallon and Becker's hands. "And make sure you contact your insurance company before you start cleaning up. They might want to see the damage as it is."

The two gendarmes folded themselves into their Renault and drove away, leaving Fallon and Becker no further ahead than when they had arrived.

"Well, my lad, it looks like I've got a couple calls to make. What do you think the chances are of having that door replaced by tomorrow?"

Becker hunched a shoulder. "It's custom made. I'm guessing it'll take longer than that."

Fallon pursed his lips and nodded, turning back to look at the broken door again. "You didn't hear anything last night?"

"Not a thing." Becker had run himself to exhaustion just after midnight and had been dead to the world within minutes of crawling into bed. "But I can assure you that I won't be sleeping so soundly tonight."

Fallon chuckled. "Don't lose too much sleep over it. If whoever broke in felt any animosity at all, it was clearly directed at inanimate objects."

Becker's mind was on the task ahead more than on his own safety. "We can't adequately repair the hole in the wall in the time we've got left," he said. "The best I can offer is to hang something over it for now, until we can get new sandstone blocks cut and installed."

Fallon's eyes lit up. "I'm sure Thérèse has something splendid that would look just stunning there."

Becker smiled. "I'm sure she does."

"That's it, then. Though Thérèse is not going to be pleased."

The mere thought of Thérèse's reaction had Becker smiling more broadly. "Break it to her gently."

"I'll be the epitome of British diplomacy, my lad!"

24

AUGUST 1944

THOUGH THE EVACUATION of the manor had started as a slow and meticulous process, by midafternoon it had escalated into something approaching mayhem. Marie had spent a couple of hours packing up two of the residents, trying to keep them calm but knowing too little to truly assuage their fears. They wanted to know what was happening, when the Américains were going to reach Lamorlaye, and what would happen to them when they did. All Marie could tell them was that Kommandant Koch wouldn't let any harm come to them. She wondered if the expectant mothers could hear the uncertainty in her voice.

It was just past 3 p.m. when an officer carrying a portable radio rushed across the lawn from the communications office and stormed up the stairs to Koch's office. He hadn't been there more than a minute before the Kommandant came out into the hallway and began barking orders. "Get the women into the cars! Pack the remaining boxes into the trucks and fill the rest of the space with whatever artwork you can take off the walls! You!" he yelled at Marie. She'd been helping a panic-stricken Elise down the stairs. "Leave her and fetch Frau Carpentier instead. She's in the solarium. You can take care of your friend when the other women are out of harm's way!"

Marie froze. She couldn't just abandon Elise, not while she shook with fear, pale-faced, terrified of what the next twenty-four hours would hold. "But—" Marie began.

"Now!" Kommandant Koch bellowed, making Elise whimper and Marie start.

"I'll be quick," she whispered. "Can you make it to the couch? You go sit there while I find Frau Carpentier, and I'll be right back. Okay?" Elise didn't respond. She just stood immobile, three steps up from the bottom of the stairs, slightly bent and clutching Marie's arm. "Elise?"

The eyes she turned on Marie were glassy. "I think . . ." She couldn't formulate the words, but when Marie's eyes traveled down to her friend's feet, she instantly understood. Elise stood in a small pool of fluid.

"Oh no," Marie said, her own panic rising at the sight. "Elise . . ."

"It's too soon," Elise murmured, her voice tremulous, one hand protectively covering her belly. "What if . . . ?"

"Fräulein!" Kommandant Koch yelled from the top of the stairs. "I've given you an order!"

"But Elise is—"

"Now!"

Marie stood immobile for another couple of seconds before launching into action. Her legs felt wobbly and her mind was numb with the riot of thoughts clashing in it, but she knew she'd have to be the one making decisions for her friend. "Elise," she finally said, her voice as firm as the hand that gripped her stricken friend's arm. "Go sit on that couch. Right now. Your water broke, but you still probably have hours before the baby arrives, and the sooner I get the other residents squared away, the sooner we can get you to the castle!"

Elise didn't budge.

"Elise!" At her wits' end, Marie half dragged Elise down the last few stairs and to the sofa near the window. "I'll run upstairs and get some fresh clothes for you. Change into them and stay here. You hear me? Stay here until I come back."

Elise's eyes were filled with tears when she looked up. "Are they going to take my baby?" she asked, the words barely above a whisper. "Are they going to take my baby, Marie?"

"Fräulein!" came the Kommandant's voice again.

"No," Marie said hastily. "They're not."

"But—"

"We'll figure something out, Elise." She grabbed the terrified young woman's chin and forced her to make eye contact, hoping her gaze held little of the panic she felt. "We'll figure something out," she repeated.

This time, Elise nodded.

"I'll be back with your clothes," Marie said, backing toward the stairs. "Just take deep breaths, okay?"

While the remaining residents prepared for their departure, the military personnel gathered every document they could find and filled large boxes to the brim with the paperwork of the twelve months of the Lebensborn's existence. There was no organization to their methods. They threw the documents into boxes pell-mell and carted them out to the front of the manor as quickly as they could. This was not the rigorously metronomed labor Marie had come to expect from the Germans, and their haphazard efforts to vacate the manor only accentuated her conviction that something was terribly wrong.

An hour later, the last of the expectant mothers had been helped into a limousine and sent off to the château. When Marie reentered, she found Elise still sitting on the sofa where she had left her, a look of abject despair mixed with surprised pain on her face.

"Elise, are you all right?" she asked, hurrying over to her friend's side.

"I think I'm in labor," Elise said, wide eyes begging Marie to contradict her statement.

"You probably are."

"Fräulein!" Kommandant Koch barked from the library's entrance. "You will finish emptying the library before tending to your friend."

Marie bristled. Though she'd been a willing employee for over a year, the imminent liberation of her town gave her courage. "No, Kommandant Koch," she answered calmly, standing to face him. "I will not empty the library. Not until I've taken my friend outside for some fresh air. She's in the process of giving birth to the Führer's child, and the least you can do is allow me to walk her out the door and find a place to sit."

There was a brittle silence while the Kommandant considered Marie's words. She stared him down, hands on hips and eyes blazing.

"Fine," he finally clipped. "Take her out the side entrance." He motioned toward the delivery doors at the side of the manor. "Then report straight back to the library!"

Afraid that he might change his mind if she hesitated again, Marie hoisted Elise to her feet and walked with her in the direction the Kommandant had pointed. A small Citroën cargo truck waited outside the door, nearly full with the boxes of documents, books, and small works of art the soldiers had been carting out of the manor for the better part of the afternoon. Marie ushered her friend toward the double doors open at the back of the truck.

"Come on," she said. *"We're getting in there. I'll help you climb into the back, and you'll be at the château in no time."*

"I'm going in a truck?" Elise wailed.

Marie grabbed her friend by both arms and shook her. *"Listen! There are no more cars out front. Frau Carpentier took the last of them. I don't think the Kommandant has any plans to take you to the castle."*

"But the other mothers—"

"Are carrying SS children," Marie said, disgust in her voice. *"Yours is the child of a stable boy, Elise. It doesn't matter to them whether you're in a safe place or not when your baby is born."*

Elise stared at her friend, paralyzed by dread. When she finally spoke again, it was in a broken voice. *"But they told me they'd take care of me. . . ."*

Marie shook Elise again, conscious that the Kommandant might come searching for them if too much time passed. *"They're* boches, *Elise. They'll do anything to preserve the Reich, and you and your baby don't count for much in that equation right now. So either we get into this truck and hope the drivers will take us to the castle, or we stand here and wait for the Kommandant to come looking for us."*

"There's no room in there for me," Elise said, her voice rising again as she glanced into the packed truck.

"Shh," Marie soothed. *"We'll make room."*

Elise's hand gripped Marie's arm so tightly that she flinched. Glancing at her friend, Marie saw the pallor of her face and the rigid set of her jaw. *"Contraction?"* she asked.

Elise nodded mutely, her eyes filling with tears of pain. *"I think the baby's coming,"* she said, horror and awe dueling in her voice. *"What am I going to do?"* she begged. *"Marie—what am I going to do?"*

Marie climbed into the truck, quickly stacking some boxes and repositioning others until she'd carved out some room. She moved a small trunk to the center of the space and motioned for Elise to come forward. "Here," she said, pulling her friend up into the truck. "You sit on this, and I'll stand behind you, okay?" she coaxed, wondering if the stacks of boxes would withstand the bumps and turns between the manor and the castle.

At that moment, two guards came hurrying around the side of the building, headed for the truck. When they saw the young women—one sitting, one standing—in the back of the vehicle, they came to a simultaneous halt.

"Was machen Sie hier?" the taller one asked.

Marie stood as tall as her five feet four inches allowed and, in as authoritative a voice as she could muster, said, "This is the last of the residents. Kommandant Koch's orders are that you get us to the castle now."

The men hesitated, suspicion in their eyes.

"Listen, you can go back in there and check with the Kommandant if you'd like, but she might have her baby in your truck if you wait any longer!"

The mention of Koch's name and the prospect of childbirth in their presence sent the men into action. They hurried to the truck, taking a good look at the precarious stacks of boxes surrounding the young women and, with an uncomfortable glance at each other, closed the girls into the back of the vehicle.

Though the small windows on either side of the truck were partially obscured by boxes, there was enough light in the close confines for Marie to see her friend's pain. "We'll be there in a couple minutes," she said as the engine roared to life and the truck lurched forward. One of the boxes slipped and narrowly avoided falling on Elise's head. Marie pushed it back into place and held it there with an outstretched arm. "Speak to me, Elise," she said.

Her friend looked up at her with so much torture and fear that Marie nearly let go of the box to grasp Elise's hand. "You can do this," she said instead, trying to infuse confidence and energy into the words. "We'll get you to the castle, and the nurses will be there to help you. You can do this, Elise. You hear me?"

"It's too soon," her friend said, a sob catching in her throat. "It's five weeks early, Marie. Five weeks! Even with the nurses there, it might not . . ." Another sob interrupted her sentence. "And what about Karl?" she wailed. "What if he gets sent to the front? What if I never see him again? What if . . . ?"

"Premature babies survive all the time," Marie said, the optimism in her voice not quite believable. "And Karl loves you. He'll find his way back to you. He will. I know he will."

"Don't let them take my baby," Elise pleaded, wracked by guttural sobs. Marie crouched down next to her friend in the crowded space and tried to soothe her. As the truck made a sharp turn, the box that had threatened to fall before toppled, hitting Marie's back and rolling off onto the floor, scattering manila folders around the girls' feet. As another contraction seized Elise, she rocked back, her head against the row of boxes behind her, biting her lip so hard that blood pearled around her teeth. Marie rubbed her arm and shushed her while her eyes skimmed the manila folders on the floor. Elise's name, at the top of one of them, caught her eye.

With one hand still stroking her friend's arm, she reached for the folder and flipped it open. Among lineage charts and medical reports were two pictures, one of Elise on the day she was admitted, a genuinely joyous smile radiating from the black-and-white paper. And one of Karl, standing erect in uniform next to an impressive stallion he held by the headstall. Marie handed the picture to her friend. "Look," she said. "Look at what I found!"

Elise focused her eyes on the small photo in Marie's hand and hiccupped, nearly smiling before a contraction sent her backward again, clutching her stomach and groaning. Marie pressed the picture into her friend's sweaty hand and folded her fingers over it.

"Hold on to this," she said. "Hold on to Karl."

And while her friend cried out in agony, Karl's picture crunched in her balled fist, Marie gathered the rest of Elise's file together and slipped it into the waist of her skirt, under the white shirt of her uniform.

25

THE CASTLE GLOWED under the falling darkness of dusk. The dining rooms and ballroom were bright with the crystal-speckled light of Thérèse's magnificent chandeliers. The Fallons' guests strolled the ground floor with champagne glasses in their hands, taking in the period-perfect details that made of the once-lackluster rooms a vibrant showcase for historical objects, antique furniture, and the *"nouveau vieux"* juxtapositions of Thérèse's visionary artistry.

Becker had spent the better part of the afternoon convincing himself that he had to attend the party, when all he'd really wanted to do was stay out of sight and observe the festivities from afar. He'd never been much for formal gatherings, and this one—at which he knew only the Fallons, Thérèse, and Jade—was particularly uncomfortable for him. When he'd placed a call to Gary the day before, he'd still had the firm intention of bowing out of the castle's inaugural celebration.

"Are you kidding me?" Gary had asked.

"It's just a party."

"Yes, it is," Gary said with emphasis. "It's the party that marks the completion of T&B's first project in Europe. So get your sorry self into that ballroom tomorrow night and drum up some more business, will you?"

Becker sighed. "Fine. But next time we do something like this, you're flying over. This is more your kind of gig than mine."

"You happy with the results?"

"Yeah. Although I could have done without the last-minute drama."

"Any news yet on the break-in?"

Becker chuckled. "If you'd seen the cops they sent out to investigate . . ."

"Not France's finest?"

"Tweedledee and Tweedledum. Make that *dumb* with a *b*."

There was something familiar and comforting about Gary's chuckle as it reached Becker across the ocean. With his part of the château project now virtually completed, his future gaped like a void before him. It was a destabilizing feeling that had made his resolve teeter and tomorrow's champagne seem a little too appealing.

"You booked your return ticket yet?" Gary asked.

"A week from yesterday. That'll give me time to tie up loose ends before I leave."

"Don't work too hard, you hear? You've earned a little R&R."

"We'll see."

After a few seconds of comfortable silence, Gary said, "Hey, try to enjoy the party."

"Yes, Mom."

"Wash your hands before you eat, stay away from the champagne, steer clear of ill-intentioned females, and don't bite anyone's head off. That cover all the bases?"

"Shut up."

Now, standing in the shadows at the foot of the grand staircase, Becker nursed the goblet of sparkling water he'd snagged from a passing waiter and observed the scene. Haute couture–clad guests stood in the entryway, their eyes taking in the graceful staircase, now restored to its original grandeur, the refinished marble floors, and the art Thérèse had tastefully hung in strategic places on the limestone walls. They wandered through the sitting room on their way to the dining rooms, oblivious to the story of the hanging tapestry that covered a portion of the wall. In the dining rooms the guests found impeccably restored floors, crown molding, and wainscoting, elaborate wall designs filled with period wallpaper, and window dressings that framed views of the circular drive completely surrounded with lanterns that flickered in the evening breeze. There was something magical about the atmosphere, but nowhere more so than in the ballroom.

Becker forced himself out of the shadows and made his way there, the lure of appetizers stronger than his reticence to socialize. The elegant room was bedecked with linen-covered, candlelit tables where trays of small sandwiches and other *amuse-gueules* were displayed. Guests mingled as they observed their surroundings, taking in the fine details of the remodel and complimenting the Fallons on the completion of their project.

Fallon and Sylvia stood by the fireplace, where a mellow fire burned orange. Sylvia's flowing empire-waisted floor-length gown in a stunning shade of red draped her form to perfection. She was radiant, her face aglow with pleasure. Next to her, Fallon beamed in a black tuxedo. He caught Becker's eye and motioned for him to join them. Becker shook his head.

"Come on, my lad," Fallon insisted, his voice jovial and loud. "No use being shy when you're the star of the show!"

Heads turned in Becker's direction, preventing him from beating a hasty retreat. He forced a smile and walked over to the Fallons, shaking the hand his employer extended.

"Becker, I want you to meet Yves and Marilène Claudot," he said in his British-laced French. "They're quite impressed with what you've done here."

"Thanks," Becker said, eager to get away. "I'm pleased with the results."

"Is that a *québécois* accent I hear?" Marilène asked, her interest piqued.

Becker saw his chance at escape slipping away. "I was born in Montreal. . . ." He paused as his eyes fell on Thérèse. She stood just outside the closed French doors that led from the ballroom to the small terrace, looking in through the glass, her bright-yellow dress vividly outlined against the darkness. Her face, slightly obscured by the reflections of light on the windowpane and the darkness beyond it, bore an expression of such intense emotion that Becker quickly excused himself and made his way out of the ballroom, entering the terrace through the doors under the grand staircase. When he got there, Thérèse was gone.

"Thérèse?" he called, somehow disturbed by his glimpse of the woman's face.

No one answered. Beck walked over to the spot where Thérèse had stood and looked into the ballroom, taking in the animated conversations, the coming and going of champagne-bearing waiters, and the muted strains of the string ensemble that played just inside the ballroom's doors. The scene might have belonged in a historical movie, framed as it was by tall windows and French doors, the long gowns and tuxedos of the guests lending an old-world glamour to the picture. Becker wondered what it was that had kept Thérèse frozen to that spot, contemplating the celebration with a look of utter sadness on her face.

The caterer's maître d' bustled into the ballroom and whispered something in Fallon's ear. With the kitchen part of the remodel not yet begun, the Fallons had enlisted the assistant chef and waitstaff of an upscale Parisian restaurant to cater the event, and the meal was about to begin.

Fallon turned toward the guests and bellowed, "If I might have your attention!"

Becker found his place at the round table where the Fallons sat and eyed the empty seat Thérèse should have filled. As the guests were escorted to their places, Jade and the children entered from the office. They'd been sequestered in the north wing of the château since the portrait shoot that had taken place earlier in the afternoon. Becker had stood by and watched the family posing on his staircase—not his, theirs—and had felt something akin to satisfaction spreading in his chest. It had been a long time since anything that warm or positive had crossed his emotional landscape, and the realization sobered and discomfited him.

The first four courses went by unbearably slowly, though each was exquisitely prepared and displayed on elegant china plates. The sommelier hired for the evening paid special attention to the Fallons' table, coming again and again to refill their wine glasses and extol the praises of the new bottles he introduced with every course. Tension mounting, Becker covered his crystal goblet each time the sommelier leaned his bottle over it, but by the time the cheese course came, he'd had enough. He pushed his chair back so hard that it groaned against the parquet, startling nearby guests into a moment of silence. "Sorry," he said, raising a hand in apology. "I was just . . ." He caught Jade's eye across the table and felt a pang of rebellion at the look of warning on her face. Without another word, he left the room.

Beck went straight from the dining room to his apartment, his heart beating too fast and his hands clammy. He threw himself down onto his bed, covered his eyes with his arm, and concentrated on calming his breathing. The combination of social stress and the sommelier's repeated visits had pushed him frighteningly near to the limit of his self-control. The frantic busyness of the past few days had kept him too occupied or too exhausted to give much heed to the static that occasionally arose, but now that there were no more deadlines to meet or damages to repair, the static was becoming a more formidable enemy.

When his heartbeat had slowed and the initial intensity of the episode had passed, Beck levered himself off the bed and went to the window, opening it to let the fresh night air cool his body. Some of the lanterns around the drive had begun to go out, and the gap-toothed appearance of the interrupted circle seemed contradictory to the sounds of the Fallons' lavish party reaching him from below. He saw a figure passing under the juniper trees that stood like sentinels along the stately stables and leaned forward, squinting into the night. Probably Jojo on his way back from the neighbor's again. Beck wondered how much time he spent over there at night, calming the horses with his presence as he had on the boulevard weeks ago.

A creaking floorboard alerted Beck to someone's presence in the apartment. He turned to find Jade standing in his doorway, looking uncomfortable. Neither of them said anything for what felt like an interminable moment. Beck fought down the sarcastic remarks that always seemed at their most vicious when his cravings peaked, and Jade looked surprised to find herself standing there.

"Did you want something?" Becker finally asked.

"The kids wanted to know why you haven't come back to dinner."

Becker raised an eyebrow, giving her time to amend her statement.

Jade rolled her eyes. "Fine," she said with a self-deprecating head shake. "I was wondering too."

Part of Beck wanted to bark at her that he didn't need a guardian. The other part was somewhat heartened by her statement. Before he could decide which of the two would win out, Jade said, "Mr. Fallon wanted you to know that you don't have to come back down. He said something about forcing a square peg into a round hole and suggested that you'd be happier up here than sitting at the table."

Beck nodded. "Thank him for me. The only thing that could talk me into going back into that dining room is exactly what made me leave in such a hurry."

"I'm sorry about the sommelier," Jade said, her gaze honest. "It's just that a French dinner without wine . . ."

Beck held up his hand. "No need to explain. The problem's mine, not Fallon's."

The silence stretched until it became uncomfortable again. Jade finally broke it. "I'll put some dessert aside for you when it's served. The chef's crème brûlée is the reason the Fallons chose him, so . . ."

"Thanks," Beck said, feeling stupid as he stood there staring at her with nothing to occupy his nerves.

Jade turned to leave, and Beck took a quick step toward her. "Wait!" he said, before he'd had the time to think of what he'd say next. Jade turned and looked at him, inquisitive. All Beck knew at that moment was that staying alone in his apartment would probably not bode well, and with the guests now moving out to the patio for fresh air between the last two courses, a frantic run around the property was out of the question. "Can you just . . . ?" He moved to the chair that sat against the wall by the window and pulled it forward. "Could you just sit? For a while? It's just that—" He shrugged, embarrassed but determined.

Jade glanced down at his hand, which was trembling as he gestured toward the chair. "Maybe for just a minute," she said. "The twins are—"

"With their parents," Beck completed her sentence.

Jade moved to sit in the chair as another awkward silence settled over the room. When she looked up at Beck, it was with direct eyes. "Tell me what it feels like," she said. Then, with a smile, added, "And feel free to sit down first."

Beck raked his fingers through his hair and dropped onto the edge of his bed. "You want to know what the craving feels like?"

Jade nodded, shifting on her chair. "It's not something I can relate to," she said. "And it looks . . . it looks like it's pretty heavily on your mind right now."

Becker propped his elbows on his knees and clasped his hands to keep them from shaking. He glanced at Jade and saw nothing but curiosity in her face. Looking away, he tried to formulate words that would adequately describe the turmoil that wracked him with involuntary spasms. "It's like . . . ," he began, but the words failed him. He thought for a moment longer before saying, "It's like there are a million spots all over my body and inside my body that have a constant low-voltage current running through them . . . like a hum or static. It feels like exposed nerve endings, and . . ." He couldn't find the words. "It's like those nerve endings send these . . . these urgent orders to my brain—to yell, to throw something, to run, to cause myself enough pain in some other place so I won't feel their power anymore, to—"

"To drink," Jade said.

"Yes, but it's not for what I get from the booze. It's for what the booze takes away."

Jade leaned forward. "What stops it? What at least makes the craving bearable?"

Beck stood and walked to the window, looking out at the sputtering lanterns around the drive. "Depends. Sometimes just getting busy. But sometimes being busy makes me want to drink more. I don't know. Most of the time, nothing makes it more bearable. I can run until I pass out and still wake up reaching for a bottle. It's—" He paused, again unable to formulate the feelings into words. "It's brutal," he said.

Jade let the silence stretch. Then she asked, "How many days?"

Beck glanced at the project calendar thumbtacked to the wall above his bed. "Eight days," he said, both pleased and threatened by the number.

"Is that as long as you've gone?"

"In the past couple of years, anyway."

"Becker . . . ," Jade began. Then she stopped herself.

"What?" Beck said, turning from the window. "What were you going to say?"

Jade sighed and met his eyes. "If you need to keep yourself busy in the next few days before your flight, you're welcome to spend time with the children and me. We're not very exciting, but we might be better than the four walls of your office."

Becker was a little surprised by the invitation. "You sure?"

"It's . . . the least we can do."

Given the tenor of previous conversations, Becker knew the invitation had cost her dearly. "And that wouldn't be infringing on any of your 'boundaries'?" he asked, drawing imaginary quotation marks around the final word.

"You're leaving in six days—I think I'm safe," she said with a slight smile. "Besides, I don't want your relapse on my conscience."

"Thanks for the vote of confidence."

She smiled more broadly. "You're welcome. By the way, Mr. Fallon wanted to know if you'd be willing to come downstairs at the end of the meal. He wants to introduce you to his guests."

Becker nodded his agreement.

"Good. I'll send Philippe up when Fallon is ready for you."

She turned and left the apartment, her high heels clicking on the hardwood floor.

Fallon stood in the doorway between the dining rooms, a glass of champagne in his hand, addressing the hundred guests he'd gathered for his wife's fortieth birthday.

"My father brought me up to avoid mixing business with pleasure," he said, "but on evenings like this one, the two are inseparably linked. There are, of course, different types of pleasure represented here tonight, the foremost of which is my beautiful bride's fortieth birthday. Now, most women might prefer to keep their exact age quiet for fear of being labeled 'old,' but I think you'll agree that Sylvia's pregnancy is doing what no amount of plastic surgery and fibbing about her age could—it's keeping her young and vibrant and more exquisite than ever." As the audience chuckled and agreed, Fallon lifted his glass toward his wife. The guests followed suit. "Thank you, my love, for being born forty years ago and for spending the last ten with me. All that I knew and dreamed was empty before you." Tears shimmered in Sylvia's eyes as he concluded by saying, "Happy birthday, Sylvia."

There was a chorus of well wishes from the diners through which Eva's "Happy birthday, Mom!" cut brightly. Sylvia acknowledged her guests with a nod and bent over to kiss the top of Eva's head before blowing a kiss to her husband.

Fallon raised his hand to request silence and continued. "I must also acknowledge that this celebration marks the end of the long and tedious renovation project that transformed this castle into the banquet site you see tonight. There's more to come, of course. The hotel rooms upstairs are well on their way to completion, and the stables will be renovated after that. But this—this masterpiece," he said, pointing his glass at the grandeur of the dining rooms, "is something to be celebrated."

There were sounds of agreement from the guests.

"When Sylvia and I first dreamed up this evening," Fallon continued, "it was with the sad certainty that our plans were probably too grand to actually be accomplished. And then . . ." He paused dramatically. "And then I met a man by the name of Gary Tyler at a conference in Connecticut. Imagine my astonishment when he turned out to be one of the two owners of T&B construction, an up-and-coming company from the United States' east coast that happens to specialize in historical renovations! Gary gave me his card, assured me that our dreams were not unrealistic, and suggested I send him a more detailed outline of my French ambitions. And the rest, as they say, is history."

Motioning for Becker to join him, he added, "It is my pleasure to introduce Marshall Becker to you, the other half of the T&B team, the man whose vision made my dreams a reality and whose expertise in the field made of Lamorlaye's tired old castle the luxurious landmark it is today. Mr. Becker," he said, raising his glass, "I thank you."

Becker didn't hear the murmurs of appreciation or the smattering of applause. His eyes were riveted on the glow he could see through the French doors—a flickering golden light that seemed to be coming from the windows of the stable's first floor. Before the applause had died down, he'd made it to the French doors and thrown them open, now certain that something was seriously amiss in the castle's old stables. He grabbed the fire extinguisher that hung on a hook beside the curtains flanking the doors and looked over his shoulder at Fallon. "Call the fire department," he said.

Becker ran toward the stately building with the extinguisher, seeing as he approached that the door at the center of the building was ajar. By the time he reached it, the smoke pouring through it loomed thick and black. Becker shrugged out of his jacket and ripped some of the buttons off his shirt in his haste to open it. Then he pulled the neck of his undershirt up over his nose and pushed the door farther inward as he entered the building.

The fire had engulfed most of the wooden stairs just inside the door, its flames devouring wood and old carpeting as it went. Becker began to spray white foam on the flames with the extinguisher, but the fire was too vast and too well-fed for the small measure to hinder its destructive power. Outside the door, he could hear Fallon yelling orders to some of the men. "Get the hose from the garden shed, René! François, keep everyone back!" Becker knew there was a tap just outside the dining rooms that had been used in the past to water the flower beds, and he hoped the garden hose would extend from there to the stables to check the flames' progress until the fire department arrived.

Beck set to work again with the fire extinguisher, putting out the flames on the bottom steps and slowly climbing, hoping the stairs would hold his weight. He thought he glimpsed one of the lanterns from the drive lying sideways on the landing above and wondered if that was the source of the blaze. He was only five steps up when he heard the sobs. At first, he thought he'd imagined the sound, but when it came again, he stopped firing the extinguisher and stood still, ears straining. Though the fire's noise was growing, Beck could hear a whimpering at the top of the staircase, and much as he tried to convince himself that it was a trapped bird or rat, he knew it had to be human.

"Hello?" he called. He listened again, but this time he heard no sound over the crackling of the fire. "Hello? Is someone up there?"

Fallon, his jacket held over his mouth and nose, appeared at the foot of the stairs, his eyes defeated but purposeful. "Get out of here, lad," he said, gripping Becker's arm. "The fire department's on its way."

Becker shook his head, his eyes watering from the smoke, and pointed upward. "I think there's someone up on the second floor," he yelled over the sound of the fire.

"Someone . . . ? How do you know?"

"I heard something. I'm almost sure I did!"

The two men listened for a moment. "Probably just a—" Fallon stopped abruptly as unintelligible whimpers rose above the chaos once again. "I heard that," he yelled. "There is someone up there."

Becker pulled his employer out the door where they could hear each other better. "What's the layout on the second floor?"

"It's a long hallway with bedrooms on either side, but it's been sealed off at the ends."

"Is there another way up there?"

Fallon pointed toward the stables' entrance. "Just those stairs. I'm afraid they're beyond use already."

At that moment, the cries from the second floor grew loud enough to reach the men where they stood. They might have been the guttural, frantic call of a caged animal, but they ended with a desperate "Help me!" that made both men pale.

"There's got to be another way!" Becker said, his eyes on the flames blackening the windows of the floor above. His lungs felt scorched from the smoke he'd inhaled. He coughed and nearly threw up from the exertion.

"I don't think so," Fallon answered, his face gaunt with dread. "With the communicating door boarded up, the only way to the second floor is up those stairs!"

Jojo appeared so quickly that he startled Becker. He grabbed him by the arm and started to pull him toward the far end of the building.

"Wait!" Becker said, trying to pry his arm free, stunned at the power in the smaller man's grip as he dragged him away from the flames. "There's someone up there! We need to—"

"There's another way," Jojo said in French, spearing Becker with a look that afforded no discussion. "Follow me." With that, he let go of Becker's arm and set off at a trot toward the entrance at the far end of the building, an axe gripped in his hand. Becker might have hesitated or argued, had he been given the time to think, but there was something so authoritative about Jojo's words that he launched into a run without question and yelled back at Fallon to keep using the fire extinguisher on the stairs. He thought he heard the sound of water gushing from a hose and hoped he was right.

When they reached the end of the building, Jojo tried the door and found it locked. He made short work of breaking the lock off with his axe and pushed inside, quickly moving through two rooms of dilapidated living quarters to a narrow staircase at the back. He took the steps two at a time, so quick and agile that Becker was hard-pressed to keep up, but the memory of that whimpering voice pushed him on, up the stairs and into a hallway that was filling with smoke.

"Step where I step," Jojo instructed, his voice the sandpaper equivalent of his appearance. "You step anywhere else, you fall."

"The hallway's blocked!" Becker yelled at Jojo. "They barricaded the door to keep people out of this part of the building!"

Jojo trotted off into the smoke, holding up his axe in answer to Beck's concern. Beck mimicked every move the older man made, staying just a couple paces behind him. There were segments of the floor that had completely rotted away and others where the ceiling had collapsed into a heap of plaster and termite-weakened wood. But Jojo didn't pause. He made his way down the hallway as if he were walking on rocks in a stream, knowing exactly where to step next and which areas to avoid.

When the two men finally reached the boarded door, Jojo motioned for Becker to step back and swung his axe—again and again—until he'd obliterated a large portion of the wood, allowing even more smoke into the narrow corridor. Then he used the butt of the axe to whale on the boards on the other side that had anchored the door closed. Using his powerful hands, he did away with the remaining obstacles until a large-enough opening had been made for him to pass through. He turned back to Becker and handed him the axe, yelling, "Make a wider space!" Then he disappeared into the smoke.

Becker, once again, didn't dare question the man's instructions. He set to work widening the opening in the door, trying to keep his T-shirt over his mouth and nose and using his bare hands to tear away the last of the boards that blocked access to the other side of the hallway. Once the barricade had been removed, he ventured deeper into the smoke, praying that the floor under his feet wouldn't send him plunging into the flames below. "God," he murmured out loud, his voice rough from inhalation. "God, help me."

The smoke was so thick and black that he nearly collided with Jojo. "Get back!" Jojo yelled. "The floor's giving out!" He pushed past Becker without another word.

Jojo held a motionless woman draped over his shoulder. He carried her as if she weighed nothing at all, holding her in place with one arm across her legs and using his other hand to feel along the wall, as the smoke was too opaque to see through. Even in the blinding, painful billows, he placed his feet as precisely as if he were playing a game of hopscotch, his unerring memory of the space a salvatory gift.

As he followed, Becker recognized the canary-yellow fabric of the dress the woman wore, but there was no time for questions now. The sound of sirens pierced through the crescendoing roar of the flames as the two men stumbled down the stairs and out into the clearer night air. Jojo deposited Thérèse's unconscious form on the grass under a patch of lilac trees with a gentleness that astonished Becker. Then, rather than disappearing into the darkness as Beck expected him to, the old man sat on the grass next to Thérèse, took her hand in his, and began to stroke it.

"Becker, my lad!" Fallon exclaimed as he hurried to his employee's side. "Is everything all right?"

Behind Fallon, firemen aimed powerful hoses through the broken windows of the first floor. The guests stood on the terrace overlooking the front of the castle's grounds, watching the flames gutting the old building. In the center of the crowd, her red dress glowing in the reflected light of the flames, was Sylvia, a hand over her heart. Eva pressed up against her legs, crying, and Philippe stood stoically at her side, Jade's protective hands on his shoulders. If Fallon had wanted a memorable evening, he'd certainly succeeded in that.

"Everything's fine," Becker told the British man who stood disheveled and untucked beside him. There were smudges of soot on his clothes and face. He pointed his chin toward Thérèse. "Jojo got her out."

Just then, a large portion of the second floor of the stables caved in, sending a spray of sparks and flaming debris cascading out through the windows and down onto the trees. Becker and Fallon stumbled back, along with the firefighters who had been standing at the entrance, planning their strategy.

"All okay?" one of them yelled.

"All okay!" a couple of the men answered. They pulled back a little, adjusted their aim, and began to pour water through the two largest windows above the stairs. A second truck came to a halt behind the first, extending its hydraulic ladder and beginning to douse the smoking roof of the stables.

"I'm really sorry, Mr. Fallon," Becker said. "I don't know how this—"

"We're all safe," Fallon interrupted, laying a hand on the younger man's shoulder. "That's all that matters right now. We'll deal with the rest in the morning." He gave Becker's shoulder a warm squeeze, then turned and stepped toward the lilac trees, where Thérèse still lay, two paramedics at her side.

The hair on the right side of her head had been partially burned away, leaving raw, blistering skin. Jojo stood not far from her, his attention on the words and actions of the paramedics caring for Thérèse. They used a gauze pad to gently remove some of the singed hair that clung to the burned skin above her temple, seeking to evaluate her injuries, and exposed a small, heart-shaped birthmark that had until then been hidden by her hair. Jojo stepped forward, and his legs seemed to buckle for just a moment.

Fallon walked to where Jojo stood and extended his hand. "Thank you, Jojo," he said. "I don't know how you did it, but . . . thank you."

"You in charge here?" one of the paramedics asked.

"Yes, I am. How can I help?"

"We need to take her to the Chantilly hospital. Are there any relatives you can call?"

Fallon looked back at Becker. "Anyone you know?"

Becker hunched his shoulders. He'd never even considered a life for Thérèse outside of the château project. He was sobered by the realization.

Fallon finalized arrangements with the paramedics and saw Thérèse safely into the ambulance. Jojo never took his eyes off her. A muscle clenched in his jaw, and there was a softness in his eyes that Becker hadn't seen before.

"You saved her life," Becker said as the ambulance drove out through the gates. He smirked in spite of the dire circumstances. "You realize Philippe is never going to let you out of his sight again. You're a real-life hero now."

Jojo shook his head, a gleam of tears in his eyes. "I am no hero."

"You risked your life getting her out of there. That's more than most people would do."

The older man shook his head again. "It's what any father would do."

For a moment, Becker wondered if he'd misunderstood. The man's French was as rugged as his skin—harsh and clipped, the *r*'s too pronounced and the consonants too strong. Becker looked more closely into the old man's eyes, their expression nearly obscured by the starless night. Jojo tried to smile, though the contortion looked painful and awkward on his age-ravaged face. His steel-gray stare was as honest as anything Becker had seen before.

26

AUGUST 1944

THE CASTLE BRISTLED with activity and tension. When their driver opened the back doors of the truck, Elise and Marie were shaken from the ride and still braced against the tall walls of boxes. It had only taken a few minutes for them to get from the manor to the château, but those minutes had been interminable for Elise. Her face was ashen, her hair matted with sweat, and her eyes frantic.

"Find Karl," she wailed as soon as the doors were opened. "Find my Karl."

Marie hopped down from the truck and tried to pull her friend to her feet. "First, we get you inside. Then I'll find Karl."

Elise shook her head, a bit of hysteria in the motion, and pulled back, holding her stomach as if determination alone would keep the baby from being born. "No!" she yelled, the veins in her neck protruding. "No! Find Karl! I'm not having this baby until you find him!"

283

Marie was about to launch into a speech about how the drivers needed to unload the truck when Frau Heinz pushed her aside. "She's in labor?" she asked, one hand mechanically going to Elise's wrist to check her pulse while the other settled on her stomach, feeling for contractions. The head nurse's firm, no-nonsense attention seemed to calm Elise's panic.

"Her water broke around three," Marie explained, nearly reduced to tears by the relief of having someone else taking over Elise's care. "I'm not—I'm not sure how far along she is. We had to hide in the truck to get here—Kommandant Koch didn't want her transported with the other mothers. . . ."

Frau Heinz's eyebrows drew together in disapproval, but she didn't verbalize her feelings. "Contractions?"

"Every few minutes, I think."

The large German woman walked around the side of the truck and found the drivers leaning against it, lighting cigarettes. "You," she said, pointing. "Get up to the second floor. We've set up the infirmary in the room just to the right of the landing. Get a gurney and come back down. We need to get this girl out of your truck and into the castle."

One of the drivers took the cigarette from his lips and pointed at Frau Heinz with it. "This is not—"

"Go!" she said so loudly and so authoritatively that the two men jumped, then scurried up the steps to the castle.

Within minutes, Elise had been carried up the curving staircase and installed in a bed in a large room that had been converted into a haphazard medical space. Boxes of instruments lined the walls, and a delivery table stood near the middle of the room. Frau Heinz examined Elise, her eyes darting over her shoulder to make contact with Marie's. "Your baby is presenting sideways," she finally told the young mother. "Now, you're still at the beginning of your labor, so *there's a chance it will turn on its own, but we'll need to keep an eye on it." She turned to Marie. "Help your friend into one of the gowns in that box over there, young lady. You got her here—you might as well make yourself useful."*

Elise had been relatively calm as she'd been carried up the stairs and installed in the room, but as soon as Frau Heinz mentioned her baby's difficult position, she went from quietly frightened to panic-stricken again. "It's sideways?" she asked as Marie tried to help her out of her clothes. She grabbed her friend's hands and pulled her down, whispering harshly. "Marie . . . Marie, I can't do this. I need Karl. I can't have this baby without Karl!"

Marie sat on the edge of Elise's bed, prepared to soothe her, but Frau Heinz stepped in before she could. "Listen to me, young lady," she said to Elise. "Whether you like it or not, this baby is coming out. It might turn on its own or we might have to turn it ourselves, but you're giving birth either way. Now I realize that these aren't ideal circumstances, but they're what you've got."

"But Karl . . ."

The whining exasperated the nurse. "Your Karl," she said firmly, "is out there somewhere preparing for whatever the next day or so is going to bring. He's a soldier, not a nursemaid, and his place is with the rest of the men trying to secure this castle. Understood?"

Elise shook her head and released a low moan that grew into sobs. There was so much abject despair on her face that the stern nurse realized there'd be no calming her. With a disapproving grunt, she turned her back on her patient and focused on setting up the delivery table.

Marie stroked her arm, leaning in close to whisper, "Just breathe, Elise. Just breathe." But Elise could not be comforted. The pain of labor and the difficulty of the impending birth had combined into a toxic jumble in her mind, and what little grip she had on reality continued to fritter away as the afternoon wore on.

"*Please don't take my baby,*" she begged, her contractions neither speeding up nor slowing but intensifying with each passing minute. "*Please don't take it away.*"

"*Nobody's taking your baby,*" Marie said again and again, lowering her voice to a soothing pitch.

Frau Heinz was called away to deal with the urgent business of preparing the castle for whatever lay ahead. She recruited a young nurse to watch over Elise, leaving her with firm instructions to check the baby's position every hour and inform her if anything changed. "*If the child or the mother are in distress or if the baby hasn't turned within the next handful of hours, find me,*" she said. "*Unless I hear from you, I'll assume things are progressing normally.*"

Though the head nurse's interactions with Elise had been firm, they'd held an undertone of sympathy. That was not the case with Nurse Grüber, who replaced her during the afternoon and evening of Elise's labor. Whatever attention she paid to the pain-wracked girl was reluctant, and she spent more time outside the delivery room than inside.

Marie continued to stroke her friend's arm and assure her that everything was going to be all right, but she lived in private dread that Kommandant Koch would arrive at the château, track them down, and put them out on the street. As Elise's labor intensified, however, there was little more she could think of than the agony her friend was enduring. Elise rocked her bent legs back and forth, gripping her stomach, her head thrown back, alternately moaning and screaming with the pain of contractions. Marie wiped her brow with a cool cloth and gave her sips of water, but she was powerless to do more to ease her suffering.

"*Don't let them take my baby,*" Elise said again, after the sky outside the tower window had darkened into night. She gripped Marie's hand with both of hers, sweat beading on her forehead, a pain- and *exhaustion-fueled dementia tightening her features and widening her eyes. "Don't let them take it! Promise me! Promise me, Marie!"*

Marie made shushing sounds, but they didn't calm her friend. Elise arched her back as another contraction gripped her, her voice broken as she screamed, "They're going to steal my baby! They're going to steal my baby!" Her eyes clung to Marie's. "You won't let them, will you? Please? Please, Marie, tell me you won't let them!"

"Elise," Marie soothed, "first, you need to have this baby. We'll figure out what happens to it afterward, okay? Concentrate on bringing it into the world first."

Elise shook her head with such vigor against the pillow that her hair fell over her face. "I'm not going to be there," she said. "I'm dying. I know I'm dying!"

Marie gripped her friend's shoulders, as she'd done so many times before, and gave them a firm squeeze. "No, you are not!" she said, enunciating each word clearly. "You're in a lot of pain—I understand that—but you are not dying."

Elise continued to shake her head against the pillow, eyes closed, repeating unintelligible pleas over and over.

It was just past midnight when Marie realized that the nurse hadn't been in to check on Elise in a couple of hours. Her friend's agony had increased to an unbearable level. She looked ashen, her face swollen, her eyes wide and terrified, her lips slowly turning a frightening shade of blue. After several hours of mumbled moaning and a lethargic submission to the pain wracking her body, she seemed to regroup for just a moment. She grasped Marie's hand with her last shreds of strength and sucked air into her constricted lungs. Staring at her friend with wrenching clarity, she half screamed, half groaned, "It hurts. It hurts, Marie! Please—make it stop!" Then she slid into unconsciousness, her body seeming to sink into the mattress as her tense muscles unclenched.

Marie laid a hand on her forehead, then felt for a pulse. Her skin was cold and clammy, her pulse fast and weak. She'd never seen a birth before and had no idea whether Elise's unconsciousness was something to be worried about, but she had a feeling in her gut that she should get some help. Marie went out into the darkened hallway hoping to find a nurse, but it was deserted. Increasingly eager to have her friend examined, she crept down the stairs toward the sound of voices rising from the large room to the west of the entryway. She approached it quietly, her ears trained on Generalmajor Müller's voice.

"Our best estimates have them arriving in Lamorlaye in four days. That's if they don't drop parachutists on the town before then. We've received instructions to hold our position at least until tomorrow evening. After that, we'll either brace for battle or evacuate east." His voice was weary, though he tried to mask it with clipped words and an authoritative tone.

Marie peered into the room, trying to remain mostly out of sight, and saw that it was filled with soldiers of the Wehrmacht, Frau Heinz, Kommandant Koch, and the German personnel who had, until that day, run the château and the manor. There was a deep feeling of apprehension in the room that she'd never witnessed before, not in all the months she'd worked at the manor. Though these soldiers were putting on a brave face, it was obvious that they knew the immediate future would not be clement.

Marie scanned the crowd and thought she saw Karl sitting two rows from the back. She longed to take him upstairs to Elise, but there was no way of getting his attention without drawing some to herself. What she needed more was for the young nurse to resume her duties, but there was no sign of her among those assembled for the briefing. She retraced her steps and skirted the staircase, wandering noiselessly over marble floors as she followed the sound of voices coming from the other end of the castle.

The dining rooms were dark, and though Marie was spooked, she wasn't swayed from her mission. She eventually made it to the brightly lit kitchen and found the nurse and two maids gathered around a wooden table in its center, smoking hand-rolled cigarettes and playing a card game. Marie entered the kitchen with a confidence born of anger and stared pointedly at the nurse who had been caring for Elise for most of the afternoon. "My friend's been in labor for ten hours and is passed out from exhaustion, and you're down here playing cards?" she asked, the angry edge to her voice unmistakable in the sudden silence. "We need you upstairs," she said, adding a firm "now" for emphasis.

The nurse straightened in her chair and raised her chin in defiance. "Go back to your slut friend and leave me alone," she sneered. "I'm not wasting my time on a stable boy's baby."

Marie felt fury burning through her veins, but before she could retort, Frau Heinz's voice lashed through the kitchen with cold precision. "Go upstairs!" she ordered, her tone razor sharp.

The young nurse flashed Marie a contemptuous smile. "Yeah, go back up to your slut friend and—"

"I was speaking to you, Fräulein Grüber," Frau Heinz said, taking a step into the room and aiming a glare that held disgust and command at the nurse. "Get back to your duties before I inform the Kommandant of your reckless neglect of the Führer's child! Move!"

The nurse got up so quickly that her chair fell backward. She didn't pause to straighten it but rushed out of the kitchen, red-faced and humiliated, taking the back stairs quickly on her way to the second floor. Marie left too as Frau Heinz's voice rose in a diatribe against the maids still in the kitchen. She followed the young nurse down the long, darkened second-floor corridor and stopped only when she'd reached her friend's room. The nurse, still smarting from the dressing-down, went promptly to Elise's bed and felt for her pulse. She shifted her fingers on the young mother's wrist, eyes vacant. Pulling back the sheets, she examined Elise's belly, pressing here and there. Marie saw her jaw clench as she pulled the sheet back up and used her knuckles to apply pressure to Elise's sternum, trying to wake her. "Elise!" she said so loudly that she startled Marie. "Elise!" she repeated, applying more pressure to the patient's chest and checking her eyes with her other hand.

"How long has she been like this?" the nurse finally asked, lifting Elise's fingers and noting their purplish color. "How long?" she repeated more harshly.

"I . . . I don't know! A few minutes, maybe. She's been bad for hours—hours! But Frau Heinz said you'd let her know if anything was wrong, so—"

"Go get her," Nurse Grüber ordered, though it seemed a reluctant command. "Get her now!"

Marie felt the breath whoosh out of her lungs. She didn't ask any questions. The look on the nurse's face was enough to send her careening down the corridor again, her pulse loud in her ears, her legs unsteady. She found Frau Heinz coming up the back stairs and stammered, "Please come. P—please!" Though the older woman was far from lithe, she moved with surprising speed, covering the distance between the stairs and the birthing room rapidly. As soon as she entered, she was pulling on gloves and barking questions at the nurse. "What's her status?"

"I think she's gone into shock."

"What do you mean, she's in shock?"

"I don't know how it happened. She seemed fine last time I—"

"When was the last time you examined her?" the older nurse asked as she quickly ascertained the progress of Elise's labor.

"I don't know—maybe an hour?"

"It's been longer," Marie said, her voice rough with fear. "At least three."

Frau Heinz didn't say anything. She speared the younger nurse with a glare that made her step back and look away.

"I got busy," Nurse Grüber said, her trepidation audible.

Frau Heinz removed her gloves. "You were to tell me if the baby hadn't turned by the time she was fully dilated!"

"I know, I—"

"Be quiet! We'll have time for your excuses later. Right now, I need your help."

Marie stood in the doorway, nausea overwhelming her, her breathing ragged and her mind in a panic. She watched as the two nurses stripped back the sheets and began to apply firm pressure to the sides of Elise's belly, slowly rotating clockwise, then repeating the same procedure. There was a red stain growing where Elise lay.

"Is she all right?" Though she'd formed the words, no sound had escaped Marie's lips. She took a deep breath and tried again. "Is she going to be all right?"

This time, the nurses heard her. Frau Heinz glanced over her shoulder to the doorway where Marie had stood since the beginning of the crisis. "I'm not sure," she said. "If she has relatives—anyone—in Lamorlaye, now would be a good time to summon them."

"She doesn't," Marie said, the nurse's words knocking the wind out of her. "I mean, she does, but they moved to Brittany several months ago, and—"

"Who's the father?"

"Karl. He's downstairs in the meeting."

Frau Heinz shoved the younger nurse toward the door. "Go down there and get him. And don't come back unless he's with you!" she ordered, her attention back on the pale and motionless young girl in the bed in front of her. "This isn't good," she said to Marie.

Marie's composure shattered. Sobs shook her body as she sank to her knees in the doorway, afraid of entering the room and being a witness to her friend's death. "I told her she wasn't dying," she sobbed. "I told her she'd be fine. . . ."

The sound of boots racing up the stairs temporarily distracted her from her anguish. Karl came rushing into the room, still in uniform at nearly one in the morning. He stopped so abruptly when he saw Elise on the bed that he lost his balance and had to grab for the edge of the birthing table that stood in the middle of the room. He said nothing, staring horrified at the pale form in the bed. "Is she . . . ?"

Frau Heinz shook her head. "No—but she's critical."

"What happened?" He was as pale as Elise, staring at her with so much shock and disbelief that his face seemed frozen in a contorted rictus of pain. "She was doing fine when I saw her last week. . . ." He motioned toward her and shook his head.

"Her baby is in a transverse position—sideways. We thought it might turn on its own, but . . ."

"Weren't you watching her?" He turned on Marie, confusion and anger dueling in his eyes. "Weren't you watching her?" he asked again.

"That young lady never left her friend's side except to get help," Frau Heinz said, casting a withering glance at the young man, who hadn't moved from the center of the room since he'd stormed in. "I've almost got your baby rotated," she said, turning back to Elise and applying so much pressure to the outside of her belly that Karl cringed. "Get over here, Nurse Grüber. This is going to take both of us, and the baby is in too much distress to wait any longer."

It took them less than a minute to finish rotating the baby. Elise regained some consciousness, moaning from the force being exerted on her body. Once the baby was in position, Frau Heinz ordered Karl out of the room and instructed Marie to sit behind her friend and prop her up. *The young mother's eyes were open but unfocused. "Tell her to push," the nurse instructed Marie. And she did just that, urging her friend to bear down with any amount of strength she had left, while both nurses used their hands to apply more pressure to the top and sides of Elise's belly, pushing the baby down and out with enough force that Marie feared the procedure itself would kill her friend.*

The baby didn't make any noise after it was delivered. The younger nurse immediately whisked it away to another room. "What . . . ?" Frau Heinz murmured when a rush of bright-red blood began to pour from Elise's body. She reached for a towel to try stanching the flow. "Nurse Grüber!" she called. "Nurse Grüber, get in here this minute."

"What's happening?" Karl asked, entering the room at the tense sound of Frau Heinz's voice, his eyes riveted on the frightening quantity of blood spreading into the sheets. "Why is she bleeding so much?"

"Her uterus has torn," Frau Heinz answered, her voice a combination of anger and defeat. She discarded the soaked towel and reached for another one, applying pressure but looking as if she knew that it wouldn't be any help. "The labor was too hard, and the delivery . . ." She shook her head. "The pressure was too much."

"What are you saying?" Marie pleaded. "What are you saying?"

The nurse slowly took her hands from the blood-soaked towel she'd been using to absorb the hemorrhage and wiped the sweat from her forehead with her wrist. "There's nothing we can do," she said quietly.

"What?" It was a gut-wrenching cry. Marie covered her mouth with her hand and stared, horrified, at the nurse.

There was a moment of silence before Karl asked, "Is she dying?"

"Young man . . ." In a gesture of uncharacteristic kindness, Frau Heinz left Elise's side and took Karl by the arm, guiding the unsteady soldier closer to the bed. "We're not set up for this kind of emergency,"

she said. "And even if we were . . ." She glanced down at the pale young mother in the bed. "There is nothing—nothing we can do. A torn uterus is . . . I'm sorry."

The young woman's blood had soaked through the thin mattress of the bed and was dripping to the floor beneath it. Karl reached out and touched Elise's arm with his fingertips, seemingly too frightened to do more than establish that tenuous contact.

Frau Heinz, who had been using a stethoscope to listen to Elise's heart, straightened and laid a hand on his shoulder. "You need to say your good-byes," she said, including Marie in the instructions.

Marie swallowed the bile rising in her throat and tried to take a deep-enough breath to fill her lungs. "No," she breathed, but there was more confusion than conviction in the sound.

Karl took a shuddering breath as his shoulders sagged, and a low moan escaped his lips. "Why can't you save her?" he asked. "Why can't you save her?"

"I'm sorry," Frau Heinz said.

Karl didn't move as the nurse listened to Elise's heart again, then took the stethoscope from her ears. "She's gone."

27

BECKER SPENT MOST of the night watching the firemen trying to rescue the stables. All that remained of the building by morning was its shell, the majority of the interior having been reduced to a smoking pile of ashes. The firemen had battled the blaze until nearly dawn, on a couple of occasions thinking they'd tamed it before another hot spot burst into flames.

Fallon hadn't left the scene. He'd observed the firefighters' efforts from the sidelines until the police had arrived, then spent an hour or so discussing the circumstances of the fire while the detectives took notes. Becker had been brought into the discussion when they'd covered Jojo's rescue of Thérèse, but he'd found there were few clear memories in his mind aside from the stark urgency and the opaque smoke. And the expression in Jojo's eyes when he'd identified himself as Thérèse's father—Becker remembered that, too.

Fallon headed home around nine on Sunday morning, knowing

further investigation of the fire would have to wait at least a few hours for the ashes to cool. The firemen rolled up their hoses and drove their soot-covered trucks out the castle's gates, and Becker went inside to soothe his tense muscles and warm his fatigued body under the spray of a hot shower. When he exited the bathroom several minutes later, he found a breakfast tray waiting for him on his bed, the croissants and pot of coffee such a welcome sight that they made his knees go weak. The physical and emotional exertion of the night had sapped his strength and left him feeling hollowed out. The sole silver lining of the events was that the fire hadn't jumped the small space between the stables and the castle.

When Becker went downstairs, Jade was nowhere to be found. There was a pot of stew simmering on the stove and a note next to it that read, "Will come by later. Jade."

Unwilling to linger in the empty castle with nothing to do to occupy his mind, Becker pulled on a light jacket and headed out the gates. He walked along the fence that framed the château's property until it ended, then continued into town, past closed boutiques and storefronts.

At the edge of town, Becker passed a small church with a placard outside that read, *Église évangélique de Lamorlaye*. Music reached him through the redbrick walls, the sound of singing voices wafting out in nearly visible threads of something that felt like serenity. It was a small building, not much larger, it seemed, than a two-car garage, and Beck gauged from the volume of the singing that the people inside must have been stacked like cords of wood.

On a whim, he pulled the heavy door open, a wall of thick, warm air pushing past him as he stepped inside. Beck had never been prone to spontaneous acts of party crashing, so the impulse to enter the church took him by surprise. There was little he could do to backtrack, however, when he found himself standing just inside the doors with several pairs of eyes looking over their shoulders at him.

Beck cast a polite smile at a middle-aged woman who nodded in his direction, reaching behind him for the handle of the door in the hope that he could beat a hasty retreat, but just as he was turning to leave, he felt a hand on his sleeve and looked down into familiar brown eyes.

"Don't go," Jade said, her expression serene. "There's a seat by me."

Beck suddenly thought with fondness of the desolate quiet of the castle, wishing he'd stifled his need to flee. Empty rooms and the lingering smell of smoke now seemed a much more bearable fate than the packed interior of Lamorlaye's diminutive Protestant church, yet with Jade's invitation and the attention his presence was drawing from the other people present, there was little Beck could do but concede defeat. He ducked his head and followed reluctantly as Jade led him to two seats in the last row.

It had been nearly two years since Beck had attended a church service. On the previous occasion, he'd found a seat on the sparsely populated floor of the Cathedral of the Holy Cross in Boston, drawing comfort from the ten-story-tall granite pillar that rose from floor to ceiling beside him. Built to seat two thousand, the church had welcomed only a couple hundred visitors that Saturday, though their social rank and political clout had made of the gathering a who's who of New England's elite.

Becker had slipped in late, correctly predicting that the bride and groom would be safely facing the high altar when he entered. No one had paid attention to his arrival. He'd flashed his invitation at the door, sent to him, no doubt, out of spite—the same spite that had landed him in court for a protracted divorce trial that had hobbled his career and smeared his reputation. The same spite that had gone after his stakes in T&B and nearly bankrupted the young business. Gary hadn't wavered in his support—neither during the trial for battery nor during the divorce—but Beck knew he'd spent anxious hours poring over company ledgers as they'd sunk into the red, crippled by the greed of Beck's trust-fund wife.

There were few clear memories of the Boston wedding in Beck's mind as he sat in the tight confines of Lamorlaye's *église évangélique*, listening to a casually dressed man addressing the congregation. He remembered only the startling white of Amanda's wedding gown in the shadowy vastness, the muffled drone of the archbishop's voice, and the stifling constriction that gripped his lungs and mind as he witnessed the barely audible exchange of vows between his statuesque ex-wife and her tall and lanky new husband.

Becker was used to the solemnity of liturgical services. He'd found comfort, until two years ago, in the predictable, metronomic flow of organized worship, in the once-removed intimacy of confession and the sanitized conventions of scripted religion. He'd found his uncertainties and worries muted after soft-spoken services in which lofty sermons had settled his emotions.

Sitting in the Lamorlaye church on that Sunday morning, however, something began to tighten in Beck's chest as the speaker moved from reading the Scriptures into another segment of singing. Beck stood when the rest of the congregation did, but he didn't join in the choruses. As each song ended, he hoped for a reprieve, for a break in the flow, but there was none. And as voices all around him rose in a joyful, carefree expression of their faith, he felt his own mind shutting down. An impenetrable blanket descended over the fragile edges of his damaged faith and hardened into anger. He would not succumb to the naïveté of mass hypnosis. He would not allow the soothing words and joyful tunes to weaken his resolve. He would not fall for that manipulative drivel again.

When the singing led into a time of prayer, Beck felt a prickle inch down his spine. He was seized by the urgent need to do something—anything—to remove himself from the saccharine sincerity of the duped believers. He wanted to yell at them that they were praying into a void, that they had fallen prey to the oldest scam known to man, and that they wouldn't realize the depth of the deception until their time of greatest need.

When Jade began praying, Beck had a reaction so visceral that he felt his body start to shake. He saw flashes of red as his muscles constricted and his jaw locked. The physical rebellion was so over-whelming that it was all he could do to keep from flinging his chair across the room and screaming obscenities at the assembled believ-ers. Only Jade's voice kept him from acting on his impulses.

Frantic to get away from the oppression of the service, Beck rose and strode toward the exit, his legs unsteady and his breathing labored. He flung the door open and rushed out into the sunny morning, the blinding light merging Boston and Lamorlaye in his mind. He didn't bother to close the door behind him. With a frenzy born of desperation, he tried to put as much distance between him and the small church as he could, launching first into a jog, then into an all-out sprint. It didn't matter to him that people stared. All he knew was that he needed to outrun it—whatever it was—or be devoured by it.

He'd made it several yards past Marcel's when his feet slowed, his mind automatically registering the relief that beckoned from the techno-saturated, smoke-encased bar. He retraced his steps, his breathing labored and his muscles weak. Inside the bar there were only two patrons, both of whom he'd seen on previous vis-its. Neither of them was talkative, which suited him just fine. He pushed the door open and stepped inside.

He wasn't sure how long he'd been there or how much he'd drunk. All he knew was that he wasn't completely surprised when a shadow fell across the floor.

"That's what I call a dramatic exit," Jade said.

Becker looked up to find her standing beside him, her expression a combination of disappointment and pity.

"Leave me alone," Beck said, surprising himself with the vehemence of the order. The other patrons glanced over, intrigued by the exchange.

"I just wanted to make sure you're okay," she said.

"I'm fine."

"Well, you broke about four Olympic records making it from the church to Marcel's, so yes, I'm inclined to agree that you're physically fine. . . ."

"Good. Now go home."

Jade shook her head and took a step closer, eyeing the shot glass in front of him. "Why are you doing this?" she asked.

"Go away."

"No."

Beck turned on his stool and aimed an icy stare at Jade. "Go—away," he said again, his tone harder this time. "Find somebody else to fix."

"Becker . . ."

"Will you make up your mind?" Becker yelled, this time earning himself a warning glare from the bartender. "Will you just decide whether you're going to shun me or save me? Because this Ice Queen versus Mother Teresa act is really getting old!"

Beck saw the benevolence in Jade's face fade, replaced by something that looked more like defiance. "You're an idiot, Mr. Becker."

"Yes, I am. There. Now can we call this intervention over?"

Jade wasn't finished. She climbed onto the stool next to him and leaned in, her voice low enough that the other patrons wouldn't hear her over the music blasting from the speakers. "You're also a blustering, cursing, ridiculous coward, and the only person you're hurting is yourself."

She spun around and stalked away, but Beck was close on her heels, arms wide in disbelief. "Excuse me?" he bellowed.

Jade stopped at the door, her back still to him.

"I'm the coward?" His voice came close to cracking with incredulity. "You prance around here running hot or cold depending on your mood, climbing on your high horse every time things get a little too close to home, and lecturing me about my failures while refusing to acknowledge your own, and I'm the coward?"

Jade turned on him. "What are you implying?"

He speared a finger toward her. "Oh, I'm not implying a thing! How dare you waltz in here and tell me I'm a coward when you're just as boarded up as I am? At least I have the honesty to admit to it!"

She looked at him with incredulity. "Boarded up? Me?"

"Yes," Becker exclaimed, arms still wide at his sides. "You!"

"Hey, could you two take this outside?" the bartender asked.

Jade swiveled on her heel and exited the bar, grabbing the bicycle she'd left leaning against the front window as she marched off toward the castle. Becker dropped a bill on the counter and followed her into the deserted street.

"Oh, you do a great job of hiding it, spending time with the twins like you're all about helping them, but the moment things get a little sticky, you run toward moral superiority like I run toward the bottle."

Jade stood on the sidewalk, shaking her head. "I'm not like that," she said, her voice hoarse.

"Then why won't you let anyone in?"

"Because the 'anyone' in question," she replied, pushing her bicycle with Becker on her heels, "is either drunk or angry or dangerously sober!"

Becker followed in silence for a moment. They passed through the square in the center of town, store shutters drawn and parking spots empty, then moved on toward the château.

"How 'bout others?" he finally asked. "Are there any other people you've let in?"

She was livid. "I have plenty of friends!"

"Then why not me?" Beck asked, surprised to hear the rough edges in his voice.

Jade kept moving forward, her eyes on the castle's gates as they came into view. "I think we've already covered that."

"Well, what if I tell you that . . ." He paused, panic-stricken at what he was about to say. He cleared his throat as they passed through the gates, Jade still pushing her bike and Beck trailing behind. "What if I tell you—and believe me, it's against my better judgment—that I'm attracted to you and that—"

Jade froze, then began to laugh. Beck walked around her, ready to lay into her for mocking him, but the look on her face held no hilarity. The tears coursing from her eyes held nothing but pain.

"You're . . . attracted to me?" she asked, her voice high-pitched and sharp. Her bicycle fell to the ground as she covered her face with both hands, her laughter dying into sobs. She stumbled blindly toward one of the small guard towers and leaned against its wall.

Beck was at a loss. The topic he'd chosen to distract Jade from his drinking had led to the kind of brokenness he'd never seen in her before, and he blamed himself—his cowardice—for pushing her into such emotional turmoil. Unsure of what to do, he stood there for a few moments, then moved to where she stood, undone. "I'm sorry. I pushed too hard. I—"

But Jade didn't hear his attempted apology. She turned weakly, her tear-soaked face blotchy, her eyes impossibly dark and huge, her voice broken when she said, "How can you be attracted to me?" Her eyes filled with fresh tears. She swiped at them with both hands. "I'm a freak—a breastless freak with a death sentence hanging over her head."

"Jade . . ."

She held up a hand to halt him. A sob spasmed in her throat. "I'm just a walking, deformed corpse. That's what I am. . . ." She sank slowly to the ground, her hands over her face.

Becker stood motionless for a few moments before sitting down across from her. He sat there while her sobs receded and her breathing slowed. He sat there until she took her hands from her face, looking everywhere but at him. He sat there until she drew in a deep breath, rolled her eyes, and attempted a tremulous smile.

"You wanted honesty? You got it. Happy now?" she asked.

Becker felt the wind knocked out of him. "You really think I'd be happy about—" he motioned to her—"this?"

She shrugged, biting her lip, eyes downcast.

"Jade—"

"No," she said softly, looking up at him. "Just once, can you not say anything?"

Something in Beck understood. There were some emotions that tolerated no commentary.

Minutes passed.

"Boy, that'll teach you to go to church, won't it?" Jade finally said, wiping the last remnants of tears from her face, traces of her old feistiness back in her eyes.

"You didn't give me much choice in the matter," Beck said, smiling.

Jade cocked her head as her eyebrows—what remained of them—came together in question. "What are you talking about? You walked into that church on your own steam. No one was more surprised than me to see you standing there."

Beck didn't like the reminder. He cursed the impulse that had doomed him. "You made me stay."

"I made you stay? You're really going to put this on me?"

Beck stood and held out a hand to help Jade up. "We're not talking about this."

"Oh, come on. . . ."

"No."

"I'm just curious."

Beck was amazed. "Don't you ever tire of arguments?"

"What happened in there that scared you so badly, Becker?" Jade asked, standing just in front of him, eyes red, arms crossed.

"Nothing."

She smirked. "Care to be more specific?"

"You were there—you figure it out."

"I've been there every Sunday for years and haven't gone running from it, so you're going to have to help me out."

Becker considered the sincerity of her expression and wondered what self-destructive purposes pushed her to ask questions she knew would cause contention. "The whole religion thing is a load of . . . garbage," he finally said.

"But you didn't always think so—you told me you used to go to church."

"I haven't always questioned the Easter Bunny's existence either."

Jade smiled and walked slowly toward the bicycle that still lay on the grass at the edge of the drive. "I know that I haven't exactly been the poster child for sanity since you've been here, but I assure you that if I'd gone through all of this without . . . without faith in someone bigger than this disease . . ."

"The Native Americans have their totem poles, the Hindus have their cows, and you've got your God. It's a pretty predictable cry for help, but that doesn't make it real."

Jade picked the bike up and pulled some blades of grass off the handlebars. "He's very real."

"Let's not talk about this, okay?" Beck said, holding up his hands. "It's a topic I tend to get a little riled up about, and there's been enough of that today."

Jade ignored his plea. "What do you have against God?" she asked.

"You really want to get into this?"

"I do."

"Fine." Beck paused for a moment, gathering his thoughts. The shots he'd had at Marcel's hadn't been enough to inebriate him, but they'd softened the periphery of his consciousness. "How many times did you pray for healing?" he asked, looking into Jade's weary eyes. "I mean—with what you said earlier—I have a bit of a better idea of what you've gone through . . . what you're going through. How many times did you ask your God to heal you, Jade? And how can you still believe in him when he hasn't come through for you when you needed him most?"

"I—"

"Why did you get sick? Why does anyone get sick, for that matter? And look at this place," he said, pointing toward the burned-out shell of the stables. "Does it look like God protected it? The Fallons are good people—why did this happen to their property?"

"You came out alive. So did Jojo and Thérèse. That's good enough for me."

Becker nearly laughed at the simplicity of her faith. "You're way too easily satisfied," he said. "This world's circling the drain, and you're . . ."

"Grateful for what doesn't happen. Things could always be worse."

"You're naïve."

She raised an eyebrow. "Are you seriously saying that to a woman who has breast cancer? I'm naïve?"

Becker attempted a sheepish smile. "Would *deluded* be a better word?"

Jade shook her head. "We live in a world where people get sick and buildings burn down and memories force us into habits we can't break," she said calmly, her gaze unflinching. "I'm not enough of a fool to believe that praying will always change the course of life on a broken planet."

"And yet you just keep at it," Beck said, trying hard to control the sneer the thought evoked.

"Sometimes my prayers get answered," Jade said. "And sometimes the praying gets me through the rough patches. Either way, I win."

"Either way, you're putting stock in an illusion."

"If you want to believe that, it's your choice. But this thing you call an illusion—it changes me. It strengthens me and comforts me, whether it's answered or not. Even when . . ." She looked over her shoulder at the guard tower that had witnessed her grief. "Even when life throws me some unexpected punches." She cocked an eyebrow and smiled with some of the old fire back in her eyes. "You ought to try it sometime. Larger-than-life challenges require larger-than-life assistance."

"Whatever."

Jade laughed, though it was tinged with sadness. "Now you sound like Philippe." She shook her head. "There are mile-wide cracks in your bravado, Mr. Becker. Pity you can't see them as clearly as the rest of us do." She turned her bicycle toward the gates. "I'll be by tomorrow with the children."

"What—so we can do this again?" Becker demanded. "We spend way too much time getting into each other's face."

Jade smiled and straddled the bike, placing a foot on its pedal. "But it's an effective distraction from your demons, isn't it? I can put up with this for a few more days if it'll keep you out of Marcel's."

A muscle pulsed in Becker's jaw as he took a step closer. "You know what really galls me?" he said, his eyes narrowing.

"I'm sure you're going to tell me."

"You get under my skin like nobody's business, but much as I'd love to cuss at you and order you to stay away—" he leaned in, his face inches from hers—"I can't seem to stop thinking about kissing you."

Jade pulled back abruptly, nearly toppling her bicycle in her hurry to put distance between her face and Beck's. "Oh—well . . . ," she stammered. "Oh," she said again, eyes averted and cheeks flushed.

Beck raised his eyebrows. "Really?" he said. "That's what it takes to stop your preaching? If I'd have known, I would have broached the topic a long time ago."

Jade still wasn't meeting his gaze. She tucked a strand of hair behind her ear and pedaled off toward the gates.

"Who's the coward now?" Becker yelled after her, hating himself for the impetuous and childish tone in his voice. Jade didn't look back.

Becker stood glaring after her, refusing to let anything she had said take root in his mind. He turned slowly to make his way to the castle and came up short when he found Jojo standing a few feet away from him. He didn't know what to say. Just a few hours before, they'd braved the flames and the stables' treacherous hallways together, but in the light of day, though there were myriad questions in Beck's mind, he couldn't seem to find a way to ask them.

Jojo stepped forward and extended his hand. Becker hesitated to take the object the older man held out to him. It was large—about the size of a football—and all smooth, carved lines and polished sheen. Jojo insisted by shoving the work of art at Becker again. Beck took the intricate piece into his hands and turned it, observing the workmanship that had caused a perfectly executed horse's head to emerge out of the block of cherrywood that was still partially rough-hewn. But it wasn't the exquisite detailing of the sculpture that gave Becker pause. It was the hand, carved out of the same block of wood, that lay across the horse's snout. It rested there with a weight and a warmth that Beck could nearly feel.

Jojo leaned in close, the smell of his dirty clothes and unwashed body stinging as Becker breathed them in.

"You rear up like a horse," Jojo said in French, his voice raspy and broken but his gaze direct. "Be still," he said. "Accept the hand."

"What, Jade's hand? Jojo, you don't understand. She isn't in any shape to—"

"Not hers."

"Then—"

"The one you scream for from the forest floor in the middle of the night. That hand," Jojo said, his wizened eyes piercing.

Becker racked his mind, trying to understand what the old man was referring to, and he finally remembered the midnight run that had ended in his screaming expletives at the sky. He laughed, though there was little humor in the sound. "Jojo, I wasn't asking for help. I was telling him off."

The old man closed his eyes for a moment, then opened them again. "We yell at those we need the most," he said.

As the old man turned to leave, Becker called after him. "Wait! Jojo!"

He turned.

"I—did you . . . ? This is your work, right? You carved this—and the other horse . . . from the woods?"

Jojo nodded.

"You're good," Becker said, admiration in his voice.

Hunching his shoulders, Jojo merely said, "I have time," and turned to head toward the gatehouse.

"Can we . . . ?" Becker wasn't sure how to proceed. Jojo turned back toward him. "The police were looking for you. They have questions about last night."

Jojo nodded.

"If you'd like to tell me what you saw, I could probably pass it on to them. I know you don't like talking much, and . . ."

"No."

"They're going to want to know. You were there. You rescued Thérèse. . . ."

"No."

Suspicion sent a shiver down Becker's spine. "Jojo . . . you didn't set the fire, did you?"

The old man leveled a long stare at him. Then, in the voice that sounded like gravel, he said, "First, I must see my daughter."

"Come again?" Becker wasn't sure he'd heard correctly.

"First, I see her. Then you can have details."

Beck ran through the options in his mind. "Sure—we'll figure something out. Maybe tomorrow morning? I could get you to the hospital tomorrow. . . ."

Jojo seemed to square his shoulders and force himself to stand a little taller. "Today. This afternoon."

28

AUGUST 1944

MARIE FOUND KARL in the stables, crouched down in the corner of a stall, his face in his hands. It had been several hours since Frau Heinz had returned to the birthing room with his baby. She'd commented, as she'd examined the tiny infant, on the heart-shaped birthmark just above her temple.

"That's a good omen," she'd said to the stunned young man who stood nearby, his body visibly shaking. Her voice was as soft as Marie had ever heard from the usually gruff woman. "Birthmarks like this presage a strong constitution and a long life."

Karl hadn't answered. He'd watched, pale and mute, while Frau Heinz had wrapped the infant tightly in a blanket, barking orders at the younger nurse to clear the room and prepare Elise's body to be taken. The order had sent Karl into a panic. Where would they take her? What would they do with her body? Who would bury her?

311

Frau Heinz had tried to explain to him that there was no time for a proper funeral with the Allied forces moving closer and no family members nearby, but Karl wouldn't hear of it. He'd finally begged, hysterical, that Elise be taken to the Catholic church and given over to the priest, and Frau Heinz had agreed, exasperated.

The rest of the night had passed in a blur. Karl had disappeared while Marie had gathered up her few belongings and tried to make sense of the events of the past hours. The younger nurse had gone about her business in sullen silence, covering Elise's body with a sheet after she'd given it a perfunctory cleaning, and then had left the room, dropping the crumpled picture she had taken from Elise's hand into Marie's lap. It was the photograph of Karl her friend had clutched since the harrowing truck ride that had brought them to the castle. Marie flattened it against her thigh, Elise's most precious possession now a wrinkled and somehow inconsequential relic. She drew a chair up to Elise's side and sat—stunned—while minutes, then hours crawled by. The irrevocability of death was a vise constricting her lungs and crushing her skull. She forced herself to breathe. To blink. To swallow. She retraced the events that had led to her friend's death and tried to imagine what might have saved her, what might have allowed her to meet her own child, what might have . . .

A hand on her shoulder had startled her out of her morbid fixation. The village priest stood behind her, flanked by two men who carried a rough-hewn casket. He stepped closer to the bed where Elise's body still lay and pulled back the sheet, revealing the ashen face and sunken eyes of Marie's closest friend. He pronounced last rites, waving his hand over her in the sign of the cross, then covered her again.

He turned to Marie. "It's time, my child," he said, fixing her with a look of such compassion that she burst into the sobs she had contained since the baby had been delivered. The priest continued to pat her shoulder as his two acolytes lifted Elise, sheets and all, from the bloodstained bed and placed her gently in the pine coffin. They lifted it off the ground by its handles and awkwardly exited the room, Marie's sobs crescendoing as the priest gave her shoulder a final, firm squeeze and followed them out.

Minutes later, she stood in the shadows of the stables, listening to Karl's breathing and wondering what she could possibly say to make sense of the night's horror. All around them, soldiers went about their business, preparing for whatever the immediate future held—either battle or flight, depending on the Kommandant's command. The tension and apprehension on the castle grounds were palpable. There was little talk and even less laughter. They were all strung tight in wait for the unpredictable and unfathomable. Only Karl seemed unmoved by the urgency.

Marie entered the stall, absentmindedly patting the horse's flank as she moved past it, then crouched down next to Karl, her back against the stone wall. Karl didn't move. He breathed behind his hands, his inhalations and exhalations amplified as they hissed through his fingers.

"Karl," Marie said, her voice rough with brokenness. He took another deep breath. "Karl," she tried again, a little more firmly this time, "the priest came and . . . and took Elise to the church. Just like you asked." Karl nodded. "I went down to the ballroom," she said. "They've turned it into a nursery. The baby's . . ." Her voice broke.

Karl whipped his head around, his hands finally falling as he stared into Marie's face. "What?" he croaked. "What's wrong with the—"

Marie held up a hand to quell his fear. "The baby's fine!" she said, squeezing his arm to accentuate her point. "The baby's fine," she said again, new tears filling her eyes. "And she's beautiful. Karl, your baby girl is beautiful. . . ."

The young man, barely more than a boy himself, nodded.

"Karl . . ." Marie hesitated. "Karl, she made me promise. Elise made me promise that . . ." She hesitated again, unwilling to cause the grieving young man any more pain, but determined to stand up for her friend's last wishes.

"What?" Weariness muffled the word.

"She made me promise not to give them the baby. Not to let them take her."

Karl stared at her, eyebrows drawn. "What . . . ?"

"When we were driving here—she made me promise that I wouldn't let the Germans take her baby and place it in some Nazi home somewhere to be raised like . . . like . . ."

"Me? That's what you mean, right? To be raised like me?"

She shook her head, flustered. "No. No, Karl. She never considered you a Nazi. You were . . . You were the man she loved. But she didn't want her baby to be raised by strangers. I think she wanted her raised by someone who knew her mother, and—"

"My daughter is a child of the Führer. She was conceived for him and she will be raised by him."

"Karl . . ."

"No!" he yelled, pointing his finger at Marie. "My daughter will be raised as I was. She will be raised by a good German family and will grow up to understand that only the powerful—"

"Karl!" The ferocity with which she said the word stopped him short. "Elise is dead!" she cried. "Elise is dead! Do you understand that? It doesn't matter what you think—what matters is what she wanted before she died giving birth to your child!"

Stunned, Karl stammered, "But . . . she knew why we were having it."

Marie leveled a disgusted look at him and threw up her hands. "Do you really believe that? Karl, do you really believe that Elise was having this baby for the Reich? She was having it for you! She was having it because she loved you and wanted that love to produce something beautiful. She might have played along with your loyalty to Hitler and your desire to give this child over to him for a while, but I assure you that the woman who rode in that truck with me yesterday had only one thing on her mind, and that was saving her daughter." She let the words sink in before adding, "We've got to do that now. You and me. We've got to get your baby girl out of the castle before she's shipped off to some halfway home with the rest of them."

Karl hadn't moved since the beginning of her diatribe. He seemed torn between anger, surrender, and grief. The emotional tug-of-war was imprinted in the dark shadows under his eyes and the creases in his forehead. "She's a child of the Reich," he said, the conviction he'd shown earlier gone from his voice. "She's . . ."

"She's Elise's baby," Marie finished for him. "You've got to help me, Karl." When he didn't move or answer, she said his name loudly enough to cause the horse to whinny. "Karl!"

He shook his head as if to clear it and covered his face with his hands again, running them up into his hair as he threw back his head and growled at the stall's ceiling. "Fine," he finally said. He turned his head against the stone wall to look at Marie, defeat in his gaze. "Fine. I'll help you."

"I need to be sure I can trust you. I need to be sure you're not going to get some kind of attack of the conscience and turn both your baby and me over to your commander."

Karl sighed. "I promise you," he said after a moment. "If this is what Elise . . ." His voice caught and he swallowed hard. "I promise you," he said again, his chin unsteady.

Marie stared at him for a while longer. She had no other choice but to trust him. "Okay," she said. "This is what I've been able to figure out. According to the radio, the Allies won't be here for three or

four more days. I checked with the kitchen, and there's a farm deliv-
ery scheduled for Friday. The farmer's wife used to be my mother's
best friend. I'll go over there tonight to see if they can smuggle all
three of us out after the delivery."

"Wait—"

"Getting to their farm will be the hard part. After that—I don't
know. We can try to catch a train to Bordeaux. My mother's been
living there with an aunt for a couple of months. She loves babies
and will be able to help. . . ."

Karl shook his head, and his mouth tightened into a sharp line.
"Not me," he said, all traces of fragility gone.

"What?"

"Not me. I'm not running off like a coward."

"But, Karl, this is your baby!"

"I'm not!" he barked. "You can take the baby if that's what Elise
wanted, but I'm a soldier. I'm staying with my comrades until we
see this through."

Marie was incredulous. "You're a stable boy, Karl! Not a soldier."

He hitched his chin up a notch higher as a muscle pulsed in his
jaw. "I'm a soldier," he repeated. "I—will—not—desert."

Marie stared at him. "You'd abandon your daughter for the sake
of the Führer?" she asked, stricken.

"I've devoted my life to the Reich. This can't—this won't—change
anything."

Several moments passed before either of them spoke.

"So . . ." Marie was at a loss. "So I'm supposed to raise your
daughter for you?"

Karl clenched his jaw. He didn't look at her when he said, "For
Elise."

"Karl—"

He turned icy eyes on her. "Do it for Elise."

Marie looked at Karl in disbelief, but there was no sign of conflict on his face. Only certainty and a fatigue that seemed to hollow out his eyes and gray his skin. "Are you sure?"

He nodded, looking away. "It's better this way."

Marie nodded. "Friday," she said. "I'll try for Friday."

29

Jojo seemed to feel threatened by the stark white walls and bustling noises of the small hospital. Becker led the way down the hall, eyeing the number plates next to each door.

"Care to explain why you hopped in the cab with us?" he asked Jade under his breath, conscious of Jojo trailing just a handful of steps behind.

She shrugged. "Mr. Fallon told me about Jojo visiting Thérèse, and . . ." She drew her eyebrows together in thought. "I like them," she finally said. "I like them both. And if I can help them to—I don't know—communicate . . . I just want to be here, that's all."

Becker paused outside the door marked 244. He turned to Jojo with what he hoped was an encouraging smile. "You ready?"

Becker saw the old man swallow convulsively, then raise his chin in defiance of his own fear. "I'm ready," Jojo said, his words slow and a little rough around the edges.

Jade knocked softly on the door and pushed it open.

Thérèse was propped up in bed, her body drowned in the folds of a white hospital gown. Her head, wrapped in a bandage, was turned toward the window, and it wasn't until Jade cleared her throat that she realized she had visitors. Thérèse's hand immediately went to her hair, patting here and there in an attempt to make herself presentable, but the thin gray tendrils were mostly covered in gauze and bandages. Her eyes darted from Jade to Becker. Then they fell on Jojo and held. He stood near the door to the bedroom as if he were poised for a quick escape.

Becker saw a look of panic pass over Thérèse's face, quickly followed by a desperate sort of curiosity that trumped her fear.

Jade stepped back to where Jojo stood, stooped and so tense that he appeared brittle. "Come on in, Jojo," she said, gently guiding him farther into the room. "I hope you don't mind us coming unannounced, Thérèse," she said to the woman whose eyes had not left Jojo. "Jojo wanted to see you, and . . . well, Beck and I did too. So here we all are."

She'd drawn Jojo to the edge of the bed as she spoke. Beck pulled up a chair from the corner by the window, and the old man sat in it without protest. There was a tightness to his jaw that Becker hadn't seen before, and though he'd watched him single-handedly subdue a frantic stallion, he was fairly sure that Jojo had never been more challenged than at this moment.

"Are you doing okay, Thérèse?" Jade asked, filling the vaguely hostile silence. "The Fallons said you might be going home in a couple of days."

Thérèse looked at Jade and blinked, the world seeming to come back into focus as she did. "Silly doctors," she said, her voice raspy. "A woman gets a bit burned and inhales a little smoke, and they strap her to a hospital bed for days."

Beck smirked. "You're not exactly strapped down."

"That's only because their shrink didn't get his way. That old owl seems convinced that my adventure in the stables was an attempt to take my own life." She raised her eyebrows and pinched her lips. "Take my own life? If I were going to do that, I'd find a less unpleasant method than smoke and fire!"

No one quite knew what to say for a few moments. Becker looked away, hoping that someone else would find a lighthearted means of moving the conversation away from Thérèse's near-death experience, but the silence stretched uninterrupted until Jojo drew himself up in his chair, his back as straight as his scoliosis would allow, and, in a voice laced with courage and relief, said, "My name is Karl-Joseph."

All eyes converged on him, and Thérèse's hand fluttered toward her mouth to press a handkerchief to her lips.

Jojo looked directly at the woman lying in the bed, a flush of red in her cheeks, and added, "I . . . believe . . ." He faltered. "I believe I am your father."

Thérèse remained remarkably calm. Alarmingly so. She shook her head. "How can I believe you? I've been looking for you for . . ." Thérèse was engaged in a mighty battle between relief and recrimination, but it looked as if her need for answers was going to win this round. "Where were you?" she begged, eyes wide and disbelieving. "Where were you all these years?"

"Ich war hier," Jojo said in tremulous German. "I was here—and I've been waiting . . . waiting for Marie to find me."

Jade sat on the edge of the bed and patted Thérèse's arm as Beck drew up another chair and sat just a couple feet from her.

Thérèse turned imploring eyes to Jojo. "Please," she said from behind the handkerchief. "Please—tell me what happened."

Jojo pinched his lips together for a moment, then let his eyes drift up toward the only window in the room. He took a deep breath and squared his shoulders. "I met your mother on June 16,

1943," he began, darting a glance at Thérèse, then looking back toward the window. "She was . . ." He paused, his face growing softer with the memories. "She was—captivating."

Becker wasn't sure how much of the story Thérèse already knew, but she didn't interrupt or press Jojo as he recounted his first meeting with the woman in the yellow dress who would irrevocably mark the remainder of his life. It was doubtful that the old man had ever spoken so many words in one sitting, but the pent-up story that had haunted him for nearly sixty years had finally found its audience, and he left nothing out, though he often stumbled and searched for words to describe the events. Thérèse nodded as he spoke, occasionally dabbing at her eyes with her handkerchief or gripping Jade's hand. Her gaze never left the elderly survivor who had spent the better part of his adulthood wandering the castle grounds at night, waiting for this moment—or one like it—to make sense of his life.

Becker sat, fascinated, as Jojo told of the tragic night of Thérèse's birth and her mother's death, of the arguments Marie had used to convince him to relinquish the child, and of the day when their plan had been accelerated by the imminent arrival of the Allies in Lamorlaye.

"We'd planned on Friday," he said, taking a sip from the glass of water Jade had handed to him several minutes into his account. He spoke slowly, deliberately, his accent evident and his French rusty. "Marie knew the farmer who delivered vegetables and eggs. She was to escape with him. But . . . something was happening on Thursday. The Kommandant spent the day speaking with his highest-ranking officers or on the radio. To the Wehrmacht headquarters. In Germany. The order came that evening. 'Prepare for immediate evacuation.' We were told to collect anything of value and load it into the trucks. The rest was to be burned. The bonfire behind the castle lasted all night."

"Where were you headed?" Thérèse asked in a small voice.

"Paris. Our commanders still believed they could defend the city."

There were so many small details that were beginning to make sense to Becker. He heard it now—the German intonation of Jojo's speech. The guttural *r*'s and the clipped consonants hadn't been obvious giveaways before, as Jojo hadn't ever spoken much. But now that he was speaking steadily, the accent was easily recognizable. There were other clues, too. Evidence that he spoke the truth. His nose had the same regal slant as Thérèse's, and his cheekbones were high and defined, like hers.

Becker felt himself drawn into the narrative, and he could see that Jade was too. Her hand never ceased its comforting motions, patting Thérèse's or holding it when Jojo's story got difficult to hear. Jade listened with rapt attention, her eyes sometimes welling with tears, her gaze often darting to Becker and holding his for a moment before moving back to Jojo.

"What happened?" Thérèse whispered. "On the night I escaped from the castle—what happened?"

Jojo let his eyes drift shut and leaned almost imperceptibly back in his chair. He took a calming breath and said, "Marie was . . . the most courageous person I've ever met."

30

AUGUST 1944

MARIE HAD NO DOUBT something big was afoot. Though she'd been confined to the nursery for the past three days, mostly because she'd convinced Frau Heinz that she needed her assistance, she couldn't help but notice the ceaseless activity of the Germans as they packed the castle's contents into boxes and crates, then loaded them into trucks and onto horse-drawn carts. She found Karl in the carriage house behind the stables, sorting through piles of saddles, bridles, and horseshoes.

"What are you doing here?" Karl hissed.

"What's happening?" she whispered back. "Why is everyone packing up?"

"I don't know! I think . . ." He paused, looking out into the late-day sun to make sure no one was within earshot. "I think we're

moving out—tonight. The Kommandant hasn't given the order yet, but—"

"Tonight?" Marie felt the quickening of her pulse. Panic constricted her chest.

"I think so. What have you heard from the radio?"

"Nothing!" Marie said, throwing up her hands in exasperation. "I don't ever get into town anymore to ask! With Frau Heinz ordering me around and your baby needing to be fed every couple of hours . . ."

Karl stopped what he was doing and looked at Marie. "Is she all right?"

"She's fine."

He nodded and got back to work packing bridles into a wooden crate.

An officer came trotting up to the carriage house, and Marie crouched down and pressed against the wall, only partially shielded by a stack of old tires. "We're leaving at dawn!" he barked, pointing at the crates that littered the floor. "Get those finished and bring them around to the front of the castle for loading." He left as briskly as he had arrived.

Marie straightened, a look of horror on her face. "Tomorrow!" she said, incredulous. "Tomorrow? How am I supposed to get the baby out of here before then? There are guards at the gate and along the entire perimeter of the grounds. What am I going to . . . ?" She swallowed panic and stepped forward to grasp Karl's arm. "You have to help me, Karl. You've got to help me get her away from here—it's what Elise wanted, and if you ever . . . if you ever cared about her at all . . ."

Karl's eyes were on the floor of the carriage house as he took several deep breaths, a muscle working in his jaw. "I'll do what I can."

It wasn't much, as commitments went, but Marie had no choice but to take him at his word. "How can we do this?" *she asked, a little breathless with fear.* "How can I get the baby to safety with all the guards and the commotion? What is the best—"

Karl turned on her and held up his arms in frustration. "I don't know!" *he said so loudly that Marie feared someone might have heard him.* "I don't know," *he said again, a bit more quietly.* "There's no time. Too many guards on duty. Maybe you should wait until we get to Paris. . . ."

Marie shook her head, appalled by his cowardice. "I'm not going to Paris. If we're going to save your baby, it's got to be tonight," *she said.* "What if I try to get away with her before everyone leaves in the morning? I can take the night shift in the nursery and maybe . . . maybe . . ."

Karl was back at work, throwing saddles around with more vigor than was necessary. "How?" *he asked.* "You're going to march up to the guards at the gate and say you're taking the baby for a walk in the middle of the night?"

"I could hide her in a bag, or . . . or something."

"Why would you be going anywhere in the middle of the night? With or without a bag? They'll know."

"I could try climbing over the fence in the back woods. . . ."

"The guards are watching every square meter of the property."

"Maybe we could hide somewhere until everyone is gone. . . ." *She racked her mind for a viable option.* "In the cellar under the ballroom. Or—or . . . in the storage room above the stables!"

Karl's face contorted into a sneer. "Or I could just lower you both down the well. That's as safe a place as any." *There were tears in Marie's eyes when Karl finally looked at her, tossing one last saddle onto a stack against the wall.* "What?" *he asked.*

"What is wrong with you?" *she pleaded, shaking her head at the young man's ridicule of her. She swiped a hand across her eyes and* stepped right up to him, planting her fists on her hips. "One of us promised Elise the baby would be safe, and I'm not going to break that promise!"

Karl was stunned into immobility by her outburst. He dropped his chin and stared at the ground for a moment, offering neither apology nor strategy.

"Help me, Karl. Think. There's got to be a way of getting out of here without being seen."

Karl stalked to the other side of the carriage house, deep in thought. He paced back and forth several times while Marie watched the sun dip out of sight and prayed the night would be long enough and dark enough to permit an escape.

"The river," Karl said.

"The river?"

"They'll be watching the land—the woods, the islands, the bridges. But they might not be watching the water. If you can follow the river through the woods and past the wooden bridge, the embankments on either side are tall enough that maybe . . ." He looked up at Marie. "Maybe you can make it out."

"What if the baby cries? What if she starts to cry while I'm in the river?"

"Can you give her something to make her sleep?"

Marie looked at him in disbelief. "She's three days old, Karl!"

"Well, how am I supposed to know?"

"Maybe if I time it to leave right after one of her feedings. She seems to be in a deeper sleep then. . . ."

"The guards work in four-hour shifts. They're usually less attentive toward the end of the four hours, so if you plan on leaving around three, you'll be hitting the end of the midnight shift and still beating the dawn."

Marie's eyebrows drew together. "Is this really happening?" she asked. *"Am I really trying to escape with a newborn by wading into a river in the middle of the night?"*

"Looks like it," Karl said, back at work sorting through the boxes surrounding him.

Marie tried one more time. "You're sure you don't want to come with us?"

He shook his head with conviction. "I'm a soldier of the Third Reich," he said, his voice firm but his hands unsteady. "My place is with my comrades."

Marie stared at him for a moment longer before turning on her heels and walking away.

31

A NURSE CAME clanking in, pushing a metal cart loaded with drinks and startling all four occupants of room 244. "Same as this morning?" she asked Thérèse, oblivious to the undercurrents that moved, slow and powerful, between Jojo and his daughter. Thérèse nodded, and the nurse poured her a cup of chamomile tea, leaving the room as quickly and noisily as she'd entered.

The silence that followed was loaded with hesitation and unasked questions. It was Jade who finally said, "What happened?"

Before Jojo could answer, Thérèse took a deep breath and began to recite the details of her story as if reading from a script. "Marie made it into the river with me. I was just three days old and light enough to hold above the water. But she couldn't risk taking the files and getting them wet."

Becker leaned forward. "What files?"

Jojo cleared his throat. "Marie found Elise's files in the truck on the way to the castle. Her family history was there—everything the Lebensborn had collected for her application to the residence program."

"And pictures," Thérèse added. "One of my mother and one of my—" She stopped, her eyes darting to the elderly man who seemed to have shrunk as he'd sat in the plastic hospital chair recounting his story. "And one of Karl," she amended.

Becker wasn't sure, but he thought he saw tears brimming in the older man's eyes. He wanted to do something to comfort him, but there was little that could be done to defuse the ravages initiated by the war and sharpened by the passage of time. "You okay, Jojo?" Beck asked, leaning forward in his chair as he noticed the sudden paling of the older man's already-gray skin.

Jojo raised a hand in response, nodding imperceptibly and swallowing hard. He appeared determined to see his tale through to the end. He cleared his throat and turned his eyes toward the window. "Marie found me around midnight," he said, pronouncing her name with a rolled German *r*. "I was helping to load the trucks. Boxes and boxes of documents—and all the artwork they could pull off the walls. She shouldn't have been there. If anyone had seen her . . ." He coughed, his slight frame convulsing with the effort, then took a deep, raspy breath. "If anyone had seen her," he continued, "they'd have become suspicious. It was strange enough that a French girl had volunteered to live at the castle when all the other villagers had gone home. But Marie . . . Marie was a loyal one. Stubborn, too."

AUGUST 1944

Karl was walking down the stairs to the foyer, carrying a painting under one arm and a box of ledgers under the other, when Marie stepped out of the shadows and grabbed his arm, swinging him around and down into the dark space under the well-traveled steps.

"Are you out of your mind?" Karl hissed, his eyes darting feverishly here and there in fear of being discovered. He lowered the painting and the box to the floor, then raked unsteady fingers through his hair.

"Listen to me," Marie said, her lucid and determined gaze finding his. "I'll be leaving with the baby at 3 a.m., but I can't take these." She pressed a manila folder into his chest.

"What is it?" He flipped the folder open, leafing through the pages of information and pausing when he reached the two pictures. "Where did you get these?"

"They fell out of a box."

His eyes narrowed. "You can't keep them."

Marie stared at him in incredulity. "Are you kidding?"

"They belong to the Reich."

"No, Karl, they belong to your daughter. That folder is the sum total of everything she'll know about her mother, and you're going to help me preserve it for her."

"I won't. I won't defy the Kommandant's orders. Take it out of here yourself."

"In the river? What if it's too deep? Or if I fall and get it wet? No. Karl—Karl, listen to me!" She grabbed his arm and shook it. He was so focused on the sound of boots going up and down the stairs above them that he couldn't concentrate on what Marie was saying. His eyes darted back to her when she shook his arm, and she continued in quiet, hurried words. "Take these with you when you go. Pack them with your stuff or tuck them into your trousers or . . . whatever. Just take them with you, okay?"

"And then what?"

"And then send them to me. Whenever you can." She took the

folder from him and showed him the handwritten address on the inside of the back cover. "Send them to me here. It's the address of the aunt my mother is living with."

"I don't know. . . ."

"She's your daughter. She's your daughter, and this is the only thing I'm asking you to do for her. Karl—"

Somewhere above them, a voice asked if anyone had seen Karl-Joseph. "Try the latrine," another voice called. "He's been hiding like a scared little girl all afternoon."

Karl snapped his head around, aiming a panicked look at Marie. "Fine," he said, snatching the folder from her. "Fine. But if you get caught, don't mention me. Don't say my name to anyone, you hear?"

Marie shook her head, and a look of disgust crossed her face. In a soft voice, she said, "I don't know what Elise ever saw in you, Karl, but what I'm looking at now . . ." She paused, studying him. "What I'm looking at now is a far cry from the man she described."

Karl stared her down for a moment before taking a couple steps and glancing around the edge of the staircase, eager to reenter the stream of dutiful soldiers carrying the boches' *loot out to the trucks. He came back to Marie, pulling up his shirt and stuffing the folder into his trousers. "That's the difference between you and Elise," he said, tucking his shirt back in. "She knew I was a soldier and didn't expect me to be anything else."*

Marie let out a humorless laugh. "How convenient for you." She handed him the painting and helped him pick up the box of ledgers. "Promise me you'll do it," she said. "Promise me."

He turned, his ears trained on the coming and going of soldiers. "Sure."

"Karl!"

The expletive he let out reverberated too loudly in the shadowed space beneath the stairs. Karl froze, holding his breath, but Marie had no time for fear. "Promise me," she said.

Karl turned icy eyes on her and hissed, "Fine! I promise!"

Thérèse took a sip of chamomile tea and smiled sadly at Jade. "Marie made it out of the castle grounds with me the night the Germans evacuated Lamorlaye."

Jojo took over. "It was just before dawn when the order came. Generalmajor Müller said to fetch the babies and take them to the trucks. Frau Heinz oversaw the procedure and never mentioned the missing baby to anyone. She seemed completely . . . unaware that Thérèse was gone."

"How could she not have known?" Jade asked.

Jojo smiled. "She was the last one onto the last truck," he said, "and just as I was closing the doors on her, she said, 'You might be a better father than I thought.'"

"She knew," Becker said, captivated by the story emerging as the two points of view converged.

"She knew," Jade agreed, squeezing Thérèse's hand. "Did Marie have any trouble getting to her mother's? I mean—with the liberation under way, I presume it had to be difficult to get anywhere. . . ."

"What happened to her?" Jojo asked, leaning forward as his eyes brightened with intensity. "What happened to her? I wrote to tell her that the papers had never left the castle, but . . . I never heard from her again."

Thérèse looked at Jojo with so much bitterness that his face went slack and he grasped the armrests of his chair. She took several breaths before answering his question. "All I know I heard from my mother." She stopped, holding a hand to her forehead. "My adoptive mother. But not Marie. Marie was not my . . . Marie didn't raise me. I grew up thinking of her as a sister. It was her mother who took care of me. And it wasn't until—it wasn't until last year that I found out about . . ." She took another deep breath and pulled herself up straighter against the cushions.

Jade squeezed her hand again. "If you need to take a rest . . ."

"No," Thérèse quickly replied, shaking her head. "We might as well get it all out now. And Jojo . . ." She looked at the man whose lips were pressed together in dismay. "Jojo has waited long enough."

Becker wasn't sure he wanted to hear the rest of the story. From the look on Thérèse's face, it wouldn't be pleasant, and he wondered how much more Jojo could take.

"Marie made it to the bridge at the back of the property, following the river and holding me above the water. But when she got there, she saw soldiers watching the grounds on the other side and she knew she'd be seen if she tried to forge ahead. So . . . she stayed hidden there for nearly an hour." Thérèse's fingers wrung the handkerchief she held. She took a moment before continuing. "It appears that I woke up while we were hiding there. I was a newborn—there was little she could do to quiet me. And when I began to cry . . . when I began to cry, Marie placed her hand over my mouth. To save me. To save us both. She held it there so tightly and for so long that I lost consciousness." She looked directly at Jojo. "She thought she'd killed me—suffocated me to death. You can imagine what those moments before I breathed again felt like to her."

Thérèse seemed to gather courage before continuing, her gaze turning inward again. "Eventually, some kind of disturbance near the castle gates made the guards move away for just a few minutes— enough for Marie to carry me the rest of the way to safety. We made it to the Catholic church and waited there until two days after the evacuation. She didn't want to take the risk of encountering any Germans who might have stayed behind. The priest finally took a stroll into town and confirmed that they were all gone."

She paused, closing her eyes for a moment as her hand fluttered to her neck. "Marie's plan was to make it to Chantilly with me and take a train from there in the direction of Bordeaux. Even if there were no trains going all the way there, she wanted to get as far away from Lamorlaye as she could on that first day. She'd figure the rest out wherever she got off the train."

Though Marie had walked from Lamorlaye to Chantilly on many occasions, she'd never done so with a newborn in her arms. All she carried with her was the evaporated milk formula she'd stolen from the nursery and enough fresh cow's milk, donated by the priest and packed in ice, to last for the day. As they entered the town, the sounds of celebration grew. People filled the streets, singing raunchy songs about the boches *and screaming crude chants at the top of their lungs. Children danced around light poles while adults gathered in squares and on street corners, many with glasses of wine and bottles of beer in their hands, telling tall tales about what they'd witnessed. The Allies hadn't arrived yet, but the scene was set for their victory parade.*

As she rounded the corner to the train station, Thérèse tightly bundled and sleeping soundly against her chest, Marie saw that she hadn't been the only one with a desire to leave in the first days after the Germans' evacuation. The station was crowded and pulsed with a nervous energy that briefly made Marie reconsider her plans. But when Thérèse stirred and whimpered against her, she squared her shoulders and stepped into the line leading to the ticket counter.

She'd been standing there for just a handful of minutes when a woman she vaguely recognized grabbed her arm and pulled her out of line.

"Filthy tramp!" she cried, her pupils dilated and her cheeks flushed. "You worked up there in the baby factory with the Nazis!"

"Leave her alone," a man said behind Marie.

"She's a traitor!" the woman screamed, pointing at Marie and scanning the crowd to gauge their reaction. "Go ahead! Ask her. Ask her if she worked at the manor!"

Marie felt fear crawling up her spine. Though she sensed movement in the crowd around her, her eyes narrowed into a sort of tunnel vision filled by the angry woman's flushed face. "I'm—My name is Marie Gallet. I live in Lamorlaye," she stammered, trying to establish a connection that would cut through the postliberation hysteria.

The woman's lips curled inward as she moved so close that Marie could feel her breath on her face. "You worked for the boches—probably slept with them too. You're a slut, girl, and we don't like your type around here." She cleared her throat and spit in Marie's face.

Marie was momentarily paralyzed with shock. She held Thérèse more tightly and looked around for help, finding only averted gazes and disapproving glares. The woman still stood there, her finger pointing at Marie, uttering vulgarities, but there was no hint of rescue in the faces Marie scanned. She wiped the spit from her eye and cheek and opened her mouth to protest, but her attacker wasn't finished yet.

"You're a tramp. A filthy traitor—working for the boches and servicing their men! Shame on you. Shame on you, you foul pile of trash!"

Others began to mumble their agreement as Marie moved slowly away from the large woman. She backed toward the door, hoping to make it out into the street before the situation escalated any further, but the liberation frenzy that had gripped the town took a rapid turn toward violence. She'd nearly made it to the door when a middle-aged man took his turn spitting on her.

"Whore!" he cried, shoving her so hard that she stumbled and had to catch herself on the wall, Thérèse cradled in one arm.

All around the small station, voices began to rise in vicious tirades.

"But—I'm not German!" Marie cried as someone grabbed her arm and began to drag her into the square outside the station. "I only worked for them to feed my family! I'm—"

"Shut up, you slut!" another man yelled, pushing her to the cobblestones, her elbows taking her full weight as she braced to protect the baby.

"Wait!" Marie cried, pain shrieking up her arms. "Wait—I'm one of you! My name is Marie! Marie Gallet! I'm not a traitor! I'm not a—"

She didn't know where the blow came from. A foot connected with her stomach, narrowly missing Thérèse, and left her gagging and writhing, in so much pain that she couldn't speak. The crowd around her was growing, and as she squinted through tear-blurred eyes into the faces of her tormentors, she was horrified to find familiar ones among them. An elderly lady stepped forward and snatched a bawling Thérèse from her grasp.

"No!" Marie cried. "No—not the baby!" Another kick, this one to the kidneys, knocked the air from her lungs and left her semi-conscious, struggling to breathe. She wanted to protest. She wanted to beg for mercy. She wanted to plead her case, but the screams around her were so loud and the blows were coming so close together that she couldn't do a thing in her own defense.

Someone finally grabbed her by the hair and pulled her to her feet. Her stomach and ribs burned with agony. The voices swirled around her, the faces swam before her eyes. Someone yelled, "Here! Bring her here! We'll show her how we feel about traitors." She stumbled as they pulled her across the cobblestone square, and when her legs gave out, they pulled even harder, dragging her by the hair toward a restaurant across the way. And there, as the voices of her tormentors rose in a hysterical cacophony of mass malevolence, she saw scissors in someone's hand and felt them plunge into her hair. The laughter and cheering that arose were the last sounds she heard as her mind finally succumbed to unconsciousness.

✠

It was a full day later when Marie woke. She'd come to a few times before, but never enough to take stock of her surroundings. With consciousness came full awareness of her pain, and the ache in every part of her body doubled her over. She leaned over the edge of the couch on which she lay and retched onto the floor.

"Now, now," came a soothing voice. A hand patted her shoulder. "Try to take deep breaths and it'll pass."

Marie couldn't open her eyes. They were too swollen, and the light in the room was too bright. But there was a kindness in the voice that she instinctively trusted.

"The baby," she mumbled through tumid lips. "Thérèse."

"Your baby's safe," the voice said.

Marie felt a cool, wet rag being placed on her forehead and was grateful for the relief.

"There wasn't much I could do to stop them from hurting you," the wispy voice said, tinted with sadness, "but I didn't think anyone would turn on an old woman for rescuing your baby."

Marie struggled to open her eyes and finally got one eyelid up far enough to see the frail, kind-faced woman who sat on a chair next to the sofa where she lay. "You took the baby—I remember you."

Something painful passed over the lady's face. "Oh, dearie, how I wish I could have spared you, too. But the anger . . . the anger and the violence . . . they were just so . . ."

"You couldn't have stopped them," Marie said. "I saw the look on their faces." She closed her eyes again and moaned at the shooting pain in her abdomen.

Thérèse let out a soft gurgle somewhere in the room. "You see," the elderly lady said, moving to the bassinet by the window, "she's just fine. Your baby is just fine."

And at those words, Marie slept.

32

JOJO STOOD BY the window as Thérèse spoke. He'd moved from the chair as she'd begun to describe the assault, his gait unsteady and his jaw clenched. Jade still sat on the bed, her hand on Thérèse's arm, and Becker sat in a chair at the foot of the bed, too stunned to do much more than remind himself to breathe.

Marie stayed with Madame Sajot for another month while she recovered, spending her waking hours writing down her memories for Thérèse to read when she was old enough to understand. It was as if she knew that her story would only exist for a limited time in her mind before it became lost in a miasma of survivor's guilt. When Marie grew too tired, her kind, compassionate rescuer took over for her, writing down the harrowing events Marie recited in great detail. She was still determined to get on a train to Bordeaux just as soon as she was strong enough, but she didn't want to take the memories with her when she left. After the first few days, she

343

began to speak less, retreating into silence as her hair began to grow back and her bruises began to fade. Much as Madame Sajot tried, there was no rescuing Marie from the lethargy she slipped into. After a couple of weeks, the older woman began asking questions in town about the Gallet family that had moved to Bordeaux, and it wasn't long before she had located them. Marie's mother got there days later, frantic with worry. As soon as it could be arranged, she took Marie and Thérèse home to Bordeaux with her.

Jojo turned toward Thérèse, tears in his eyes. "Marie," he said. "Did she . . . ?"

Thérèse took a deep breath and smiled faintly. "She had good days and bad days. . . ." She hesitated. "I'm not sure what was worse. The chronic pain in her body—or the pain in her mind. I think I was five when she packed a suitcase and left. She'd come by every few months but never stayed long. She died in a hotel room in Quimper when I was twelve. Pneumonia, they think. Mother packed up her room and never spoke of her again."

"I didn't know," Jojo said, still standing at the window. He seemed to sway, and Becker jumped up to steady him, but he brushed the helping hand aside. "I'm fine," he said, his tone hard and his words clipped despite the frailty of his voice. "I'm seventy-four years old and fine. Marie never really made it past seventeen. . . ." When he swayed again, Becker took his arm and escorted him back to the chair.

"There's nothing you could have done," Thérèse said to Jojo, and it was obvious that the comforting words cost her greatly. "Even if you'd known."

He raised his head and said, "The letter. I sent a letter to the Bordeaux address nearly a month after we left Lamorlaye. Did she get it? Did your mother?"

Thérèse's eyes clouded over. She pursed her lips and clasped her hands tightly in her lap. "I—found out only last year about your letter. My mother died in the seventies, and I kept her house as a summer retreat." After another sip of her now-cold tea, she continued. "I decided to sell it last year, and as I was preparing some of my mother's antiques to be appraised, I found your letter and Marie's written account behind one of the drawers of her bureau. She must have found them when Marie died and left them there—I'm not sure why. She hated the *boches*—hated the Germans so much for what they'd done to Marie—but maybe she still thought that someday she'd find the courage to tell me the truth. I guess she died before she'd made up her mind." She coughed a little from the exertion of so much speaking and leaned back on the cushions. "Your letter—it started me on a journey that ended in the stables last night. I had to know. I had to know."

Jade looked at Jojo. "What did your letter say?"

"I told her that—"

"'Dear Marie,'" Thérèse interrupted, eyes closed as she quoted Jojo's letter verbatim. "'I trust you and the baby made it safely to Bordeaux. Unfortunately, I cannot send you the papers as you requested. On the morning we evacuated, Generalmajor Müller ordered a thorough search of all the personnel who left the castle. I couldn't risk being caught.'"

This time, it was Becker who voiced his disappointment. "You left them there?"

Jojo's eyes fired up. "I left the folder in a place she could find. She still had friends in Lamorlaye. I thought—if she ever came back—she'd be able to locate it."

"But your instructions were too cryptic for anyone other than Marie to understand," Thérèse said.

"I needed to be sure that no one else would intercept the letter. I needed to keep those documents safe—for you."

"There wasn't anything selfless about it," Thérèse said with disdain. "You left those papers there for the same reason you abandoned me in the first place and let Marie—a seventeen-year-old girl—take on the responsibility of raising me."

A heavy silence settled over the room. "Yes," Jojo finally said, eyes averted. "I did it all to spare myself."

Thérèse seemed destabilized by his admission. Her indignation was less virulent when she addressed Beck and Jade, quoting more of the letter. "'The folder is still at the castle. I left it in the small, dark hiding place we discussed as we were planning your escape. The place I suggested I hide you. If you know where to look, you'll find it with no difficulty.'" Thérèse looked over to where Jojo sat, head bowed. "Do you know how many small, dark places there are in a castle? If Marie's mind had survived the escape, she might have been able to find the folder, but since she was nearly killed for her association with you . . ."

Her words had the desired effect. Jojo leaned forward in his chair and covered his face with his hands, breathing harshly.

"Thérèse," Jade whispered.

"He did what he could," Beck interjected, his eyes on the broken man now rocking slightly back and forth in his chair. "He was a seventeen-year-old boy playing at grown-up war."

"He—was—my—father," Thérèse said, every word articulated with venom. "And he threw me away."

The taxi ride back to Lamorlaye was silent. Jojo sat in the back next to Jade, his vacant eyes on the blurred trees and houses rushing by. Nearly sixty years of waiting for Marie to return had not yielded the relief he had hoped for, but a grief so miserable that it shrank his frame and blanked his expression.

"When did you return to Lamorlaye?" Jade asked gently.

Jojo didn't move. A minute passed before his tired voice said, "As soon as I could without being recognized so easily. I wanted to be here if . . . if Marie came back."

"But why?" This from Becker, in the front seat. He turned so he could see Jojo's profile as he stared out the window. "You'd made it clear that you wanted nothing to do with Thérèse. Why did you come back?"

Another silence, weighty and somber, lumbered by. "When the war ended—" He coughed, a deep, rasping sound that garbled out of his sunken chest. "When the war ended," he began again, straining for the right words, "I found I had nothing. No family. No . . . what do you call it? Dignity. No honor. No friends. Nothing that belonged to me. Nothing. And I—I couldn't get the baby out of my mind. Nor her mother. I couldn't . . ." He paused, his jaw working. "I couldn't understand why I had cared so little."

"You could have gone to Bordeaux," Jade said quietly. "Tried to track her down. You had the address she'd given you, didn't you?"

He nodded and took another wheezing breath. "I wrote to her. Many times. From Germany. And there was never any response. And then—I tried to send a telegram but was told the address was—" he paused, racking his mind for the correct term—"no longer valid. I hoped . . . I hoped the letters had reached her and that she was just having trouble coming back here for the papers."

"So you waited?" Becker asked.

He felt an almost physical punch to the gut when Jojo's gaze, tired, hollow, but impossibly keen, connected with his. The elderly man spoke his next words with as much strength and conviction as his weary body could summon. "She was my daughter. I learned too late what that means—what that should mean. We are made for . . ." He paused, intent on using the right words to define his journey. "We are made to be connected—to be intertwined with others. We are made for belonging. Unless we have that—unless we allow that—we have nothing."

Becker glanced at Jade, whose face seemed cast in stone, then back into the sharp blue-gray eyes that hadn't strayed from his. He felt something implacable softening inside. The sensation terrified him.

The police returned to Jojo's gatehouse the next day to close the file on the château's fire. Becker and Fallon joined them, as much to support the old man as to ask a few questions of their own. When they exited the small structure a little over an hour later, they found Jade and Sylvia waiting for them on the steps of the castle while the twins played by the river.

"Did you have an interesting conversation?" Sylvia asked as the men walked up to the steps.

Fallon chuckled and sat down next to his wife. "You have no idea, my dear. That man's life is fit for the movies."

Becker propped a foot on the bottom step and gazed up at the château's facade. "For a man who hasn't spoken much in decades, he's sure been talking a lot."

"Well, don't keep a good story to yourself," Sylvia coaxed. "What fascinating tidbits did you learn?"

Becker sighed, raking his fingers through his hair. "Those noises I've been hearing at night?"

"Jojo?" Jade asked, turning to face Beck.

"Yep. But only because he was following Thérèse."

Sylvia was appalled. "What was a woman like Thérèse doing scrounging around a castle in the wee hours of the morning? That's preposterous."

"The folder," Jade said.

"The folder." Beck smiled a little at the futility of it all. "All Jojo told Marie was that he'd left it in a small, dark hiding place they'd discussed . . . and Thérèse spent her nights looking in every small, dark place she could think of. Officer Vivier didn't say much about it, but there's a bit of a psychiatric history there."

It was all coming together in Jade's mind. "The crawl space under the patio? Was that her too?"

Fallon shook his head in reluctant admiration. "And the well, and the cellar under the ballroom—it must have taken true desperation for her to climb out of there with the rope."

Beck nodded. "And all the while, the file was in the gatehouse, with Jojo. He'd removed it from the well himself when he returned to Lamorlaye after the war."

"That still doesn't explain the fire," Sylvia said.

"Did Thérèse start it?" Jade asked.

Fallon nodded. "She wanted to give the stables one last search. That's where the soldiers had been billeted, after all."

Becker took over. "The cops said she took a lantern from the drive while the rest of us were celebrating in the dining rooms. She was on the landing of the second floor when the wood gave out beneath her. She fell through to her waist, and the lantern landed hard and shattered."

"You can imagine how fast the wood floors and wallpaper caught fire," Fallon said. "She pulled herself out and got as far from the flames as she could, but those hallways were blocked off years ago. She must have passed out on her way to the other end of the corridor."

"That's where Jojo found her," Becker finished.

"Jojo . . . ," Jade said. "His name was Karl—how did he become Jojo?"

"That's what I wanted to know," Fallon said. "His full name is actually Karl-Joseph Gerhard. He gave up the Karl to erase that part of his past. When the police tried to evict him in the early fifties, the village rallied around him and Joseph became a sort of folk hero named Jojo."

"And he's been here ever since," Jade said, her eyes on the gatehouse.

"Squatter's rights," Fallon explained. "The French are rather militant about them."

Sylvia raised an eyebrow. "You got all that information in the hour you were in there?"

"It was a very informative hour," he said with a chuckle, standing. "And an exhausting one at that." He moved toward the river. "Philippe! Eva!" he called. "Put down those stones. We're going home."

33

"IT'S TODAY! It's today! It's today!" The kids came stampeding up the stairs with simultaneous shouts. They crashed into the hallway of Beck's apartment and came to a sliding halt just inside his bedroom door.

"It's today!" Philippe yelled, his eyes wide as saucers and his cheeks rosy with excitement.

"Yep," Eva chirped, her red curls bobbing as she nodded her assent.

"You're that excited to get me out of here, are you?" Beck asked, a grin belying the seriousness of his tone.

"Huh?" Philippe cocked his head to the side and considered the bewildering man in front of him.

"Mr. Becker thinks you're excited because he's leaving this morning," Jade said as she appeared in the doorway. "And by the way, you two, did you stop to knock before you came careening in here?"

"Uh . . ." Philippe attempted to dodge the question with a feigned lapse of memory.

"Nope!" Eva said, effectively disarming her brother's ploy. "My mommy's having a baby!" she yelled, taking a couple steps forward so she stood just inches from Becker. "She's having it right now in the hospital!"

"Yay! Yay! Yay!" Philippe chanted, stepping just as close to Becker as his sister and pumping his fist in the air.

Becker took a step back and glanced up at Jade. "Really?"

Jade nodded. "Three weeks early, but the doctor assures us everything will be fine." Grabbing the children's heads, she turned them around to face her and crouched down in front of them. "Are you listening carefully?" They nodded simultaneously. "We will go to the hospital just as soon as your father calls, but until then, you need to go down to the kitchen and color the cards you made for your new brother. Okay?" Another nod. "Okay. Now, scram!"

They left as discreetly as they'd come, their clatter as they descended the stairs doing strange things to Becker's heartstrings.

Jade glanced at his suitcases. "Finished packing?"

"All but the carry-on."

"You travel light."

Beck laughed. "Yeah, I'm a firm believer in leaving ample space for duty-free booze."

Jade narrowed her eyes at him.

"Joking," he said, holding up a hand to ward off her diatribe. "Although the airport bars and the free wine on the plane are going to be . . . a challenge."

Jade nodded. She'd spent enough time with him in the past three months to understand the power of the addiction.

"So," Beck said, steering the topic into safer territory. "If the Fallons are at the hospital . . . ?"

"Mr. Fallon apologizes for not driving you to the airport himself. He had me order a taxi for you. It should be here at noon."

The silence stretched until she laughed and smoothed a tendril of hair. "You know, for all the awkward standing we've done in this room, you'd think it would have gotten less uncomfortable by now. . . ."

"I'm not going to keep in touch," Beck said, soft determination in his voice as he leaned back against the window frame and folded his arms across his chest. "After I leave," he added. "I'm not going to stay in touch."

Jade was silent for a moment as the words settled into finality. Then she seemed to draw herself up taller as she said, "Did I ask you to?"

"No, but . . . I just wanted you to know."

She squared her shoulders and moved to stand directly in front of Becker.

"What's with you people and personal space?" Becker asked before she could say anything.

She completely ignored his question, squinting at him. "Lest you missed it the first fifteen times I said it, Mr. Becker, I don't want you to keep in touch."

"Because of the cancer thing?"

She raised her eyebrows. "Because of the cancer thing?" she repeated. "Yes, Mr. Becker, because of that thing."

Becker pushed off the window frame and took her by the arms, moving her determinedly backward until she sat in the chair next to the dresser. He didn't release her as he crouched down in front of her and said, eyes ablaze, "You're not going to die."

"What—?"

"You're not going to die. You're going to beat this cancer. You're going to get your energy back and you're going to stop being afraid of getting out there and living life."

Her words were slow and measured, her eyes narrowed. "Who do you think you are to be lecturing me on quality of life?"

"No one," he answered, releasing her as he stood. "I can no more lecture you on quality of life than you can lecture me on vulnerability, and yet . . ." He shook his head and looked out the window in amazement. "We've been doing nothing but that since the day you first walked through that door and I mistook you for Mrs. Fallon."

"What are you saying?"

"I'm saying—and I've been giving this a lot of thought, trust me—I'm saying that I'm a messed-up freak of a man who isn't fit to live around others." He hurried to add, "But I was—once. I was able to . . . I was able to do everything I can't do now. Trust, love, commit, expect success. And then I got kicked in the gut, completely broadsided, and . . . well, you've seen the results."

Jade hadn't moved a muscle since he'd deposited her in the chair. She stared, mute, her lower lip pinched between her teeth.

"See, I had this big speech prepared for you. I was going to order you around like some kind of despot. I was going to tell you to stop worrying about dying and to forget about your hair—it'll grow back. And to keep telling yourself that, with or without cancer, you've got to keep fighting for all you want from life—"

"With or without breasts, too?" she asked quietly. "With or without those physical attributes men can't seem to live without?"

Becker quelled the surge of denial and frustration that threatened to escape his lips. He saw the emptiness in Jade's eyes, the sag in her shoulders as she spoke the words, and realized how very deep her anguish went.

"With or without breasts, too," he said, his voice no louder than hers. "And I'm not saying that because I can relate in any way. I'm saying that because—because you're Jade. You're not a body part—you're a feisty, frustrating, loving, supportive, and . . . and exasperating person who is worth fighting for."

A tear escaped the corner of Jade's eye and rolled down her cheek.

"Wait—no," Becker said, reaching out a hand to stop her. "This was supposed to be a pep talk, not a . . . not a . . ." He raked his fingers through his hair, incapacitated by her emotion.

"And then what?" she whispered. "I live my life, I finish my education, I get a great job, and . . ." Another tear followed the first. She swiped at it. "And I wonder every day if the cancer is really gone or if it's just lying in wait. And then I meet a man and fool myself into thinking he won't mind my—deformity. And I tell myself that I might have beat this thing after all, and I have children, and . . . and suddenly the cancer is back or the man moves on or my daughter discovers she has cancer too, only she got it from me. And then what, Becker? Tell me what the fighting's for if it only leads to that?"

Becker leaned back against the wall, appalled by Jade's pain, then slid down to sit on the floor. His eyes were on the ceiling, on the window, on the tacky framed paintings, but not on Jade. Not on the pain she'd managed to hide for so long that was now agonizingly clear and running down her cheeks in wet streaks. He ran his hands over his face and let out a loud, defeated sigh.

"I'm no good at this," he said. After a moment, he added, "Every time I try to . . ."

Jade smiled through her tears and hunched a shoulder. "You gave it your best shot," she said.

"No, I didn't."

"Becker . . ."

"That thing I was saying before? About you lecturing me and me lecturing you and neither of us being really qualified? I don't know how to help you. I want to. But I don't know how to. Mostly because I'm too warped to figure myself out, so how am I supposed to be—I don't know—be solid for you?"

Jade wiped her cheeks with the palms of her hands and released a deep sigh. "What are you trying to say, Becker?"

He leaned forward where he sat, elbows on his knees, and said, "I'm sorry. I've been a jerk. I've been a drunk. I've been a coward."

"Beck . . ."

"I've climbed on that wagon a dozen times since I've gotten here, absolutely sure that I was going to pull it off this time, and I've fallen off hard every single time, mostly right on top of you. And I still managed to convince myself that I was in control."

"Becker, you don't have to apologize. . . ."

"And the bottom line of what I'm trying to say is that I know I can't do this on my own. I know that now. I can't do it alone. And the first thing I'm going to do when I get back to the States is figure out who I need and what I need to get to the other side of this, and I'm going to fight for it. I want to fight for it this time—with everything in the arsenal. But I'm not stupid enough to think I can be here for you too right now. So I need you to fight for yourself, because . . ." He stopped, depleted by the honesty that had become so foreign to him.

Jade shook her head, afraid of what might come next.

"Because Jojo waited almost sixty years in that gatehouse and never gave up. Because Marie held on to that baby while the mob was shoving and kicking and nearly killed her. I've never failed as much in my life as I've failed here. Mostly because I've never attempted as much in my life as I've attempted here. And I've gotten nowhere because I've been trying to do it on my own terms—on my own steam. But there's hope. I know that now—I feel it. There's hope when I'm dying for a swig of something strong, there's hope when I can't picture a life free from dependence, and there's hope when all I can do is cuss at God because this isn't easy enough. I'm ready to fight for that hope and to—to accept the hand."

"Accept the hand?"

He shook his head, a small smile curving his lips. "It's a Jojo thing," he said. "The old guy might not say much, but when he does . . ." Beck looked over at the larger of his two suitcases, knowing the coarsely cut hunk of wood with the horse's head emerging from it was safely tucked away inside. "I'm ready now," he said. "I really am. And I'm through hurting people like you in the process. I'm through using you. And I'm willing to face whatever it takes. But I need to know, while I'm battling my demons, that you're battling yours too because . . . because I might be ready in a while to meet someone and risk loving her, and when that day comes, I'll hope that it's . . ." He paused, his breath catching in his throat as he looked into the limpid brown eyes of this woman who had mesmerized and infuriated him every day for nearly three months. "I'll hope that it's someone who's fought for her life and won the battle. I'll hope that it's someone like you."

"Becker."

A horn sounded near the carport. Becker stood and moved to the window. "Taxi's here," he said, turning back to Jade. He shook his head, unsure of how to say good-bye, mostly because he knew it was the last thing he wanted to do. "I'm sorry," he said. "I'm sorry for all the times I hurt you, and I'm sorry for . . . everything."

Jade rose, a hand against her trembling lips, her cheeks wet with tears.

Becker moved around her to the dresser and made short work of stuffing the remaining odds and ends into his carry-on bag. He swallowed hard past the knot in his throat and blinked away the tears that blurred his own vision.

They walked down the stairs and through the kitchen together, Jade with his carry-on bag and Becker with the suitcases. The children weren't there.

"Somebody's going to spend a while in the time-out chair," Beck said as they exited the kitchen and moved toward the Peugeot taxicab waiting in the courtyard.

Jade nodded her head toward the sound of laughter reaching

them from the woods at the back of the property. "It's a special day—I'll make an exception just this once."

They stood facing each other while the driver stowed the luggage. It was Becker who finally stepped forward to embrace the woman who'd been his ally and his nemesis. She felt frail in his arms. "Will you fight?" he whispered into her ear. "Please. I need to know you're fighting too."

Jade nodded against his chest and pushed away, her eyes downcast and brimming with tears. Beck lifted her chin and ran his fingers over her face, memorizing each feature, then turned and got into the cab. He didn't look back as it drove past the coach house, the stables, and the guard towers. He didn't turn to watch the castle disappear as the car rounded the corner. He swallowed hard, squared his shoulders, and faced resolutely forward.

A NOTE FROM THE AUTHOR

THOUGH MANY ELEMENTS of this novel are fictional, the places featured in it are not. The Meunier manor, hidden away in the hills above Lamorlaye, does indeed exist, and it really was the site of France's only Lebensborn until the Germans evacuated in 1944. Most of the documents that might have helped to reconstruct the WWII period of the manor's history were destroyed as the Nazis left, but there is no doubt among historians that many children were indeed born there during the final months of the war. Unlike other "Founts of Life," Lamorlaye's seems to have been reserved for women who entered the program voluntarily. Others across Europe were much more sordid, their babies the product of rapes and kidnappings committed in the name of expanding the Third Reich.

When I was thirteen, I started attending a small school that met in the Meunier manor. The property belonged to the Red Cross at the time, and it housed a rehabilitation center for physically handicapped children. I was part of an integration program that allowed a handful of students from the village to study with the residents of the center. I have vivid memories of reenacting the entire *Les Misérables* musical on the front steps of the manor, of playing soccer in a clearing in its woods, and of taking "field trips" to its Japanese gardens.

Lamorlaye's small evangelical church is real too—my parents were among its founding members. And the White Queen's Castle is one of my favorite places on earth. I spent many afternoons there, picturing myself as the owner of the diminutive and exquisite architectural wonder and trying not to watch weekend fishermen shoving worms onto metal hooks.

I have no childhood memories that don't involve Lamorlaye's other landmark, the château. Until I moved away at the age of sixteen, I spent much of my leisure time on the grounds of the castle, which housed the European Bible Institute from 1960 until 2001. While my parents taught inside, I played on the islands and went on treasure hunts in the woods. My brother and I came *this close* to burning the building down one afternoon as we lit matches on a stack of mattresses stored in the back stairwell. I've crawled under the castle's patio and imagined grand events in the ballroom we called a chapel. Beck's Château de Lamorlaye was home to me. It nursed my childhood aches and fueled my romantic élans. Its grand staircase remains a defining feature of my growing-up years. I dearly miss my castle days.

Today, though the château's grounds have become a much-visited botanical garden, the building itself is locked and empty, slowly succumbing to the ravages of time. Yet even in its less pristine condition, it is graceful and strong, a silent sentinel whose towers and arches guard mute vestiges of the lives that once breathed within its walls.

Much more information, including photos of the castle and other sites in the novel, can be found on my website, www.michelephoenix.com.

DISCUSSION QUESTIONS

1. Was Gary right to send Becker to France? What were the potential risks and benefits?

2. What do you think of Marie and Elise's decision to work for the Nazis who had taken over their town? What were the benefits and the dangers of cooperating with the Nazi regime? What challenges faced those who refused to cooperate?

3. What is your opinion on Jade's decision to abandon her studies and care for the Fallons' children? How might you respond to a similar medical diagnosis or other unforeseen life change?

4. Which do you feel is more logical, Beck's rejection of God or Jade's relentless faith? Why?

5. Do you agree with Sylvia Fallon's statement, "We never, at any age, outgrow the rules that apply to children. We need to feel known, we need to feel loved, and we need to feel safe"? Why or why not?

6. As you read about the suspicious nighttime events, whom did you suspect was the culprit?

7. If you were Thérèse, would you be able to forgive Jojo's behavior as a young man? Why or why not?

8. How do you envision Beck's future directly following his departure from France?

9. How can addictions, such as the one Beck struggles with, prevent people from developing healthy relationships? What are some things that could help a person fighting an addiction? What are some of the challenges to overcome?

10. Which of the characters in the book shows the most courage?

ABOUT THE AUTHOR

BORN IN FRANCE to an American mother and a Canadian father, Michèle Phoenix is an international writer with multicultural sensitivities. A graduate of Wheaton College, she has spent twenty years teaching music, creative writing, drama, and English at Black Forest Academy, a school for missionaries' children in Germany.

In 2008, Michèle fought two different forms of cancer and endured ten surgeries in four months. This dual battle caused her to reevaluate the direction of her life. Armed with a desire to make her remaining years count, she returned to the States in 2010 to launch a new ministry for and about missionary kids (MKs).

Now living in Illinois, she serves with Global Outreach Mission as an MK advocate and spends her time speaking, writing, and educating the North American church about the unique strengths and struggles of missionary kids.

TURN THE PAGE

FOR A LOOK

AT THE NEXT EXCITING NOVEL

FROM MICHÈLE PHOENIX

In Broken Places

AVAILABLE IN STORES

AND ONLINE SPRING 2013

TYNDALE
FICTION

www.tyndalefiction.com

1

"She's beautiful, Shelby."

I stared at the social worker's face and wondered what *beautiful* had to do with the present circumstances. There were other words that described my dilemma. Strange? Yes. Disconcerting? Yes. Completely and horrifically out of control? Absolutely. But beautiful? No—it was not an adjective that belonged in this particular conversation, no matter how accurate it might be.

"Dana . . . ," I began, shaking my head and raising my hands in utter dismay and incredulity, "I can't . . . I mean . . . Seriously? You're being serious here?"

This was only the second time Dana and I had met, but given the circumstances, we'd abandoned the formalities and gone straight to first names. She was old enough to be my mother, and there had been a frantic moment during that first meeting when all I'd wanted to do was curl up in her well-padded lap and have her shush me into oblivion as my mom had done when I was a child, but the official nature of our encounter had kept my instincts in check and my pride intact. Besides, I was sure not even the competent and sympathetic Dana would have known what to do with a thirty-five-year-old woman trying to crawl onto her knees.

Weeks later, I didn't remember many of the details of our first meeting. Only the general gist of the conversation and the mystification that had plagued me every day since then. My dilemma had done for my prayer life what trans fat–free fries had done for my fast-food consumption. I was cranking out prayers as fervently as I was shoveling in fries, and though my decision hadn't gotten any simpler to make, my ability to use a drive-through window without guilt had vastly improved. But I hadn't given up on my praying. Not yet. This impassable imbroglio had proven two important facts to me. First, I was helpless. A lifetime of learning to be strong and independent had left me more debilitated than I'd ever felt before. And second, my praying had gotten rusty. The first few times I'd tried to utter something profound, I'd sounded like a glossary of antiquated King James clichés. I was pretty sure God laughed at my initial attempts, but I figured he could use the entertainment as much as I could use the practice.

"I need you to make a decision," Dana now said, reaching across the gray Formica tabletop to press warm fingers around my frozen disbelief. Her oversize gold rings sparkled in the morning sunlight, somehow incongruent with the muddiness in my mind. "The paperwork is drawn up, and we can get this procedure started just as soon as you give us the go-ahead."

The go-ahead. Such an innocuous term. But in this case, it carried life-altering ramifications I couldn't even fathom. I grasped the edge of the kitchen table and found comfort in its realness. It was solid and predictable, scarred by time and use, but there—measurable and palpable and familiar. It seemed at that moment that everything else in my life had catapulted off a cliff, exploded like a clay pigeon into thousands of jagged fragments, and fallen, scattered and unrecognizable, into the dark abyss below. Giving anyone or anything the "go-ahead" while the pieces of my life were still settling in the muck of incredulity seemed about as wise as diving into a piranha-infested lake with pork chops strapped to each limb.

"Dana . . ."

"I know it's frightening," she said, tightening her grip on my hand, "and I know you have no point of reference for making this decision."

"It's just . . ." I searched her eyes for answers. "How did this happen? I mean, a month ago my life was . . . And now it's . . ."

"Kaboom," Dana said matter-of-factly.

"Exactly." I sighed and retrieved my hand long enough to rub at my eyes and rake at my hair. Dana returned my gaze, unflinching, and I tried to absorb some of her calm as it wafted across the table toward me like the fragrance of cinnamon or freshly cut grass or White Shoulders on my mother's chenille robe.

"Will you at least come to meet her?"

"No." The word shot out like a reflex.

"I'll stay with you."

"No."

"We won't even tell her who you are. . . ."

"I can't."

"Shelby." Her expression was compassionate, but her eyes scolded my cowardice. "There's more at stake here than just you. I know it's overwhelming, and I know you're still reeling, but think outside yourself for just a moment."

I laughed at that, mostly because it seemed preferable to curling into a fetal position under my mom's old kitchen table and praying to God for the Rapture to come quickly. This was a choice of cataclysmic consequences, and I was known to get stumped by a

Dunkin' Donuts display. How was I supposed to decide this so soon when glazed versus frosted could keep my brain in a knot for days?

"She needs a mom," Dana persisted.

"I'm not her mom."

"But you can learn. Even if you're not her real mom, someone's got to raise her."

"No." I shook my head as if the gesture would rid me of the excruciating decision. "I'm not mom material. He made sure of that."

"And yet it's you he wanted for his daughter. No one else."

I laughed again, though the sound was completely devoid of humor. "He doesn't even know who I am. . . ."

"But he chose you."

"I can't do it."

"What other option do we have, Shelby?" Her voice was soft, but her words slammed a vise across my lungs that threatened my ability to breathe. "What other option does Shayla have?" She leaned across the table, her eyes seeking my averted gaze. "Take a deep breath, Shelby." She waited while I obeyed. After a few moments, she smiled and added, "If you don't let it back out, you're going to pass out."

I expelled the breath in a rush of frustration and helplessness and fear, tears stinging my eyes. "I feel like I don't really have a choice at all."

"Sure you do. Technically. But if you're feeling like there's only one right choice—I think that might be true." She fished a Kleenex out of her giant purse and handed it to me as if she'd done it a thousand times before—which she probably had. "I suggest you and I go for a little ride. We'll drop in and see her—just as casually as you'd like—and then maybe you'll be able to wrap your mind around all of this." She pushed her chair away from the table and rose.

"I'm not sure I can do this." I swallowed past the boulder in my throat and bit my bottom lip to steady it.

"I believe you. But you still need to."

"I'm scared, Dana. What if . . . ? What if . . . ?"

"You don't have to decide today. Maybe seeing her will help you, though."

"Help me what?"

"Help you to know."

"You won't tell her who I am?"

"It'll be our little secret."

"And you'll stay with me?"

Dana nodded and hung her purse over her shoulder. "You ready?"

"No. . . ." My laughter only almost masked my terror.

"You'll be fine," Dana assured me, coming around the table to squeeze my shoulder as I stood. "I'll be with you—and we'll take it nice and slow."

"I need to brush my hair."

"I was hoping you would."

"Don't insult me—I might change my mind."

"Then you're absolutely beautiful," Dana said sweetly.

"And you're a lousy liar."

"Hey, if it gets you to the car . . ."

"I need a donut."

"There are three Dunkin' Donuts between here and Dream Acres."

"Good," I said bravely. "We'll stop at all three."